Romantic Suspense

Danger. Passion. Drama.

Hunted On The Trail
Dana Mentink

Tracking The Missing
Sami A. Abrams

MILLS & BOON

HUNTED ON THE TRAIL
© 2024 by Dana Mentink
Philippine Copyright 2024
Australian Copyright 2024
New Zealand Copyright 2024

First Published 2024
First Australian Paperback Edition 2024
ISBN 978 1 038 93904 3

TRACKING THE MISSING
© 2024 by Sherryl Abramson
Philippine Copyright 2024
Australian Copyright 2024
New Zealand Copyright 2024

First Published 2024
First Australian Paperback Edition 2024
ISBN 978 1 038 93904 3

MIX
Paper | Supporting
responsible forestry
FSC® C001695
www.fsc.org

Published by
Harlequin Mills & Boon
An imprint of Harlequin Enterprises (Australia) Pty Limited
(ABN 47 001 180 918), a subsidiary of HarperCollins
Publishers Australia Pty Limited
(ABN 36 009 913 517)
Level 19, 201 Elizabeth Street
SYDNEY NSW 2000 AUSTRALIA

Cover art used by arrangement with Harlequin Books S.A.. All rights reserved.

Printed and bound in Australia by McPherson's Printing Group

Hunted On The Trail

Dana Mentink

MILLS & BOON

Dana Mentink is a nationally bestselling author. She has been honored to win two Carol Awards, a HOLT Medallion and an RT Reviewers' Choice Best Book Award. She's authored more than thirty novels to date for and Harlequin. Dana loves feedback from her readers. Contact her at danamentink.com.

Books by Dana Mentink

Security Hounds Investigations

Tracking the Truth
Fugitive Search
Hunted on the Trail

Pacific Northwest K-9 Unit

Snowbound Escape

Rocky Mountain K-9 Unit

Undercover Assignment

Alaska K-9 Unit

Yukon Justice

Love Inspired Trade

Trapped in Yosemite

Visit the Author Profile page at millsandboon.com.au
for more titles.

Repent ye therefore, and be converted, that your sins may be blotted out, when the times of refreshing shall come from the presence of the Lord. And he shall send Jesus Christ, which before was preached unto you: Whom the heaven must receive until the times of restitution of all things, which God hath spoken by the mouth of all his holy prophets since the world began.

—*Acts* 3:19–21

To Grandma Mentink, Junie the Wonder Dog
misses you, and we do, too.

Chapter One

"Bad idea. Very bad. The worst." Garrett, Stephanie Wolfe's twin, sounded much farther away than the three-hour drive to their family ranch house in Whisper Valley.

"You're wrong, it's a fabulous idea," she said firmly. "Finishing in the top three will net Security Hounds more cred." *Way more.* The four-day Lost Sierra Tracking and Trailing Competition would be yet another proving ground for Steph and her champion bloodhound, Chloe. From the back seat, Chloe flapped her ears in support of the idea.

"We're doing okay," he said.

"No, we're not." Their investigations firm took private cases and also did search and rescue for the county, and neither end had generated much activity of late. He knew it, she knew it and so did their other three siblings.

A windblown pine needle splattered against her SUV. The movement caught Chloe's attention and she slopped a giant tongue out the partially open window to capture it. Stephanie smiled at her canine passenger. Best dog she'd ever worked with, bar none. The purebred bloodhound, Duchess Chloe Cleopatra Rosamond, had been discarded by her breeders when she was discovered to have a flaw. In Steph's mind, her only flaw was her previous owners. "We won't get killed. Promise."

"Not funny."

"I leave funny to you, so put down the tennis ball and get going. I'll do the same."

He paused. "How do you know I'm fiddling with a tennis ball?"

"Please. I can tell you what you had for dinner."

"You can't."

"Cheese quesadillas with salsa and sour cream, no cilantro," she rattled off.

"I..." He stopped. "Well, there was no sour cream so I went without, for your information. Steph, I just feel uneasy about you tackling the Lost Sierra alone."

"You're gun-shy." He should be, after his last case. "And I'm not alone. I've got Chloe and the competition assigns you a partner." Because Garrett was right about one thing—the sprawling Northern California wilderness that spanned the Sierra Nevada crest was way too rugged and isolated to tackle solo, dog or no dog. Before he could rally a response, she brought out the big guns. "Catherine needs you to be with her when she testifies at the trial." An understatement, after his girlfriend had almost lost her entire family—and Garrett too—before they'd wrapped their last investigation.

He huffed. "Okay. I concede. I'll only be gone five days, tops. Roman and Chase..."

"Are away, leaving Mom, Kara and Steph, the poor delicate females, to manage on their own."

"Don't kid. Weather's bad. The storm's gonna be a doozy."

The November forecast was grim. "Which will be an excellent test of Chloe's skills, and mine. Our cases don't always occur on lovely balmy days, right? It's only three nights."

He huffed. "The timing with Ferris's release..."

"Don't." She tried to smooth over her caustic tone. "I'm

here. I'm doing this." *Read: I'm living my life and no one is going to stop me, especially not Ferris Grinder.*

His sigh was bone-deep, weary, which made her feel bad about adding to his worries.

"I got this, Garrett. Trust me."

"I do. Love you."

"Ditto."

She put away thoughts of Ferris and tackled the steep road up the mountain. There was no sign of any human activity, only a wide sprawl of granite slope, heavily wooded. Had she taken a wrong turn?

Her brother's comment jangled. *The timing with Ferris's release...*

A memory crept in before she could shield against it.

The day in court, the trial for Maurice Grinder, Ferris's father.

Ferris had walked by on his way to the courtroom, passing where she stood in uniform. Chloe was there too. Her brother Chase had brought the dog as part of the ongoing training process, to accustom her to the sights and smells of a public building, and also, Steph suspected, as a show of moral support. Ferris stumbled and sent a chair flying at them, which clipped Chloe. Though there was no way to prove it, she knew Ferris had done it intentionally. Chloe reacted with a yelp and a spate of barking unlike she'd ever heard from her dog.

They'd convicted Ferris's father for his fraudulent business practices, the fake trucking company that he used to steal freight and fence the goods. But there hadn't been enough evidence to get Maurice for what she believed deep down he'd also been responsible for: ordering the murders of an employee and his family after the clerk made plans to blow the whistle. Maurice had died in prison.

Ferris was shortly thereafter convicted of fraud, theft and assorted small crimes. If she'd been allowed to take on his case, maybe she could have gotten him for murder since she was sure he'd been the one to carry out his father's deadly contract. But Vance Silverton, her boyfriend at the time, who'd been promoted to detective instead of her, hadn't gotten the job done.

Steph eyed the roiling clouds as she drove deeper into the wilderness. Ferris had been paroled only three weeks earlier. There was no proof that he was behind the series of calls she'd received, anonymous promises that she and her dog would soon be dead. Former cops acquired lots of enemies, didn't they?

Teeth gritted, she drove on.

When she finally saw the tiny mile marker, she turned off toward a narrow bridge that spanned a river. To her relief, the metal security gate that barred access was unlocked and pushed aside, an indication she was heading the right way.

It was confirmed when she saw a short man with an orange vest on horseback. He waved her on. Abreast of him, she rolled down her window and he craned to look at her. His full beard almost covered the shiny ID tag on a pristine lanyard around his neck... Evan, volunteer.

"Here for the competition?" His gaze roved to her back seat. "Is that a liver-and-tan hound?"

"She is."

"A champion, huh?"

"Yes."

He laughed. "That's what they all say."

Rude. "With my dog it's the truth."

He pointed. "'Bout a half hour to go. I'll bring up the rear since you're the last pair."

Precisely thirty-five minutes later, they arrived at a small registration table, where a woman stood bundled against the cold, a banner with Lost Sierra Tracking and Trailing Competition snapping in the wind behind her.

Another woman sat nearby in a parked Jeep, poking at her phone.

Stephanie unloaded Chloe and approached the table. The registrar beamed her a smile from under the hood of her raincoat and they made their introductions.

"Excellent," Elizabeth said. "You're our last team. We've got your starts staggered, of course. Don't worry, winners are calculated strictly on elapsed time and course completion."

"How many teams are competing?"

"You're the tenth and final duo."

Perfect. She'd have a great shot at reaching the top three.

The woman pawed through a box under the table and handed her a pack. "We've got six volunteers from the various tracking clubs to monitor the checkpoints. At the first checkpoint, you'll receive your tent and sleeping bag, as well as a GPS tracker. If you need to quit because of the storm at any time, have your partner radio and drive you back to your car. Your safety and your dog's is the first priority." She gestured as the woman in the Jeep got out. "Here she is. Her name is…" She sighed. "So sorry. I've forgotten. It's been a busy day."

The petite woman with a neat braid hastened over and pumped Steph's hand. "No problem. Gina Johnson. Pleased to meet you." She kneeled and scrubbed Chloe behind the ears, sending the dog's tail whipping. "You look like a winner to me, baby."

"She is," Steph said. "Many times over."

Gina grinned. "Well, let's go add another feather to her cap, shall we? I'll drive us to the starting point."

Volunteer Evan remained atop his horse, watching. "How about I escort you ladies to the first checkpoint?"

"No thanks," Gina said.

"Mighty rugged out there," Evan said. "Dangerous."

Gina waved him off. "I think we got this."

With a shrug, he dismounted and turned to help Elizabeth load supplies into her car.

Stephanie was about to follow Gina when she noticed a vehicle pull up and park under a tree. Her curiosity turned to shock as she watched a man get out. Tall, stubbled chin, and with a dimple on the right side of his mouth that would show if he'd been smiling.

He wasn't.

She couldn't make her brain believe he was standing there.

Not him.

Not now.

Vance Silverton realized his jaw was hanging open and closed it with a snap. *Steph? Here?* That changed everything. His brain spun through the ramifications.

The woman with the braid who looked to be a volunteer strode to the Jeep and got in. Steph hadn't moved and was staring daggers at him. Stomach quivering, he freed the dog from the back seat to give himself a moment before he sauntered closer to Steph.

"Best behavior, Brutus," he muttered to the sluggish hound. "Hi, Steph." Friendly, casual. Maybe they could ignore the big fat white elephant of their past lazing between them. That notion immediately popped like a soap bubble.

"What are you doing here, Vance?"

"I was going to register."

"*You* were going to register? For this competition?" She eyed his dog incredulously. Brutus flicked one of his ears, the one that stood upright, before oozing like a puddle to the damp ground. Were a dog's legs supposed to spread out in all directions like that?

"You and him?" Steph looked as though she was not sure which point to tackle first. "Since when are you into tracking and trailing?"

Since never.

"I'm sorry, sir, but the competition is closed," the registrar called out. "We're not taking any more last-minute entrants because of the unfavorable weather forecast."

He was going to press his case, but there were other fish to fry now.

"Steph." He kept his voice low and took a step closer to her. "I need to talk to you. Privately."

A drop of rain landed on her short dark hair. She opened her mouth, closed it and then started in again. "No, you don't. I have no idea why you're here, but whatever it is, I don't want any part of it, or you."

Direct, like she'd been since they were colleagues. "Listen to me..."

"Elizabeth," Steph called over his shoulder to the woman in charge. "We're ready to roll."

Elizabeth finished shoving papers into boxes. She was too preoccupied to notice the awkward body language between him and Steph, but the other lady hadn't.

"Everything okay?" she called from the Jeep.

"Yes, one second, Gina," Steph said. "Let's go, Chloe."

He took her wrist. "Steph," he said urgently. "I really need to talk to you."

She jerked away from his touch. "I don't buy for one red-hot second that you're here to compete, so that means you're lying. I don't talk to liars."

He'd expected fireworks, but he thought he'd be able to at least explain before she shut him down. "Two minutes. It's important. I'm concerned about you."

"*Now* you're worried? That's real nice, Vance. You sure didn't spare many feelings about me when you took my job. Didn't care much then, did you?"

"I didn't..." He trailed off, snatching his baseball cap from his head and whacking the raindrops against his knee. But he had, actually. He'd done everything he could to get the detective promotion for reasons he couldn't tell her then. While he was trying to work out just what to say, she turned her back on him and trotted with her dog to the Jeep.

"Steph..." He'd taken a few steps when the registrar stopped him.

"Sir, this team has to get going before dark. Is there something else I can help you with?"

He eyed her box. "Aren't you going to stay until the event's over?" Three nights of sleeping under the stars, he'd read in the brochure. An eternity.

"Only until they reach the first checkpoint because they're the last team and the others are hours ahead. I'll wait in my car for their text and then go join the staff at the finish line camp site. We'll dispatch help from there if any is needed." She looked dubiously at Vance and his dog. "You're going to leave too, right? Storm's only getting started."

"Sure," he said faintly. "After one more pit stop for Brutus."

She arched an eyebrow at his lounging animal. "Um, don't be offended when I say this, but you might want to get your dog into better physical shape if he's going to compete."

Vance kept his expression neutral. "He's got a lot of inner-core strength."

To her credit, she did not laugh. "Okay." She loaded the carton under her arm into her vehicle along with the small table and climbed into her car.

Stephanie and Gina took off. The Jeep's headlights punched weakly into the gloom.

He rubbed a hand over his jaw. Maybe he was wrong. Maybe Ferris hadn't come to this pocket of nowhere and Vance had misread the clues he thought he'd found. But Stephanie Wolfe was here and that could not be dismissed as a coincidence. He thought he'd been tracking Ferris. Now he had the sinking feeling he'd been played.

A spatter of rain hit his forehead. The isolation struck at him as he lost the distant sound of the Jeep. Just two women and a dog in a great big wilderness. He fingered his keys. Wouldn't hurt to add two more to the mix, and he probably had enough supplies to keep him and Pudge from starving for a while, just long enough to be sure she was safe. He could pretend to leave, then loop around and follow Steph and Gina without Elizabeth knowing. Steph would have a blowup of epic proportions if she found out he was trailing her.

But what she didn't know wouldn't hurt her.

He grinned down at Brutus. "All right, fella, it's time to follow our guts, and certainly you've got a lot of guts to follow."

The portly dog whipped his tail at him.

Whatever the fallout, he wasn't going to live with another failure. If he was wrong, he'd suffer the consequences. But if he was right...

He hoisted his dog into the car and cranked the ignition.

Gina drove slowly, keeping the Jeep in the center of the rugged trail, though the branches scraped the sides as they passed. Time was moving in painful slow motion.

Steph kept her chitchat light, to prevent thoughts of Vance from creeping in. The shock still shuddered through every bone and sinew, but she wasn't about to reveal that to her companion. "You got the short straw in escorting the last entrant?"

Gina shrugged. "Someone had to do it, so I offered. But I should get hazard pay, since everyone else got the benefit of a couple hours of daylight and no rain. This is going to be a once-in-a-lifetime experience. Great photos for my Instagram."

As they bumped on, Steph went over the map she'd been given. "Starting point should be coming up if you take this trail east."

"Got it." Gina peered into the gloom. "Man. It's only six o'clock but it might as well be night already."

She'd thought the same. She checked her own supplies and tested her flashlight again, then transferred the contents of the competition backpack to hers.

Gina shot her a surprised look. "You don't want the official gear?"

"I like my own stuff." Her supplies had saved her life once, and Chloe's too when the dog had been bitten by a snake while searching the heavy brush of a canyon. Her gear was personalized right down to the organic snacks she brought. It all came down to rule number two—your gear is the second most important thing for a successful search and rescue.

Gina shrugged. "Suit yourself but take this." She handed Steph a metallic pouch. "The contest sponsors provided it. Dog food. All organic or some such thing."

Steph took it to be polite, but she wasn't going to give Chloe any on account of rule number one—your dog is your most precious colleague. Chloe ate only what Steph had purchased or prepared with her own hands. She loved Chloe, had adored her since the moment her mom handed over the scrawny, underfed bloodhound who'd been dumped by the unscrupulous breeder in a shelter in Southern California. Five years ago, Chloe had been more ears than dog, but she'd grown and become a champion tracker and Steph's best friend. Sometimes she felt like her only friend, since Vance was no longer in her life. The miles stretched on, fifteen minutes bleeding into a half hour and beyond.

Stephanie rechecked the map and squinted through the rain-speckled windshield. "I wonder why I don't see any lights. Elizabeth said the checkpoint would be easy to spot. Oh, wait. There it is," Stephanie said. Off to their right, where the trail dipped down into a flat bowl of grassland and trees, shone a speck of white light.

"Whew. I was worried I'd gotten us lost." Gina drove them off the road and through a rutted path of grass. Stephanie held the door handle against the jostling, glad she'd tethered Chloe securely in the back seat. After a teeth-rattling twenty minutes, they arrived at the edge of a pine forest.

Stephanie let Chloe free and headed toward the light. "Hello," she called as they ducked under the trees. She'd expected to see a table, or at least a volunteer with a vest on, but there was no one, only a solitary lantern, beaded with moisture, hanging on a branch. Wind swirled the pine needles, speckling her with cold droplets. Goose bumps erupted on her skin. "I don't see a GPS tracker anywhere around, do you? Or the supplies?"

Gina frowned. "No. Maybe we did make a wrong turn and this isn't the spot. I'll grab my radio from the Jeep. Elizabeth is going to have to drive up here and help us out." She hurried off.

What was there to get wrong? They were supposed to receive their scent article, a sleeping bag and tent, and take a GPS tracker to carry along. Possibly they'd made an incorrect turn but why would there be a lantern hanging in some random place? Had there been a mix-up?

That probably explained it. She'd been a late entry and likely been left off a list or something. She texted Elizabeth with no response. Chloe was still sniffing, her sides gleaming in the twilight since it was now almost totally dark.

Stephanie looked closer. The lantern swung slightly in the breeze, sending the shadows crawling. Foreboding pulled at her stomach. No reason to jump to conclusions, she told herself. There was no threat here that she could detect. Chloe was calm and curious. She listened for the sound of Gina's return. Where was she? She would have had time to make it to the Jeep and back. Steph prickled with the desire to get out of the dark woods.

"Chloe." The dog immediately trotted to her side. She wanted to call out for Gina, but something made her stay silent as they hurried on. Branches cracked at the edge of the clearing.

They froze, listening. Chloe began to growl, nose quivering. Immediately, Steph pulled her weapon as they scurried back to the Jeep. Gina wasn't in the vehicle.

As she searched the ground for footprints, bullets erupted from a spot in the trees, spraying into the vehicle and carving chunks from the dirt. She grabbed her pack and yelled to

Chloe, and they stumbled around to the other side. The shooting continued in a steady stream.

Semiautomatic, her brain told her. She cradled Chloe as the rear window glass showered down around them. Her ears rang with the torturous noise. The shots were sporadic, the noise growing closer.

The shooter was moving, closing the gap, coming to murder her. *Plan?*

She would not stand much of a chance at returning fire with any accuracy in the dark with the shooter firing at regular intervals. He'd edge around to get a better angle until his bullets penetrated the vehicle and cut them in half.

Her mouth and throat were dry with fear.

A noise behind her position spun her around.

An accomplice closing in from the rear? She fought down the bubbling panic as she clutched Chloe close.

All she could think of was how right her brother had been.

Chapter Two

Vance's pulse hammered as he called over the rifle fire. "Steph, it's Vance."

"Vance?" she hissed.

"At your twelve, in the bushes. Stay low. Run to me when you can. I'll cover."

When he was sure she'd gotten onto her belly, he squeezed off cover fire, his shots peppering the trees and ringing across the valley at what he believed to be the gunman's position. The shooting stopped abruptly, but Vance continued until Steph and her dog tumbled into the bushes next to him. In the distance, he heard the firing of a motor, then the gunman flooring the pedal, moving rapidly away. *Coward.*

He breathed hard and lowered his weapon, wiping the sweat from his brow with a forearm.

Safe. For now. He offered a hand to help her up, but she ignored it. Before she could launch the inquisition, he went on the offensive. "Yes, I followed you. Yes, you can rip me to pieces later. But what's going on right now? Aside from the fun little shootout, I mean." He pointed over her shoulder to the Jeep.

She hesitated.

"Come on, Steph. Now is not the time to withhold." *Even from me.*

"There was no one at the checkpoint," she said. "No scent article or tracker. Gina went to get the radio out of the Jeep and now she's gone. No keys in the vehicle, but I didn't check closely because of the obvious."

Every sentence caused his stomach to cinch tighter. "Go get in my car. I'll check the scene, make sure Gina's not hurt somewhere, and we'll clear out."

"I don't think so." Steph pulled a silver pouch of dog food from her pocket. "Chloe and I will find Gina. Her scent is on this."

He bit back a comment. Of course she wasn't going to take the sensible option. It was the stubborn, totally fearless attitude that annoyed and attracted him in equal measure. Maybe not completely equal, because at the moment she was stomping on his last nerve. She offered the pouch to the eager blood-hound pawing at her knee.

"Find." Her tone was calm, but he noted her hand was trembling.

"This isn't safe," he said as she attached a long lead to Chloe. She ignored him and followed the tugging dog.

"It's Ferris," he called.

She stopped. Finally, she turned around. "Explain that."

"I'm not gonna stand here and lay it all out right now, but I know he's behind this. He's here. Close. Maybe he snatched Gina or shot her."

"You *know*?" Her mouth tightened, chin went up. "You're going to fill me in on how you came to that conclusion after I find Gina. She probably panicked and ran this way when the shooting started. Where's your dog? I can give him the scent too. Double-team it."

"Uh, he's in the car. He's a little...green."

Green and spectacularly unqualified. His new canine partner of two whole weeks, whom he'd recently renamed Brutus, likely hadn't located anything more significant than a dropped potato chip. Mercifully, Stephanie's dog tugged her away so all he could do was run after them, grateful he'd kept up the fitness regimen after leaving the force.

The dog beelined for the river that roared through a shrub-covered ravine. Vance gripped his own weapon as they sped along, taking up a flanking position while trying to avoid the branches clawing at his jeans. If the shooter—he knew down to his eyeteeth it was Ferris—was doubling back, they didn't have much time.

Stephanie plunged on, undaunted. The safest plan was to leave immediately, but if Gina was wounded...

Chloe stopped abruptly and he bumped Steph, catching her shoulder to keep from knocking her over. She jerked away as soon as she'd recovered her balance, shining a penlight from her pocket onto the ground. It took him a moment to spot it.

A footprint.

Steph didn't have to command her dog. Chloe had already resumed her search. He felt as if the forest had a million eyes, watching them. Hairs on the back of his neck tingled as he tried to track all the shadows and noises, which were soon swallowed up by the roar of rushing water.

They'd reached the edge of the riverbed. Stephanie stopped Chloe from charging over the lip of the rock and into the chasm. The dog whined.

He flicked on the flashlight he'd brought with him and angled it down into the water, the glow catching on the rocks and wild current. There was a narrow ribbon of earth paralleling the river, big enough for a motorbike or very small vehicle with a very confident driver.

"Did she double back maybe and we missed her?"

Steph shook her head. "Chloe would have tracked that." She looked again into the waves and he knew they were both thinking the same thing. If Gina had fallen in, she'd be no match for the current. Had she been shot?

New game plan. Steph was going to do the smart thing and lock herself in his car while he searched, whether she liked it or not, but the words died on his lips as he spotted the figure at the bottom.

"There she is," Steph said.

Her light was barely sufficient to catch Gina's outline. The woman was lying on her side, holding on to a branch with both hands, resisting the pull of the water that threatened to snatch her.

He didn't wait for Stephanie's action plan. He holstered his gun, shoved his cell phone at her and plunged down the bank. Rock and dirt shifted, and he struggled to stay upright. "Hold on," he shouted over the waves. "I'm almost there." Her torso was being dragged by the flow, away from solid ground. As he neared, he detected the trembling in her arms.

"Almost there." He had to move faster but the ground near the bottom was mucky, suctioning his boots, and he fought for every step. The darkness concealed her face, but he caught the gleam of her profile as he approached.

He'd reached the water, extending to grab her wrists.

As he made contact, the whites of her eyes widened in the gloom.

And then she was gone.

He blinked in shock. He hadn't noticed her lose her grip, but she was whisked away, the feel of her wet sleeve lingering on his fingers.

No. He lurched a step forward. Steph shouted.

"Don't, Vance."

He wanted to ignore her, but she was right. He shouldn't leap into that violent water in the dark and leave Steph alone to fight Ferris. He stood peering into nothing, awash in fury and grief. If he'd moved faster, been stronger... She called again and he finally roused himself and scrambled back up the bank.

"I couldn't get her."

Steph touched his shoulder. She didn't say anything because

she knew there was nothing to offer that would help. They'd navigated the cop life together, where people lived and died, and justice was a fleeting phenomenon. Knowing how to put aside the grief was the only way they could do their jobs. Gina would be added to the arsenal of memories he stored away in the dark places for the bleak moments when he could not keep them submerged.

"Steph, let's go to my car. Now." The urge to get her out of this place and call for help swamped him. Maybe Gina would be able to grab another branch downstream, haul herself out. A delusion, probably, but it helped for the moment.

Her expression was unreadable in the gloom. "Okay."

Limbs weary, he moved them to the edge of the trees, which provided some cover at least, and they hurried through the darkness. The moment they left the Lost Sierra, they could sort it through, talk to the police, figure out what happened. The "they" might be optimistic, but at least he'd make sure Steph was clear on every single detail before they parted ways again.

He led them to the spot where he'd parked the car in the trees that overlooked the meadow.

Steph pulled something from her pocket and groaned.

"What?"

"My satellite phone is broken. It was in my pocket when I dove for cover. I have my cell too, but no bars."

He checked his own. "Same." And he didn't have a sat phone.

He fisted his keys. "Exit plan. I'll turn around. The bridge is the quickest way out, and we might get some cell reception there when we pass the trees. Registration area's right there too. Elizabeth should be there still, and she's got a radio and sat phone, no doubt. We'll fill her in, then we all get out as fast as we can."

No argument from Steph. She opened the back door before he could get there and looked inside. "What's your dog's name?"

"Uh, Brutus," he said quickly.

"Move over, Brutus," she said. The dog wagged his tail, his bulk spread across the seat. He tilted his head at Chloe and quivered with excitement, but he didn't move.

"Over, Brutus. Scooch over," Vance ordered.

The dog wagged harder, his crooked tail whamming into the seat, his gaze riveted on the new arrival.

Vance hurried around, opened the other door and hauled his dog to the far side. Steph loaded Chloe, and the dogs gave each other a good sniffing before they settled in together.

"He's, you know, green, like I said."

"Uh-huh." She got into the passenger seat, poking at her phone. "Still no reception. I'll text Elizabeth, but I'm not sure it will go through. If she's left for some reason, the contest coordinators will realize something's wrong when they can't track the GPS we were supposed to be assigned."

But how long would that take?

"Texting Security Hounds too."

Security Hounds was her private-eye business, he knew from his internet snooping. "Is there maybe a separate tracker in the gear they gave you?"

"No."

He focused on driving as fast as possible, which wasn't very fast at all considering the conditions. Wet, dark, cold. He felt her gaze riveted on him and he resisted the urge to squirm.

"Are you ready to tell me the truth?" she said.

He challenged, "Are you ready to listen?"

Waves of acid floated at him from the passenger seat. Fine. He had some feelings of his own. If she'd given him two minutes before she launched into this competition...

"My call to Elizabeth went through but she isn't answering."

"We'll get across the bridge and phone her again. If she doesn't answer, you can drive until you get a signal and I'll run back to the registration area and see if her car's still there."

"That's silly. Let's drive there together now. Check. Hit the bridge after."

But his instincts were hollering their loudest.

Get Steph out of here.

He swung to the left, having almost missed the turn.

"Vance." She didn't exactly clutch the door handle, but she looked like she was thinking about it. Back-seat driver, always had been. They'd constantly battled about who would drive whenever they'd had to travel together as cops.

She'd accused him of driving like a sixteen-year-old who was afraid of scratching his father's Buick. He said her recklessness made him feel like he was a passenger in a getaway car. He almost smiled as the steep slope to the bridge came into view. Steph held on as he made the perilous descent. He was about to launch into the explanation of his presence when he braked hard.

"What...?" Steph's question trailed off.

They both got out to take a closer look.

His headlights caught the gleaming metal gate, which was now stretched across the bridge and secured with a padlock. They were sealed off from exiting, this way at least.

Stephanie blew out a breath. "Maybe Elizabeth left, locked it to prevent any more last-minute arrivals on her way out."

"I don't think so."

Shoulder-to-shoulder, they stood in silent thought.

Someone wanted them trapped here, cut off and vulnerable. And he knew exactly who that someone was.

Steph chewed her lip. Vance no doubt had the same thought she did. *Ambush.* "Back to the registration area. My car's there and there's an old satellite phone in the back we can power up. Hopefully Elizabeth will be there safe, too. We have to warn her the bridge is locked and there's a shooter."

Vance juggled the wheel. "She had to have wondered why you haven't checked in yet. She might have called it in already."

She ripped open the map again, shining her penlight on the paper as he spun the wheel in a tight arc and floored it. "If

Elizabeth has left, our next best exit option is north of here. A road that cuts through the valley. It'll eventually take us to the highway."

"Copy that," he said.

The phrase was so natural and yet so much a part of their shared past that it stabbed her like an ice pick. She didn't like the pain. Anger was better. She clenched the map. "Start talking."

"Oh, *now* you want me to talk?" His nostrils flared, his biceps flexing as he detoured around a mudhole. "We could have avoided this if you'd listened to my talking earlier."

She goggled at his audacity. This was her fault? "You blame me for not wanting to chit chat with you, Vance?"

He rolled his eyes. "It wouldn't have killed you to listen for two minutes. I told you it was urgent and you should have believed me. I guess now you do, huh?"

She couldn't see his eyes spark green fire, but she knew that's what she would have noted, light permitting. He had a point, unfortunately. Her emotions at seeing him had overridden her good sense, and anger wasn't going to get them out of whatever jam they were in. She took a breath. "Vance," she said calmly as they hurtled along, chasing the last flicker of gray in the blackening sky. "Give me a sitrep. Please."

Her attempt at control worked. His wide shoulders resettled. The fringe of his crew cut brushed the roof of the car and the wheel looked like a toy in his hands. Why had such a big man chosen such a small vehicle? Vance was always the tallest in the room, a full eight inches above her, which made her head tuck nicely under his chin when they'd hugged during their six months of friendship that had turned to romance. *Focus, Steph.*

"Short story is, I took early retirement after Ferris was locked up. I'm a bounty hunter now. Have been for a year or so."

Fortunately, the gloom covered her look of surprise. "Okay." She desperately wanted to know why he'd quit the force, especially after betraying her to steal her job, but it was more important to get the facts. "And you're tracking Ferris because…"

"He skipped out on his probation officer three weeks ago, but I've been sticking my nose into his business since the day I quit the force."

"Why?"

He snagged a look at her. "Because he's a killer who never got what he deserved."

A killer whom they believed helped his father execute his clerk and family. She suppressed a shiver. Without sufficient evidence to try Ferris for murder, the department had settled for what they could get like they had for his father, Maurice. Settling was never her go-to. Vance's either.

Vance's skull thunked the roof as they bounced over a rough spot. "We missed something. *I* missed something and Ferris got away with murder. I decided I'd use my bounty-hunter status to keep him on my radar while I searched for more info, some witness that overheard Maurice and Ferris planning the murders, an inmate who might have caught a comment from Maurice before he died in jail. I'd feed whatever I uncovered to the cops. When Ferris ditched his parole officer, I had legal permission to go after him. At least I could send him back to jail for *that* minor offense while I kept digging."

Surprising. She'd assumed Ferris was one of those losses they'd both had to swallow whether they liked it or not. "How'd you track him here?"

"I followed him to the Shasta Cascade region, then the Lost Sierra specifically. A couple weeks back I found some brochures he'd looked at about the competition in a hotel room he'd vacated. He's a slob, by the way. Left trash everywhere and not even a tip for the housekeeper. My aunt Lettie would have been disgusted. The brochures were about this tracking-and-trailing competition. Made no sense that a man like him would be interested. I tried to do my undercover thing—enter, to poke around—but I was too late. Then I…saw you."

His voice throbbed when he said it. *Saw you.* He'd certainly awakened a reaction in her too, but she wasn't about to admit that.

Vance let out a huge breath. "Steph, at first I thought Ferris skipped out on parole and I was tracking him until I realized you were here. Now I think he knew I was following him and he left the clues for me to find. Ferris wanted us both here at the same time. I think he's trying to make us pay."

"Us? Why me? It wasn't even my case when Ferris was convicted. It was yours." The words were hard, like river stones.

"Yeah, Ferris was mine, but you got it started and you helped the detective seal the deal on his dad. Maurice went to jail kicking and screaming and died there. My new theory is Ferris blames us for that and he's going to even the score. Maurice's life for yours and mine."

She considered the comment Maurice Grinder had flung at her at the sentencing.

You crossed the wrong family. It had been followed by a string of expletives fired directly at her before he was removed from the courtroom. She suppressed a shiver. "So you think he's lured us both here because he's got some plot cooking to kill us? Why now? Why risk his freedom when he was legally released?"

For a moment there was only the sound of the rain driving against the window. His gaze drifted to hers. "Know what date it is?"

"November fifteenth. What does that...?" Her words died away. The year before on November 15th Maurice Grinder had died in prison, where she'd put him. Her throat went dry.

He turned up the wiper speed to match the increasing rain.

"Walk me through it. How did you land at this event, Steph?"

"I got an email last week, telling me there was an unexpected opening because a team dropped out."

"From whom?"

"A generic Gmail account. The message included basic info and a phone number."

"And?"

"And I called, and I entered."

"Anything out of the ordinary about that process?"

"No..." She reconsidered. "Actually, I did think the registrar, Elizabeth, seemed surprised. She asked me how I'd heard about it and she said she didn't know their publicity person had reached out personally to anyone, nor was she aware of a team dropping out. They were happy to have me and she handled the application, even after the deadline had passed."

"Likely it wasn't their publicity person who contacted you. Easy to create a fake email account."

"But to lure me into a contest to kill me? Us? Drop clues for you to follow here? It would be a lot of work for Ferris. Kind of an elaborate plan. Why not just take us out in Whisper Valley someday? I'm regularly out with Chloe on some trail or another and you're fishing all the time. A quick shot and we're dead."

"I'm not fishing all the time, but never mind that. He chose here because he's not going to have witnesses, or any trouble getting in and out unnoticed. What better place to do it, Steph? On the anniversary of the day his father passed away?"

Hundreds of acres of wilderness. No communication. A hard knot began to form in her belly.

"He'd have to assume I had a sat phone. No way for him to predict it was out of commission. I could simply call for help."

"Unless he figured you'd be dead before you could do that. He'd planned to end it at the first checkpoint. Kill me too, maybe, along the road in or out."

Vance could be wrong. She didn't want to believe it, that she'd fallen so easily for Ferris's lies. If it was Ferris, she'd been blindsided and her unwillingness to listen had delivered her squarely under his control. She wasn't going to share that little kernel with Vance.

Ruthless, that was exactly how she'd describe the Grinder family. Lawrence Harlow, the man who ran one of Grinder's warehouses, realized Grinder was maintaining a fictitious trucking company from which he'd dispatch various criminals to steal freight he then resold.

Harlow had been prepared to go to the police. Another employee named Jack tipped off Grinder and the Harlow family—four people—was dead within hours, gunned down by an assassin that was never caught.

Steph believed Ferris had pulled the trigger on the Harlows himself, but there was no physical evidence to prove it. For some unaccountable reason, Lawrence Harlow had opened the door for his killer. She'd never been able to figure out why.

Maybe if Vance hadn't wanted to stroke his own ego by taking the detective's job…

Let it go. You're happy to be rid of police work, remember?

That much was true. Mostly. God was growing her up in a new direction, as her mother often reminded her. And she'd been glad to be clear of Vance too, until he landed in her sphere again like a meteor falling from the sky.

"When's the official finish to this competition?"

"Saturday evening." And it was only Wednesday.

Brutus whined from the back seat.

"Can you turn on the radio?" Vance said. "The country station? Brutus gets nervous when he's riding and then he throws up, but music seems to help."

"This doesn't seem like a good time for music."

"It's not a good time for upchucking either and he ate a bag of cheese puffs I had stashed in my hotel room so that's not gonna be pretty."

"Are you kidding?"

"Dead serious."

She shook her head. "You were never dead serious."

"I was. A lot."

"Like you were the first week I transferred into the department?" He'd snuck into her assigned car and set the emergency lights, siren, radio, wipers, air-conditioning controls, signals and anything else he could find to turn on when she started the engine. She'd finally gotten it all deactivated and found the other three members of her shift laughing at her. She'd laughed too because teasing meant you were part of the brotherhood... even if you were a sister. Vance had always been able to make her laugh like no one else. And cry.

"Got your attention, right?"

"It did.

"It was a little welcome-to-the-force gesture."

And his wide smile and deep baritone laugh had sparked a connection between them that had grown deeper and wider, like water funneling to the sea. They'd dated only when they were in separate supervisory chains, on and off, two and a half years before. Vance, in fact, worked a graveyard shift and their time together was stolen moments that seemed all the sweeter for it. They'd started in on that relationship that lasted six lovely months until the Harlow family was murdered.

After that, her work to convict Maurice became so engrossing she'd not noticed them begin to edge apart. Vance turned his focus on Ferris and his desire to put him away was all he ever talked about.

They'd both been consumed. She'd assisted the lead detective to convict Maurice while a preliminary case was being assembled against Ferris. She knew they'd get Ferris too and it was part of what she looked forward to when she'd applied for the detective slot. Vance said she'd be great. And then he'd also applied and let spill personal details about her that blew up her chances. His betrayal hurt like nothing else she'd ever experienced, and she'd left the force.

Thunder sounded in the distance and Brutus howled.

"The radio," Vance insisted. "Or he's gonna hurl and I just got the back seat clean."

Steph fiddled with the knobs, glancing at the dogs. Chloe

had scooted over, draping her head over the shivering Brutus. "Good girl, Chloe." She noted Brutus's ample belly oozing out from under Chloe's muscular frame. If that dog was a trained tracker, she was the Queen of England.

"I'm gonna need some backstory on Brutus."

Her cell phone pinged.

"Saved by the bell," Vance muttered as a fork of lightning split the sky.

Chapter Three

Steph peered at the phone and pumped her fist. "We must be able to get a connection here. It's a text from Elizabeth." She let out a cheer. "'Team located volunteer, Gina, injured but alive. Transported to hospital. Holding at registration area until you get here.'"

He felt a ponderous weight lifted from his heart and he breathed a silent thanks to the Lord that Gina had survived. He was going to make sure all four of them did too. Now that task would be a ton easier with help on the way.

Steph's fingers flew and she dictated her own follow-up message. "'Are you advised shooter at large in vicinity?'" After a moment Elizabeth replied and Steph sighed. "She said affirmative. Police dispatched. Gina must have told her."

They both flopped back on the seats, buoyed by the knowledge that they were no longer cut off. Rescue was imminent. All they had to do was wait with Elizabeth. Between them they had enough firepower to fend off the shooter if he showed up again.

Police on the way. Gina found. He tried to assemble the sequence in his mind as he guided the car toward the registration area. Had Gina been spotted and rescued by a competitor?

Unlikely, since the other parties were several hours ahead. New scenario. She'd crawled out of the water on her own and contacted Elizabeth…how? There was limited connectivity in the area and whatever phone Gina had been carrying had been inundated when she fell in the river. Could have been in a waterproof case, he supposed.

Steph was still tapping keys. "Ugh. Lost the signal again before I could send the text to Security Hounds."

They drove in silence for a few minutes. He looked over to find her drumming her fingers on the knee of her jeans. Finger tapping. A tell he'd seen before.

"You're tapping."

"And you're tugging your earlobe."

He realized he was doing exactly that. She wasn't the only one with a tell. His honorary Aunt Lettie would have noticed it too and teased him about it. "I'm giving the situation the sniff test."

"Me too."

"And it smells funny."

"Uh-huh."

"Last I saw Gina she was being swept downstream, away from the competition course."

"Elapsed time?"

He checked his watch. "That was probably two hours ago by my calculation, maybe a little more."

"Two hours," she repeated.

"So Elizabeth's team had time to locate Gina, get her out, move her by vehicle to a hospital before Elizabeth contacted us?"

"Could be they had a medical vehicle standing by."

"Uh-huh." No choice but to say it. "It's also possible that Elizabeth and Ferris are partners. He might have threatened or bribed her into cooperating."

Steph continued to tap. "Or it's not her we're messaging." She stared for a moment. "I'm thinking about my days in the academy. I had a training captain who used to drum into me 'by failing to prepare we're preparing to fail.'"

"Yep."

"All right," she said slowly. "If it's actually Ferris or his accomplice who we're driving to meet, how about we have a little surprise ready for him?"

"My thoughts exactly." He couldn't stop the slow smile that spread over his face and the tickle in his stomach at her grit. She was tough and he'd been enchanted by it and by her, once upon a time. They'd dated in fits and starts, but he was always drawn back to her, no matter the tug of their careers. Toward the end of their months of casual dating he'd started to fall in love with her until he'd thrown it all away. Not the moment to wade through that again, but he could admire her, couldn't he? Nothing wrong with that. They had a plan together in under a minute, stopping a quarter mile from the staging area where the whole debacle had begun.

Brutus was reluctant to leave the car, but when Chloe exited, he decided to follow. They led the dogs to a deeply shadowed pocket near a tower of rock, overlooking the staging area.

"Elizabeth's car's there, parked under a tree near yours."

Even with their night-vision binoculars, they could not make out if anyone was behind the wheel. Dogs in tow, they took a slow route through the trees, creeping closer. Elizabeth's car was still and dark under the trees, while Steph's vehicle was fifty feet away.

"Will Brutus maintain a silent stay?" she whispered as they stopped at a thick cluster of shrubs that separated them from Elizabeth's parking place.

"Yes," his mouth said. *We'll find out*, his brain corrected. "If Ferris shows up, I'll initiate contact."

She looked as though she was going to argue, but instead she nodded. "I'll cover."

Brutus whined.

"It's okay, boy," he whispered. "Sit. Stay." That sounded

more or less how Stephanie and her siblings would command their dogs.

The dog's whine turned into a yip.

"Quiet," he admonished as loud as he dared.

Chloe looked at her compatriot and slathered a tongue over his snout. The dog quieted for a moment, but then with a pitiful cry he hauled himself up and dashed away into the bushes.

"Brutus," Vance called. Great. Now was the worst moment possible for the animal to show an independent streak. The dog was plenty slow so Vance only had to jog between the shrubs, but he got slashed in the face by wet branches for his effort. He was moving too quickly to adjust when he came upon Brutus standing like a stone, and he somersaulted over the top of him, landing on his face in the wet pine needles at the edge of the clearing, not five feet from Elizabeth's car.

Steph appeared with Chloe. "What is going on?" she whispered. "Is this your idea of stealth?"

He got up and froze as he saw the heel of a boot protruding from under the shrubbery.

He gave Steph a hand signal and she immediately stopped in her tracks.

Chloe did too. Through the branches, he could see both cars, quiet, beaded with raindrops. He drew his gun and skirted around Brutus, who was shaking and whining, attention fixed on the boot.

The dripping shrubs covered the person wearing the boot. Brutus whimpered softly as Vance pressed closer. Maintaining cover until the last minute, he kicked the branches away.

Elizabeth was lying on her back, eyes staring, the dark spot of a bullet hole gleaming in the center of her forehead.

He reached down and checked for a pulse. He knew he wouldn't find one. Elizabeth was dead. Before or after he locked the bridge, Ferris had probably wormed his way into her car somehow while she waited for Steph to check in, killed her, then used her phone to text them, or something else along those lines. He might be getting a bead from a hidey-hole right now, ready to shoot them.

"Steph…" He stopped talking at the sound of movement right behind him.

Steph gripped her weapon, palms slick. Chloe barked savagely. She'd thought they had the upper hand, since there were two of them, but the tables had turned in a moment.

Neither of them had reacted quickly enough before Ferris charged out from behind a tree.

Before either could get off a shot, Ferris had the pistol to Vance's temple. He swiveled to face Steph, using Vance's body for cover.

Chloe kept on barking.

"Shut that dog up," Ferris snarled.

"Chloe, silent." The dog settled into plaintive whines, which were echoed by Brutus. Steph clenched her gun and sized up her options, adrenaline igniting her nerves. "Drop it, Ferris."

"Sure. Let me just do that right now, Officer Wolfe." His voice was exactly as she remembered—high-pitched, nasal. "Anything to accommodate."

The watery moonlight left him in shadow, but she saw with a jolt that he was wearing a Kevlar vest. Vance was right. Ferris had been plotting. Her bullets wouldn't make a dent, not where he was shielded anyway.

He'd come prepared. *Failing to prepare meant preparing to fail.* She hadn't prepared and her own gullibility sickened her. Would Vance die because of her failure? Would she and the dogs be killed too?

Vance was a tense silhouette, his gun still gripped in his raised palm. Maybe they had a chance if they could distract Ferris.

But Ferris pressed his gun hard into Vance's temple and stripped Vance's revolver loose with the other hand, tucking it in his waistband. She resisted the fear that crept along her spine. Vance was unarmed, nothing between him and a bullet to his brain except her.

She mulled over the options as Chloe stood quivering at her side. The dog wanted a command, something to tell her what to do, but Chloe was not an attack dog and Steph could only tell her "steady," which hopefully would keep her from jumping into the line of fire. Brutus cowered on the path, alternately trembling and growling in terrified uncertainty.

Vance locked gazes with her as he talked to Ferris. "You left an easy trail. It was a piece of cake to follow you. What happened to the great criminal mastermind?"

Ferris laughed. "That's a cop thing. You always believe you're the smartest people in the room. What arrogance," he said, emphasizing the point by smacking the gun into Vance's brow. "That's the thing I can't stand about cops."

"It's not arrogance. We really are smarter than you," Vance said through gritted teeth.

Why was Vance goading the man who had a gun to his head?

"So smart you let me lead you right here so I can kill you both," Ferris said. "Geniuses, you two." He held up a bunch of red wires. "Your spark-plug wires, Officer Wolfe. Disabled your vehicle just in case you made it back to your car before I was ready." He tucked them in his pocket.

"Put down the weapon, Ferris," Steph commanded before Vance could antagonize him any further. "Cops are coming. You have no way out."

He rolled his eyes, pale glimmers in the darkness. "Do they have a class in cop school to teach you how to lie? I always wondered that. There's no one coming. You know it, Officer Wolfe, and so do I."

"The contest coordinators will miss us when we don't check in."

He laughed, a hearty guffaw. "You don't get it, do you? I'm checking in as Elizabeth using her phone. Already alerted the officials that you and Gina decided to back out due to the storm and you've left the area. For good measure, I told them you'd decided to check into a hotel to wait out the storm. If your family calls to check on you, that's what they'll be told. No one will know that anything's wrong. By the time they do, it'll be too late."

Too late. The words chilled her.

He tapped the gun against Vance's cheekbone. "Now that I think about it, maybe I am a criminal mastermind."

Steph eased an inch to her left, desperate for a clear shot that wouldn't kill Vance. "All this. Just to punish me? Because I put your father in prison?"

"Originally, to punish you, yes, but when Officer Vance here decided to follow me, I figured two birds, one stone, right?"

"You were a free man," she said. "You served your sentence and you're throwing that all away because you're upset that you and your dad got caught for breaking the law?"

"And why would I be upset about that, Officer Wolfe? Because you harassed my family? It was humiliating for all of us. We couldn't show our faces anywhere. My favorite cousin had to move out of town to avoid the shame of it."

Vance smiled. "'Whatever is begun in anger, ends in shame.' That's a Ben Franklin quote. I read it on a cereal box. You should read more, Ferris. It would do you good."

Shut up, Vance, she wanted to shout at him. "Your father got what he deserved."

"You forced my father to spend his last days in prison, where he *died*. Sharing a cell and a toilet in a six-by-eight-foot space with cement walls. And *you* sent me to jail so I couldn't even visit him before he passed." His grip trembled on the gun as he pressed it to Vance's brow. "Nothing upsetting about that?" he spat, the saliva spraying out at her. "Maybe you'd understand better if it was your family. All those precious brothers and sisters, your sweet mommy."

With effort, she let the comment deflect off her. Another half inch and she could risk it. She leaned as slowly as she could.

"Cops are all alike," Ferris said. His grip tightened on the trigger and a vein in Vance's jaw jumped. He held one finger up out of Ferris's field of vision, a signal.

Panic flared in her. This was a lose-lose scenario. This close, people would die—Vance first. *Don't you dare try something reckless*, she mutely blazed at him.

Run, Van mouthed to her.

The muscles in his arms bunched. He was going to make a move anyway.

She squeezed the trigger.

Her shot caught Ferris in the fleshy part of his shoulder, less than an inch from the Kevlar covering. He spun back with a grunt. Vance scrambled away and bolted toward her.

"Away," she shouted to the dogs, praying Brutus would follow Chloe's lead. She squeezed off some shots, which sent Ferris retreating behind Elizabeth's vehicle. While she was deciding whether she had enough of an advantage to outgun him, a rattle of semiautomatic fire sprayed the trees as Ferris appeared over the hood. Vance yanked her by the arm.

"Come on."

They sprinted down the path after the fleeing dogs. When they reached his vehicle, Vance flung open the rear passenger door and Steph and the dogs dove in. He did the same in the driver's seat, then jammed the key in the ignition and gunned the engine.

Bullets fractured the rear window, glass ricocheting. She grabbed for the yelping dogs.

"Stay down," Vance yelled.

Unnecessary. She was flat on her stomach, one arm around Chloe and the other anchoring Brutus. Ferris's next round of bullets would have cut Vance down if he hadn't floored the gas, getting them far enough away that the shots sheared off the side mirror and punched into the doors.

With them out of range, Ferris would have to return to Elizabeth's vehicle or Steph's, or perhaps he had another stashed somewhere. They'd have a precious head start, but not for long. She quickly checked the dogs.

Vance's anxious gaze caught hers. "You hurt? The dogs?"

"We're okay, except Brutus looks a little green around the gills."

Vance flipped on the country music and the dog immediately relaxed.

Steph gaped. If they hadn't almost been murdered not two minutes before, the situation would have been positively comical. Running for their lives with a carsick dog and someone singing about a pickup truck and a high-school sweetheart.

She grabbed a blanket and brushed the glass off the seat, covering the sharp bits with the floor mats to protect the dogs' paws. Then she squirmed her way into the front.

Vance was heading for the bridge, which would have been the quickest exit if it wasn't locked up. They'd have to try ramming through. A bruise was rapidly forming on his brow and blood trickled from a cut that flowed into his eyes. She pulled a piece of gauze from her pack and pressed it to his wound. "Hold this."

He did with one hand, shooting her an incredulous glance. "I can't believe you took that shot."

"Really?" She taped the gauze in place. "You can't?"

He blinked at her. "Actually, I can believe you took it, even though my skull was in the vicinity."

"I'm a crack shot."

"Fortunate for me, but it wasn't necessary. I was working on a diversion."

"Saved you the trouble." Her words were cool, but her stomach muscles quivered.

Truthfully, she didn't want to consider what the negative

consequences of her actions might have been. A hair to the right and... She'd known, somehow, that God wouldn't let her fail in that moment, wouldn't let Vance suffer at her hand. Was it simple hubris or faith talking? She wasn't sure, and not being sure was uncomfortable.

She returned the gauze and tape back to her pack.

He continued to ride the gas. "We're outgunned unless you have a rifle in your backpack."

"Negative."

"Elizabeth's car isn't a four-by-four. Mine's better for off-roading so that's an advantage, at least."

"Uh-huh." She narrowly avoided smacking her head on the side as he pivoted around a boulder in the road.

"He's probably not far behind us. Lots of spots near the bridge where he could pick us off." The blood had begun to seep through the gauze. He looked at her. "Run or hide, Steph?"

Everything relied on their decision. Sweat pricked her forehead. "I need to think."

"Think fast."

It annoyed her to be pressed, especially by him, but the seconds were flying away like birds startled from a nest. "I say run. Ram our way through the bridge gate, get high enough that we can snag a signal. Do you agree?"

Vance maneuvered around a fallen tree, eyes flicking to the rearview. "I say we hide. Let him pass us. Double back to the bridge and see if we can spring the lock. I have a trick for doing that."

"Dodgy."

"Yes. Pluses and minuses." He held up a fist. "Rock, paper, scissors?"

Was he serious? "You know I can't stand that when you throw it all to chance instead of—"

"Making lists? Calculating outcomes? Convening committees? Steph, we've got about five minutes tops before he's on our tail. There's no time for a spreadsheet on this one."

"I don't make spreadsheets," she snapped.

"Yeah, I remember when you enacted your coffee-room campaign. You'd been there less than a week before you created an Excel spreadsheet and had us all slotted in to man the supplies and tend to the coffeepot."

"That needed to be done. Half the time there was no coffee and everyone was in a panic when there wasn't time to DoorDash Starbucks."

"True story. Never was an upset coffee drinker after that. But you gotta go with your gut here. Stop overthinking."

She bridled at his tone, but they'd come to the steep descent that would ultimately end at the bridge. He pulled the car deep into the shadowy shoulder and reached for his belt.

"Where are you going?"

"Recon. Keep the dogs quiet."

"Vance," she snapped, but he'd already headed for the rock, crouched low with the night-vision binoculars pulled from his pack.

Her mouth was open to retort. Both dogs looked at her expectantly from the back seat, eyes wide and trusting in the darkness.

Was delaying the best plan? She had no idea, but she wasn't going to sit idly in the car and wait for the big, strong man to figure out their next move.

"Stay," she said quietly. Chloe sat obediently, but Brutus looked as though he might howl. She fished a couple of sticks of jerky from her pack and presented one to each dog. Brutus sniffed cheerfully and gently took the offered treat. At least he had good manners.

She snuck out and joined Vance where he was crouched, peering down at the road. No need to ask any questions. She hunkered next to him and waited in silence, ticking off the seconds in her mind.

The crunch of rock under tires sent her pulse spiraling.

Elizabeth's car rolled past their hiding place, Ferris in the driver's seat, his head swiveling back and forth. He might be able to track where they'd left the road but she didn't think so. The ground was rocky enough to resist tire prints and she grudgingly admitted that Vance had chosen the perfect spot to leave the trail. Ferris drove toward the bridge, stopped, waited, then reversed his direction and rolled onward until he was obscured by trees.

She heard Vance exhale. "We'll give him four minutes and then beat it to the bridge. Okay?"

"Vance, you're obviously going to do whatever you want. Don't bother asking for my opinion."

He chuckled softly. "It gets your goat when I'm right, doesn't it?"

She wanted to smack him in the shoulder. "Even a broken clock—"

"Is right twice a day," he said, finishing her thought. "Quick. Time for your part of the plan. Let's go before I'm wrong again, huh?"

There was no choice but to hurry after him and pray they got to the bridge before Ferris found them.

Chapter Four

Steph's legs ached from bracing them against the floorboards. Vance had to keep the car to a crawl since he didn't dare turn on the headlights. The wind had risen to a howl, which would help smother any sound of their progress, and the undulating canopy of branches overhead couldn't hurt either. She prayed Ferris had continued in the direction they'd seen him take. So far there was no indication he had an accomplice.

The wheels spun in the mud for a heart-stopping moment until they broke free. To minimize the risk of being spotted, Vance was driving on a trail that wasn't meant for vehicles, that much was clear. At one point the path narrowed so severely, with drop-offs on either side, that she had to get out her flashlight and direct his progress.

As he navigated the descent, Steph held on to the doorframe, wishing she'd taken the time to tether the dogs. They slid and scrambled as they tried to stay on the seat. At the bottom, she could see it now—the gate secured by the shiny new padlock.

Bolt cutters. What she wouldn't give for a pair. Normally she'd carry a small version if she was going on an extended search with Chloe. No telling where she might encounter a livestock fence to keep trespassers out. Trespassing was never her preference, but if Chloe indicated there was a lost child or confused senior on the other side of the fence, she'd cut locks first and ask for forgiveness later. Why hadn't she brought cutters along?

Because you were bamboozled into thinking this was a competition. "Bamboozled" was a word her father would have used. *Too gentle, Dad*, she thought. "Duped" sounded more like it and she'd not suspected a thing.

The ease with which Ferris had tricked her caused her stomach to churn. If she'd listened to Vance… That brought the churning to a whole new level, which was only going to make things more difficult. *Fix the immediate problem, Steph.* Shooting out the lock might draw Ferris's attention if he wasn't too far away. She finally realized Vance was trying to get her attention.

"Under your seat." He pointed. "Toolbox."

She grabbed it out. "You have bolt cutters in here? Why didn't you say so?"

"Not bolt cutters, my second gun. Take it. You'll need two rocks to deal with the padlock, but there are plenty around to choose from." He stopped her question with a quick look. "It's a cheap padlock. You whack both sides with the rocks at the same time and it'll pop open." He pantomimed how with his palms and the gearshift.

She lifted her brow. "How'd you learn that trick?"

"Retired United States Marine, remember?" He wriggled his eyebrows. "We do things, and we know stuff."

She didn't argue with that. Vance did seem to know about an endless variety of topics from how to restring guitars to the best way to boil an egg. It had been a constant source of amusement to their police squad, and to her.

"Why didn't we do that earlier when we first found the bridge locked?"

"Because, if you recall, we thought it was a trap and we were going to be picked off like ticks on a coonhound."

"We might be anyway."

"The difference is now we have no choice."

No choice. Just the way Ferris wanted it.

He drove the last steep yards to the bridge, put the vehicle in Park and yanked the emergency brake. He left the engine running but the lights off. "Gonna find a high point and recon while you're at the bridge. Texting's probably still spotty. Whistle if you can't handle the lock."

She bristled. "I'll handle it, one way or the other."

"Well then, whistle when you clear it. Dogs in or out?"

"Chloe can stay in with the window down in case I need to give her a command."

He lowered the rear window while she collected her pack. In case his rock trick didn't work, she was going to try dismantling the gate hinge and she'd brought a few small tools of her own from her backpack. It'd take far too long if she had to go at it with her meager equipment, but desperate times...

Brutus yipped and they both yanked a look at him.

"I'm doubtful your dog can stay quiet if he's not snacking," Steph grumbled.

"You wound us with such aspersions." The comment was glib, but Vance actually sounded a bit offended.

Brutus was already starting to dance anxiously from paw to paw. It wouldn't do to have him baying in panic. That sound would carry for miles.

"He's quiet when he's close to me and I can keep my hands free," Vance said. "I'll sling him along."

She blinked. "You'll do what now?"

He rolled his eyes. "I know it sounds weird, but I got one of those baby slings for him because he gets tired and he's too awkward to carry on my back."

"A...baby sling?"

Vance ignored her astonishment and grabbed a blue cloth sling from the between-seats compartment. The material was cloud patterned. He threaded Brutus inside. The dog's gangly

legs overlapped the edges and he seemed deliriously happy
to be so close to Vance. Such a load would be ungainly for a
smaller man, but Vance seemed unfazed.

"This gets weirder and weirder," she muttered.

"Cut the chatter and move out, Wolfe." With a roguish wink,
he turned his back on her and strode toward the rocks.

"Be right back, Chloe." The dog's droopy gaze riveted to
Steph as she got out and found a couple of rocks before she
hurried to the bridge. "All right. Wonder if this trick will actually work." The first whack of the rocks accomplished nothing except that she banged her knuckles.

"Owww."

The second blow seemed to loosen the lock, or maybe it
was wishful thinking.

The third hit sprung the locking mechanism loose. Her
mouth fell open. Incredible. The rock thing really did work.
She felt like pumping her fist but instead she pocketed the
padlock and opened the gate. She shoved it wide, the metal
squealing. Combining with Chloe's bark, the sound carried
in the thin air. Chloe's bark turned to a howl.

The dog was standing on the back seat, head shoved out,
yowling for all she was worth. Reacting to the shriek of the
gate? Signaling danger? From where?

She pulled her weapon and did a 360.

From somewhere up slope she heard the sound of crackling branches.

"Steph," Vance shouted from a distance. "Incoming."

Incoming from where?

As she struggled to figure out what he meant, Elizabeth's
car appeared above on the steep slope. Ferris had figured out
their ruse.

The vehicle was rolling, picking up speed on a direct col-
lision course. He was going to ram them? He'd risk dying in
order to punish her? She lunged for Vance's car.

Elizabeth's vehicle careened on, tires crunching. Terror

balled her nerves as she ran. There wasn't enough time. She wouldn't be able to open the door and get Chloe to safety before impact.

"Chloe, out," she hollered.

The dog leaped through the window, landed hard on the muddy ground and bolted toward Steph. There was nowhere to go as the oncoming machine plowed into the back of Vance's car, the impact forcing both vehicles onto the bridge. Glass broke with a pop. Momentum fueled the wreck as it was propelled right toward her and Chloe, a massive metal monster. The bridge was too narrow for them to evade the spinning wreck. The opposite end of the bridge was also secured with a sturdy locked gate. Trapped.

Only one answer. Steph leaped onto the metal rail. Below them the water churned, white whorls gleaming. She heard the scream of the tangled vehicles bearing down on them. How deep was the water? How cold? Would she break bones? Be knocked unconscious and drown? Would Chloe be injured in the drop?

No choice.

"Up, Chloe."

The dog did not hesitate to hurl herself into Steph's arms.

Another glance to spot any sign of Vance.

But he was nowhere to be seen.

Chloe clutched tight, Steph dropped into the water.

Vance's muscles burned as he ran, hunching over Brutus. He tried to keep to the trees as gunfire rattled from the other side of the trail, the spot where Ferris had positioned Elizabeth's car to careen into his. Likely he'd jammed the gas pedal down somehow. Vance hadn't been able to tell if the crash had caught Steph or Chloe.

He leaped behind a thick trunk as bullets sheared off bits of bark. Brutus trembled. Another round of bullets bored into the trees. Ferris wasn't going to give him the opportunity to take a shot.

He removed Brutus and set him down next to the sling. The dog's brown eyes were pleading. Vance's heart lurched. What had he done dragging a hapless dog into this situation?

"I gotta leave you here, buddy. It's too dangerous for you."

Brutus's whine was pitiful.

He cupped Brutus's hairy muzzle and kissed him on the nose. "I'm real sorry I got you into this, baby. You're a good dog and you should be sitting on a couch next to a fireplace somewhere." He swallowed, moved away and said in his sternest voice, "Stay."

Brutus shivered, but he remained still.

Vance crouched, weapon drawn, and waited. There was no way Ferris would come out in the open and give Vance a shot. He needed a distraction, something to draw Ferris's attention long enough to gain the upper hand.

From the bridge below came the pop of an exploding tire.

Good enough.

Vance put his head down and sprinted for higher ground, where he could get a bead on Ferris.

A bullet whistled by his ear, so close he could feel the heat trail.

"Next one's in your skull," Ferris called. "Drop the gun."

Running game over. Vance stopped. Slowly he turned, hands up, but he didn't relinquish his weapon. The gun was his only chance to survive long enough to get Steph and the two dogs to safety. He strained to hear any noise from the bridge, praying they'd somehow evaded the crash. The smell of smoke indicated there was a fire burning. That didn't bode well.

Ferris advanced on him, gun held in a neat two-handed grip. "Think your lady's still alive? Or is she a bloody pancake?"

Vance saw a red mist creep over his vision. "You won't win."

"Arrogant, just like I said." Ferris laughed. "Where should

I shoot you first? Don't want this to be too easy, do we? More fun when it lasts a while."

"A real party." Vance faced him full on. He was going to take his shot one way or another, though there was zero chance he'd survive. He'd buy time for Steph.

Ferris fired, and Vance grunted as the second bullet whistled by his temple. Ferris laughed.

Something rustled in the bushes.

Ferris darted a quick glance, long enough for Vance to regroup, but as he brought the gun into firing position, Brutus broke from the trees, galloping, the sling caught on his rear leg.

Vance was struck speechless with surprise, unable to shout at the dog to stop. Ferris didn't have time to take proper aim before Brutus bore down on him, barking savagely, saliva dripping. The dog was less than three feet away when the sling finally tangled around his rear paws and he stumbled, somersaulted and crashed right into Ferris's ankles.

They went down in an heap, the gun flying out of Ferris's grip. Brutus scrambled upright again, making a beeline for Vance.

Before Vance could get off a shot, the dog rose up on his hind legs, sling and all, to leap into Vance's arms. *Stop. Sit. Stay.* All the words got fouled in Vance's mouth as the dog hit him like a cannonball. He barely managed to keep on his feet, clutch the animal and maintain his hold on the gun. He finally slapped the drool from his eyes, cinched Brutus under one arm and raised his weapon.

Ferris was gone. His gun too. Vance put Brutus down, then scanned the shrubs. He bit back a shout of frustration. The coward only felt comfortable when he had every advantage. But he hadn't gone far, that was for sure.

Though he longed to charge into the woods after Ferris, he had other priorities. He stuffed the sling into his pocket, called to Brutus, about-faced and sprinted to the bridge.

His pulse was out of control. *Please, Lord, don't let me find them hurt...or worse.* But when he pulled up at the wreck, there was no sign that Chloe and Steph had been caught in the crash. His smashed car was crookedly wedged between Elizabeth's burning front bumper and the bridge supports. The steering wheel was compacted clear to the dash and the two front tires were hissing air. There would be no driving it. Or Elizabeth's car, even if they had the chance. The hood was billowing smoke.

Their transportation was now gone, but his thoughts were rushing in one direction only. He allowed himself five seconds to reach in through his fractured rear window and grab his pack.

He held his breath against the acrid smoke as they rushed to the far end of the bridge, which provided a wider view. Maybe his movement would broadcast his position to Ferris, but he didn't see many options. Steph and Chloe weren't on the bridge, which meant they'd somehow escaped.

"Steph," he called in a low voice, but louder than the tumbling waves.

The only answer was the roar of the water. Fear flashed like a grenade through him as he scanned. Was the river deep enough for them to have jumped? She'd been wearing heavy boots and clothing. What if...? He freed a flashlight from his pack and swiped it across the dancing surface. The current was ferocious and it might have swept them away, like it had done to Gina. He thought of Gina slipping through his fingers, the strange look in her eyes. Resigned? Angry at her fate?

He was anything but resigned as he shoved down his rising panic. "Steph," he called again, louder. Above the tumult, he heard something. His imagination? But Brutus heard it too. He hauled himself up to brace his front paws on the railing. Vance moved to the dog and craned to look over the side.

"Down here." The voice was barely audible.

The words electrified him, filled him with an eruption of

emotion so strong it could have blown off the top of his head. "Where? Where are you?"

"Here," Steph called again.

He almost bent in half over the railing and finally spied her, clinging with trembling arms to one of the cement posts underneath that supported the structure. Chloe was draped across her shoulders and she'd managed to keep hold of her backpack. Brutus shoved his snout around Vance's shin and barked. He felt like barking too.

Steph called up. "Was it Ferris?"

Good question, but not the most important one. Ferris or not, how was he going to get Steph and her dog out? "Coming for you."

With Brutus over his shoulders, he climbed over the barrier and down onto the brushy slope, sliding through mud and debris until they reached the river's edge. He took off his pack. The center support where Steph and Chloe were perched was ten feet from the bank, a stretch of roiling water separating them. He couldn't reach her, even with his long arms, and if he tried to swim, the current might catch him. He was Steph's only chance. And he wasn't convinced that Brutus wouldn't dive right in alongside him. Could the dog swim? He had no idea.

Work smarter, not harder. His gaze raked the underside of the structure.

Bridges required maintenance, tools, equipment. There had to be something he could use. It was almost completely dark, but his flashlight beam provided enough light for him to assess. He spotted a ladder affixed to the underside of the bridge. When the water was lower, it would provide a way for workers to inspect the infrastructure. He slogged through the mud and climbed onto the cement support. A closer inspection revealed the ladder was rusted in places. It flaked under his palms as he grabbed and pulled. The metal groaned but did not come away, so he braced his boot against the cement and heaved again until his joints popped. When he thought his muscles would snap, the ladder broke loose and he stumbled back, clutching a section that had torn free.

Elated, he hauled it to the bank, planted one end down on the ground and levered the other over to Steph. She snagged it and laid it on top of the cement piling. Dangerous, the whole setup. If he crawled over to her, the ladder might not hold under his weight. If she crawled to him with Chloe on her shoulders, they both could tumble in.

And there was the Ferris wild card to consider also.

He turned to Brutus, who was fidgeting uneasily in the mud. The dog hoisted himself up against Vance's thighs, leaving mucky paw prints. "Okay, fella. You were amazing back there with Ferris. If you get a whiff of him, you gotta bark and tell me. Copy that?"

Brutus shot out his tongue and slopped it over Vance's cheek. "All right, well stay out of the way, at least."

"Let's do this," he called to Steph.

Steph lowered herself to hands and knees and eased awkwardly onto the rungs. It lurched under her weight, so he threw himself on his end to hold it steady.

She was breathing hard, her lithe body taut with the effort. Chloe appeared unperturbed, her nostrils sampling the air as the two of them inched along. Did bloodhounds ever give their noses a rest? The metal wobbled and he tensed.

"Almost there," he said through gritted teeth. "Last part's a cakewalk."

She grunted. "Speak for yourself."

Her arms trembled violently now, each lurching movement an extreme effort.

Brutus shook his ears and whined. Was that a Ferris alert? Or Brutus's anxiety spilling out?

Without warning, a rung snapped under Stephs's palm and she flailed. Chloe yipped, sliding. Steph barely grabbed a more secure rung and managed to keep them from plunging into the water. The ladder groaned and twisted, rust flaking off into the darkness. The stressed metal would not stay intact much longer. He felt it begin to snap in half.

He dove, stomach first across the span, desperately holding the failing pieces together. "Climb over me. Quick."

Steph didn't hesitate. She flung herself forward. It required all his strength to maintain his grip. He got her elbow in his ear, a boot in his neck and her knee squarely in his kidneys, but he held on and somehow the ladder stayed in one piece long enough for Steph and Chloe to make it across.

Steph immediately grabbed him by the belt and helped him scramble off. The metal gave way the moment he touched land, breaking into pieces, and was sucked into the maw of the river.

They both doubled over, heaving in oxygen, while Brutus shoved his nose into Chloe's face and began to lick her muzzle. Vance couldn't allow them much recuperation time. Instead, he hustled them under the cover of the thickest tree with the most branches that he could find. He listened hard, but with the water and his own labored breathing, he heard no sign of their stalker.

"What?" she panted. "Ferris?"

He provided the main points of his previous encounter as he stripped off his jacket and wrapped it around her.

Steph's eyes were enormous as she listened to his whispered report. "You're saying…" She looked at Brutus. "That dog took on Ferris?"

Of all the things he'd said, *that* was the one that shocked her? "Yes." There was no need to bring up the fact that the dog had been tangled in the sling and almost wiped Vance out in his exuberance along with Ferris. "But the main point here is Ferris hasn't gone far and we need to move. Are you hurt?"

She shook her head, but she was still staring at Brutus in

utter bewilderment as she removed a towel from her water-proof pack to scrub Chloe dry. "He actually attacked Ferris?"

"Plans, Wolfe," he snapped. "We need plans. Focus, would you?"

She heaved out a breath. "What do we have for weaponry?"

"My handgun and yours. Extra clips. Dunno what else you brought."

"Just my Glock. Hopefully still operational." She stowed the damp towel. "Options are to skirt the canyon and bypass the bridge. Get to the main road."

"Sketchy," Vance said. "He's the kind of guy who travels prepared. It's possible he's got another vehicle stashed and he's got the spark plugs for yours. We're both wet and we've got—"

"Two backpacks, a tracking dog and..." She waved a palm at Brutus. "Another dog."

He arched an eyebrow. "New idea. We go for Gina's Jeep."

Steph was quiet for a moment. "If we could make it, it'd get us some wheels. But maybe your car or Elizabeth's is drivable. At least we should check for a working radio."

He shook his head. "They're both burning and it's not worth the risk. Ferris hasn't gone far."

Her chin went up. "It is worth the risk. I can sneak up there while you watch the dogs. Neither one is alerting right now. Ferris probably went to higher ground to spot us."

"Probably?" He fisted his hands on his hips. "I disagree but if you're going to be all stubborn about this, I'll go."

Brutus shook himself and yowled.

Chloe stiffened, nose to the air.

Vance's gut knotted and he went for his gun. Neither plan was going to make a difference if Ferris was in a good firing position.

Ferris's shout drifted down from above. "I'm going to kill both of you."

Vance couldn't see him, but he guessed Ferris was perched on a rocky outcropping twenty yards above their location. Fortunately, he wouldn't be able to spot them from his vantage point thanks to the canopy. Hopefully.

Brutus started to let out a bark, but Vance clapped a hand over his muzzle.

"I'll let you linger on a while, like my father did in prison," Ferris called. "He died. You'll die. No help, no other search and rescue teams around, no Elizabeth. How's that feel?"

Steph locked eyes with Vance. He knew she was calculating the distance, possible escape routes, formulating and rejecting plans like he was.

"I'm going to enjoy every minute of your suffering." Ferris laughed. "Not so cocky without your radios and equipment and your squad, are you? Just two mice with a cat on your tail—a big, nasty, feral cat."

She held up a finger and pointed behind herself, to a gap in the brush that would take them away from the bridge. He nodded, shouldered his pack and settled Brutus under his arm. Their situation was coming into dire focus.

They truly were alone in the Lost Sierra with no vehicle, no communication, only the supplies in their packs, two dogs and a cold-blooded killer on their trail.

Outgunned.

Minimal chance of survival.

Maximum exposure and risk.

He heard Lettie's words, the ones she'd whispered over him as he hunched on his knees, sobbing. *Keep your eyes on the Lord, not on the difficulties.*

Steph was looking at him. He squared his shoulders and answered her slight nod with one of his own. *Lord, here we go.*

He followed her into the trees, Ferris's laughter ringing in his ears.

Chapter Five

They didn't speak. It took all their faculties to move through the thick trees, skirting rocks and avoiding the thorn-studded clumps of shrubbery. Steph's half-frozen brain struggled to take it all in. One moment she was looking forward to a competition challenge and the next she was fighting for survival. And not by herself either.

Vance plowed along with apparent ease, which made her pick up the pace a tic in spite of the numbness of her limbs. She wasn't about to lag behind.

God must have a rich sense of humor to put her into this situation with Vance. Anyone else would have been more welcome than the big man striding along in front of her, muttering reassurances to his nervous wreck of a dog. Was she supposed to learn some lesson about being forced to cooperate with the guy she'd sooner leave in the dust? She slapped at a branch. There would be no learning, only tolerating. Temporary allies, that was all. Or more like cooperative enemies.

Their silent hike lasted two hours, with only occasional stops for reconnoitering and sips of water. Sprinkles turned into drizzle, freezing drops chilling whatever parts the dive into the river hadn't. She had hand and feet warmers in her pack, but there was no sense activating those until they stopped. Her toes had gone numb the moment she'd jumped off the bridge into the water.

Chloe was undaunted. Keeping her canine companion cool during sweltering days was more of a concern than the opposite, but the dog was no doubt tiring, since Steph wasn't hauling her up the steep stretches like Vance was doing for Brutus. They were easing along a rugged uphill section when Chloe lost her footing and began to slide. Steph caught her harness and pulled her close.

"Gotcha, Chloe." The dog licked her face. Steph used the break to take a quick peek at the map, cupping the light with her palm and checking her compass.

"Jeep's another two miles," she said, heart sinking. "Uphill."

He swatted a bug from his brow. Now that he was facing her, she was gratified to read fatigue on his features too. Her body was screaming for rest and warmth, relief of any kind.

"We gotta stop," he said. "Find a place to hunker for the night. Hope Ferris has done the same."

Thoughts of Ferris's chilling promise made her want to keep moving, but Vance was right. It was almost certain that she or Vance or one of the dogs would get hurt trying to navigate. And the drizzle had morphed into a downpour. She could no longer control her shivering. Since Vance had given her his jacket, his sweatshirt was soaked. He had to be freezing as well. Brutus was no petite canine and lugging the dog was a workout. Rest was imperative. *No alternative, Stephanie.* Jaw clamped, she nodded in agreement.

Vance pulled a flashlight from his back pocket and she was going to caution him when he shielded it with his hand as he beamed it around. Unlikely as it was that Ferris could detect the meager gleam through all the foliage, they couldn't take the risk. He explored the shrubs and rocks beyond while she shifted from foot to foot to try to restore circulation.

An eternity later, he reappeared. "Found a place. Come on."

Knees shaking, she followed him through the sheeting rain.

He pushed aside the wet foliage and led them toward a cliff of rock. At first, she could see nothing through the increasing rain, but he guided them to a cleft of granite, a dark pocket shielded from the elements by a jutting slab above. He bent almost in half and disappeared inside. She followed with Chloe.

The interior was cold, the rock ceiling no more than six feet high, but the ten-foot patch of earth that served as a floor was dry and she was deliriously delighted to be out of the rain. Chloe flapped the water from her ears and sank down next to Brutus. Both dogs were tired to the point of exhaustion, much like their humans.

She tried to channel the water funneling from her borrowed jacket into an out-of-the-way spot.

"You have a change of clothes?" Vance hunched to keep from banging his head.

"Of course. You?"

"Yep. You first." He turned his back and she slunk into the darkest corner of the cave, rifled through her pack and swapped her wet clothes for the dry ones. It was pure bliss to yank on the socks and her backup boots, even though she could hardly feel her feet. She returned the jacket to Vance. He changed his own clothes, exclaiming as he banged his elbows and head in the cramped space. They both rubbed down the dogs with dry towels. Chloe submitted gracefully. Brutus rolled onto his back, legs splayed, and begged for additional tummy rubs, which Vance supplied.

"You're Daddy's good boy," he crooned. "Tough as nails, right?"

Her watch read almost 10:00 p.m. Seemed like they'd been hiking a lot longer than that. She began to unpack some of her supplies, jittery at having Vance so close. Normally on a mission, it would be only her and Chloe. All of her siblings, with the exception of Kara, preferred working alone. Different case now. While she knew she would be twice as vulnerable without Vance, her nerves refused to settle. He seemed to take up so much of the space in the cave, his presence impossible to ignore. She caught the scent of the woods that clung to him, the droplets that hung from his shorn blond hair. Was that an empty snack-food wrapper that had fallen from his pocket when he changed?

A memory lit her consciousness like a streetlamp turning on at dusk.

Cookies.

One of their fellow officer's kids, Jaycie, had been trying to sell cookies for her Girl Scout troop, but there was stiff competition in her neighborhood from a group of girls who'd bullied Jaycie at school. Vance had immediately purchased all seventy boxes of cookies on the spot, spending his entire monthly food budget. After that, she'd known whenever she was invited over for dinner they would be eating boxed mac and cheese with Scout cookies for dessert. The memory left a complex aftertaste, both bitter and sweet.

Why was she thinking about that now? Her business was survival. No bandwidth for anything else. "I'm disoriented, but at first light I'll climb and get us a bearing."

He didn't argue, kneeling and rifling through his pack. He pulled a packet free, unfurled a packable bowl and dumped in kibble for Brutus. It pleased her that he'd prioritized the needs of his dog. She suspected he'd taken on Brutus to help his cover when he entered the tracking competition. So was Brutus merely a means to an end, or a companion? She'd get the truth about him one way or another.

Brutus gazed at Vance as he filled an additional water bowl while she did the same for Chloe.

"Go ahead, Brutus," Vance said. "Eat up."

The dog cocked his head, unmoving.

Vance shifted and spoke louder. "Brutus, chow time."

Chloe munched her food and they both eyed Vance and his dog.

Brutus didn't seem inclined to move. "He's your cover, isn't he? You got him recently? He's not a tracking dog, obviously."

"Well, no. Not exactly a tracker. I got him at the shelter. Figured if I showed up at the competition without a dog, they'd get suspicious."

Bingo. Typical Vance, making an impulsive decision. Did he realize that Brutus was now his lifetime responsibility? He'd better. No way would she hear of him dumping the dog if they managed to survive.

Brutus was still staring at Vance. "Maybe he does have some training," Steph said. "He looks like he's waiting for you to give him permission to eat."

"We're still getting to know each other. It's only been a couple of weeks. Permission granted, Brutus," Vance said. "Eat, huh?"

Instead, the dog laid his fleshy head on his paws and stared forlornly at Vance, who rubbed a palm over the back of his neck. "I, uh, actually, I think maybe I've confused him."

Whatever the issue was, Vance was not keen on telling her. Silently, she waited.

He looked everywhere but at Stephanie. "The thing is, his name's not actually Brutus, according to the shelter."

"What is it?"

"I, um, I'm not sure I can recall."

She folded her arms and skewered him with a look. "Don't lie."

He searched for a spot on the ceiling and exhaled. "It's Pudge."

The dog looked brightly at Vance, tail wagging. Vance sighed. "Sorry, boy. Wrong of me to change that on you, wasn't it? Eat, Pudge."

The dog practically dove into his food bowl. Kibble flew as he wolfed it down noisily.

Stephanie giggled. "Now that name suits him."

Vance rolled his eyes. "Yeah, well, what self-respecting

champion tracker is named Pudge? I had to think of something else."

Her giggles turned into guffaws and escalated from there until tears streamed down her cheeks. Probably a release from the tension they'd just experienced, but she couldn't stop for several minutes.

Vance laughed too. "Pudge has had a tough transition. He lived on a fishing boat and it was a quiet life, you know? But his owner passed away and he landed in the shelter and no one wanted him for some reason. And there was this big, alpha dog in the cage next to him, and Pudge is, you know, sensitive. I could see he had potential, though."

"He's..." She was going to remark that Pudge had a snowball's chance in the desert of turning into a tracking dog, but instead she cleared her throat. "He's got some good instincts."

Vance beamed, looking like a schoolboy who had won the spelling bee. "Really? You think so?" An errant bit of kibble dropped from Pudge's fleshy lips and he gobbled it up before wagging his tail at Vance. He massaged Pudge's neck until the dog's rear leg pistoned in pleasure. "I thought he looked intelligent. Mostly desperate, but with undertones of intelligence."

Steph watched the tender smile play across Vance's lips. He obviously did care about this animal. A strange feeling of fondness crept over her for this big, muscled man with a heart of butter. What? Hard stop right there. No matter how much of a dog lover he turned out to be, he was also a manipulator who'd betrayed her and decided to track Ferris on his own without seeing fit to let her know. Even if she had blocked his calls, he could have gotten her the message.

Didn't think she could take care of business herself?

A misperception she'd fought her whole career. Women had to walk a tightrope in the workplace that men would never encounter. Come across too tough and you were seen as abrasive. Too emotional and you were a liability. He wouldn't ever understand because police work was still a largely male profession. That's why it was even more painful to be cheated out of a rare chance at promotion.

What was all this useless cogitating while they were being hunted like animals? She brought out her topo map and spread it on the ground, examining it with her penlight. Her cheeks were tight with cold. It would be amazing to light a fire, but she didn't feel confident they'd put enough distance between them and Ferris. She still wondered about the guy on horseback too—Evan from the registration area. Something about him bothered her. His rude comment felt out of place with the enthusiastic, positive people who usually participated in search and rescue events.

Vance began rattling things around, but she was determined to focus and ignore him as much as possible. She located the ambush spot where Gina's Jeep was parked. But where were she and Vance, exactly? She could hazard a guess, but she wouldn't be certain until daybreak, when the rising sun would be an advantage and a hindrance. If she could get a view of the area, so could Ferris. But all she needed was some intel and a few seconds of signal to text her family. Once they alerted Security Hounds, she and Vance could evade Ferris until help arrived. Her mother, Beth, and siblings Kara, Garrett, Chase and Roman, and their assorted dogs would move mountains to get to them.

A sizzle of lightning lit the cave. Seconds later thunder rolled overhead and Pudge yelped. Since Vance was still busy with something or other, Pudge scooted next to Chloe who laid her head over his neck. Both dogs closed their eyes. If that wasn't adorable.

Don't get attached to Vance's dog, Chloe. This isn't a permanent thing. Pudge certainly had no such reservations. He practically had cartoon hearts in his eyes when he gazed at Chloe. She covered both animals with a lightweight blanket from her pack.

Finally, she looked up to find Vance tinkering with a portable butane stove. She watched as he poured water into a metal bowl and turned up the flame. As if her limbs had a mind of their own, she found herself moving toward that comforting glow.

"What are you doing?" she said.

"Making dinner for the humans."

Dinner? Food felt like a trivial matter in light of their situation, but her stomach was growling like a bear coming out of hibernation. Wouldn't do them any good to starve. She had more than enough for the competition, but it didn't hurt to be cautious with their supplies. No doubt Ferris had packed enough food to see him through his deadly mission. Besides, if Vance was willing to cook, she was happy to gobble down whatever he provided.

He might as well have been a scientist fusing atoms, so closely did he watch the bubbling water. After a few minutes he turned off the flame and poured the hot liquid into metal cups, then ripped open two packets of instant oatmeal and dumped them in. He sank a metal spoon into both and handed one over.

"Oh, wait. One sec." From another bag, he sprinkled M&M's into the oatmeal. "For flavor," he said.

Her eyes flew wide. Vance was an unrepentant sugar addict. She'd schooled him on the subject repeatedly, along with other warnings, but as the warm oatmeal melted the chocolate into colorful swirls, she could think of nothing else she'd rather eat.

They sat cross-legged with her small solar lantern partially covered between them.

"Thank you, Father, that we're alive, the dogs are alive and You've provided this food." He added a plea for their safety and for the families of Elizabeth and Gina, which made her eyes pool. Ferris had killed two women, if Gina had succumbed to the river. And he was ready to kill two more people if they gave him the chance.

"You should have told me you were after him."

He sighed. "We already skied that slope."

She hesitated. "My brother warned me not to enter this contest. Now I wish I'd listened, but Ferris would have found me anyway." She shrugged. "I got some anonymous threats. No doubt it was him."

"Did you go to the cops?"

"No." She countered, "Did you ever fill them in on your investigations? Did they know you made it your personal mission to get the dirt on him?"

He looked down. "No."

"Why not?"

He dragged his gaze to hers. "I didn't get Ferris when I should have. That's on me. I..." He swallowed. "I did a lot of things I regret, Steph. None more than how I treated you."

Warmth crept up her neck. "We don't need to go into that."

"I'd like to. I have some damage to repair," he said softly.

"What makes you think it's repairable?"

The silence magnified until it filled the whole space.

She shrugged. "Let's just eat, okay? Before it gets cold."

They dug into the oatmeal. The creamy mass was sweet and comforting. It was all she could do to keep from moaning aloud as she savored. She ate every morsel, the warm goo restoring her an inch at a time.

Vance sighed as he scraped up the last remnant. "Wish I could have seconds, but that should take the edge off."

"Thank you, for...you know, cooking dinner."

He smiled, showing the dimple in spite of his five-o'clock shadow. "You're welcome. Glad I bought some of those pre-made camping-meal packs. The candy was my brilliant addition, of course, and not to toot my own horn but that really made the meal."

She wouldn't say so, but he was right. Her supplies were nourishing, top notch nutritionally, but the chocolate was still dancing on her tongue.

He reached for her and her mouth went dry. What was he...?

He eased a twig from her hair. "Brought some of the forest with you."

She ducked her chin, mortified, because in that moment she realized she'd wanted him to touch her, to trace a finger along her cheek like he'd done when they dated. She gulped and found a wipe in her bag to clean out the cups. He tried to stop her.

"Only fair I do the dishes," she insisted, "since you cooked."

He yawned and tried to stretch, but there wasn't room. "I'll keep watch. You get some shut-eye."

"I..." Rest was imperative. They had a long hike to the Jeep. Exhaustion was already dulling her senses. "Okay." She set her watch alarm. "An hour. Then we switch."

"Two."

"Do you have to argue about everything?"

"Two," he insisted, "or you'll be cranky."

And in that maddening way of his, he moved on, smoothed out a spot in the dirt for himself to sit and zipped his spare jacket. He crammed on a black ski cap.

"'Night, Steph."

"Good night."

While she wiped out the cups, his comment twirled through her mind.

I have some damage to repair.

He acknowledged he'd done wrong. She suspected that was the reason he'd called her endless times, leaving messages on her cell that she'd not returned. *Fool me once*, she'd told herself. What would he have said if she'd allowed him to speak? she wondered. And how would she have felt about it?

The chill from the stone permeated her clothes and left her squeezing the emergency blanket tighter around herself. She didn't think she would be able to sleep with the cold and Ferris and the hard floor. But for some reason, as she stared at Vance's silhouetted profile, her body eased itself into oblivion.

Chapter Six

Vance dimly remembered taking over the watch from Steph in the wee hours. He must have dozed momentarily, yanking himself awake to find Pudge curled up beside him, Chloe and Steph gone.

His heart lurched until he realized it was nearly 4:00 a.m. and she'd likely gone outside to pinpoint their exact location, like she'd told him she would. He forced himself fully awake. Every muscle and joint hollered at him and it was an effort to heave himself upright. And he barely avoided slamming his skull on the low ceiling. They went outside, where he found a place for morning business. Pudge meandered through some wet foliage to stretch his legs, but he didn't go far. The temperature was enough to make his teeth chatter, the heavy atmosphere oppressive. The rain was sparse, but the air was thick with the promise of more. Watery pockets of moonlight peeked from behind undulating clouds. The gist of it was they were going to get pounded today. No getting around that.

"Hope you don't mind being wet, fella."

Pudge flapped his ears. One stood up and the other was at half-mast. Nothing about that dog was perfectly symmetrical. Chloe hadn't seemed to care. "I think you might have a shot with Chloe, you know, if you mind your p's and q's." The canine relationship was moving more smoothly than his and Steph's, but he was fairly certain they'd crossed a barrier the day before. At least she was speaking to him. And he no longer had to try and keep up his dog's alias.

He tried his phone. No bars.

Steph and Chloe appeared. Pudge scurried up to sniff his dog partner.

Vance raised a hand in greeting. "Success?"

"Yes and no. Got our location. Still not able to call or message. It's about a mile and a half to the Jeep. Steep."

He tried to hold in his groan. That was an hour hike in the best of conditions. "How exposed is the route between here and there?"

"Concealed until we reach the lip of the valley where we have to drop down into the meadow. That's going to put us in plain view for a solid quarter mile unless..."

"Unless?"

"We can take another route that loops around to the eastern side and access the meadow that way, but it's rugged and longer. It will add on an hour minimum, probably two."

Another couple of hours for them to be discovered and killed. Would they be better off extending the time until they could secure transportation or get there faster with greater risk of being spotted? A coin flip, at best. "All right. We can delay that decision until we reach the edge of the valley though, right?"

"Agreed."

His stomach growled. "More important question before we break camp. Breakfast or no breakfast? I've got M&M's and two more packets of oatmeal left if we can spare ten minutes."

A flicker of moonlight drifting between the clouds softened her expression, or maybe it was his imagination.

She chuckled. "Always the chow hound."

He grinned and stretched his bruised muscles. "I learned

a long time ago, if I'm going on a hike with you, best to fuel up first."

Her smile remained for a moment and he held his breath. He'd lived for that smile in the past, ached for it after she'd left the force, left him. Her mind might have been drifting through the memories too because her smile drained away, tucked behind a serious get-it-done look that shut the door on their intimacy. *Just as well. Wasn't it? Bigger fish to fry, Vance? Stuff like survival?*

"We shouldn't take the time for us to eat. Just feed the dogs. We can have a snack later," she pronounced.

His protesting stomach disagreed but he offered a thumbs-up. They packed quickly, fed and watered the dogs, checked their weapons and departed. He was happy to let her lead. He could read a topo map just fine, but she had way more experience in the wilderness than he did. Steph was smart and strong. And funny, at the most unexpected moments, like the time she'd whipped three clementines off the staff-room table and showed off the juggling skills her brother Chase had taught her. The performance earned her the nickname of Steph the Magnificent. A random moment that he couldn't stop reliving.

He zipped his jacket and fell in behind her.

Pudge seemed content to walk today, as long as he was within touching distance of Chloe. Vance appreciated the break for his biceps, which still ached from lugging the dog the day before.

The route was uneven, puddled with rainwater that threatened to soak them to their ankles if they didn't pay attention. The dogs had the uncanny knack of avoiding the squishier areas and he only had to help Pudge off an unsteady rock once while Chloe waited patiently, wagging her tail in encouragement. Maybe Pudge was going to turn into a more confident canine after all, under her tutelage. They kept on until the rain started again and they pulled up under some dripping trees for a rest. Pudge immediately scooted with Chloe under a thick mat of branches.

Steph looked as winded as he felt. Water funneled down her hood, dampening the fringe of dark bangs as they joined the dogs under the shelter.

"Breakfast break?" he asked.

"Something quick."

While he fished through his pack, she pulled out a lined, water-repellent vest and fastened it around Chloe. "Didn't you bring rain gear for Pudge?"

He frowned. "No. I didn't think of it."

She blew out an exasperated breath. "When you have a dog, you have to plan ahead, Vance. It's like bringing a child along."

"I did plan, kinda, but it didn't occur to me we'd be stuck in a downpour."

"Planning for the future isn't your forte," she muttered.

He felt a lash of irritation. "I was busy thinking about killers and such, you know?"

She wiped the water from her hood. "That excuse won't hold up. It's your modus operandi, Vance, and you know it."

"What is?" He was uncomfortable now, cold and hungry. Not the best time for the argument she'd started.

"A lack of preparation." She shoved her wet hood back from her brow.

He stared. "Just because I don't overthink every life decision like you do, doesn't make me—"

"You lease cars and get rid of them. You never wanted to talk about settling down in a place. You spend every dollar you earn."

Not the first time he'd heard her say that. It had been a bone of contention between them during the six months they'd dated. He looked at the strange assortment of things he'd shoved into the backpack and at his dripping dog. Arguing, especially about this topic, was not helpful. He tried to turn it into a joke. "Spontaneous. That's what makes me the life of the party."

No return smile. She wasn't going to be diverted and she shook her head, which annoyed him further. So he wasn't a seasoned wilderness searcher. He'd brought candy for the oatmeal and kibble and water, hadn't he? The most important stuff. He took a deep breath and let it out. "Okay. So the future is the last thing on my mind sometimes. Is that a crime?"

She faced him, fists on hips. They stared at each other, ire simmering between them until she surprised him by heaving out a defeated breath. Her expression wasn't as much angry as desiring an answer. To what question, he wasn't sure.

"Why, Vance? The reluctance to entertain the future and long-range plans and all that. Why was it always the last thing on your mind?" Moisture spangled her lashes and a raindrop landed on her cheek. Without thinking, he reached and thumbed it away, her skin like chilled satin to his touch.

She didn't move, just stood still, waiting.

He was uncertain how to reply. "Because I didn't... I don't..."

She continued her silent stare. He was not going to get out of answering. Might as well come clean. Could be the only chance he ever got to do so. "I used to have everything planned out when I was in the Marines. I saved up my pay and invested it, believe it or not. Stocks, bonds, 401(k), the whole nine."

Clearly, she didn't believe it from the sudden dropping open of her mouth.

"My plan was to take care of my mom. She was my hero. My dad took off when I was three and she managed everything herself my whole life. We were really close." He fought down the lump in his throat. "I knew when I enlisted it would be hard on her, having me away, but I had this plan, see? I'd come out with a nest egg, use the GI Bill to pay for school and buy Mom a nicer place, with the garden she always wanted. I'd take care of all the maintenance and yard work and everything." He almost threw the words at her. "See that? Buttoned-up, adult-type plans, right?"

She cocked her head. "But it didn't happen."

He stared, unfocused, at the lashing rain. "No." The weight of his mother's situation crashed down on his soul again, pressing the anger away in a well of defeat. "I came home and two months later she was diagnosed with Alzheimer's. Four months after that and she didn't know me. I could have handled it I think, except that it changed her whole personality. She acted as if she hated me." He swallowed the bile. "She...called me a loser, accused me of trying to steal her money. Threw shoes at me. Who knew she had a killer throwing arm?" Not funny, but he'd tried.

Steph recoiled. "That's awful, Vance."

"Yes. Nothing to be done about it. It wasn't her, it was the disease, but..." He took a breath. "I promised her since I was five years old that I'd take care of her and never put her in a home. I tried so hard." He kept his voice steady in spite of the pain. *So. Hard.*

She touched his hand and he stared at their connection, the small, strong fingers.

"Sounds like you didn't have a choice." Her tone was so soft it made him ache inside.

He shook his head. "I managed for a year, with Aunt Lettie's help. You remember me talking about Lettie?"

Steph nodded. The older lady, not actually a blood relation, had become somewhat of a mother figure to Vance, she knew that much.

"Lettie came over every day after her son, Jack, left for work. She cooked and helped me cajole Mom into going to her doctor appointments, sat with us while we watched the same recorded game show over and over. Showed me how to sneak Mom's medicines into foods she liked. She'd play the piano, which soothed Mom usually. When it got too dangerous and Mom went to the facility, Lettie still came over, every single day." His cheeks burned. "I was drinking a lot then, and she'd come and pray over me and make sure I ate. After Mom passed, she even drove me to meetings until I could stay sober on my own."

He didn't want to meet Steph's eyes, fearing what he might see. "After that..." He lifted a shoulder. "I don't know. It seemed like my plans all went up in smoke. I couldn't keep my promise to my mother. I lost my taste for thinking about a future. Lettie said someday God would give me a reason to look ahead again." Now he dared a glance and did not find pity or scorn in her expression, which heartened him. "And then when I couldn't keep my promise to Lettie about putting Ferris away..."

Her brow furrowed as she put the pieces together. "It was her son who tipped the Grinders off that their employee Harlow was going to talk to the cops."

He scrubbed a hand over his face. "Yes, it was. Jack was her only child. Ferris pressured him into spying on the Grinders' employees if he wanted to keep his job. Jack felt he had no choice but to report that Lawrence Harlow was going to contact the police. Then they wound up killed. After the family was murdered, Jack couldn't take the guilt. Lettie found him after he overdosed on sleeping pills."

Steph exhaled. "Tragic. Lettie must have been devastated."

"After everything she did for me, I couldn't ease her pain in any way but one." Now he held his breath as he watched her.

"You promised to make sure Ferris went to prison for what he'd done," she said finally.

"I was desperate to make it happen. I got the detective's job, but all I could hang on Ferris was fraud. No solid proof that he was responsible for the executions. No physical evidence to put him at the scene."

"Lettie doesn't blame you for not getting Ferris for murder, does she?"

"No. She doesn't have to." Because he blamed himself.

The moment had come. God had made it happen in this bizarre set of circumstances. He'd have his chance to say what he'd been composing in his heart for a year and a half. "For what it's worth, Steph, and I know that's not much, I am sincerely sorry for taking the job that you should have had. More than that, way more, it was wrong of me to share your personal information to better my chances, telling the chief you were interviewing elsewhere. I still can't believe I actually did that. I'm ashamed. It was wrong. I'm sorry."

Her lips went tight and she looked down at the sodden ground. The silence stretched long between them. He'd apologized. She hadn't accepted. When he realized she wasn't going to reply, he started up again.

"Hey, what am I going on about? You asked why I'm no good at adulting and I'm blabbing my life story." "Blabbing" was the right word. He couldn't stop the nervous gush of speech now. "I'm working on being a better grown-up. Probably won't impress you that I opened a savings account and drew up plans to build a house on a piece of property my uncle deeded me in Whisper Valley."

She jerked a look at him. "Really?"

"Yeah. Going to build a mother-in-law unit too, if I can convince Aunt Lettie to come live in it." He forced a smile. "Doing some adulting, right? Better late than never."

"Yes."

She fiddled with the zipper on her backpack. He resolved to keep to the important details and stuff the personal comments down deep.

She finally spoke without actually looking at him. "But just doubling back, your plans collapsed, but the important thing is your mother knew you loved her."

Surprised, he gaped at her. "How do you know?"

"Know what?"

"That my mom, even with the way she was, knew I loved

her? Because I was so frustrated, angry when she'd go at me. How would she know?" He yearned for her answer.

"She saw what you did, the actions."

"But she sure didn't appreciate some of them."

"Maybe not, but deep down she knew. We think love is a feeling, but that's not the whole truth. Love is action, behavior—it's what you do when you aren't feeling the good feelings."

He cocked his head at her, wanting more.

"You cared for her when she threw shoes at you."

"Yes."

"You showed her she was special, cooked for her, read to her, turned on her favorite game shows even though they were repeats and you'd probably seen them a million times."

"Uh-huh."

"That's God's kind of love, Vance. Honoring and respecting in spite of your feelings, not because of them."

He wanted to touch her shoulder, turn her to face him. Instead, he stood beside her, lost in wonder. "Who taught you that?"

"Mom's a big one for the Bible stuff. Let's redistribute the wealth here." She bent and removed Chloe's rain vest, stripped off the underneath liner and put the outer layer back on her. Then she stopped to fasten the inner part around Pudge. It barely held around his stocky tummy. "There. We'll improvise so they'll both stay somewhat dry."

"Thank you." He grinned at his ungainly dog. "You like it, Pudgy?"

Pudge flapped his ears and wriggled his tush.

Steph gave each dog a jerky treat, which they accepted with tail wags. She fidgeted with her bag of goodies. "I'm sorry I badgered you about the planning thing," she said finally. "I can be bossy to the point of meanness. Something I need to work on. And..." She gazed at him with those smoky eyes and his heart lurched. "I'm truly sorry about your mother, Vance. You did everything you could and she knew that deep down."

And then she hugged him. He had to be dreaming, but there she was, her arms encircling him. His head dropped and he laid his cheek on her shoulder. She held him close. He took it in, the comfort of her presence, a flood of connection that made him want to sob and laugh at the same moment. All too soon, she let him go, busying herself stowing her materials.

He steadied himself with a deep breath. Though she hadn't actually accepted his apology verbally, somehow he felt they'd reached a precarious place of understanding. Strange that they'd attain it here, in the middle of a manhunt, one step ahead of an assassin.

To hide his discomfiture, he snagged two items from his backpack. "Peanut-butter crackers. Acceptable breakfast?"

"I've got some protein bars..."

"No offense, but these are going to taste better."

He held one out to her, but a sound made him tense.

She looked around. "What?"

He put a finger to his lips and whispered. "Thought I heard something."

They stood motionless for several minutes. Wind spit rain under the branches at them. Chloe cocked an ear, alert but not overly so. "False alarm, I guess."

He offered the crackers again. "Would be better with grape jelly."

"It'll do." She took the crackers, touched his biceps with her free hand and squeezed, her fingers tracing warmth throughout his body. Another physical gesture? He must be on a roll. Or she was getting loopy from hunger and exertion.

"I love peanut-butter crackers," she told him. "Maybe there's something to be said for letting the seat-of-the-pants guy plan the meals."

"Score one for the Marines."

"Don't get your ego puffed up about it."

"Too late."

He wished they could stay like this, enjoying an easiness between them he'd never dared imagine he'd experience again. She unwrapped the cellophane and popped a cracker into her mouth. The ground was wet, so they leaned with their backs against a smooth tree trunk, which kept them mostly sheltered from the elements.

He was devouring his second cracker when Chloe leaped to her feet, nose in the air. Pudge followed suit a moment later. On high alert, all four of them stared into the rain. The noise became more defined, the same low buzzing he thought he'd heard earlier.

Now he could not ignore the facts.

The buzzing was not from anything in the natural environment.

Fifteen feet away, the black metal drone appeared and disappeared, skirting the edge of the forest like a man-made dragonfly.

His stomach dropped.

They were about to be discovered.

Steph silenced Chloe with a signal and put a palm on Pudge to keep him quiet. She and Vance slowly drew the dogs back farther into the bushes, the wet branches clawing and scratching. In her haste to snatch up their belongings, she prayed she'd not left anything that might be visible to the spy.

Ferris had a drone. Why should she be surprised? The lightweight flying machines equipped with cameras were still a fairly new phenomenon when she'd left the force, so she only knew the rudimentary facts, but they'd grown to be outrageously common. Her brother Chase had a toy model that he sometimes took on training runs to track their bloodhound's progress. Drones were equipped with high-tech cameras that streamed real-time videos and could be purchased on the cheap. They could be flown anywhere by a skilled operator, as long as the batteries remained charged. Some had fancy thermal imaging to detect body heat. If this drone had that capability, their goose was cooked.

"It's a low-grade model," Vance whispered in her ear, tickling her cheek. "Probably has a four-hundred-meter range."

The number made her gut quiver. That meant the drone operator, the man who wanted them dead, was less than a half mile away. A thought occurred to her. "Is it possible he has an accomplice?"

Vance frowned. "I didn't want to bring that up, but it occurred to me too."

"Could be Ferris himself flying it, or the guy I encountered on the way in. Evan. He was on horseback. Something about him rubbed me the wrong way. What was it?" She closed her eyes trying to recall him in detail. "I got it. His name tag was pristine, the lanyard too. Elizabeth's was banged up. Obviously she was with the group a long time."

"Not conclusive, but food for thought."

She peered at the drone. "Do you think it spotted us?"

"We'll find out pretty soon."

They crouched in the scratchy, dripping shrubbery and waited. She had her arms around the dogs and they were intensely focused on the whining intruder, but quiet, as she'd directed them to be.

"Good dogs." She stroked their heads. "It'll be okay."

But would it? If Ferris knew exactly where they were?

The drone whizzed along, approaching the trees but not moving too close to the canopy.

"He can't risk clipping a branch so he's got to keep clear," Vance said.

She realized she was holding her breath and forced herself to exhale. Her watch ticked off the minutes as the drone hummed around them. Five, eight, ten, twelve. Her calves cramped and a drop of freezing water slithered down the neck of her jacket.

The whining motor hitched into a slightly different octave.

"Battery's low," Vance murmured. "Cheap ones can only last about forty minutes before they have to be recharged or switched out for a new one."

Vance was a whiz on this drone stuff.

The drone completed one more erratic search and then retreated, vanishing behind the distant hillside. With one finger, Vance gave her the wait signal. They remained immobile until he unfolded himself and crept free from the bushes. She followed suit with the dogs, but they remained beneath the shelter of the trees.

Vance peered at the sky. "Don't think he spotted us."

"But we can't risk taking the exposed path to the Jeep. Not with a drone in the picture."

Distracted, he pulled a broken peanut-butter cracker from his jacket pocket and ate it in one bite. "Looks like it's the long way around for us, huh?"

She heaved a sigh. "'Fraid so. We'd best get moving before he has his drone operating again."

They cautiously eased back onto the path and soon tackled the sharp slope that would lead them in a circuitous route to the meadow.

"It'll all be worth it if we can get ourselves a set of wheels," Vance said.

With a vehicle, they'd stand a chance.

But if Ferris could track them with the drone, would he suspect they were headed for Gina's abandoned Jeep?

If so, they were on their way to another ambush.

And the chances they'd survive diminished with every passing moment.

Chapter Seven

Vance and Steph stopped regularly to rest, water and feed the dogs and refresh themselves. Twice they dove into the bushes when they thought they'd heard the approach of the drone, but both occasions had turned out to be nothing but delays.

His calves were screaming at him, along with various other body parts. Hopefully, he'd done a fair job concealing his aches and pains throughout their arduous march. Going uphill was a tremendous effort and he'd had to carry Pudge, who'd become exhausted in spite of his stiff-upper-lip attitude. At least Vance's thoughts were a good distraction from the physical misery.

The hiking provided plenty of time to consider what had transpired between him and Steph since he'd shown up at the competition starting line. He still wasn't sure exactly how to categorize their conversations. Healing? Confrontational? Cathartic? He'd never wanted to tell her about his mother, but she'd reacted with surprising understanding and tenderness, and he felt lighter for it. She'd accepted his apology, and though she'd clearly not forgiven him, she'd at least listened. As he reached to help her and Chloe over a sharp spine of rock, he imagined what it would feel like to hold her hand on a regular basis. She braced against his arm as she climbed over the obstacle. His fancy, no doubt, but he thought she might have allowed her fingers to linger in his for a moment longer than was necessary. *How about putting survival at the top of the agenda, buddy boy?*

When they next stopped to rest, he recounted the supplies in his pack. Three bottles of water and six food pouches. With two adults and two dogs needing constant hydration, they were going to outstrip his supplies. Fortunately, Steph would have toted along more than enough for the competition. The rain was falling and they could collect that to drink to supplement if necessary, but they'd have to stay in one place for an extended period and that was akin to painting a nice bright target on their backs.

Did Steph have a better idea? He was going to ask her when she pumped a fist in the air.

"I got a bar."

He looked up from his jumbled supplies, distracted. "Chocolate?"

"No, phone," she snapped, shoving the cell at him.

"Better than chocolate." Nerves zinging, he took a knee next to her as her fingers punched in a number. His own phone was still not showing any connection whatsoever. Why hadn't he purchased a satellite phone?

"It's ringing," she said. He scrunched his face close to hers, hearing the phone chirp unsteadily as if it was struggling to connect them to the outside world.

Come on, little signal. Hang in there. You got this.

A woman answered. "Hello?"

He bit back a crow of triumph. Finally.

"Kara," Stephanie almost shouted. "I'm in the Lost Sierras with Vance Silverton. Ferris Grinder is here hunting us. No one knows we're—" She pulled the phone away from her ear in dismay. "It cut out."

He tried to tamp down his disappointment. "How much do you think she heard?"

"No idea. Not even sure she finished her 'hello' before it quit." Fatigue shadowed Steph's face and snuffed out what had been a joyful smile. His heart ached at her downcast expression.

"It's okay. Even if she only got one word, it could make her start to question what's going on."

She sighed. "Maybe."

He nudged her elbow with his. "Come on, Steph. This is your sister we're talking about. When we were together, you used to tell me how hard she was working to save her chickens from being eaten by coyotes. Think how much harder she'll work to find you once she realizes something's amiss."

She didn't smile, but the corners of her mouth turned up slightly. "Yeah. The coyotes are still a problem for Kara. I've been trying to help her with a plan to protect her birds that doesn't involve her staying up with Dad's shotgun all night."

He cajoled her into eating a handful of M&M's. "Another half hour and we'll be at the rim of the valley. And the rain's holding off."

She held out her palm for more M&M's. "And we've got candy, which is better than my healthy options. Food of champions, right?"

He laughed, delighted that her spirit had revived somewhat. "Yes, ma'am." He poured some out for her and tossed a few into his mouth. Strangely, they tasted better than any he'd ever eaten before.

When she was ready, they struggled on. Undeniably, their pace was slowing. Steph had a blister on the back of her heel so she'd changed back into her regular boots, but they hadn't dried out from her plunge into the river. Her feet had to be as cold and painful as his. Pudge's fatigue made him clumsy to the point that Vance picked him up again, securing him close with the sling.

They sojourned on until they arrived at a spot to rest, just before they'd plunge down into the meadow. He freed Pudge, took out his binoculars and climbed onto a rock. Body complaining, he lay on his stomach and scanned. His watch told him it was past lunch time, but the atmosphere was gloomy and dim. They'd been trekking steadily since before sunup.

The meadow was alive with wind-rippled serpents of grass. The Jeep was parked where they'd abandoned it. There was no indication of any human presence. It might have been an eternity ago he'd encountered Steph at the first checkpoint, pinned down by gunfire, frantic to find her escort, Gina. The memory brought back pain. Gina, the feel of her hand snatched loose from his, that last look before she vanished... If he'd been quicker, more agile...

A rock poked him in the belly, bringing him back to the present. Mentally he put away the failure with Gina, shoved it into that vault where all of his worst defeats were locked away. He adjusted the lenses and continued his sweep of the valley, the trees beyond, the steep slope and the sharp drop-off that would take them out of the meadow and on their way to rescue. A blip of color caught his attention amid the muddy brown of the trees. He looked again, fingers strangling the binoculars. His mouth went dry.

"Steph," he snapped. "We've got a complication."

She immediately climbed up next to him. "More complicated than a killer with a drone?"

He handed her the binoculars. "At your eleven."

She hissed out a breath as she saw what he had. A horse, tail swishing, barely visible as the rider guided it into the trees. She groaned. "This is unbelievable."

"Your instincts were right. Evan the cowboy's a player in this game."

"He's operating the drone for Ferris?"

"I think that's what's in the black bag he's carrying."

She shook her head. "This is like some kind of ridiculous TV show. We can't catch a break."

Ferris. Two women victims. Now Evan added to the mix. The complications were stacking up and they all worked in Ferris's favor. Vance ran through their plans, searching for ways to adjust in light of the new threat.

"We can scrap the Jeep idea. Climb higher and see if we can get another, stronger signal. Head for..."

Steph shook her head. "I'm tired, Vance. We all are. There's no way we can hike out of here. We need that Jeep."

He heard the tinge of desperation in her words. He felt twinges of it himself, though he'd walk over coals before he'd articulate that to her. "The positive in this is that Evan's heading away from us, into the trees. Ferris probably directed him to keep tabs on the Jeep in case we returned for it, but he's finished his check for now. I think he's going to use the remaining daylight hours to find a spot to hole up for the night. It'd be dangerous for him to ride in the dark in this terrain, right? We can stall, give him some time and distance to move away. Sneak into the meadow after dark. If we can't find the keys, I can hot-wire it." Unless Ferris had returned and disabled this vehicle too.

"If Evan's close enough, he'll hear the engine. Put up the drone and alert Ferris immediately."

"That will take time for him to realize what's going on and launch. All we need is five minutes to get out of the meadow. If we see any sign of the drone, we can hide the vehicle or you can shoot down the drone, if it comes to that."

"Now that would be satisfying," she admitted.

"Worst case, Ferris and Evan are immediately on to us. I know we can get to the Jeep before the horse and I'm a way better driver than Ferris, that's certain." He added a cocky grin and gave her a mock punch to the shoulder.

She grabbed his wrist, playfully, but then she laced her fingers through his. "Thanks for trying to lighten the mood, but the truth is, we don't really have many options, do we? We're not going to survive much longer on foot."

He gripped her fingers and pulled her knuckles close, kissing them.

"We're going to make it out of here, Steph."

"And you're certain because..." She leaned an inch closer, her lips near his. "Marines know things..."

"And we do stuff." Before he could rethink it, he closed the gap between them and kissed her. His brain struggled to catalog the feelings, the warmth, softness, a touch full of life and tenderness. All the emotions flooded and flashed their way through him like sunlight reflected off moving water. She leaned into him for the barest tic, allowing the kiss to continue, and then she sat back.

He was unsteady, unmoored.

Her breathing appeared a bit off-kilter too.

"Vance..." she began.

His spirit dropped as he heard her unspoken message. It wasn't what she wanted. He wasn't what she needed. "I'm sorry," he mumbled.

She stared at him, tucked the hair behind her ear and shrugged. "It's okay. Strange times, right?"

The strangest, because the truth was, he wasn't the slightest bit sorry he'd kissed her. Unfortunately, she did not feel the same. "Yes, ma'am."

She grabbed her pack and rifled through it, her way of reinserting an appropriate distance between them. "If we're going to wait until dark, might as well eat. It's my turn to make dinner. No steak and lobster, but I'll see what I can do."

He sat quietly as she made preparations.

She opened packets, poured water, accepted his propane burner.

He watched and wondered, trying to cement the memory of what was undoubtedly the last kiss he'd ever share with Stephanie Wolfe.

* * *

When the hour came for the dinner meal, she did her best, but it was not as satisfying as the oatmeal. She'd reconstituted her supply of organic beef stew, which they spooned right out of the packets. To add a flourish, she'd gone so far as to plop a dollop of it into each dog's kibble and they'd gobbled it like it was a fine filet.

Vance also appeared to enjoy the meal and it pleased her to provide it, glad it brought out the dimple in his smile, happy to feel his fingers brush hers as he accepted it. She rued her own thoughts. Vance might be comfortable entertaining notions that they could get back together again, but she wasn't.

Why not?

The thought rested like a stone in her stomach.

Why not? Because he'd hurt her. He was a man who'd consider betrayal if the stakes were high enough, his devotion to Lettie stronger than his affection for her. That's what her wounds told her anyway. Was it true?

She stiffened. And was that the real root of it? That Steph hadn't been first in his heart? Her own words poked at her.

That's God's kind of love, Vance. Honoring and respecting in spite of your feelings, not because of them. And hadn't she personally witnessed him honoring and respecting her wishes even under the extreme duress they'd been experiencing?

Her mind flashed back to a police call two winters prior, to which they'd both been dispatched. It replayed in vivid detail. An elderly lady had run into the street, hysterical after finding her husband deceased in his living-room chair. They'd been on their way home from a training event, where Vance had volunteered to be the "bad guy" and gotten roughed up by a police dog. His pants were torn at the knees and there was a smudge of dirt on his forehead. One minute they'd been discussing purchasing some steaks to grill for dinner, and the next, the lady had lurched into the street almost in front of their vehicle. Steph had slammed on the brakes and called it in while Vance ran into the house with the frenzied woman.

By the time Steph had made it into the residence to join him, Vance had guided the woman into a chair and sat next to her at a scarred kitchen table. He'd caught Stephanie's eye, given her the barest shake of his head, indicating he'd checked and there was nothing to be done for the woman's husband.

"What am I going to do?" the woman wailed, breath coming in terrified pants as she twisted the cross around her neck with arthritic fingers. "We've been married for fifty-two years. What am I going to do?"

Vance clasped her small hands inside his big ones and scrunched his tall frame to look directly into her stark face. "I'm going to stay here with you. We're going to pray together until your family comes. Would that be all right?"

She'd nodded and Steph watched in utter awe as Vance calmed the woman with sweet prayers of comfort. The moment had embedded itself deep in Steph's soul too. She had grown up a believer, but she defaulted to herself she realized, not God. Problem? She'd fix it and pray about it later.

But Vance had done the reverse in that small space of time. There wasn't anything they could have fixed. No way to alter any of the stark facts. The woman had clutched his fingers as personnel arrived to transport her husband. He'd led her into the kitchen before the medics did their job, preparing her a cup of tea to spare her witnessing the removal of the body. His entire purpose had been providing comfort and support until her son arrived. Then Vance had kissed her on the cheek and scrawled his personal cell-phone number on her notepad. "If you need anything at all, Mrs. Brubaker, you can call me anytime." And he'd meant every word.

She'd called from time to time. He'd brought her a box from his supply of Scout cookies. When she cooked pot roast he was always invited.

Steph had started to fall for him then, in the terrified woman's kitchen—the man with the torn pants and the dirt on his forehead.

Maybe there was an answer for her tucked away somewhere in those memories that she couldn't grasp at the moment. At the very least, she could show care and respect for Vance in spite of her feelings. She didn't have to accelerate all the way to love. It certainly wasn't the time for that development. Plus, she and Vance had tried couplehood and she was wise enough now to know it wasn't going to work out. *Care and respect. Stick with that.*

And she did care, she discovered. More than she could have imagined two days before.

He leaned back against a tree trunk and stretched until his spine cracked. He was disheveled, a new hole in the elbow of his jacket. "Something wrong?"

She jerked, realizing she'd been standing like a silent lump with her empty stew packet, gazing at him. "Uh, no. I was…" She floundered until she noticed the cooling water. "I'll pour this back into the bottles. I have tablets, by the way—purification tablets, so we can collect river water and make it potable if our supplies run low." If they were stuck there much longer, water might be the least of their difficulties.

"Excellent. I didn't want to mention the water thing, but it was climbing to the top of my list." He held up his half-empty bottle and capped it carefully.

Once their bottles were full, she poured the remainder of the cooled water into the dogs' bowls and they both drank heartily.

The scant sunlight disappeared from the sky as she stowed the trash and repacked. Vance returned to his position on the rock, switching to night-vision binoculars as the valley plunged into velvety darkness.

Ten more minutes and he gave her a thumbs-up.

"No return of Cowboy Evan. Rain's holding off. All factors trending in our favor," he reported with a goofy grin.

If that was the case, why did she have a sickening sense of foreboding?

She scanned the gloomy landscape, the Jeep nestled innocuously in the grass below like a resting beetle.

Was Ferris lurking there too? Had he already disabled the vehicle? Planned a trap?

She stroked Chloe's ears. "I know you'll tell me if Ferris is nearby, won't you, girl?"

Chloe's head was a soft pillow for Steph's cold cheek. Her siblings would have been there in an instant, if they only knew of her predicament. She prayed Kara had gotten enough of her frantic report to start investigating. But with Roman and Chase working cases, and Kara helping their mother recover from back surgery, would she be able to rally the troops quickly?

Not in time to face the upcoming challenge. One way or another, the next few hours would change everything. She looked up to find Vance watching her. Silently he reached out a hand.

She took it, and together they prayed.

Chapter Eight

Vance took the lead just after midnight, closing in on the Jeep in a slow crouch that made his knees crack. As he reached the point where he'd have to step out of cover, he gave Steph a raised fist to stop her progress with the dogs. A glance behind told him she'd slowed to a halt, still sheltered by the rocks. They'd argued about the plan, but there was no denying she was better at controlling the dogs than he was; smarter for her to bring up the rear. Suited him fine. He'd do the initial recon and if Ferris was hiding, ready to pounce, Steph would have a chance to either back him up or get away. He hoped she'd take off at the first sign of trouble.

Who was he kidding? She wasn't about to turn tail and leave him to die. Love—in this case the generic type of tenderness for a fellow human—was about action, she'd told him. She would act to assist him, instead of protecting herself.

And that worried him. Deeply.

He'd cost her enough and he didn't want to contemplate her taking a bullet for him. Or anyone. The mere suggestion that she could get hurt made his stomach heave. It wasn't love, he figured, since that would be a one-sided proposition for sure. It must be that same generic-tenderness-for-a-fellow-human thing again. But he could not quite breathe away the prickly cascade of emotion he felt for Steph.

"Lord…" he whispered.

The rest of the prayer was a silent conversation. He slunk forward, leaving the brush and crawling through the grass with his gun in one hand. The movement was both awkward and painful when his knuckles, knees and elbows encountered rocks. Wind threw drizzle in his face, down his back, further dampening his already clammy jeans. The Jeep was in sight now, windows beaded with moisture on the outside but not clouded on the interior. All right. No one breathing inside. Ferris wasn't hunkered down waiting to kill them.

Encouraging. But that didn't mean Ferris hadn't left another deadly snare in place for them to find.

Steph would be scanning the wider area with binoculars while he focused solely on the vehicle. Reaching the driver's-side door, he tried the handle. Unlocked. On his feet now, he eased open the door and checked the interior, gun cocked and ready. As he'd thought. No concealed killers. A relieved sigh escaped his lips. The keys were gone, of course, but all he needed was two minutes to overcome that problem. He prayed the engine would work.

He gave Steph a signal and slithered into the driver's seat. The cold material permeated his spine. With the screwdriver from his backpack, he pried off the ignition panel and exposed the wires. A quick snip with his cutters to sever and reconnect the electrical system brought the interior lights to life. His excitement surged at the soft glow. This might actually go off without a hitch.

He darted a look to see Steph moving fast now, the two dogs racing next to her. He cut the starter wire, stripped the ends and touched them together. The engine chugged to life with a sound more beautiful than music. He tore off two pieces of tape and covered the live tips. By the time he'd finished, Steph had thrown the rear door open, loaded the dogs and flung herself into the passenger seat. Her breath puffed white clouds as she continued to do her reconnaissance job while he put the Jeep in gear and rolled it free from its grassy nest.

A moment later the wheels caught and spun in the soft earth. *Not now. Please. Not stuck. Please do not do that.* The engine noise would have alerted Ferris or Evan if they were close. They couldn't be trapped here in the mud. Five heart-stopping seconds and the Jeep pulled free. Sweat rolled down his temples. He kept the lights off, moving to the more solid ground that led to the steep grade out of the valley. He prayed they would not fall victim to any mud pits.

His elation was so great he didn't feel her tugging at his arm, peering at the dash. "Vance," she said. "There's..."

She stopped as a figure stepped into view dead center in the path in front of them.

Whatever she'd been about to say died on her lips.

Ferris strode forward as confidently as if he was going to accept an award, the rifle aimed at the front windshield. Steph gripped her gun, but firing at Ferris would require her sticking her head out the window. Same story in his case. Just what Ferris would want—two easy kill shots.

Vance stopped, engine idling. He had to turn the tables to give them a chance. Desperate measures... "Count of three, you turn on the brights, Steph."

"What? No." A vein jumped in her jaw. "Whatever you're planning, forget it."

She looked completely fierce as she stared him down—fierce and beautiful and brave and perfect. He grabbed her hand, felt her tremble. "Three," he said, throwing himself from the car as she scrambled to turn on the headlights. The dogs barked madly.

Ferris flung up an arm to shield his eyes and Vance took the precious advantage. At an oblique angle, he fired. Ferris flinched, the bullets missing him. Vance was moving too fast to aim properly, so he dove headfirst at Ferris, only managing to catch one ankle. Ferris sidestepped and kicked at him, connecting with Vance's chin as he scuttled backward.

White-hot pain almost immobilized Vance but he rolled and staggered to his feet, weapon still clutched in his fist. Ferris did the same, ready to fire. Rifle versus revolver. Two men determined to get off the lethal shot.

"There's no way you're going to survive this," Ferris said.

"Funny, I had the same thought about you."

Ferris cocked his head. "You keep on persisting in the face of inevitable failure. It's refreshing. Honestly I thought you'd both crumble without your badges and reinforcements. It's been more satisfying than I'd imagined, this plan of mine."

Sweat trickled from his throbbing forehead. Where was Steph? Still in the Jeep? "We're scrappy."

Ferris smiled. "So here we are, both armed and dangerous. Like a standoff in the Old West. You can almost hear the tumbleweeds rolling along. Dad and I loved watching those old black and white movies."

Vance's palms were slick with sweat as he gripped the gun, trying to visualize the possibilities. If Ferris fired, it could easily penetrate the Jeep. If Vance fired, he'd have one chance to immobilize Ferris, who had the Kevlar advantage on his side. Unlikely he'd succeed. There had to be a better way.

"The difference between you and me is," Ferris said, a smile spreading, "I brought backup."

The cowboy stepped from the bushes holding a long-bladed knife. Enemies doubled.

Vance caught the sound, the barest tap on the accelerator, Steph's warning to him. He chuckled. "Would you look at that? Looks like I did too."

As the Jeep plowed forward, Ferris and Evan dove into the grass. Vance barely managed to avoid being run over. He executed a clumsy tumbling roll that knocked the wind out of him. Somehow, he regained his footing as the Jeep showered him with debris. The closest door was the driver side and he leaped in, Steph scooting over. Ferris and Evan were upright now too.

He punched the gas. The Jeep rattled and rumbled over the ground. "Stay down," he yelled at her. There was no way to keep clear of the men with the trees and jagged rocks on either side.

He caught one quick glimpse of Ferris as they zoomed past.

Smiling? Why not shooting? Maybe he'd been hurt trying to avoid Steph's onslaught.

Rocks zinged from under the tires and he prayed they didn't have a blowout. The grade was steep, but the sturdy vehicle took it well. The dogs were bunched together on the back seat. Pudge whined as the wheels bounced and they slid to the other side.

"I can't believe you did that." Steph twisted to track Ferris out the back window. Her anger was palpable.

"There was no other way."

"Running him down with us both safe in the Jeep might have been an option," she snapped.

"Not with his rifle skills, and I might point out you took a risk there too. You almost flattened me."

"No chance of that with your catlike reflexes."

"Not the time for sarcasm, ma'am."

She braced herself against the door. "Why didn't he shoot us when we went for the Jeep in the first place?"

"He's enjoying himself too much." He kept to the middle of the narrow path, but the vehicle was still wide enough to take out branches on both sides. "He's trying to see how much torture he can apply before he ends us."

"Vance…"

"Hold that thought for a minute, okay?" He was forced to slow as the steep slope gave way to a perilous drop that made the dogs whine and his own stomach lurch. After getting up and over the peak, the Jeep was tipped, nose down, until he was practically standing on the brakes. "Couple more yards and it bottoms out again," he said through gritted teeth. "There's another area of grassland ahead, which leaves us exposed but we'll punch our speed as much as we can. Unlikely he can take us out while we're moving. More cover after that with the trees."

"I don't think so. There's..."

He gripped the wheel as the Jeep slammed up and over a fallen branch he hadn't seen. "We can either make for the competition finish line, where there will likely be people around, or the main road, whichever comes first."

She slapped a palm on her thigh. "Neither one of those is gonna work, Silverton."

What was that tone for? Now he was getting miffed. "Just because you're mad about my methods doesn't mean the plan is bad."

"It's not going to work," she insisted, stabbing a finger at the dashboard display.

"What?"

She directed him to the gas gauge. "Look."

He flat-out gaped.

"That's what I've been trying to tell you." Steph's tone flattened from angry to discouraged. "Chloe alerted just before we got in. Ever since the courthouse she can sense when Ferris comes into our proximity. She detected that he'd been around the Jeep sometime recently and she let me know. She was right."

He could hardly make his eyes believe what he was seeing. They'd come so far, risked so much. But the little red needle pointing to E was undeniable. They were nearly out of fuel.

She heaved out a breath. "Ferris outguessed us, figured we would head for a working vehicle since he disabled mine, yours and Elizabeth's. He siphoned the gas. We're going to stall out in open country and he knows it. Just his way of prolonging the game. Like you said, he's enjoying it too much."

Vance stared.

The needle fluttered even lower.

Ferris had indeed outguessed them. They were outguessed, outgunned and running out of time.

He pushed the Jeep, gas pedal to the floor, but it was only gravity pulling them along now. The trees thinned out around them, the sparse canopy allowing the rain to hammer the roof as the engine began to sputter.

A howl of rage built inside him.

Ferris had won again.

Steph had her backpack on before the motor completely fizzled. The dogs needed no command to exit the car. They sensed the urgency and catapulted free as soon as she opened the door for them. Pudge immediately looked around to find some avenue to escape the pounding rain.

Vance recovered from his shock enough to quickly search the Jeep for anything useful that might aid their survival. Steph was too numb and disappointed to help him. She couldn't imagine what would make their current situation easier and Ferris had probably stripped out anything that might be of use anyway. Ferris had wanted them to experience hope so he could rip it away.

Vance was an optimist though, even now. She felt no such emotion. They were in deep trouble and it was only getting worse. Ferris would double back to his own vehicle, hers maybe, and pursue them, relishing every moment, no doubt. Worse yet he had Evan on horseback to track them too and she'd seen the knife so Evan wasn't merely a spy. He'd kill them if Ferris gave him the command. They'd seen his face and could testify as to his role in the murder plot. She spared one precious moment before they ran to the trees to glance at her phone. No signal.

He reached the sheltering branches a moment after she did.

"The Jeep plan went up in smoke. Now what? River or mountain?" he demanded.

She blinked away her stupor and tried to focus. Their two options were ominous. The Feather River thundered nearby, funneling off the high mountain peaks of the northern Sierra Nevada. The river's main forks and offshoots snaked through precarious canyons, with Class 3, 4 and 5 rapids made worse recently by a historic spring snowmelt. Unlikely they'd find any kayakers in the wild waters to help them, not at this time of year, and not in a nasty storm.

She cast a look at the stern granite peak rising above the trees. Climbing would be arduous, impossible even. They'd never reach the other side, but the choice held the hope they might encounter a rough weather hiker or an empty camp- ground where they could find shelter and a possible signal. Most significantly, Ferris would assume they'd follow the wa- terway, which would lead them to one of the tiny towns dot- ted here and there throughout the Lost Sierra. He'd be sure to complete his executions before they set foot in any of them.

"Mountain," she said, explaining her reasoning. "Unless you have another idea."

"Not at the moment." He rubbed a bump on his forehead. "My last plan wasn't worth much, was it?"

"I didn't see it coming either." His demeanor was different, worrying her. "You all right?"

He waved off her question. "Ready, dogs?"

Pudge and Chloe both wagged their tails. Vance took the lead position.

She figured they didn't have long before Ferris regrouped. Evan would send up a drone to search the meadow, the trails. Though it was still far from sunrise, it was possible the drone had low light tracking capabilities. At least the bits of granite and leaves covering the ground would conceal their footprints. Maybe the violent rainfall would make it harder for the drone to spy on them. They would need any slim advantage to sur- vive long enough to get help.

She moved as fast as she could, keeping up with Vance's

quick pace in spite of the growing agony in her feet. The gush of warmth indicated her heels were bloody, but there was no question about stopping to treat her wounds. She could hear her wild brother Chase's slogan echoing in her brain. "Pain is never permanent," he'd said while recovering from the various injuries he'd sustained as an Army Scout and his often reckless behavior in his leisure time.

And it wasn't going to be permanent now. She straightened and pushed on.

Vance tripped once, catching himself. His gait was less fluid than normal. Had he suffered a head injury tackling Ferris? Or was it merely fatigue and the uneven trail? She suggested a moment of rest, but he declined.

Chloe stayed by her side, vaulting over rocks and fallen logs. Steph was thankful she kept up Chloe's exercise regimen regardless of the season. Pudge maintained a better pace than she'd thought possible. He'd need to be carried eventually...if they survived long enough. If Vance was too tired, she could lug him for a while, maybe borrow the sling. He was such an ungainly dog, the opposite of her beautiful bloodhound, but he was a loyal, dedicated soul who was quickly taking up a big spot in her heart. The guilt she felt about ensnaring Chloe into their perilous situation must be something Vance was grappling with too with his dog. What would happen to Pudge if and when they got back to civilization? Vance had a tiny apartment with a no-pet policy.

She was encouraged when they stumbled upon a mile marker almost covered by overgrowth. "We're on an official trail of some sort, thankfully." When she unfurled the map to check, Vance bent over to shield her and the flapping paper from the driving rain.

"Yes, here it is," she said. "It leads..."

Vance shushed her and they went still. He pulled her into the crook of his arm. She could feel his heart thud against her shoulder. The drone zoomed above them, its metallic eye searching. She pressed her face to his chest.

"I'd give a week's pay to shoot that thing down," Vance muttered.

"Same."

He kept her close and for a moment she forgot the circling drone and the pain in her heels and the hunger and bone-deep fatigue. There was comfort in his touch, the way he held her close enough to protect her, but gently too. He'd treated her throughout their ordeal with enough respect to communicate that he valued who she was, and what she thought, and the decisions she made. Every breath he took encouraged her to relax against him. So comfortable, she thought. So right.

You're reading into this, Steph. Running for your life isn't helping your mental state. But she absorbed the warmth anyway while the moments ticked by, as if she was powerless to separate herself. They remained motionless until the drone moved off to search another area.

She bit her lip as they stepped apart, covering her jumbled emotions by sipping water and offering some to the dogs along with a jerky snack. Ahead was a crooked switchback that appeared to lead straight up at a merciless pitch. Vance slumped as he perused their path.

He had something to say, something important. She waited.

"Steph, even with the drone gone, we're in a dog's breakfast here."

One of Vance's favorite expressions when they were on the force together. A dog's breakfast was the remains of whatever the chef had ruined and made unfit for human consumption. She didn't like the flatness of his tone, the rounding of his impossibly wide shoulders.

"Speak for yourself," she said lightly. "My dog eats the finest quality breakfast."

Her joke didn't work. He faced her with hands on hips.

"I think we should separate."

She recoiled. "What?"

"I'll move away, draw them off, divert them long enough that you can find someone to help, or at least hide. You've got rations and I'll give you mine too. That will allow you a couple more days."

She folded her arms, scared but determined to firmly and calmly talk him out of his notion. "No. We're not doing that."

"Steph, we're running out of options and time."

The bruise on his cheekbone was dark purple and she noticed dried blood in his hairline.

His mouth was set, brow furrowed. If he decided the best way to save her was sacrificing himself, she wouldn't be able to change his mind, so she let her instincts take over. She lifted her hands to his cheeks, thumbs brushing his lips.

He put a palm over hers, eyes closed as he cupped her hand to his face.

"Listen to me," she said softly.

He didn't look at her so she pressed her forehead to his. "Vance? I need you to hear me."

He leaned back slightly and opened his eyes.

She maintained their connection. "The only reason we're still alive is that we've stuck together."

He grimaced. "I should have sent the cops in the first place, not gone after Ferris myself. Insisted you quit the competition."

"The cops have other things to do besides chasing people who skip out on parole." She gently eased up his chin until she was looking into his eyes. She remembered the soft green, the color of rain-soaked spring leaves. "And regarding your idea that you should have forced me to quit the competition, when was the last time you were able to force me to do anything I didn't want to do?"

His fingers tightened on hers. "He's already killed two women. I—"

"Vance." She pulled their joined hands to her and squeezed tight until he stopped talking, willing him to listen and accept, praying he would not leave her. "We're partners again right now, like we were back on the force. Partners don't abandon each other. Ever."

He stared at her, drew her hand to his lips, pressed his cold chin against her skin. Her heart fluttered as he kissed her knuckles one at a time. "I can't bear it if you get hurt," he said softly. "I've taken a lot in my life, but I cannot survive that. I won't survive it."

The words were so precious, considering. She'd been hurt, deeply wounded by this man, but love was action and he surely was behaving as if he loved her still. Or maybe again? Could they be discovering each other in a new way?

She forced a smile. "Improvise, adapt and overcome, isn't that what you Marines say?"

He blinked.

"Didn't think I'd remember?" she asked.

"Didn't think you listened."

"I listened to every word you ever said to me." Every word, every nuance, every look had been written on the pages of her mind until the book had slammed shut between them. Shut for always.

Without warning, he scooped her in an embrace and rested his chin on her head. "I dreamed of reconnecting with you over and over, but not this way."

Dreamed of reconnecting? She felt the pressure of his hug, the breadth of the muscled shoulders that had made him a champion swimmer in college. But that's all this was, a surreal dream. Nothing real existed between her and Vance outside this nightmarish bubble. Did it?

She and Vance were partners for the moment. And running through the Lost Sierra an inch away from a killer hadn't changed anything.

Survival.

That was all they had to worry about.

Survival, and making sure Ferris got the punishment he deserved.

She pulled away from him and he let her go. "We stick together. Period."

With a sigh, he took off his cap, wiped his brow and gestured with it. "All right then. Ladies first."

She could not restrain a giggle as she forced her body into motion.

"What's so funny?"

"Your cap. You still write your passwords inside your hat because you can't remember them."

He rolled his eyes. "I remembered them just fine when I had the same one for everything."

"Getmeasandwichasap?" she asked as she skirted a puddle the size of a manhole cover.

"Yeah, that one, until it got hacked and you made me promise not to use the same passwords for everything." He slapped at a low branch. "Letters, numbers, symbols, uppercase and lower? Who can remember all that? I'm not into codes and stuff. What can I say?"

So true. His motto was I Don't Math in Public. Again he reached to clear a branch, this one low-lying, to assist Pudge.

"What are you going to do with Pudge when the case is over?" she asked.

He frowned. "What do you mean?"

"Are you going to return him?"

The look he tossed her was pure disgust. "You actually think I'd dump him back in the shelter? Are you kidding me?" Vance glared at her and covered Pudge's ears. "Don't let him hear you say a thing like that. You think I'd discard him like some sort of ugly sweater?" he whispered. "I hope he didn't hear you. He's sensitive."

She was struck silent with a combination of amusement and awe. "You're keeping him?"

He uncovered the dog's ears. "Well, of course I'm keeping

him. Good grief, Steph. You've accused me of lots of terrible things but that's got to be the worst."

"I apologize."

He blew out a breath, clearly still offended. "I understand I broke your trust and you figure I'm a scoundrel, but I promise you I would never dump Pudge. He was in the shelter next to a kind of intense roommate like I told you about. Hence, Pudge stayed in the corner. When I showed up, he waddled over and pressed himself to the bars with these pleading eyes, as if he was saying 'Please take me home and we can be best friends forever.' How could I walk away from that?" He bent and kissed the dog's fat wedge of a head. "You're Daddy's Pudgy, aren't you? We're friends for life, right?"

She tried to take in the sight of the big man who'd broken her heart, crooning baby talk to an overweight mutt as if the animal was a precious infant.

Pudge happily slurped a tongue over Vance's nose. "I guess I got us both into a lot of trouble here, didn't I?" Vance said. He locked eyes with Steph. "I should have tried harder to contact you before the event, tell you what I was up to."

Something inside her loosened. "And I should have listened to you when you showed up at the start line."

"I'm sorry," they both said at once. Pudge lathered Vance with another dog kiss.

"But you can't keep him at your apartment, can you?" she asked.

"No, but I didn't like that place anyway. Terrible parking and the air conditioner isn't up to snuff. And those weird curtains were never my style. Who puts roosters on curtains? We've been staying in pet-friendly hotels while tracking Ferris, but when I get back, he'll bunk with Aunt Lettie while I pack up the apartment." He arched an eyebrow at her. "Pudgy is mine now. Forever." He stalked farther ahead, obviously still miffed at her.

And you misjudged him. Maybe it was better to have him

annoyed with her than trying to start up a relationship again. Grateful that at least she'd rekindled a fire in him, she smiled in spite of her discomfort as her new view of Vance settled into her soul.

Vance wouldn't let Pudge down and he wouldn't let her down either. Not again. He'd fight to the last breath, the final moment. He was brave enough to stay the course, strong enough to apologize for what he'd done wrong.

Her heart was still fluttering at an accelerated rate from their physical connection. What in the world? She had to be suffering from dehydration or stress or low electrolytes to be imagining things about Vance, a delirium born of danger. Any moment the drone could pinpoint their location again. Ferris's rifle shot might find them from behind a rock or tree, no matter how fast they pushed on.

How were they going to escape?

Friday morning was nearly upon them. The weather was worsening. The chances that they'd run into anyone who could help them was slim to nonexistent.

If they could only get a signal...

Her phone was juiced up thanks to her solar charger.

One text or call and the whole game would change.

Just keep moving, Steph.

But she could feel her body weakening. Vance was slowing too and she'd barely talked him out of separating.

Did they have enough stamina to outlast Ferris Grinder and company?

Soon their physical state would leave them at his mercy, no matter how great their determination.

Chapter Nine

They'd been hiking the whole day along a ragged trail which Steph was sure would connect to a bigger path in the space of twelve miles. Twelve miles might as well be a thousand, he thought. On the plus side, there had been no further drone sightings and the way they were going would make it unlikely Ferris could follow in a vehicle. But the minuses still overshadowed the pluses. Vance had been carrying Pudge for the last mile and he'd stumbled so many times he feared he'd drop the dog. Areas of thick mud forced them to stop and chew up time going around. The day elapsed in painful increments until finally the sun was low in the sky. Vance's nerves began to prickle as the daylight disappeared behind the mountain peaks.

Even Chloe was lagging, though they'd stopped regularly. The competition allowed only for daytime participation, since the terrain was rugged. Smart rule. Marching around in the dark and cold was stressful and hazardous, especially without the prescribed rest hours in a nice, watertight tent. At least they had enough supplies, though he probably hadn't packed enough of something.

When Steph tripped and went to one knee, he hurried to give her a hand up, and she leaned heavily on him. Chloe slurped an anxious tongue across Steph's cheek, but it was clear the dog was depleted too.

"We gotta camp until morning. Rest and refuel." He figured she'd argue but she didn't. Telling.

"Where?" was all she said.

"I'll find a spot—and you're gonna love this part." He yanked the slender bundles from his pack. "Two ultralight sleeping bags I swiped from the Jeep."

Her eyes lit in a way that made his breath hitch. "Really?" she squeaked. "Ferris left them there?"

"They were stowed behind the seats. I think it was meant as extra competition gear. Or Ferris is simply making things more sporting. Anyway I figure a human and a dog per bag and that's gonna be tight, but warm. We can lay them over there, down in the hollow. Don't think a drone can get close with all those branches and fortunately they're black so they will be even less visible. What do you say? I can even toss in a meal to sweeten the offer."

"Perfection."

Pleased with himself, he enjoyed a spurt of energy as they hurried to the small depression in the ground. Thick pines added a carpet of needles. Together they spread out the bags and arranged their makeshift camp.

"Food or sleep first?"

"I'm too tired to eat," Steph said.

"Sleep it is. It's almost five o'clock," he said. "We'll overnight here, aim to move out again at three a.m. I'll take the first shift while you sleep."

She crawled into the sleeping bag and held the side open so Chloe could burrow in next to her. Pudge tried to join them.

"You got your own bag, buddy." He unzipped his and smoothed it out a few feet from Steph and Chloe. Pudge slithered inside down to the bottom.

Steph wriggled a few times until she and Chloe reached some sort of comfortable compromise. Something missing, he thought. The sling would do. He folded it into a small rectangle and kneeled next to her.

"Use this for a pillow."

She lifted her head and he slid it under her cheek. And because he was tired, or out of his mind, or maybe just too uncomfortable to deny his craving, he bent down and kissed her on the lips. "Sleep well, Steph."

She smiled as her eyes closed.

Vance returned to his sleeping bag and sat atop it, away from the lump of Pudge, back against the tree. He checked his gun and laid it next to him.

"Vance?" Steph's voice was small and delicate in the great big emptiness.

"Yes?"

"You promise you won't leave me?"

That tiny little-girl voice coming from that strong-as-a-lion woman made a lump form in his throat. How could he put his ferocious surge of emotion into words? He swallowed hard. "No, honey. I will not leave you. I promise."

And he wouldn't. Not until there was no breath left in him, or worse, until she asked him to. It wasn't until that very moment that he understood how big and deep and wide were his feelings for Stephanie Wolfe. "Get some rest, Steph," he whispered.

When he heard the sound of her regular breathing, he committed some time to prayer. The only way they'd get out alive was with God's intervention. As much as it pained him to admit it, he was weakened, failing by the hour, and Ferris had outwitted him at every turn. He tried to settle his spine against the rough tree trunk. No matter how he squirmed, some sharp bit dug into his back.

Maybe the pain would help him fight off the sleepiness.

Because Ferris wasn't sitting back for a snooze.

He had no doubt about that.

No doubt at all.

* * *

Vance lurched awake, reaching for his weapon and his senses. His eyes were gritty, his limbs stiff and cold, as he processed the misty air all around him, the black outline of trees, the branches crackling overhead. They'd been exchanging watch duty and currently he was supposed to be on, according to the schedule. He threw off what was covering him and found he was still lying on top of his bag with Pudge burrowed at the bottom, snoring softly. He rubbed a hand over his foggy eyes and heaved himself to a standing position.

Steph came into focus a few feet away, kneeling next to his propane burner. Chloe watched the proceedings, droopy head on her tidy paws.

Steph snagged a look at him. "Hi."

He exhaled in relief that she and Chloe were okay in spite of his failure to keep watch. "What time is it?"

"Almost three."

"Why didn't you alert me for my shift?"

"You were sleeping so soundly I couldn't bear to wake you. It got really cold, so I covered you with my bag."

His cheeks burned with mortification. "Sorry."

"Don't be."

"Can't believe I did that. I'm awake now if you want to get some more shut-eye."

She tucked a section of hair behind her ears to better watch the burner. "We're okay. Unbelievable how rest can bring a person back to life."

He wasn't sure he'd qualify himself as fully in the living category, since his back was aching and muscles all over his body twanged like banjo strings, but he definitely felt a good deal better. More alert. Pudge squirmed up the length of the bag and shoved his head out.

"Hey, buddy. All rested up?"

Pudge wriggled free and snuggled against Vance's shins, then accepted a good ear rubbing before he went to inspect Chloe.

Vance sniffed. "Does my nose deceive me or is that the incomparable smell of oatmeal?"

She giggled. "I helped myself to your pack. Hope you don't mind."

He pointed at a smear of chocolate on her lip, visible in the tiny glow of the burner. "I see. Sampling the ingredients too?"

Now it was her turn to blush. "They might go bad if we don't eat them."

"Of course. It was only prudent. Back in a minute." He went into the woods, where he made a quick stop and then located the small stream he'd heard nearby during his night watch. He splashed his face and hands with water so frigid it made his molars throb. How long would a person survive if submerged at that temperature? Not long. He pictured Gina for a moment before he shut off the thought and tried to squeeze the feeling into his fingers.

When he returned, the dogs were munching kibble mixed with a dribble of oatmeal and each had a container of fresh water.

"I got some from the stream and purified it," Steph said. "Refilled our water bottles."

"I missed a lot while I was conked out." He took the warm mug of oatmeal and rolled it between his cold palms, inhaling the steam as if he could feed on the vapors themselves. Warmth was a thing he'd completely taken for granted in his normal day-to-day. He never would again. "Only a few candies for me," he said. He wanted to be sure there would be enough left for her to snack on. She sprinkled in a half dozen.

After a prayer, they spooned up the hot oatmeal, illuminated by Steph's tiny penlight, which she was careful to keep partially covered. Their breath steamed the air, the clinking of their spoons mingling with the trill of some distant insect. The air was incredibly pure; the stars that peeped through the clouds shone bright as gemstones. His taste buds sang with the most intense appreciation of the humble meal. How could his senses feel so alive, more than they ever had before, when he and Steph were so close to dying?

And why, oh, why did he want to do nothing but sit in that miserable place and stare at her? Check that. He wanted to get her somewhere warm and safe and settled…where he could look and listen and laugh. With her.

He blinked, realizing she'd asked him a question.

"Come again?"

She inclined her chin at him. "I was saying I want to hike that way. There's a clearing and maybe I can snag a signal. What do you think?"

He nodded, still lost in the pleasure of the warm oatmeal hitting his famished stomach. His grin grew wider.

"Why the grin?"

"I was thinking three days ago you'd have rather shoved me aside than asked my opinion of anything."

"Three days was a lifetime ago."

He agreed.

"It's a fairly clear path so I can go check for the signal before we decamp."

She was back to her all-business approach. He should be too, except he was thinking about kissing her, the softness of her lips and the way they fit against his so perfectly.

Steph suddenly became intent on examining the sky. "I—I hope you don't… When I asked you not to leave me last night, I was tired, and exhausted, not my usual self. You understand, right?"

"Yes, we were both at the end of our ropes."

She relaxed, relieved.

"But to be clear, I told you I wouldn't and I won't." *Please tell me that's what you still want.* He watched her eyes, shifting in every direction except toward him. His spirit lagged when the moments ticked by. So it had been fatigue or fear that caused her to want him near. *Desperate times…*

She sprinkled some dog treats on the ground. He followed suit and Chloe and Pudge gobbled them up.

She picked up the cups. "I'll wash them in the stream."

"I'll go with you."

"No need. I got it. Give me yours and I'll do both while you deal with the campsite."

He got the message and handed it over. *Pack up and stay clear.* Not surprising, her attitude, but it disappointed him anyway. Hadn't they bonded over what they'd survived? And hadn't he sensed a certain reciprocal enthusiasm in their kiss? Obviously not. Self-delusion or pride. But she was right, likely. If they were going to survive, their attention had to be on the mission, not some flighty romantic notions he'd dreamed up. *Simmer down, heart. Brain's in charge now.*

He rolled the sleeping bags and placed them into his pack again. Everything was stowed in neat, military fashion when she returned. He shouldered his pack and helped her shrug into hers, though she appeared a little squirmy from the gesture.

Manners. He could show her that much, couldn't he? Though there was undoubtedly another storm wave approaching, there was no rain at the moment. Fortunate, because the trail was murky without the benefit of daylight. The route she'd selected took them from their sheltered glen up and over a peak and onto a higher area of forest, where the trees were spaced wider apart, like gap teeth protruding from a bed of soggy, pine-needle-covered gums.

Steph had her phone out, waving it this way and that. He didn't see much sense in doing the same, but it wouldn't hurt to ascertain if he could snag a precious signal with his phone. He was digging in his pocket when he heard her gasp.

"No way," she said.

Not a signal, her expression indicated. Nothing but bad news loading. The dogs confirmed it with their rigid attention before he detected the low whir of a motor. Out of the fog emerged their old mechanical foe, the drone.

It dipped low and flittered under the canopy, yards from their location. Evan had found them. Again.

He felt his self-control snap like a flag in a freshening wind. No more would he hide like a cowering rabbit. "That's it," he growled. "I'm done."

"Vance," Stephanie hissed. "What are you doing?"

He bent to lock gazes with her. "I am tired of hiding from this drone. I won't if you tell me to stop, but I want to flip the script here. What do you say?" She'd know what he was really asking. Did she trust him?

The moment lingered and he held his breath.

When he thought she would put an end to his plans, reveal her distrust of him and widen the crack in his heart, she stepped back. Her small nod told him everything, flushed him with pride and purpose. She was entrusting her life and future to him. He would not let her down.

Blood on fire, he strode out of concealment.

Enough was enough.

The moment of truth.

Steph almost changed her mind as Vance strode past, stooping to pick up a stout branch that had fallen from the oak tree that towered above them. Her mouth went dry. She trusted him, in spite of everything, but he couldn't possibly be planning to… "Vance…"

He wasn't listening as he raced up on the flying contraption. The drone swiveled to face him, camera glinting, Evan remotely collecting every detail. She watched the unbelievable scenario play out in front of her like a scene from a movie. Vance took a warm-up swing with the branch, as a batter would behind the plate, and then arced it at the drone.

The branch smashed into the object with an impact that sent it spinning in a wobbly orbit. He'd actually hit it, wounded the thing. Pudge barked, but Vance wasn't done.

"Come here, you dirty spying robot." Another smash from

Vance's makeshift weapon and it plummeted to the ground in a swirl of blinking lights.

"That's what I'm talking about," Vance crowed, taking in the drone buzzing feebly in the dirt. He rushed over and crushed the heel of his boot into the metal body, smashing it flat and sending bits of plastic and a screw flying. Pudge barked again, but Steph kept him still, hardly able to believe what she'd witnessed.

When it was over, he stood panting, hands on hips, staring down at his vanquished foe.

"That," he said after an exhale, "was deeply satisfying."

She wasn't sure whether to laugh or scream. "Effective, but you gave away our location. Even if we get out of here double time he can pinpoint our general vicinity."

Vance didn't seem at all regretful. He nudged the drone with his foot before he bent to extract a big chunk. "Changing the game. Sorry. I should have told you the entire plan before I went all Babe Ruth, but I think I had what Aunt Lettie would describe as a 'red moment.' In any case, I'm tired of playing defense and you are too. Am I right?"

"Yes." She was still bemused as he handed her the hunk of drone.

"All right then. Let's put your champion dog to work."

Now she understood, and a smile crept over her face. *Adapt, improvise, overcome...* Evan had to be within a 400-meter radius to operate the drone. "We'll have to move fast since he's on horseback."

"Copy that."

She kneeled and gave Chloe a whiff of the broken piece. No doubt Evan's scent was all over it. Chloe's nostrils quivered as she went over every inch of the mangled instrument.

Stephanie shot a look at Vance while Chloe worked. "Pretty pleased with yourself, aren't you?"

He shrugged, but his grin was not at all modest. "Would

have been a home run in any ballpark in America. I should have gone pro."

She laughed. "I agree. Nice piece of hitting."

"I know."

Their laughter mingled and she felt a fresh wave of excitement and hope.

He'd just changed the game, all right, and he hadn't discussed the details with her beforehand, but they both knew they couldn't continue on much longer being hunted by two armed men. Offense was a lot more her style, and now they would take out the accomplice. Wouldn't be easy. Evan had a knife and a horse and direct communication with Ferris.

All right, God. We're gonna need a lot of help with this next part. It felt good to ask.

Chloe sat, the signal that she was done with her examination. Vance slid the piece of drone into a plastic bag she gave him in case Chloe needed a refresher.

Vance stomped the remnants of the drone a few more times. "On general principle," he said. "It's probably got a GPS tracker in there somewhere that may be functioning, so we'll leave the corpse. It would spoil our surprise attack if Evan knew we were coming."

Steph patted Chloe and cupped her fleshy chin. Everything depended on her dog's extraordinary tracking skills. Yes, she trusted Vance and she trusted Chloe too. "Ready, Chloe?"

Chloe wagged her tail.

"Find."

Chapter Ten

She clipped the long lead on Chloe to prevent her from unexpectedly encountering Evan and his knife. Chloe could perform all manner of duties, but she was completely clueless about friends and enemies. In fact, Ferris was the only person she'd ever reacted to negatively and with him it was a visceral hostility she'd never witnessed in the dog before. Everyone else they encountered was simply a collection of interesting scents that hadn't yet been sniffed out, or a potential source of treats or scratches. She wouldn't know Evan had a knife and was working with a killer.

Chloe dragged hard, urging Steph along a minuscule path with bushes on either side that clawed at her pant legs. She could see where the clusters of tall grass had been slightly flattened about halfway up the length of the stalks, probably the work of Evan's horse. Pudge yelped when he stepped on something sharp. Vance finally picked him up, earning a massive tongue slurp. He didn't put the dog in the sling, instead draping him over his shoulders like the world's weirdest cape.

She knew the reason. The sling would impede Vance's reach and he wanted to be able to pull his revolver when they found Evan. And it was definitely a "when," not an "if." Chloe was barreling onward in a familiar manner that told Steph she was latched on to a strong scent. When the dog zinged westward along a slightly more trampled path, she paused momentarily to nose at a hoofprint in the muddy margin. Steph pointed it out to Vance. He gave her a silent thumbs-up.

Confirmation. Soon now.

There was no way to keep a ninety-pound dog moving through the brush completely in stealth mode, but she hoped the brisk wind churning the leaves would muffle their progress. Chloe strained harder, yanking Steph and sparking pain all the way from her wrist to her spine. Her shoulder ached from sleeping on the ground and diving for cover every time the drone showed up. She wound the leather leash tighter around her hand. If she lost her grip now, Chloe would continue on like an out-of-control locomotive, heedless of anything but securing her prize.

The trail took them toward a grove of trees. As they drew close, she saw Chloe's body tense in that way that meant she was closing in on her target. Steph's breath caught. With enormous effort, she slowed the dog and gave Vance a fist to stop him. She pointed.

A horse cropped at a patch of soggy grass, the reins tucked loosely over the saddle horn. Steph hauled Chloe to a full stop and commanded her to sit under the shelter of a sprawling wild blackberry shrub. Vance plopped Pudge next to her. Chloe was trembling with excitement and Pudge immediately snuggled close. The horse eyed them uninterestedly and continued drifting for the next patch of lush grass to nibble.

Vance rolled his shoulders. "Showtime?"

"Yes. Evan's in there, no question."

"Then we should have our meet-and-greet." His tone was light, but his eyes shone with a simmering rage. Or perhaps it was determination. They pulled their weapons and crept slowly forward, edging past rocks and fallen trees until they could get a view of the woods.

At the same moment, they froze.

In a small circle of relatively dry pine needles, Evan was tapping at his phone, squinting at the screen, moving right and left, then tapping some more. His grizzled eyebrows were drawn together and he muttered too low for them to hear.

Vance murmured in her ear. "Flanking from the rear. Give me thirty." Before she could argue, he'd snuck off.

Thirty seconds until everything would change one way or the other.

There had been a few events in her life where circumstances had changed in a matter of moments.

Breaking her leg during a high-school track meet…

The death of her father…

Quitting the force…

And now a showdown in the wilderness with a man she'd thought was out of her life.

Twenty-nine, twenty-eight…

She rechecked her gun. Her hands shook slightly. Fatigue, stress, exposure—all those factors would work against her shooting accuracy. Would she be sharp enough to handle the situation? A year and a half away from the force added to the rust, but she'd kept her skills sharp at the range. *Get real, Steph.* Who was she kidding? A neat, stable, shooting-range target was a completely different beast to a living, breathing enemy. And there was Vance to consider. She could not risk injuring him. There would be poor visibility in these cruel morning hours with the mist and the chill and the wind. Add in the adrenaline that was swamping her senses… So easy to make an error. A round from her gun flying at 27,000 feet per second cutting through Vance… The thought made her body go clammy.

Fifteen, fourteen…

She didn't want to shoot anyone. She prayed the next few minutes would not require her to discharge her weapon. Evan might give up without resisting. Then again, she'd seen his knife. *Vance, please be careful. We have to get out of this alive, all of us.*

All of us. When exactly had they become a pseudo family in her mind? She couldn't say, but it was undeniable. They were a unit, the four of them, which was both a terrifying and comforting feeling.

Ten, nine...

The remaining seconds evaporated.

Mouth dry as powder, she edged forward and stepped into view.

"Hands up, Evan."

Evan jerked, dropped his phone and went for his pocket, but Vance appeared and took the legs out from under the man with a quick sweep of his ankle. Evan went down on his stomach and Vance pounced on him.

Her pulse was roaring as she edged closer, tightly gripping the gun while Vance pinned Evan with his weight. She expected their prisoner to resist, but after a few vigorous thrashes, he went still.

Vance pulled Evan's hands behind his back. "Hey, Ev. 'Bout time we had a face-to-face, right? Got a moment to talk or are you too busy trying to explain to your boss how your toy got busted?"

Evan's eyes rolled. "Get off. You're suffocating me."

Vance eased up on Evan's back, but only slightly.

Stephanie moved closer and tossed Vance a set of zip ties.

He caught them with one hand. "Why do you travel around with zip ties?"

She sniffed. "They're useful, as you can plainly see." Steph noted the horse had trotted off at the tumult. The dogs were still stationary, but whining.

Vance guided Evan into a sitting position and secured his wrists. "So, Ev, how did a nice fellow like you get involved with a guy like Ferris Grinder?"

Evan scowled. "Why should I tell you?"

"So that when we get word to law enforcement, we remember exactly where we left you," Vance snapped.

Evan blanched. "Left me? Come on. You're not going to do that." His tone was not as defiant as it had been a moment before.

"Ticktock, Ev," Vance said. "Gonna start storming again soon and my dog doesn't like thunder and lightning. We gotta move out. Start talking and make it snappy. How'd you get involved with Ferris?"

Evan shrugged. "Not like we're long-time buddies or anything. Didn't even know the guy before last week. He drove by my place when I was tending my horse. Got a cabin about an hour from here. He said he was looking for someone to help him with an easy project." Evan eyed Vance and Steph. "I could use the money, so I said sure. All I had to do was volunteer to pretend to help with some dog competition and then sneak off to fly the drone and track you two."

Vance's chin went up.

Evan continued. "He showed me how to use the drone. Just like flying a model airplane, more or less."

"Except that you were using it to track us, knowing full well Ferris had murder on his mind," Steph said.

"It's not my business what happened between you all."

Vance shook his head in disgust. "You were happy to pitch in with your knife though, huh? An easy sidestep from tracking to killing us?"

Evan didn't look at Vance. "Gotta represent, but I was going to let him do the killing part. He figured you'd go for the Jeep so he got there first and drained the gas. He's enjoying this whole thing a lot more than I am."

Steph waited until Vance had zip-tied Evan's ankles before she stowed her weapon, filled with gratitude that she hadn't had to use it. She felt shaky and drained. They'd actually done it. Thanks to Chloe, they'd captured one of their two enemies.

Vance checked Evan's pockets for weapons. "Only the

knife." He tucked the folded blade into his own pocket. "And this." He removed a radio and waved it at her.

She picked the cell up from where Evan had dropped it. "And this."

Vance grinned. "Now we're talking."

"Not gonna help you. Cell's pretty much useless up here," Evan said. "Should have brought a satellite phone like Ferris has. My calls don't go through and my texts are hit-or-miss too."

"Don't kid a kidder, Evan. Your satellite radio works fine and you've got a GPS tracker on it, right? So the big boss knows where you are?"

Evan scowled.

"Code to unlock your phone?" Vance asked. "I'd like to see what you and Ferris have been chatting about. That'll make some nice evidence for the cops."

Evan scowled. "You're such a hotshot, figure it out yourself."

Vance yanked Evan's hand out and jammed his thumb on the button. "This way will work." The screen glowed and he frowned. "You've been efficient about deleting your texts and voice mails. Afraid you'll get in trouble?"

He scowled. "Not gettin' paid enough to stick my neck out too much."

Vance and Steph exchanged a look. Vance's fingers danced over the tiny device and he frowned. "He's telling the truth. No texting, no calling."

"He's supposed to radio me for a report any minute now."

Vance grinned. "Don't worry. We'll make sure he gets one."

Evan stared in surly silence.

Steph cocked her chin. "Why would you throw your life away on Ferris? You don't trust him, clearly. Maybe you're afraid he's going to get rid of you when this is all over since you're a witness to his plans?"

Evan's mouth worked as he stared at his boots. "I only

wanted the money. I didn't know it involved murder. Got in over my head until it was too late to bail."

Vance whistled. "Man, I'd be scared too if I were you, Ev, to be working for Ferris. Cops think he had a family of four murdered for crossing him. Did you know that? And he killed Elizabeth, the contest coordinator, and Steph's volunteer partner, Gina. Six people dead already because of him. You'd make an easy seventh."

Sweat popped out on Evan's forehead. "I want to get out of here. Forget the whole thing. Untie me and you'll never hear from me again."

Vance smirked. "Uh-huh, I totally believe that. No way you'd tell Ferris our whereabouts in order to get your payout, right? 'Cuz you're such an upstanding, trustworthy guy?"

Steph knew that's exactly what Evan would do if they let him go. He'd put a lot of sweat and skin into the game and he'd want his pay. Plus, he was probably worried what Ferris would do to him if he took off with the job unfinished. Ferris knew where he lived, after all. Six people murdered. Vance was right. Ferris wouldn't bat an eyelash about killing Evan too.

"Where's the horse?" Vance asked. "We might have to borrow him."

"Nope. He's loose. He's used to being on his own and he's sure not going to let anyone on him but me if you do manage to catch him, which you won't."

"Fine. I'm no cowboy anyway." Vance examined the radio. "We'll be sure to send someone to collect you and your horse when the police get here."

Evan's eyes widened. "Don't you get it? Ferris is waiting for the opportune moment. He's got plenty of ammo and help. You'll be dead by the time any cops arrive."

Vance ignored him, continuing to flip through the phone. He looked over his shoulder at Steph. The gleam in his eyes intensified as a plan seemed to form. It was almost like she could see him assembling the pieces in his brain as she did the same.

"Tired of running?" she said softly.

"Beyond tired."

They smiled at each other in understanding. The only way to stop Ferris was to take control. Vance stowed Evan's phone along with the radio. "Rope?" he asked.

She tossed him a coil of white nylon. Vance used the rope to tie him to the tree. He was seated, his back to the trunk, fairly sheltered from the rain.

Evan didn't struggle, simply gaped. "You're not really going to leave me here, are you?"

"Yep," Vance said cheerfully. "Thought I was joking, huh?"

His eyebrows zinged up. "But what if you both get killed and no one finds me in time? I could starve to death or get eaten by mountain lions."

Vance considered. "Don't think they'd like the taste of you, but I guess you'd better hope Ferris doesn't win. If we don't get out of this alive, chances are you won't either."

"But..." Evan clamped his mouth closed and snorted. "So much for easy money."

Vance smiled. The smile and the sweat and the stubble somehow only served to make him more handsome.

"No such thing as easy money, didn't you ever learn that?" Vance dropped two protein bars, a pack of pretzels and two bottles of water within reach. "Make it last, Ev. We'll double back to get you when we can or send help the moment we take Ferris's sat phone from him."

Evan groaned. "That'll never happen."

"Glass-half-empty kinda guy, huh?" Vance tossed an emergency blanket over Evan's lap. He would be able to unfold it, even with tied wrists. If he was extremely resourceful, he could find a sharp rock and saw his way loose, maybe locate his wayward horse, but that would take a while and he'd have no phone or access to a radio.

"He's going to yell," Steph said as Vance stood back.

"I'd be disappointed if he didn't. With the storm, I don't think anyone will hear him, and besides—" he grinned and wiggled Evan's radio "—Ferris is gonna think good old Ev here is somewhere entirely different."

The knowledge that Ferris would be privy to their exact location made her shiver.

Vance gave Evan a salute. "Hang in there, Ev. Catch you on the flip side."

Evan's cheeks went red.

"Ready to put the next part of our scheme into action?" Vance said. She could tell he was still flush from their victory.

"I need to do one thing first." She went to Chloe and gave her the signal. Chloe bounded up and galloped over to Evan, skidding to a stop practically on his lap.

"Call it off," Evan shouted.

"It's a she and you won't be bitten. She just wants her prize."

Ears flapping and glee in every line of her body, Chloe sniffed him all over, sprinkling him with slobber. Then she circled once and sat. Victory. Steph kneeled, rubbed the dog thoroughly and gave her a handful of jerky treats. She tossed one to Pudge too. He'd been a stalwart companion. "You're a good dog, Chloe. That was a champion find."

Her elation dimmed. Now would begin the second phase and it would be an excruciating effort to bring their real enemy to his knees.

She brought out the maps and she and Vance pored over them.

Their survival depended on making the right choice.

Chapter Eleven

Vance mulled it all over as they trekked over a series of steep climbs and bone-jarring descents. It would be a long hike to the spot where they'd chosen to enact their plan. Every rise brought yet another massive slice of untouched terrain into view. The wilderness felt endless, as if they were on some far-flung planet inhabited by only two exhausted humans and their hardworking canines. *And a killer. Don't forget that.* His shins screamed from the uneven trail and Pudge was a dead weight in his arms. Fortunately, Chloe was maintaining a good clip, but Steph was struggling, though she did her best to hide it.

The tracking contest was scheduled to end that night. The fact was both a plus and a minus. With the competition con-cluded, and Stephanie still not returned after supposedly waiting out the weather in a hotel as Ferris's fake message in-dicated, her family would be in rescue mode. Unfortunately, he'd not left a hard return date with Lettie, or she might have alerted the authorities herself earlier. Nothing to be accom-plished by dwelling on that. Ferris, no doubt, would feel the hours dwindling too, as dedicated to his mission as they were to theirs. The man was determined to make sure they never set foot back into civilization, the same punishment his father had received. What a family.

"Hey," Steph said, poking at his arm.

"What?"

"You're thinking and you walk too fast when you're thinking. Besides, I want to be in on the planning." She shoved the bangs from her forehead. "No more bashing drones and surprising me."

He laughed and lowered Pudge to the ground, holding in the groan that wanted to escape. His failure weighed him down more than his overweight pal. He could avoid the issue, but it didn't feel right to cover up, not with her, not anymore. "I've been thinking about how we came to be in this predicament. Doesn't feel good to know Ferris led me here like a barnyard sheep, left the pamphlet for the competition for me to find. I did exactly what he intended, and I didn't suspect a thing. Some bounty hunter, huh?"

"I didn't suspect anything either. We were both bamboozled."

He quirked a smile. "Somehow that word makes it sound like less of a failure, but I was tracking the guy, Steph. It was my job to find him and I didn't and now we're here." *You're here, Steph. Because of me.* He could take the punishment he deserved for his stupidity, but he couldn't stomach her paying for his errors. And he didn't even want to think about Aunt Lettie finding out that the family who'd ultimately pushed her son into suicide was roaming free and spreading more terror around the world.

He was surprised when she slid her hand into his. "This isn't all on you. You tried to warn me. I didn't listen. We both got ourselves into this mess."

He laced his fingers through hers, the connection buoying his confidence. "And we're going to get out of it. Together."

"Still optimistic we can capture Ferris?"

"Absolutely. The timeline is shrinking for him to make

a move. He's only got today before people start realizing you're missing."

"I thought of that too. Also, any minute now, he's going to check in with Evan via the radio when the guy doesn't report as scheduled. Ferris will either track him down, figuring it's a communication glitch, or Evan's had an accident or…"

"Either way he's going to need to follow Evan's GPS tracker and come see for himself, which is why our plan is a good one."

"He won't be an easy takedown like Evan was," she said.

"We chose the location carefully. This campground you spotted midway up the trail. It's flat with one main access. There are bound to be places we can get a bead on him. Spot him coming." And at minimum that campground would mean shelter. A secondary consideration, but his limbs were wooden with cold and the dogs were only protected so much by their raincoats from the steady drizzle. Unfortunately, it would be a full day's hike to get to the campground. Steph was trying hard to keep the pace, but she could not disguise her limp.

Her foot landed wrong and she cried out. His sudden grab was the only thing that kept her on her feet.

"You okay?"

"Sure, but maybe a quick rest?"

"Right." The dogs sniffed the rain-washed rocks and Steph selected the flattest, driest one she could find and settled onto it. Her eyes were smudged underneath with dark circles of fatigue and her mouth was tight with pain. She hauled up the right leg of her pants. He wasn't surprised to find her sock was tinged with blood that seeped up from her heel.

He wanted to chide her for not speaking up earlier about the severity of the wound, but that wouldn't help the situation. "Why don't I administer a little first aid, since we're stopped and all?"

"I can get by. Nothing major." She fumbled with the knotted laces until he pushed her hands out of the way.

"Good, because I'm only skilled in minor stuff."

She acquiesced, no doubt her pain winning out over her pride.

He worked the double knots loose and eased her foot from the boot. The heel of the sock was adhered to the skin with dried blood. From the water bottle he poured a splash of liquid onto the material until it came loose. "Looks rough. I can see why it's causing you pain."

She shrugged. "Normally I alternate pairs of boots and change socks frequently, but this hasn't been exactly a routine expedition."

"True that." He opened the first-aid kit. "This is going to sting, Wolfe. Sorry." The antiseptic washed away the grit and fibers. She stiffened but didn't make a sound. Chloe somehow intuited her pain anyway and came over to snuffle her chin. Pudge followed suit until she had two damp cheeks and a lap full of interested canines.

"Thanks, guys," she said, wiping the doggy saliva away.

Vance dabbed an ointment onto her ravaged skin and applied a bandage. He pulled dry socks from her pack. He was going to slide them on so quickly she wouldn't have time to protest his help, but she edged her feet away.

"I can do it."

He reached out and took her hands in his, the soft ball of socks nestled between them. She was cold, so cold, and he wished his touch would lend her warmth. He caught her amber gaze for a moment, the color of rich honey. "There is nothing more important to me right now than helping you."

She suddenly looked away and he knew he shouldn't have said it, not with such earnestness, but his defenses were falling away with each mile and it was the honest truth. He would give anything to spare her from more pain. *Lighten the mood, Silverton.* "And I'm tired, but if I have to chase you around this forest and jam these socks on your pretty feet, I will."

"I..." She twisted to look at him. "You think my feet are pretty?"

She'd latched on to that? Mystifying. "Yes, ma'am. You got yourself two dainty princess feet right there."

"I always thought the toes were too long, nothing like my sister Kara's."

He regarded her toes solemnly. "I confess I've never seen your sister's toes, but these piggies are beauts."

She actually giggled and her momentary relaxation allowed him the chance to roll the socks onto her feet.

Her eyes closed for a moment and an expression of contentment spread across her features. "Can't believe a pair of dry socks could feel so amazing."

Amazing. He'd given her that with a pair of socks. He could have danced. "And for my final performance," he said, unfurling two plastic bags he'd taken from her supply and sliding them over the socks. "No way we can get your boots dry right now, but this should provide something of a barrier." He eased on her boots and rolled the extra plastic down so it was hardly visible.

When he was done, he offered his palm with a flourish and helped her to stand. "Better?"

"Loads," she said. "Thank you."

He wondered why he felt so incredible about being able to help her into dry socks and plastic bags. It was more rewarding than any bust he'd ever made, any race he'd ever won. Flushed with happiness, he gave the dogs two treats each before they hit the trail.

They journeyed on as the day slipped into late afternoon and cold shadows mingled with the rain. He tried Evan's phone again and she tried hers. No reception. No call from Ferris on the radio.

An hour passed into two and when he'd almost decided they'd made a wrong turn, Steph grabbed his arm.

"There."

The trail ahead flattened out into a wide sweep of level ground with a dozen canvas tents erected atop wooden frames. Everything seemed in good condition, buttoned up well for the winter. A river rushed behind the campground and the mountain peaks soared above, lost in the velvet puffs of clouds. It would be the ideal place for a wilderness adventure. Not that he ever planned on adventuring in the wilderness again. Only destinations with well-paved roads and good cell coverage would be his aim and nowhere too far-flung from hot coffee and washers and dryers.

He pointed. "That's got to be the office cabin to the left. Guest tents and two bathhouses. The squat building in the center is probably a dining hall or something along those lines. We'll get inside a tent, activate a lantern to draw attention. Hopefully, Ferris will think it's Evan."

Steph nodded. "The dogs and I will find another tent cabin to hole up in, where we can get a visual. I wonder how much time we'll have."

The tent they chose for the lantern decoy was musty but dry. He hauled a small table close to the window and set the lantern on it. The glow would certainly be visible to Ferris. They both flinched as the radio crackled in Vance's pocket. Stomach tight, he drew it out.

Ferris's voice was muted and tinny. "Answer me, Evan. Why are you near the campground? Why haven't you communicated with me?"

Vance put his shirt over the speaker. "Drone broke," he said. "Tracked 'em here. They're approaching." He turned the radio squawk button. "Trouble hearing you."

"What do you mean the drone broke?" Ferris demanded.

Vance played once more with the buttons, as if his conversation was being interrupted by static. "Can't...hear you."

"Just hold in place and keep them in your sights, you oaf," Ferris snarled. "I'm coming to you. Don't do anything until I get there. It'll be three hours, minimum, if I don't blow a tire on the way."

The radio cut out. Vance returned it to his pocket.

"I guess we have our timeline," he said slowly.

"I guess we do." She blew out a breath, which steamed the air. "Better go see what our accommodations look like."

The canvas tents were secured only by strong zippers. The interior of the second platform tent was stripped bare, and the raised cots sat on wooden frames with no bedding. Aged floors showed slight warping and possible rodent visitations if the dogs' sniffing was any indication. They put down their gear and walked back to the nearest bathhouse.

The door was secured by a sturdy padlock. He turned around to find Steph holding two rocks out for him. "Your padlock trick, right?"

He grinned. "Look at you, my lock-picking apprentice. I'm sure we can explain a busted lock to the park service, considering." He got in on the first whack. Inside, the bathhouse smelled of cleanser and mildew. There were two stalls with plastic shower curtains and a separate toilet area.

To her delight, Steph found the sink faucets working. Instantly, the two dogs reared up on their hind legs and shoved their muzzles into the flowing water, lapping noisily. The humans laughed, enjoying their companions' excitement.

While she dried the dogs with a paper towel, he strode to what appeared to be a closet and opened it. A fairly new hot-water heater beckoned. *If this works, it'll be a game changer.* With a match from his pocket, he lit the pilot light and continued to explore the closet, where he found a stack of towels.

"Steph?" he said.

She was washing her hands in the sink. "Yes?"

"Could I interest you in a hot shower and a clean towel?"

She whirled. "Don't even tease about that, Silverton."

"No teasing, ma'am. This is an eighty-gallon water heater, which should take about an hour to heat, by my calculation."

"How do you…?" She broke off, eyes wide. "Forget I asked. Marines do things and they know stuff. If you're right about this one, I'll bake you a cake."

He folded his arms. "What kind?"

"Any kind," she said breathlessly.

He stroked his chin, pretending to think it over. "I have specifications. Not any old variety will do. I require carrot cake with cream-cheese frosting."

"Okay."

"And the cake part should have raisins and bits of pineapple mixed in there. Not pineapple chunks, mind you—tidbits. That's what Aunt Lettie calls them."

Her mouth quirked. "All right."

"With flecks of nuts. Walnuts, not pecans. And the frosting needs to be thick on the outside and in the middle part too, where the layers stick together."

"You require layers?"

"Yes, minimum two, and back on the frosting topic, it should have those blobby swirls on top."

"Blobby swirls? You mean rosettes?"

He snapped his fingers. "That's it. Rosettes. I need rosettes on my cake."

She stopped him with a raised hand. "You're really milking this for everything you can get."

"Hot shower," he said in a singsong voice. "What's a measly cake compared to the joy that will bring?"

She laughed, a light silvery sound he hadn't heard since they'd dated. "All right. Carrot cake with two layers, raisins, tidbits and rosettes."

"And nut flecks. Don't forget those."

"And nut flecks. I can make that happen. Kara won't mind helping me out if I need a consultation."

"Excellent. While we let the water heat, how about we choose a tent for dining and resting activities?"

"Fine, but..." A frown stole the joy from her expression. "Should we be thinking about showers and cakes and resting while we wait for a murderer to arrive to kill us?"

"We have a good three hours, remember? And he's not going to kill us. We're going to neutralize him before he can make a move." He held the door open for her and the dogs. "And what's more he's not getting any cake in prison. Ever."

They decided on a tent cabin positioned so they'd have a clear view of the one below, where they'd placed the lantern, and the road beyond. Inside, Steph's teeth chattered and his hands were icy in spite of the thick canvas that kept off the wind and rain. What he'd give to make a roaring campfire outside. He'd bundle her close, and they and the dogs would watch the flames dance and the stars emerge on the heels of the storm. *Don't let your mind drift right now, buddy.* He blinked and the daydream popped and vanished. Cold tent, hungry belly, feet blistered and bloody and Ferris on the way. Those were the realities to keep front and center.

But other feelings filtered in anyway. Gratitude, for one. They were alive and Steph would get her shower and God would help them survive, like He'd been doing for the past four days. *Thanks, God. Sorry for the grumbling.*

Steph fed the dogs and offered more water, while he used the burner to heat Steph's dehydrated whole wheat mac and cheese for the humans. The abnormally orange kind out of the blue box was undoubtedly way better but he'd have the good manners not to say so. Only four packets left from her supply. He didn't have much more, just some pouches of nuts and the remnants of the candy. He could probably inhale the whole lot in one sitting and still not be full.

The salty pasta soothed his raw throat. He and Steph devoured every morsel and scraped all traces from the foil packets. He craved more but at least it momentarily quieted the major stomach rumbling. After they finished, he handed her the baggie with the remaining half dozen M&M's. "Almost done with this adventure. Might as well polish them off."

With a grin, she took the bag and began to divide them up.

"No need. All six for you, Steph." He patted his stomach. "Watching the carbs."

Her giggles turned to guffaws and he joined in. Their laughter intertwined, drifted, circled through the musty old tent. Was there ever such a joyful sound? There shouldn't be any laughter here, not now, yet somehow God made room for it.

She doled out two candies, savoring one at a time and stowing the other four. "These will be the celebration candies for the moment we capture Ferris."

"Hear! Hear!" he said. "Be another half hour before your hot water's ready. Might as well take a snooze." She nodded. He unrolled one of the sleeping bags on the raised platform bed and she lay down on it. Before he could even cover her with the other, she was asleep.

He brushed the hair from her face and snuggled the fabric around her.

He settled down on the empty bunk across from her, elbows resting on his aching knees. The risk of what they were attempting circled in his gut. So much piled up against them. Maybe they should have separated, like he'd suggested. She might have had a chance to escape. But she'd wanted them to face Ferris together. Somewhere deep down she'd decided to trust him again. The very thing he'd longed for, coveted, and now he'd gotten it and he was scared he'd let her down again. Only this time, she'd pay with her life and Chloe's.

"Lord, I've messed up so many things," he murmured quietly. "And I don't deserve any special treatment, but please let me get this woman and these dogs out of here safely. Show me how to do it and give me the strength and Your protection."

When he was done, he tried to fight the fatigue and achiness by cleaning and loading his weapon, reorganizing his pack, running the plan in an endless loop in his mind. He wasn't going to sleep, in case Ferris arrived before the estimated three hours. The dogs had no such problem, lying side by side, Pudge snoring.

The time elapsed and he touched her shoulder. "Ready for your hot shower, sleepyhead?"

She blinked, then leaped to her feet. "I'll race you."

"Not with your heel all bandaged up. A brisk walk will do."

The dogs roused themselves and trotted after their humans. Pudge applied his nose to the ground in similar fashion to Chloe. Maybe the dog was actually learning some tracking skills. Vance puffed with pride. "I knew Pudgy had hidden talents."

Steph considered. "He's done really great." She reached for his hand and squeezed. "And so have you. And I'm not just saying that because you're supplying a hot shower."

He tucked her arm in his, intending to savor their closeness until the moment she left him again. "Flattery will get you everywhere," he joked. Her arm remained linked with his until they reached the bathhouse.

"Your shower awaits, madam," he said, holding the door open for her.

"Why thank you, kind sir." She went in and he heard the sound of the shower running while he stood outside. Her ecstatic squeal of glee confirmed that the water heater was functioning properly. He wished he'd recorded that sound of her happiness.

"Am I a stud or what?" he crowed. Pudge swiped a rubbery tongue over Vance's shin to confirm he thought so too.

Still grinning, Vance watched the dogs meander through the puffs of steam that emanated from under the door. He peered up, the rain having subsided into a mist. The clouds were down to ragged wisps that revealed swaths of inky sky.

Somewhere above was a patchwork of constellations, scads of stars shining steadily, though he could only see a sprinkling of them. A memory ripped at his serenity. He recalled

standing in the front yard of his mother's home at some ridiculous hour with the stars twinkling overhead. He'd been trying to find the car keys his mother had tossed from the house
in a rage since she was up throughout the night as the disease
advanced. Even with alarms engaged to let him know if she
snuck out, she'd flung open the door and shouted insults at
him as she'd lobbed the key ring into the grass, which he'd
not had time to cut.

He'd hit bottom at that moment, crawling on hands and
knees in his frantic search with the wet grass soaking the
knees of his jeans. Her shrieks flew at him like sharp arrows,
insults piercing him from a woman who'd loved him all his
life. Why? He'd cried out to God then, for help, for strength,
for comfort that didn't come from a bottle.

And their neighbor, dear Lettie, had driven up without
warning that very morning, to soothe his mother, tuck her
back into bed with prayers and song and help him find the
keys. Lettie was the help God had sent, and he'd not been able
to repay her, except to promise he'd spend his life putting Ferris back behind bars. Ferris, the man who'd turned her son into
an informer, the person responsible for assassinating a family,
waiting for his chance to add to his list of kills.

Steph's high soprano trickled out to him and he felt such a
rush of pleasure and a deep sense of blessing that he'd been
able to comfort her. Had Lettie felt similar? Was she blessed
by being able to bless him and his mother? Did it assuage her
own pain to lessen someone else's agony?

It was a thought he hadn't entertained before. Such a refreshing idea. He'd talk about it with Lettie when he got back,
right after he told her he'd put away the criminal that her son,
Jack, had let himself fall in with. The next few hours…

His mother's words as he'd driven her to the memory care
home rang in his ears.

You hate me. You're sending me away.

He prayed Steph and Lettie were right and he'd shown his

love with actions even when his mother thought he'd betrayed her by moving her to a memory care facility, where she'd passed away. *I hope you know I only wanted the best for you, Mama. I miss you.* The grief rose outward until it engulfed him. So much pain. So many regrets.

He stopped, pulled in a breath as deep as his lungs would hold and exhaled slowly, forcing his thoughts to the here and now. The humans and dogs were alive, and Steph was relishing a hot shower. He was sober and cherished by Lettie, a woman who had no reason to step into his life except that God had prompted her to. And he and Steph were reconnecting, at least at some level.

So much love. So many memories. The good and the bad. He prayed once again they'd all live to experience more of the tumultuous journey God planned for them. He shoved his hands in his pockets and breathed deeply of the mountain air until Steph emerged bundled in her clothes again and with an expression of utter bliss. "That was the best shower of my entire life."

He chuckled. "Well worth the effort it's going to take to bake the cake?"

"Absolutely."

He reached out and touched her shoulder. "I'm glad." She turned her head to look at him and he moved her closer, feeling the warmth of her body from the hot shower.

"You okay?" she asked. "You look…pensive."

"Yeah. I was…" Nothing had been promised. The end could be nearer than either of them imagined. He felt the words welling up and decided to let them out before he thought better of it. "I was thinking. After we get clear of this, I'd like to invite you over for dinner, wherever Pudge and I find to live, I mean."

Her churning thoughts were almost palpable. Had he erred? He hurried on.

"I've learned how to cook chili after much trial and error and I have some boxes of Girl Scout cookies left. I'll buy us some cornbread to go with it. What do you say?" he asked, then rushed on. "We could, maybe, start again."

Her soft exhale was a white puff in the night. "Not sure that's a good idea."

He felt a pinprick to his soul but he soldiered on. "Why not?"

"We're different people, Vance. Completely. I had a lot of time to think about it since we broke up. I'm serious and intense. You're relaxed and fun-loving. I plan and you're a seat-of-the-pants kinda person. It's just…" Her words dropped off for a moment and she tapped him lightly on the chest. "We had our shot. Probably wouldn't have worked out anyway, right? Even if we hadn't broken up over the job."

Right? Absolutely wrong, but if she didn't want him, then it was the end of the line. The warm optimism he'd felt a moment before was smothered by the pain that bloomed in his heart.

"You're a good man, Vance Silverton. I hope we'll be friends forever."

Friends was not what he wanted and he wasn't quite ready to give up. "Opposites can be a good thing," he said stubbornly. "Would you want to date another version of yourself? Relationships are supposed to make the other person better."

She remained silent, not quite looking at him.

He was losing her; maybe he'd already lost her. The despair widened, and he stepped back and cleared his throat. "Anyway it was just a dinner invite."

"Sure. And it's very sweet, but…we should focus on bigger picture things now. A few more hours and this will all be over. Critical time, right?"

"Yes." But for some reason, the picture that kept flashing across his consciousness was one of him and her, together, safe and back in love. But that required two willing participants and she'd made her position clear. *Dream on, Vance.*

So many good memories.

So much regret.

He'd have to learn to live with both.

Chapter Twelve

Steph was practically delirious at being warm and clean, but even those sensations could not quite strip away the lingering doubt about what she'd said to Vance. He'd made it clear—he wanted to start over. She'd been given another chance to pick up the relationship that ended in pain for both of them. And she'd turned him away.

It was true, every word she'd said. They were complete opposites, wired differently, through and through. Their recent affection was the outgrowth of a bizarre, stressful situation over which they could exercise no control. That affection butted right up against the tough, invisible wall she'd built around her emotions when it came to Vance. Ironic that it was in a place with no walls whatsoever that she'd realized the overwhelming dimensions of the one she'd constructed.

As much as she felt Vance tugging at her heart, she was not ready to let him breach that barrier. Or more accurately perhaps, she wasn't willing to provide the ladder. Over that, she still had control and she'd cling to it regardless of their current situation.

But something's changed, her spirit whispered. *Vance isn't the person you knew. And you aren't the same, Steph.* Emotions new and fresh and startling were racing around her body in spite of the fact that it was absolutely the worst timing ever.

Determined to leave the thoughts behind, she followed Vance to the empty tent, where the dogs promptly fell into another snooze. She admired their ability to live in the moment. There was still no cell signal and her texts were lost in a swirl of dots that never seemed to send. "One text. Why can't I send one lousy text?"

Vance wasn't listening but was busily peering through the binoculars out the plastic-covered window. "Nothing so far."

She crept up next to him and peered through her own binoculars.

"Stay down, Steph," he said automatically, glasses swiveling to take in the campground and the wooded trail below.

She bristled, her unsettled feelings rushing to the surface. "I'm part of this team too."

"Right. I'm only saying we don't need two directors for this show. I'll take care of recon. You back me up after I corner him."

Here was confirmation of why she was right about them. Even now, after everything they'd endured, he'd dismissed her. She folded her arms and glared at him.

He finally looked away from his lenses and realized. He sank down on the plank floor to face her. "What did I say? Something dumb, judging by your expression."

She shook her head. "Never mind."

"Nope." He put down the glasses and folded his hands in his lap. "We've got a while before he'll be here. You made it clear I won't see much of you after we return to civilization." The hurt flashed in his eyes. "What?"

She unclenched her jaw. "You got all bossy."

"Oh, is that it? Sorry." He flashed a lazy smile. "Occupational hazard."

Of course. And totally acceptable, for most of the force.

The old anger rekindled and left her grasping for words. She finally landed on a reply. "Easy for a man to say that, Vance."

He cocked his chin. "What do you mean?"

Her frustration was too close to the surface but she forced an exhale. "It's not important right now, considering."

His jaw tensed. "Steph, we're not going to talk once we shake this off, except for the cake delivery, and we're about to have a knock-down-drag-out with a killer. Might get a little messy so I think there's no better moment to clear the air. Spill it."

She shoved back the bangs from her forehead. "You have no idea how hard it is to be a woman cop, do you?"

His forehead crinkled in confusion. "I can imagine some of it, a woman in what's still a male-dominated profession, but clearly I don't have a complete picture. Tell me."

A flush of heat crept up her neck and she suddenly felt ridiculous. Why was she talking about this? Now? To a man she'd just condemned to the friend zone? With Ferris closing in to trying and kill them? But the words came out anyway, as if the water had started to pour through the tiny hole in the dam, taking all the bracing with it. "As a man, you react and you don't have to overthink how you're coming across to others. A woman in a leadership role on the other hand... can't be too girly, or they'll see you as weak. Too pushy and they'll accuse you of being a harpy. Anything a male cop has to put up with is twice as hard for a woman, and you know what?" Unexpected tears welled and she blinked them away, forcing her chin up. "I was a good cop, a very good cop, in spite of all that."

"No argument there."

And she was right back in the hurt again of what had happened between them. "I was looking outside the department because I knew there were five guys ahead of me for promotion including you, three of whom were long-timers, which meant I wouldn't have a shot at detective for years, maybe ever."

He started to rebut but she cut him off.

"Whisper Valley never had a female in the detective role. Ever. There were only two women in the whole department when I left and for the past ten years all lateral transfers from other departments were male, even though dozens of seasoned women cops applied right along with those men."

"Steph, I…" He sighed. "I never thought about it that way." He slumped. "As soon as I let it slip that you were looking elsewhere, I destroyed your chance at that promotion. It didn't occur to me that it might be your only chance for a while. Never really considered that your opportunities would be fewer and farther between than mine." He waited for her to say more.

"Most male cops in Whisper Valley don't really get it."

"But I should have. I'm sorry."

She didn't want to go into the other part. He'd already apologized, hadn't he? But it came tumbling out as she stared at the warped floorboards. "What hurt most wasn't the lost opportunity, even though that was painful, but the fact that I didn't matter to you as much as the promotion did."

He grimaced. "You did, Steph. You mattered, but my pride and my plans got in the way for a minute."

"It wasn't a momentary failure, Vance. We were both applying for that job and we knew someone had to lose. I was prepared for that. But you took something I'd shared with you, my trust in you, and tossed it away. I didn't think you were that kind of person. It's hard enough to love someone…" She snapped her mouth shut. Too late. He'd heard the *L* word. Completely mortifying.

She hadn't realized until that very moment why Vance's actions had hurt so much. Because in order to be the best at what she did in a male-dominated arena, she'd striven to control every detail of her life. Loving someone, loving Vance, was the most out-of-control thing she could ever consider, and she'd done it anyway. Hook, line, sinker.

Thrown away her control.

Because of him.

He touched her hand. "Steph, I'm sorry. I hurt you. I've never been sorrier for anything in my life. And what's more, I didn't know all those things about how hard it was for you on the force. I should have. A man has to understand the realities of the woman in his life. We'd dated long enough that I should have known. And all cops should know and understand. We have enough enemies outside the force. We're brothers and sisters in blue. One family."

She was still fighting back the persistent tears. There was a possibility they were going to die, so why should it matter that they cleared the air anyway? Here she was talking about things in the past that could not be changed. She couldn't possibly control the tiniest thing about their present situation either. Instead of measuring out the words, fashioning her next comment, she let her thoughts gush out. "I know you're sorry. You said so before and I believe you were sincere. I truly do, and I'm sorry for not making things clear to you earlier and bringing this all up now. I guess... I wasn't finished being mad about it."

He extended his palm to her with the most tender look she'd ever witnessed on a man's face. "Will you forgive me, Steph? Not just about the job thing, but for breaking your heart? Your trust? All of it?"

A lump formed in her throat as she struggled to answer. Yes? No? A little of both? What was the real answer?

His eyes sought hers.

She could brush him off and turn away.

But maybe this was her only chance. God had given her a moment, one slender tick of the clock, to let Him work in her, show her how to forgive, revive her heart, which had turned to stone. Forgiveness was the only way to heal both of them. Even if her love of Vance didn't return to what it had been, this was the way forward.

She reached out and twined her fingers with his. Her silent response was enough.

His expression lit from within, as if the sun had risen inside and spilled across his face. She felt the warmth of it deep in her own soul. He bent to kiss her fingers and she felt his tears. Her anger was good and truly gone now, the soul spot it had occupied filled with something warm and soft and healing. No matter what happened, she would remember with gratitude that God had set both of them free in that wild nowhere.

Pudge intruded on the moment by jerking his head up and flopping one ear as he listened intently.

"Caught a sound, boy?"

Chloe alerted a second later too, scurrying over to Pudge.

Vance again lifted his binoculars, only now he gestured for her to join him. She squeezed close and they both scanned the terrain.

Two soft golden flickers drew their attention from deep in the woods. Headlights, definitely.

"It's him," Vance said. "He's got your car. Saved those spark-plug wires. Wonder why he's not driving whatever he rode in on."

Steph's heart slammed into her ribs. Fifteen minutes more. Maybe less? The lights flickered in and out of view along the twisted trail through the woods.

"I'm going to make my way to the pinch point, where he'll enter the campground," Vance said. "I'd love to blow out the tires, but we'll need a vehicle to get out of here. I will if I have to though. Agreed?"

She nodded. Whatever it took, they had to stop him now, gain control. "I'll be in position at your three beside the bathhouse, lay down some cover fire or take him out if I get the chance."

He grimaced. "It really pains me to know you're a much better shot than I am."

"Deal with it, Silverton."

They checked their flashlights, which would be their only means of communication if things went wrong. "Two flashes if he gets away from you since I won't have a clear line of sight from your side."

"He won't. He'll have to stop and go on foot when he hits the edge of the parking area to access the campground. Soon as he opens that driver's-side door, he's my prisoner."

My prisoner. Her skin grew cold. What if the plan went awry? Ferris already had superior firepower and plenty of ammo, a car, communication. What if Evan had gotten loose somehow? But there was no way they could have reconnected, since Ferris was tracking Evan's radio right to the campground.

Doubt still nagged at her. What if they'd overlooked something? Vance stopped her cartwheeling thoughts with a squeeze to her wrist.

"Steph, this is all going to be over soon."

The shimmer in his gaze went right through her but it didn't eclipse the fear that took hold deep in her bones. How tragic would it be if they finally reached a place of forgiveness, only to be slaughtered by Ferris Grinder?

"Just...no going after him with a branch or anything, right? If it goes sideways, we regroup and make a new plan."

"We'll see what the mood calls for," he said breezily. He pulled on his pack.

"Maybe I'll take you up on that offer," she blurted, fiddling with her own.

He jerked a look at her. "What offer?"

"Dinner, like you said. A bowl of chili when I deliver the cake. I could do some quick lessons with Pudge. You need someone to help you because he is desperately lacking in training."

Pudge looked up at his name, tongue lolling.

Vance beamed. "That'd be great, absolutely fantastic. Chili it is. But I'll have to take up the training thing later with Pudge. He's going to need a long vacation after this. I mean he went from cowering in fear of his roommate in the shelter to tracking an assassin. He probably needs a few spa treatments or something."

"Don't we all?"

He leaned down and kissed her then, lightly, as if he was afraid of jostling the fragile connection between them.

Tingles swept through her body. She cupped his cheek. "Don't get hurt, okay? Please."

He kissed her again, a little more firmly, a little longer connection.

Her stomach clenched. "If he smells our trap I'll assist in taking out the tires."

"I won't need it."

She laughed. "Yes, you will."

With one final grin, he snuck off.

With her kiss warm on his lips, he crept out into the night. His limitations were frustrating. No means to communicate with Steph save a flashlight signal. This was truly a desperate, old-school scenario. He was confident anyway, encouraged by the thought of ending the torture. Ferris was already here and all they had to do was get him out of his car. Between him and Steph, they'd handle the rest. Ferris wasn't interested in dying, only killing, and he'd surrender when he realized he was out of options.

Besides, Steph was willing to eat his chili and help his dog.

If that wasn't a green light to rebuild their relationship, he didn't know what was. *Later, Romeo. Focus.* He silently counted the passing minutes.

Steph didn't signal that she was in place to the side of the bathhouse, the dogs shut safely in the cabin tent, for fear of tipping off Ferris, but she'd had time to settle into position. The lightness in his soul was euphoric. She'd forgiven him, she'd made him understand her deepest, truest feelings, and she was going to share a meal with him.

He restrained himself from whistling as he found the perfect shrubby nook to conceal himself. Ferris was closer now, winding his way along the twisty entrance road in Steph's car. The arrogance of him to take hers when he had a vehicle in which he'd arrived. Probably stroked his ego to use Steph's. Insult to injury. Smarter for Ferris to have parked somewhere along the trail and gone the rest of the distance on foot since he'd be impossible to track in the dark, but Ferris wasn't one to do things the hard way and he wasn't expecting the trap that was coming. No, he'd gotten Evan to ride all over on horseback with his drone and feed information. Ferris would roll on up in his cushy vehicle, an assassin with all the creature comforts.

Vance yearned with everything in him to finish things. No more miserable nights in the cold with dehydrated food for dinner and every square inch of them scraped, bruised and bashed. Stephanie and her pretty toes would be out of here, along with their long-suffering dogs.

The car rolled closer, taking a sharp turn that brought Ferris out of view behind the rocks for a moment. Vance tamped down his glee at the thought that Ferris would return to jail for the rest of his life. He couldn't wait to tell Lettie. Justice wouldn't bind her heart together again, but it might help her sleep at night knowing Ferris wouldn't hurt anyone else's child.

"Come to Papa, Ferris. Just a bit further." He pulled his weapon and laid it next to him before pointing the binoculars again. The headlights bobbed and bounced, a weak glow in the face of all that darkness. He plotted it out in his mind. Ferris would pull up in the parking area, see the lantern in the decoy tent, confirmation that Evan was indeed waiting for him. He'd arm himself and get out of the car.

And Vance would make his move. Hopefully Steph wouldn't have to be involved at all. No shooting. Nice and neat.

The car slowed as it approached the last turn. Vance's fingers tensed on his gun. "Come on."

The vehicle idled as if Ferris was considering.

"What are you waiting for?" Vance muttered. He almost dropped the binoculars as the car executed a hasty U-turn. *What?*

No, this couldn't be happening. What had spooked him? Didn't matter. They weren't going to lose Ferris now. He prayed Ferris wasn't looking in his rearview mirror as he flicked his flashlight beam once. What he wouldn't have given for a working cell phone, but Steph would probably intuit what he intended. She'd have seen Ferris's abrupt retreat.

Vance holstered his weapon in his belt and picked his way over the uneven ground as fast as he could. A straight shot through the woods would put him on an intercept course with the road where it coiled around the mountain. He'd have to shoot the tires out or disable Ferris through the windshield. Both difficult in the dark, but he'd do it.

Why would Ferris wait until he was almost at the camp and then jet away? What had given their plan away? Vance stumbled on a tree root and fell to one knee, the jarring pain flashing hot through his leg as he hopped up again. There was no time to slow and no way to track where Ferris was without risking missing him. On he jogged, leaping over rocks and crashing against branches he'd not detected. The land sloped down and the wind direction changed, diverted away from the mass of mountain. His destination was dead ahead. He pulled his weapon and crept forward until he could see the road below.

Taillights shone three yards away. While he got into position to take a shot, he realized the car was idling. *Why?*

He eased to the edge and lined up on the rear tire.

The car burst into motion, the driver's foot hard on the pedal.

Vance fired a shot that glanced off the rear fender. He was going for shot two when he stopped.

Why would Ferris turn away from the campground?

Why had he appeared to idle there for a moment?

Almost as if the driver was waiting...

Vance's stomach contracted to a tight fist.

Ferris hadn't fallen into their trap...because he'd planned one of his own.

The campground... Stephanie.

Vance whipped around and sprinted hard.

Steph couldn't imagine why Ferris had suddenly departed but she knew Vance had pursued him and she wasn't going to leave him without backup. She stowed the binoculars in her pack and worked out a bare-bones plan as she hurried around the bathhouse. She'd hustle after Vance, get close enough to signal him—he'd be expecting her to follow anyway—and find a position to shoot out Ferris's tires. Vance was probably going to try the same thing, but she'd have a better chance at success. Between the two of them, Ferris wasn't getting away.

Thanks to the hairpin turns in the road, they'd have an opportunity to short cut their way to intercept by hustling through the woods.

She'd have to move fast though, because Vance wasn't going to wait around for her to catch up. He'd go blasting away. Suspicion poked at her. What had given them away? She'd just cleared the corner of the bathhouse when a leg swept out, caught her ankle. The ground rushed to meet her as she fell.

Chapter Thirteen

The breath whooshed out of her. A moment later Ferris put a knee in the small of her back and a gun to the side of her head.

No. It could not be.

His breath was hot on her cheek. "Hello, Stephanie. Not quite what you were expecting, right?"

She tried to process the ruse. Vance was chasing someone else in the car they'd thought Ferris had been in. Had he freed Evan? They must have connected somehow. She'd not thought it possible but the pain in her spine from Ferris's weight made it crystal clear they'd miscalculated. Ferris had tricked them again. A scream built inside, but she tried to control her rising panic. She clamped her mouth shut, grit digging into her chin as he pressed her to the ground.

He stripped the handgun from her waistband. "Hoping to shoot me down, neat and tidy? Kill me like you did to my father? How unsportsmanlike."

"I didn't kill your father."

"You put him in prison. Same thing." He ground the gun into her skull. "Helplessness is a bad feeling, right? You're trapped, awaiting your fate. That's how I felt in jail. My dad too."

The scent of pine was strong in her nostrils. "Killing me isn't going to change anything."

"Of course it will—for me anyway and for your kin. Family ties are strong, aren't they, Steph? Your people will mourn your death and that's justice in my book."

"Not mine."

"Don't be so pretentious. You'd do whatever for your family. Grinders and Wolfes agree on that point. That makes us the same, you and me."

"No, it doesn't. I wouldn't murder anyone for my family."

He increased the pressure on her temple until she thought her skull would splinter.

"You would, if the circumstances were right." He hauled her to her feet and marched her to the shadows under the tree near the bathhouse. He kept her in front of him, far enough that she could not flail and knock him over or deliver a satisfying head butt. If she broke away, she'd be dead in moments. In the distance she heard Chloe howl. Her heart ached. What would happen to the dogs if she and Vance died here? They would die too, likely, of starvation if they weren't discovered quick enough. Or maybe Ferris would kill them also.

Plan, Steph. What's the plan?

Ferris forced her under the dripping branches. "Vance thinks he's following me right now. Dope. Does he have Evan's radio or do you?"

When she didn't answer he spun her around and shoved her against the tree trunk. She banged the back of her head. He yanked a radio from a clip on his belt. "Vance's voice is far too deep to do a good Evan impersonation, by the way, but it was a noble effort for a dumb ex-cop."

She could only stare at him, desperate to find a way out of the deadly scenario.

He wriggled the radio. "This is where it gets fun."

Her stomach dropped.

"Silverton," he said into the radio. "It's Ferris. I'm here with your girl. Got ahead of you again and you didn't suspect a thing. You tore off after the car assuming I was the driver.

You know what they say about assumptions. No wonder you both washed out as cops. Getting tired of being played yet?"

Stephanie's throat was tight with terror as the radio crackled with a response.

"If you hurt her, you will die." Vance's tone was so hard, so fierce, she almost didn't recognize it. *Just run, Vance. Get away.* But she knew with a surge of grief and love that he wouldn't. He would do what Ferris asked in an attempt to save her. Fear at what was about to happen flashed along her nerves.

"Don't—" she began to call out to Vance, but Ferris slammed a palm over her mouth so hard she tasted blood. He stepped away a few paces but didn't lower his weapon.

"You'll come to me," Ferris said into the radio. "I want you to see her die before I kill you."

See her die. It was a nightmare.

Vance's breathing was audible over the radio. "Ferris—"

Ferris cut him off. "You'll walk into the campground up the front drive. That's what's going to happen. If you do as I say, she'll die easy, one quick kill shot. If you don't…it will be long and extremely painful, I can promise you." He paused, listening to the sound of Chloe's barking, now accompanied by Pudge. "And then I'll find the dogs and kill them and I'll make it last so they suffer too. That's your choice. I kill the woman and both dogs in the most agonizing way possible, or you deliver yourself to me and they go easily. If you decide to bolt and save your own skin, you'll be a dead man walking from then on. I'll scour every square inch of this wilderness until I find you."

"Not going to happen," Vance snapped.

"Yes, it is," Ferris said. "It's a matter of how it's going to happen and that's up to you. Ten minutes. If you're not at the entrance in ten minutes, their suffering is on your head." He fired a shot. She screamed as it streaked past, three inches from her cheekbone, boring into the tree next to where she stood.

"Ferris," Vance shouted but he turned off the radio and produced a rope.

"Turn around, grab the tree and give it a hug, Officer Wolfe."

She kept her hands at her sides, but he glowered at her. "I can tie you with your cooperation, or I can shoot you first and accomplish the same thing in a messier fashion. Either way, I need you in one place."

Stiffly, she held her arms around the trunk and he tied her wrists together, pinioning her in place. She fought back the enraged howl that wanted to force its way from her mouth. Instead, she pressed her cheek to the abrasive bark and tried to think. He wouldn't win, couldn't, not after what they'd endured, after the evil he and his father had brought on the world.

Vance would be showing up in a matter of moments. She had to figure out some way to help him or distract Ferris. The bark was rough, hardened by centuries of weather. She could use it to saw the rope if he'd turn his attention away. Breath held, she silently willed him to stop staring at her.

Her wish was answered a moment later when Ferris turned away to scan the road with his binoculars. Then he switched his focus to the trees that crowded in on every side along the sweep of road where Vance would approach. The Kevlar vest was strapped tight around his body, but he kept near the bathhouse to shield himself in case Vance took a shot.

Which was exactly what she would do in Vance's shoes, but he wasn't going to shoot wildly in the dark, at a distance. He'd have to get close enough that he was confident his bullet wouldn't hit her too. He wouldn't risk it. She scraped the rope against the bark. The abrasion caught on the nylon, biting into it.

Hurry.

She kept at it.

Chloe and Pudge were barking in unison, the sound carrying in the night air.

When Ferris spared a look at her, she had to stop.

He chuckled. "Have to admit, it would have been much faster if I'd shot you both a couple of days ago, but not nearly as much fun. This is drama, and I'll enjoy remembering it for the rest of my life."

She smothered the rage, the tears, the pain and fear. He wouldn't have the satisfaction of seeing her at the mercy of her emotions. *Look away,* she silently willed him.

He began to check his rifle. His attention diverted, she began to work the ropes against the bark once more. There was no way to protect her wrists, and blood welled from the scrapes she was inflicting. She kept on, feeling a slight give as a strand fell away. Or was it her desperate imagination? Ferris was almost finished inspecting his gun.

Vance would appear any moment around the slight bend in the trail near the tumbled pile of granite.

Picturing him walking into Ferris's sights made her work more feverishly. There would be no way Ferris could fail to shoot him dead, no way for Vance to even draw his revolver without being seen. Tears welled in her eyes from the pain in her wrists, but she kept on. Another strand. She had no gun, but she'd distract Ferris, dive at him, throw rocks, anything she could think of if only she could free herself.

Ferris picked up his binoculars and scanned the trail. "Like clockwork. Here comes the mighty Vance Silverton, meek as a kitten."

She needed more time. She sawed, frantic now. Another thread gave way. Her nerves knotted as she saw a shadow cross the path. *Vance...*

Warm blood seeped into her jacket cuffs as she scraped for all she was worth, the bark embedding itself into her wounds. *Please, God...please.*

Vance stepped partially into view. She couldn't see his expression, but she could imagine his resolve, the handsome cut of his jaw, the crow's feet around his eyes, the full mouth set in a determined line.

"If there's a gun in your hand, I shoot your girl," Ferris shouted.

Vance stopped, still cloaked in shadows. "No gun."

The rope came loose. She batted it away.

As she broke from the tree, a spark ignited in the darkness where Vance stood.

A flaming pine cone streaked through the air, thunking Ferris squarely on the side of the face.

His pinecone must have found its mark because he heard Ferris swear a moment before he began shooting. A bullet whistled past Vance's chin as he rolled to the side. He prayed Ferris kept his shots focused on him instead of Stephanie. He hopped to his feet and sprinted, gun in hand.

Ferris fired again but he was clearly still off balance from the tossed pinecone because the shots sprayed wildly. Vance charged and there was no other choice but to go full steam ahead. He did not know exactly where Stephanie was so he wouldn't return fire. Old-school. Head-on tackle.

But he didn't make it in time.

Ferris swung around, took aim. He braced for the feel of bullets carving through him but instead he heard a soft thump from in front as Ferris hit the dirt.

Stephanie had launched herself at Ferris, landing with her full weight on his back. Ferris lost his grip on the rifle.

Ferris had fury fueling him and Stephanie could not maintain her hold. Before Vance could make it there to assist her, Ferris shoved her off and darted into the trees.

Vance rushed to her, heart twisted with uncertainty and fear. "Steph, are you...? Did he...?" His prayers and questions got all tangled up in his mouth as he reached for her.

With his assistance, she got to her knees, wobbling until he brought her into his arms. He pulled her to him, reassuring himself she was alive. Unhurt. She clutched him back fiercely with a strength that filled him with joy. He relished the give of her soft shoulders, each shuddering breath as he held her steady. *Oh, Lord, thank You.* The words were wholly inadequate. He'd been near paralyzed at the thought of what he'd find at the campground, his only weapon a pinecone of all things.

She tensed and pushed him away.

"Get the dogs," she panted. "We can track him with his scent on the rifle."

He forced his brain to work. Ferris was on foot, without his rifle, though he had a handgun too. If there was any justice, he was stunned by the pinecone he'd taken to the cranium. Excellent. Too bad it didn't knock him out completely. With his jacket sleeve pulled over his fingertips, Vance lifted the rifle.

"Hurry," Steph urged. She was moving a step ahead of him, sprinting to the tent cabin, where the dogs were barking in frantic rhythm. They reached the door flap at almost the same moment. As she lifted her arm to open it, he saw the blood gleaming wetly.

He grabbed her and turned her to face him. "You're bleeding. What…?"

"Not shot. He tied me. I had to get the ropes loose."

He got only a glimpse of her ravaged skin before she pulled from his grasp and freed the dogs, who leaped all over her. Hot anger solidified in his gut, fueling his resolve as he held out the rifle while Steph clipped the leash on Chloe.

"Find," she said and he heard the emotion rippling through the word. Ferris had scared her. Hurt her. She would track him like the miserable fugitive he was and Vance would be with her every inch of the way until they got him or died trying.

She gasped in pain as Chloe tugged them into the night, Pudge staying by his shin. He yearned to take Chloe's lead and spare her the discomfort, but he didn't. She wouldn't allow it and he wasn't skilled in handling a tracking dog. Instead, he focused on keeping Pudge close by and slashing away the branches that impeded their progress as they left the campground and entered the woods.

Ferris had a head start. He might be radioing his accomplice in the car to retrieve him. When he next clapped eyes on Evan, they were going to have a conversation that Evan wouldn't forget.

Intercept mode, Chloe, he urged. *You got this.*

Chloe did not slow for rocks or shrubs or anything as she bulldozed her way through the foliage. They were on Ferris's trail. No doubt about it.

"Close now," Steph whispered, struggling to control the dog. He detected the sound of the river, at first a murmur that rose into a shout as they barreled on. Ferris might be hoping to shake his pursuers off his scent by getting to the water but he'd underestimated Chloe. She was straining now, hauling Steph along toward the rocky lip that rose above the swirling waves.

"Wait," he called. Ferris was dangerous and growing more desperate and they were about to run right into him, he had no doubt.

He tried to stop her, grasping at her arm, but whether Steph's grip was weak due to her injuries or Chloe's animosity toward Ferris was unquenchable, the dog hurtled through the trees, emerging only feet away from Ferris. Uncharacteristically, Chloe barked.

Ferris reached for his pocket.

"Hands," Vance shouted, weapon drawn, as Steph attempted to quiet her dog.

Chloe growled and strained at the leash.

"Hands where I can see them, Ferris," Vance roared.

Ferris froze, considering. Then he lifted his palms.

Vance waited until Steph had Chloe quieted and her own gun out before he moved to Ferris and secured his hands behind his back, zip-tying them with one from Steph's supply.

The satisfaction he felt at finally, finally capturing Ferris Grinder filled him to the brim.

He wasn't about to risk any further escape. Since they had no more zip ties, he settled for fastening Ferris's legs together with duct tape. "How's that feel, Ferris?" Vance asked. "Not too tight, I hope?"

Ferris didn't answer, his eyes glittering with hatred.

Vance removed the radio from Ferris's pocket, along with a satellite phone.

"Would you like to do the honors, Steph?"

Mouth trembling, she nodded. "I would."

He couldn't wait. She placed one call to the police with their location, a quick brief of the situation, and the second to Security Hounds, smiling as she waited for someone to pick up. After the agony they'd endured…it was about to be over.

Ferris looked up and heaved a deep breath. Steph's call connected. She opened her mouth to speak. Chloe went stiff. Ferris lowered his head and charged right at Steph. The phone flew from her hand as Ferris crashed into her.

Vance shouted as Stephanie and Chloe were knocked into the swollen river.

Chapter Fourteen

Water struck Stephanie like a punch as she tumbled into it. The cold stripped her of breath as she went under, then she shot up, in shock from the frigid temperature. She twisted in a violent effort to keep from being sucked below again. Her clothes acted like a sponge, weighing her down.

"Chloe," she screamed, spray stinging her eyes.

To her left she saw an upturned paw, a glimpse of her bloodhound fighting as hard as she was. *Hang on, baby.*

She bobbed forward, struggling to snatch at any glimmer of wet fur, but the waves tossed her as if she was a load in the washing machine. Chloe appeared for a heart-stopping second, then disappeared. Steph paddled in a circle, an agonizing effort, but she could not spot her dog. She screamed again. A torrent of water rolled over, filling her mouth and nose. When she broke the surface, she gulped in a breath and tried to get her bearings. *Don't panic. Keep it together.* She was moving rapidly away from the point where Ferris had knocked her in, where Vance was probably out of his mind with worry.

Would she live to see him again?

The steep bank flashed by—exposed roots, swirling waves, a glimpse of rock. That was her greatest enemy as the surge propelled her along—being crushed against one of the boulders that poked up from the riverbed. One knock on the skull and she'd be dead. Chloe too.

"Chloe, talk," she hollered, after spitting out a mouthful of the river.

Was that a faint bark she heard? She thrashed in the opposite direction.

Chloe appeared a couple of feet away. "Chloe," she called but another wall of water inundated her, and when she was done sputtering and choking, she couldn't see Chloe anymore. She fought down the fear. *You're not going to drown, Chloe. I'm not going to let you.*

"Chloe, talk," she screamed again.

Another bark. Closer.

Chloe bobbed to the surface ten feet away, paddling hard.

She tried to swim for the dog, but she was thrown on her side, sucked under the freezing water. The cold was overwhelming, but she battled free once more. In the distance she saw the outline of a massive tree trunk spanning the chasm. It rose a couple of feet above the waterline. Would she be able to catch it? Hang on and haul herself to safety?

Not without Chloe. She wasn't going to leave her best friend to drown.

"Chloe," she yelled, narrowly avoiding being impaled by the sharp end of a branch. More branches appeared between the ripples. She hooked an arm around the next one she passed and was yanked to a halt so hard she bit her lip. It was a brutal effort to cling there with the river thundering around her, but she held on, praying the branch wouldn't break. She yelled again for Chloe to talk. *Answer me, Chloe. Please.*

The bark was louder now. Ears—she saw a glimpse of those incredible flappy ears.

"Come, Chloe. Come." Her heart quivered as Chloe surged toward her, powerful legs churning. The water fought against the dog, snatching her away until she fought back.

"You can do it." Her arm stretched out until her sinews almost snapped. "Come on. Come to me, girl. Please." The last word came out as a sob.

Snout low, Chloe steamed forward like a battleship.

"Almost there. Two more feet. Push hard."

She came close enough that Steph grabbed a strap on her harness and hauled her in.

Chloe looped those ridiculously long legs over Steph's shoulders and she and her dog clung close, hearts beating wildly. The wet fur against her cheek filled her with gratitude and renewed her determination. God gave her Chloe and they'd survive this. For a moment, maybe more, they held on to each other, stationary in the wild chaos. They could not remain that way for long. Steph's arms were trembling, Chloe's added weight making it harder to maintain their position. The branch she held shuddered ominously.

Next step. Should she let go? Hold on to Chloe and let the water carry them to the makeshift log bridge? Would she be able to snag hold and get them both out? She wasn't sure what lay beyond. A safe spot to wade out or a dangerous plunge or twist?

They couldn't remain with their body temperatures dropping, sucking away their strength. Vance would come, she was sure of it, but it would take time, more than they had. So it really wasn't a choice, was it?

She kissed Chloe. Their partnership was one of ultimate trust in one another. Whatever came, they'd endure it together. "No matter what, you are the best dog in the entire world, and I love you."

Chloe licked the moisture from Steph's face.

"All right. Hold on tight, sweet girl. Ready?"

With a fervent prayer and her pulse galloping, she let go.

Vance could barely contain his fury as he hauled Ferris away from the bank and tied him to the tree like he'd done with

Evan. A furnace was burning inside him—Steph's shocked expression as she and Chloe went over was seared into his brain.

Ferris laughed. "Didn't get you, but at least I got her and her dog. Two for two, which isn't bad. My daddy always taught me to maximize the wins where you can."

Rage curled his hand into a fist and he fought the urge to use it on Ferris, to smash the wicked grin from his mouth. The seconds ticked loudly in his brain, each one ripping Stephanie and Chloe farther away from him. He didn't trust himself to speak as he searched for Ferris's phone and radio while Pudge barked and whined at the edge of the river where Steph and Chloe had disappeared.

He found the radio, pocketed it and dialed the emergency number on the sat phone. When the sheriff's department answered, he launched in with the terrible update.

"This is Vance Silverton. You just got a call from Stephanie Wolfe, but the situation's changed. I've still got Ferris Grinder secured at..." He checked the coordinates and relayed them again. "But he's shoved Stephanie Wolfe and her dog into the river. I'm going after them. Come get him and send help."

There was no need to whistle for Pudge. He was already slipping and sliding down the bank. As Vance followed, Ferris called out again.

"You're going to die too. If the river doesn't get you, I will, sooner or later, in a way you don't expect. Just know when you're dying, it was my doing."

Jaw clenched, he didn't answer, simply made his own ungainly way to join Pudge as he slid down the steep bank. They'd continue in the muddy margins as best they could, climb around obstacles when needed, follow the direction where Steph and Chloe had been carried.

He didn't feel the cold, the water droplets splashing at him, the mud oozing into his boots. All his emotion was funneled into one crystal-clear desire.

Find them.

But the freezing water was roaring, punishing the rocks and trees and anything it encountered. They had to make faster progress. He upped the pace, and Pudge maintained position at his side. When they encountered an enormous cleft in the bank, they scrambled to higher ground to skirt it, which cost them precious time.

Returning to their course along the river, he saw no sign of Steph or Chloe. He roared her name every few minutes and his heart sank lower when he received no replies. Had he and Pudge passed them somehow? Were they clinging to a rock or had they managed to pull themselves out and they'd rushed by the two? Worse thoughts threatened his sanity but he refused to give them purchase. *Keep going,* his instincts told him.

Another quarter mile, maybe a half, and he was feeling the tug of panic along with the burning in his legs. Doubt and fear overwhelmed him.

Lord, please.

Pudge dropped to his tummy, tongue lolling, but Vance could not stop. The next few yards might reveal Chloe and Steph. Pudge barked, but Vance rushed ahead, around the massive log that spanned the river. Something was nibbling at the edge of his consciousness, a change in the sound of the water. Vance's senses picked up on the information before his brain could.

Twenty yards past the fallen log, the riverbed plunged steeply, funneling into twisted rapids that pounded through a pinch point lined with sharp-edged rocks on either side. A death trap. His spirit dropped. The flow was raging with such force Steph and Chloe would not have been able to fight it. Unable to slow or stop, they would have been crushed against the rocks and been borne away.

He could not make himself believe it. It couldn't have ended that way. They must have gotten out somehow. Frantically he yanked the binoculars from his pack and scanned, praying for a glimpse of Steph or Chloe, safe on the bank.

There was no sign of either.

No Steph.

No faithful bloodhound.

It was as if the spirit drained out of him along with the last dregs of energy and hope.

He sank to his knees. Too late. He'd been too late.

If he hadn't stopped to call the police? Tie Ferris to the tree? What had he done? Had his desire to secure justice for Lettie caused him to sacrifice Steph? It was agony even to breathe in and out.

Pudge barked but he barely heard.

He couldn't absorb the enormity of what had happened. One moment, they'd been celebrating Ferris's capture, and then...

Pudge appeared at his elbow and barked again, whapping him on the shoulder with his snout.

Vance blinked, tried to focus. "What?"

Another bark. Another tap. Pudge about-faced and waddled rapidly upstream.

Upstream? Why there? The dog was definitely trying to tell him something.

But Pudge wasn't a tracker. Could this misfit dog, the odd-ball, untrained hound, know something about Stephanie and Chloe that he didn't? Pudge was a shipwreck in many ways, but the animal loved Chloe and Steph too, he had no doubt.

Should he follow Pudge or call the police again?

He clambered to his feet. "Pudge?"

The dog looked back once and let loose one loud, forceful come-here bark.

Vance summoned the strength to sprint after him. Pudge was panting, tongue lolling, when he finally heaved himself to a stop back at the spot of the fallen log. Vance used the binoculars and swept them over the span. There was nothing. Despair weighed him down.

"I don't see anything," he said to Pudge.

Pudge rose up on his back legs and head-butted Vance right in the stomach.

"I can't…"

As he straightened, he got a glimpse in the pocket of water contained by the roots of the fallen giant, a gleam, a soft shape where there shouldn't be any, the curve of an arm.

"Steph," he yelled.

She didn't answer, or maybe she simply didn't hear over the tumult. With Pudge at his side, he charged toward the tangled roots, his sight obscured by the water spraying into the darkness as they climbed up and over the mighty limb.

Pudge found them first, barking and panting, climbing and stumbling through the tangle of roots. Chloe's answering howl sent a shiver of pure joy right through him. But Steph. What was her condition?

He charged on, heedless of the roots grabbing for his ankles, hauling himself up and over piles of brush until he reached them.

Chloe sat on her haunches, shivering, her body leaning over Steph.

Steph was lying on her side in the fetal position, eyes closed.

Lord, oh, Lord, please… The words repeated over and over in his soul as he dropped to his knees and touched her face—it was ice cold.

"Steph," he whispered, searching for a pulse on her neck. No thrum of life penetrated his frozen fingertips. "Open your eyes, honey. Please, please, please."

Had she stirred? Or was it his overwhelming need confusing him?

"Steph?"

Her mouth moved. Heart slamming, he pushed closer.

"What took you so long?" she whispered.

Joy swept him up in an intense wave as he bent over her, stroking the wet hair from her face, stripping off his jacket to cover her. "You scared me, Wolfe." He gently checked her limbs for obvious breaks.

"Nothing broken," Steph murmured. "How's Chloe?"

He spared a look. "Pudge is licking her all over and she seems to be passing inspection. Can you sit up?"

She stirred.

"Slow, Steph. Take it easy. No rush, right?" But there was an urgency because she was undoubtedly becoming hypothermic. "Cops are alerted and on their way. Gotta get you warm in the meantime."

"Ferris?"

"Tied to a tree."

"Any way he could escape?"

"I'm gonna say no on that."

But Ferris's last comment echoed in his mind.

If the river doesn't get you, I will, sooner or later, in a way you don't expect.

His gut tightened. The river hadn't won and it wasn't going to. And neither was Ferris.

He bent and picked her up, her frame trembling with cold. "Chloe, are you okay to walk, girl?"

Chloe stood on shaky legs, Pudge nosing her with concern. Together, they picked their way over to a more sheltered spot, drier, farther from the roaring water. He set her down against a thick trunk and spread a silver emergency blanket from his pack, one for her and Chloe to sit on and the other to wrap around them over his jacket.

"You're cold and wet too," she said. "Take your jacket back."

He snorted. "As if. I'm a Marine, baby. We know stuff, we do things, and we never get cold." His goose bumps said otherwise, but he cheerfully ignored them. He gathered up as many dry leaves as he could find, as well as fallen bark, then piled everything up and coaxed out a flame with the waterproof matches from Steph's pack.

The blaze was tiny at first, but the way it danced life into her eyes gave him hope. More and more fuel he piled on until it was a sizable fire. It would help the rescuers find them.

"Can you feel it yet?"

She shook her head. "Not y-yet," she said through chattering teeth. He sat next to her, drew her into his arms, as close to the flames as was safe. He added another metallic emergency blanket to their pile. Chloe burrowed in on one side of Steph and Pudge squirmed under the blanket on the other, crinkling the material.

Steph laughed weakly. "Now I'm feeling it."

And he was too.

Such feelings as only God could understand.

He embraced the woman and the dogs and breathed his thankful prayer into the frigid mountain air.

Chapter Fifteen

Search and rescue found them two hours later, along with a park ranger and two cops. Steph was still shivering, but not as violently, and Chloe appeared to be comfortable.

Ferris was in custody, the cops reported. Finally. Vance provided a quick briefing, including where they'd left Evan, though he'd obviously gotten free and helped Ferris with the campground ambush.

"The horse," Steph said. "Evan's horse needs to be collected."

"Later, Steph. Let them transport you on a stretcher," Vance said.

She shook her head. "No. We'll walk to the vehicle."

"But…" His face had been so ravaged with fear when he'd carried her and Chloe out and it had struck a chord inside her that kept on sounding. Trauma, maybe, but she took his hand, gripping it tight as she stood. Pudge pranced next to Chloe, who'd been thoroughly dried, and both dogs had been given handfuls of treats from their rescuers.

"We heard from your sister. She's been trying to locate you," the cop said.

Steph sighed. "Radio her quick that we're okay, otherwise she'll have had a platoon of Wolfes en route."

The ranger looked up. "She called the competition planners after your hang-up and they reported that you'd tapped out, gone to a hotel. We'll contact her and provide the broad strokes of what happened."

She groaned. "All the while we were running for our lives, no one knew what was really going on." Ferris and his clever deceptions.

She and Vance and the dogs were loaded up into the vehicle and taken to the hospital, where they were checked over and more officers took their expanded statements. They even summoned a veterinarian to the hospital to tend to Chloe and Pudge.

"You've got some story to tell," the doctor said. "Amazing you survived."

She wouldn't have, except for the fact that Vance had been with her. She wanted more than anything to sleep for another few days, but she could not rest until her family knew the reality of her condition from her own mouth. They'd only gotten a bare bones report from the police. She dialed, and Kara and her mother answered on speakerphone.

"What happened? I want the whole story," her mother demanded. "Are you positive you aren't hurt? The cops didn't tell us nearly enough."

"You might want to sit down for this," she told them.

Kara didn't interrupt. Her mother, on the other hand, peppered her with questions until Steph promised again that she and Vance were unharmed, mostly, and they would be on their way to the ranch within the hour. She hoped Vance would agree with her plan.

"No. We'll come get you. Right now. I'll grab my keys…" her mom said.

"No need." Especially since her mom was still healing from back surgery. "I'm leaving as soon as possible. We'll be home tonight. You can track my phone via GPS if it will make you feel better."

"Okay, sis," Kara said and Steph heard the tears. "I'm so sorry I didn't suspect anything. I should have known when—"

"No way. This is nothing anyone could have foreseen. Stop that line of thinking, pronto."

"I agree," her mother said. "When you get here, we're going to have hot soup and bottomless coffee while you provide every last detail. I'm going to wait to call your brothers until after you give us the 411 or they'll all storm the castle."

She laughed. "All right. I'll message you when we leave."

Vance and Pudge showed up as she was ending the call. She'd been given a shower, which stung every scrape and cut, especially on her abraded wrists, and a set of hospital sweats and a T-shirt. Vance was dressed in his own borrowed gear, the pants slightly too short, his hair gleaming with moisture. Pudge had been wiped down like Chloe and looked much more presentable.

"What's the prognosis?" he said.

"Bandages and ointment and a few stitches. Lots of rest, blah, blah, recommended. You?"

"Similar but no stitches." He smiled at her. "Not to put too fine a point on it, but you look amazing for a woman who fell in the river."

"And you are pretty put-together too, considering you came after me."

"Steph—"

"I want to go home," she said, cutting him off. The need was so great to return to the Security Hounds Ranch, she swallowed her pride. "Will you drive me? Now? My wrists hurt too bad to steer. We can rent a car. I know it's late in the day and a lot to ask, but…"

He was already pulling out his phone. "Wireless. I'll never take it for granted again. I'll get us a set of wheels right now. What do you want? A Corvette? Rolls?"

"Something that the dogs can slobber on." She laughed, feeling lighter than she had in years. More specifically, better than she'd been since Vance got the detective's job. She looked over at him.

"I'm on hold. What's the smile for?" he said.

"Just thinking about your cake."

"Oh, yeah." He looked suddenly shy. "You said… You said you'd come over and have chili when you delivered it. Is that still okay with you? Unless you've changed your mind since we're back in civilization."

Her insides quivered. What would happen between them now that they were back in the real world? The forgiveness was cemented, she knew, but she wasn't sure about their romantic status. He clearly wanted to start over. Did she? Could she? "Yes," she said faintly. "When things settle."

"When things settle," he repeated and the disappointment rang in his voice.

She felt suddenly nervous.

"Okay," he said. "I'll get us that car."

The trip was more uncomfortable than she'd imagined, but the pain reliever they'd supplied in the hospital took the edge off to the point that her eyelids had grown heavy. Her chin hit her chest twice as she struggled to stay awake. She forced herself straighter in the seat.

"Vance, there's something I can't figure out."

"I'm listening," he said around a mouthful of licorice. He'd been eating since they left the hospital and seemed to show no signs of stopping.

"How did Ferris find Evan when we had his phone and radio?"

"I wondered that myself. And further, why did he take your vehicle to try and capture us instead of whatever he'd rode in on?"

"Questions, more questions," she said sleepily, unable to stifle her yawn.

"Important thing is we made it out."

She yawned again.

He chuckled. "The details can wait. Go ahead and rest. I got this."

She dozed, swimming to consciousness hours later when they reached the gate that led to the ranch just before sundown. It was open and she smiled. Normally, every visitor would be greeted by a baying chorus of canines, but it was quiet since Roman, Garrett and Chase and their dogs were all elsewhere. Her mom's elderly bloodhound, Arthur, was likely lazing on the back lawn. Kara was tending a dog with medical issues who was finishing up a stay at the animal hospital.

Vance parked, got out and stretched, his groan echoing her own myriad of aches and pains. He clamped a hand to his back. "I am never sleeping on the ground again. Ever."

"Agreed."

Eager as she was to see her sister and mother, she got out of the car and took a moment to smooth her hair, straighten the borrowed clothes. Her family would be worried enough. The story would have to be told in pieces to cover everything they'd experienced. Multiple times, since her brothers would demand a thorough report too, when they returned home.

Where to start?

Vance shifted, eyeballing the house. His mouth twitched uneasily. Was that a sheen of perspiration on his brow? He caught her looking. "Uh, your family, your mom in particular, well, they weren't my biggest fans when I messed things up with you."

She laughed. "You scared of my mom?"

"One hundred percent," he replied solemnly.

"Not scared of my three brothers?"

"Nah, I can take them, but your mom..." He shook his head. "Whole other level of scary."

"Go on, Marine. Take your medicine like a big boy."

With a sigh, he saluted, squared his shoulders and pivoted to the house.

As she started to follow, her phone rang.

Vance was already striding to the door, his arms full of Pudge while Chloe waited at her side.

"Go on ahead," she called to Vance. "I need to take this. It's the cop from Lost Sierra."

Vance obliged and lugged Pudge along, only setting him on his feet on the front porch before he knocked politely.

"Hello, Officer," she said into the phone.

"Good afternoon, ma'am. You asked me to call you when we found the horse."

Evan's horse. She'd been concerned about the animal running loose without care. "Is he in good shape?"

"Yes, ma'am. He was standing pleased as punch right next to his owner, who was also in fine condition before we booked him."

"Wait. His owner?"

"Yes, Evan Bowman, the man hired by Ferris. He came clean about everything. He'll be an excellent witness when Ferris is tried."

The first flush of fear pricked her skin. "You found Evan Bowman tied to the tree."

There was a pause. "Yes. Right in the location you told us about when we debriefed."

Her body went cold. If Evan had been tied to the tree the whole time, who'd been driving the car when Ferris approached the campground? Her mind spun. Who would have been able to rendezvous with Ferris? Someone who'd been in on the whole plan. But if not Evan...

"Ms. Wolfe?" The officer's voice came from far away. "Is everything okay?"

Her vision swam. Somebody who'd helped him lure her there, delivered her right to the spot where he was waiting to shoot. Her gaze caught tire tracks pressed into the mud on the side of the driveway marking the path a car had taken around the side of her home. Out of sight. "Dispatch local PD to this address," she said as she rattled off the location. "I…"

The words were swallowed up by a gunshot.

A second after the door swung open, the bullet pierced Vance's shoulder and exited the other side, spiraling him sideways into the doorframe before he hit the entry hall floor. Dazed, he didn't feel the pain as much as he experienced the shock. Blindsided, he found himself staring up at Gina, the woman he hadn't saved from the river. She stood with hands locked around a gun. Pudge howled in panic, dancing in frenzied uncertainty next to Vance.

Gina glared.

"Don't…" He'd started to call out a warning to Steph but it was too late—she was already there behind him, gripping her own weapon, advancing.

He managed to sit halfway up. Pudge pawed and barked while Chloe howled behind him at Steph's side. Try as he might, he couldn't get himself to his feet. His muscles simply wouldn't obey. The blood coursed a warm trail, soaking his sleeve, and he finally understood what had been bothering him since that moment at the Jeep. It was the look on Gina's face when he'd tried to save her from drowning in the creek. She hadn't been plucked from his grasp by the water. She'd *let go*. He'd disastrously miscalculated.

He tried to think over the pounding pain in his body. Pudge continued to bark at full volume and Steph said something, but he didn't catch it.

Gina was wearing different clothes than she had when he'd tried to rescue her, and there was an angry scratch on her neck, but it was her eyes that called the most attention—cold, filled with hate, her intention blazing. She was going to murder them. That much was clear. What had already happened to Steph's family? His gut went cold. Had she already killed them?

"Put your gun down," Gina said to Steph.

"That's not going to happen." Steph moved closer, Chloe next to her. "Where's my family?"

"I'll kill him," Gina said, pointing to Vance. "Shoot him right in the head."

"Police are already rolling." Steph stepped around him, advancing toward Gina. He tried to catch her attention, command her to stop.

But she kept her focus riveted on Gina. "Vance?" she said without looking at him.

"All fine here. A through-and-through." But the next one wouldn't be, and he was desperate to think of a plan to keep her from being Gina's next target.

"Where's my family?" Steph asked again, the urgency penetrating each syllable.

Gina laughed. "Awww. Are you worried? That's so sweet. But you deserve it, considering what you did to my family."

Steph tensed and he hurriedly spoke. "How'd you get out of the river? That water was frigid, moving fast." He surreptitiously snagged Pudge's collar with one hand, pulling the hysterical dog closer. Pudge whined and prodded Vance with his wet nose.

"I'm a good swimmer. I pulled myself out. Ferris was watching through binoculars and saw me fall in. He sent Evan to track me with the drone and pick me up. Evan set me up with a campsite and Ferris told me to wait there until he collected me."

"You were the one who drove Ferris to the campsite in my car," Steph said.

"Yeah. You were oblivious, both of you. After I dropped him in the trees and made sure you followed me, I drove to our prearranged rendezvous spot, left your car, and took off in Ferris's vehicle. He wanted me to get away clean and without being implicated." Her lips tightened. "But things clearly went wrong. He didn't show at the rendezvous. I hear he's been arrested."

Vance forced a chuckle. "If you ask me, things went exactly right. We left him all nice and trussed like a Christmas turkey for the cops to find. He sure wasn't happy about that turn of events. Grumble, grumble, grumble." Vance eased Pudge in front of him. "I take it you're the favorite cousin he mentioned. The one that had to leave town after he and Maurice were arrested?"

She glowered. He could feel Steph's tension as she aimed her gun. A standoff that would lead to death if he didn't do something.

"I had to move away," Gina snapped. "The police were all over everything, tearing apart the trucking business, making my life miserable even though I only helped with the computer work."

He watched her expression, bitter in such a young, delicate face. In other circumstances, she'd appear to be a complete innocent, a genial person whom you'd never suspect of such murderous tendencies. Another truth clicked home. It made sense now, why the Harlow family had opened the door to their assassin. They'd seen a small, harmless woman on the porch, not Ferris. "You killed the Harlows, didn't you?"

He heard Steph suck in a breath.

She shrugged. "They had it coming. And you do too. This was always our fall-back plan if something went wrong in the process of killing you two. First, we'd make Steph's family mourn, then your aunt Lettie. If Ferris couldn't complete the job, I would." Grim satisfaction rang in her words.

Steph spoke through gritted teeth. "Where is my family?"

"Locked in the basement, so I could make you watch while I killed them. Don't look so relieved. They'll die painfully too."

"None of this is going to help Ferris," Steph said. "He's on his way to prison."

Her chin went up. "Yes, it will. He'll know his father was avenged. I'll find a way to help him escape someday, but justice is the goal. It was from the beginning. Ferris says that's all you can strive for in this world."

Justice had been his primary goal too, for a while. And he'd allowed it to destroy things between him and Steph. No more.

"Gina," Steph said quietly. "This isn't…"

"Shut up."

Vance finally scooted Pudge into position. He used the dog's stocky frame to hide his actions as he reached to his waist-band and palmed his gun. Pudge tensed and whined as Gina glared at Steph. "If you don't drop your weapon, I start shoot-ing." Her fingers whitened on the trigger.

Before she could pull it, Vance let go of the dog. Pudge bolted, got his paws tangled and tumbled, his bulk sending him skidding across the floor. Vance and Steph both brought their weapons up simultaneously. Before Vance could get a shot off, Gina went over backward as Pudge rolled into her shins. Chloe raced to her friend's side and in the melee, Vance sprang on top of the pile and grabbed Gina's gun hand, pinning it to the floor. His shoulder was on fire, but he clung with everything in him until Steph pried Gina's gun out of her clawed fingers.

Vance flipped Gina over, ignoring the searing pain, and kneeled there until Steph found an extra leash to tie her hands. Pudge licked his face the whole time, and Vance put his good arm around his dog, who was whining at the blood pouring down Vance's arm.

"Good dog, Pudge," he said. "Best friend ever. I didn't know you were going to help in the takedown. I'm going to see to it you get a commendation for canine heroism and a piece of my carrot cake."

Gina secured, Steph turned to him. "Vance…" The pain in that one word. The fear. For him and for her family. His breath caught.

"I'm not critical," he said. "Go find them. I'll watch her."

He prayed with everything in him that she'd discover her family alive and unharmed. She raced to the basement door and unlocked it. Her cry of relief was overwhelming as he saw Kara and Beth Wolfe appear.

Thank You, God. His head spun with gratitude.

They hugged fiercely before the three hustled back to Vance again.

Gina remained tied and on her stomach. Pudge continued to whine and sniff at him, uninterested in the newcomers. Kara coaxed the dog a few inches away, her voice soft and soothing.

Beth took a knee at his side, assessing in the thorough manner he'd expect from an Air Force nurse.

"I sure didn't intend to meet you again this way, Captain," he said respectfully, using her Air Force rank. "I'd salute properly but..." But blood was pouring down his arm and he was beginning to feel lightheaded, his ears buzzing. *Do not pass out, Vance.* He closed his eyes for a moment and then refocused.

"Stay still," Beth Wolfe commanded. "Kara, bring me some towels."

Kara nodded, a phone pressed to her ear as she called 911 while Steph tied Gina's ankles. Gina continued to swear and scream but Chloe joined in with such an ear-splitting howl that Gina stopped.

Beth pressed towels to his wound, front and back. "Good thing you weren't standing two inches to the left or you'd be dead." He winced as she applied pressure. "Pain?"

"Hardly any, ma'am," he choked out.

"You are clearly lying."

"Yes, ma'am."

"Noted. And you're not going to give me some macho lip about denying a hospital transport, are you?"

"Wouldn't dream of it, ma'am." He squirmed. "Uh, but I'm making a mess on your hardwood. Maybe if I roll myself outside onto the porch..."

"Not necessary."

He shook his head. "Aunt Lettie spent years scrubbing

floors so I can appreciate the problem. Bloodstains are a bear to remove. It'd be easier if I bled on the porch, ma'am, where there's a hose so you could..."

"Vance?"

"Yes, ma'am?"

"Stop talking."

"Yes, ma'am."

She smiled as she pressed the towels tight, which almost made him scream aloud. He ground his teeth together.

Beth regarded him, head cocked, mouth pinched. "Vance Silverton, you behaved like an imbecile and broke my daughter's heart."

He looked at her in mute agony.

The flared nostrils communicated her disgust along with the words. "I'd thought better of you, being a Marine and all."

That hurt. He wriggled, opened his mouth and closed it again.

"You may talk now," she said.

"I did behave dishonorably, ma'am. I treated her with disrespect. I am deeply ashamed of my actions."

Beth continued to work on his bullet wound. "She left the force because of you."

"Mom..." Steph said.

He looked Beth Wolfe square in the eyes. "Yes, ma'am, and I am truly sorry for it. Sorrier than I've ever been about anything else I've ever done in my whole life. If there was one thing I could do over, it'd be to change how I treated you daughter."

Beth remained silent for a moment. "You've told her so, I gather?"

Steph busied herself checking Gina's restraints. "Yes, Mom. He has."

"And you've accepted his apology, Steph?"

Steph blushed a cotton-candy pink. "Yes."

Yes. Oh, how grateful he was for that one syllable. Steph forgave him, but her mother was a different matter.

Beth patted Vance on his good shoulder. "All right. There's no need to discuss it further then, is there? Kara's called for an ambulance, and we'll save the soup and coffee for another night."

He nodded, dizziness overtaking him as Beth went to fetch more towels. Steph dropped to his side. "We make it through four days being hunted by a killer in the middle of nowhere and you get shot in my kitchen?"

"Front hallway to be exact." He smiled through the pain. "They say most injuries occur in the home."

She brought her face close to his and cupped his cheek. He stayed still, willing himself to memorize the feel of her touch, precious as sunshine, pure as a mountain morning.

"Hold on, Silverton." Then she kissed him hard, once, edged away and then again, softly, tenderly. "You just hold on, you hear?"

He wanted to reassure her, apologize again for the wound he'd inflicted, the mistakes he'd made, to tell her how she'd never really left his thoughts in the months they'd been apart, but he felt his stamina recede.

"Pudge..." he muttered.

"He can stay here with me," Kara said. "We'll take good care of him, I promise."

Pudge whined, pulled away from Kara and bustled to his side again.

The last thing he felt before he passed out was the tingle of Steph's kiss and the slippery slosh of Pudge's tongue on his wrist.

Steph looked with satisfaction at the message on her screen from the police department as she stroked Chloe's silky head where she sat next to Steph's chair. One full week after she and Vance had almost died in the Lost Sierra, justice was finally being served. Ferris was under arrest, as were Gina and Evan. The dogs had recovered fully and Vance had been stitched up and sent home. He'd already started house hunting for a rental that would accept dogs. In the meantime, he was bunking at his aunt Lettie's and Pudge was getting way too many treats from the woman.

Vance had called Steph every day and visited so often that her brother Chase had jokingly suggested Vance was the reason he, Roman and Garrett were installing a new security system. None of them wanted to say out loud the real reason, or to consider what might have happened if Gina hadn't been stopped. She would never forget seeing Vance lying bloody on the floor, or the feeling of terror before she'd freed Kara and her mother in the basement.

Kara looped an arm around Steph and squeezed. "Okay, sis?"

"Yes." And she meant it. Nightmares aside, her heart was at peace and her body had almost fully healed, as had Vance. God had blessed her richly.

"Good. Garrett said you're not to leave the house without an escort."

"And Garrett knows full well that is a ridiculous command which will not be obeyed."

"Yep. He sure does." Kara snagged a bag of carrots from the fridge.

"Hungry?"

"No, but the chickens are."

"I haven't forgotten about them. I'm still working on those plans for a more secure coop. Vance said he knows someone who might be able to help too."

"I didn't doubt it but hurry up if you can. I spotted two coyotes last night, licking their chops." Kara exited into the yard.

Chloe raised her nose in an alert a moment before the doorbell rang. Steph stuffed down a flicker of stress and strode to answer it, checking first through the peephole since her brothers hadn't yet finalized the security system. *You're safe. No more predators out gunning for you and Chloe.*

Her pulse bumped as she took in the tall, handsome man on her porch. She opened the door. Vance stood there holding a nervous Pudge. Pudge peered over Vance's arm, down at an enormous cream-colored mountain of a dog sitting attentively on the step. Pudge shot the large dog a look and scooted farther up toward Vance's shoulder as if he was trying to escape the jaws of a hungry tiger.

For a moment, her surprise left her speechless.

"Hi, Steph." Vance juggled his ungainly dog. "You're fine, Pudge. Absolutely safe. We talked about this, remember? Man up, would ya?"

Stephanie stared from Vance to the huge white dog and back again. "Whose dog is this?"

"Funny you should ask. Uh, remember when we spoke on the phone last night, I told you I knew a guy who could help with your sister's chicken problem?"

"Yes." She examined the dog closer. "Is that a...?"

"Anatolian shepherd, yes. Handsome, isn't he? He answers to the name of Phil. He was a livestock guardian on a farm, but it sold—you know, tough times for agriculture right? A real shame. Anyway they didn't want to take him along when they moved to the suburbs, so he landed on the unemployment line at the shelter with Pudge, go figure. He's the dog I mentioned Pudge was kind of afraid of, but Phil's not aggressive, just intense. You know. Kind of like you."

She blinked, trying to absorb it all. "Why did you bring him here?"

"Phil needs a job, and you need some chicken help, or at least, Kara does. Phil's got a whiz-bang résumé, though in his previous employment he specialized in sheep. Not a problem for him. He's versatile."

"Vance..." Words failed her.

Vance took a breath and kept going. "So, you know, I thought Phil could go to work protecting your sister's chickens. He wouldn't need to be doted on like Pudge here, because he's kind of an introvert, which is why no one seems to want to adopt him. A waste of talent, right? There Phil was in a cage, and there are your sister's chickens all juicy and vulnerable..."

A chuckle welled up from a spot deep inside and in a moment she was laughing so hard she was crying. Never had she seen a more adorable man. Pudge watched her and trembled. Phil was entirely unruffled by her mirth.

"I guess," she said when she could get a breath, "we could give him a trial run."

"Excellent. A probationary period, so Phil can demonstrate his skills." Vance eased Pudge down onto the opposite side of the porch step. The dog leaped through the doorway and cowered at Steph's legs. She reached down to pet him, still giggling. "Go sit yourself on the couch with Chloe, Pudge. She'll protect you."

Pudge scuttled off to join his bloodhound friend.

When she straightened, Vance was grinning. "This is terrific. We should totally celebrate Phil's new job."

"All right. What do you have in mind?"

"Is my cake ready? The carrot one with the rosettes and the tidbits?"

"Not yet."

He frowned, considering. "And my place is all boxes so how about dinner out? We could talk about serious adulting stuff."

"Like what?"

He looked thoughtful, stroking Phil's neck in a distracted fashion. "My savings account and those plans."

"What plans?"

"The house plans. The property I bought is big enough for a three-bedroom place, two bathrooms, a yard for a garden and space for a bunch of dogs. I was considering putting in a video-game room or a home gym, but I'm not married to the idea or anything. As long as there's plenty of room for the two of us..."

She jerked. "The two of us?"

"And the dogs," he added quickly. "And a nice kitchen because I like to eat. You know I can take down a full side of beef in a week and however many carrot cakes are available. And a pantry for treats. That was Pudge's idea."

She put a palm on his chest. "Back it up, Silverton. Did you say the two of us?"

The moment stretched between them, full of a silent promise that made her heart thunder.

"Yes, I did," he said quietly, suddenly serious.

"That's going to require some explanation."

He encircled her wrist. "I meant you and me, Wolfe." A tentative smile broke over his face. "We go together like peanut butter and jelly, or ice cream and a spoon. You are the cheese to my macaroni."

"If you're making a joke..."

"I'm not," he said, applying pressure with his fingers. "Pay attention because I figure I'm only going to get one shot at this, you being the hard nut to crack and all." He locked eyes with her. "I love you, Steph. Like in that completely ridiculous, redonkadonk way that makes me want to wear socks that match and put money in a bank account and buy you roses every single time I pass the florist shop."

She gaped.

"Do you want me to list the reasons why? No problem. I came prepared." He released her wrist and pulled a rolled-up paper from his pocket. "I wrote it all down and Phil helped me edit. First, you are smarter and stronger than I am, even though my muscles are way bigger. Second, you sacrifice for other people, which is a godly quality if I ever heard of one. Third, I think you're beautiful." He looked up at her with a dopey expression as his gaze roved her face. "Like, you know, inexpressibly beautiful, from the inside to the outside, and when you smile at me it feels better than winning at basketball and that's something because I am really competitive and I win a lot. Fourth..." He squinted at the paper. "Well, I can't read my handwriting, but I think it's something to do with the fact that I never met anyone else in the whole world who impresses me like you do, and by impresses, what I mean is…" He waved a vague hand as he grasped for words.

"Vance," she finally said.

He stopped, and in that moment she saw through his genial facade how much he'd risked to profess his love, how deeply he cherished her and how precious this great big man was, with the dogs and plans and laughter and jokes.

Thank You, God. A lump rose in her throat. "I love you, too."

He pumped a fist. "I knew it." He turned in a circle and whooped to the sky. "Did you hear that, Phil? She loves me. I totally knew it."

Then he swept her into his arms and kissed her until she was breathless.

Three more kisses and they broke into laughter. Phil looked up at them patiently, as if waiting for their senses to return.

"You're hired, Phil," Steph said, still in Vance's arms. "Should we show him his new flock?"

"Yes, ma'am. No time like the present." But instead he kissed her again until she giggled.

"Are you sure Phil wants to come live at Security Hounds? It's chaotic here."

"Absolutely. He was born for it. Hop to, Phil," he said to the white mountain at his shin. "Me and the missus got to show you your new charges because we have things to do and plans to make."

So many things, and so many plans.

Thank You, God.

* * * * *

Don't miss the stories in this mini series!

K-9 SEARCH AND RESCUE

Tracking The Missing
SAMI A. ABRAMS
December 2024

K-9 Alaskan Defence
SARAH VARLAND
January 2025

Searching For Justice
CONNIE QUEEN
February 2025

MILLS & BOON

Tracking The Missing
Sami A. Abrams

MILLS & BOON

Award-winning, bestselling author **Sami A. Abrams** grew up hating to read. It wasn't until her thirties that she found authors who captured her attention. Most evenings, you can find her engrossed in a romantic suspense novel. She lives in Northern California but will always be a Kansas girl at heart. She has a love of sports, family and travel. However, writing her next story in a cabin at Lake Tahoe tops her list.

Books by Sami A. Abrams

Tracking the Missing

Deputies of Anderson County

Buried Cold Case Secrets
Twin Murder Mix-Up
Detecting Secrets
Killer Christmas Evidence
Witness Escape

Visit the Author Profile page at millsandboon.com.au.

These things I have spoken unto you,
that in me ye might have peace. In the world
ye shall have tribulation: but be of good cheer;
I have overcome the world.
—*John* 16:33

This book is dedicated to Goose, the real-life Ducky. A golden retriever with personality to spare. If he could read, I'd thank him for taking such good care of my daughter Melissa. Goose boy, you're the best!

Chapter One

Dried leaves crunched to Victoria Campbell's left, sending a shiver slithering up her spine. She jerked her head toward the noise. What critter had her in its sights? Did it have four legs or two? She hated the woods. More than that, she hated the unknown in the depths of Indiana's Wildfire State Forest—or any forest for that matter. Her deceased husband had owned the hiking and camping gig. He'd loved the outdoors and had passed that passion on to their son. So here she was, in the middle of nowhere, ready to jump out of her skin at any strange sound because she loved the teen.

The fire crackled in front of her. Sparks popped, and the flames danced and snaked into the night, chasing away the crisp fall air. The weatherman claimed lows in the midforties at night. Not the normal freezing temperatures Indiana was known for during this time of year. That's why she went ahead and planned a backpacking trip with her son and his friends. One last outing before winter hit.

The log she leaned against while sitting on the forest ground dug into her back. The discomfort mimicked her life—tolerating trials and adversity.

Never in her wildest imagination had she thought she'd be

a widow at thirty-two with a sixteen-year-old brother-in-law whom she'd raised as her own since she married at eighteen. But here she was killing it—kind of—mostly—not really. She loved nature...from the deck of a mountain cabin. The changing color of the leaves and cool air had a calming effect. But traipsing through Wildfire State Forest with three teenage boys in the middle of fall—not so much. At least the temperatures wouldn't kill her. She hoped.

"Momma T, thanks for bringing us." Joey, her son/brother-in-law, leaned in and touched her shoulder with his.

She reeled in her runaway thoughts. Her heart filled with love at Joey's name for her. As far as she was concerned, he was her son, and she'd always treated him as such. Raising him since he was two gave her that right. She plastered a smile on her face and refused to show him anything but pleasure. "There's no place I'd rather be."

Joey's friends Kurt and Andrew snorted.

"Hey." Tori picked up a twig and chucked it at the two clowns. Although, they weren't wrong.

Andrew ducked and laughed. "Seriously, Mrs. C. Thanks for bringing us."

"Yeah, Mrs. C. Thanks," Kurt chimed in.

"You're welcome, guys. I'm happy to do it." And she was. Her husband, Ryan, had died six years ago, and Joey missed his brother, the man who'd taken over the role of father, something fierce. When Joey had sunk into a deep depression a few months ago, the backpacking trip had been her way of jolting him out of his despair. The teen adored hiking—a gift from Ryan.

The fire started to die down, and the wildlife symphony grew in the background. Tori rubbed her arms. Night two of the trip and the night noises continued to make her uneasy. A twig snapped behind her. She jerked her gaze toward the sound. "What was that?"

"Probably a bear," Joey teased.

"Not funny, J." Tori glared at her son.

"Or a cougar," Andrew added to her son's torment.

Ugh, these boys would be the death of her yet.

"Don't worry, Mrs. C. It's only a raccoon or deer." Kurt came to her rescue. All three teens were good kids, but Kurt had the softest heart out of the trio.

She hoped he was right. "Since it's late, and we have a long day ahead of us if we plan to make it to the scenic point of the lake tomorrow, I suggest we get some sleep."

"Sure."

"Sounds like a plan."

The boys agreed a little too easily.

"Uh-huh." She shook her head, knowing they'd be up for hours after she went to sleep. "Help me store the food. I expect you to put out the fire when you finally decide to call it a night."

The group worked together, and within minutes the campsite appeared clutter-free from critters looking for munchies. "Don't forget to take care of the fire."

"I know, Momma T. I've done this a thousand times with Papa Ryan."

Maybe not a thousand, but she'd admit Joey's experience outweighed hers. "I'll see you three in the morning."

The teens bid her good-night.

After removing her boots and crawling into her tent, she zipped it closed. Her body ached from the hike, and sleeping on a small thin mat did nothing to help the matter, but the light in Joey's eyes was worth it. Snuggled deep in her sleeping bag, she drifted off to the quiet whispers and soft snickers of the boys in her care.

Tori jolted awake. She sat upright and tilted her head, listening for what had roused her. A bear, or a cougar. Wait. Did Indiana have bears? Yeah, she had no idea.

Feet scuffled, followed by a crash. But it was the muffled cry that had her rushing from her tent.

The flap flew open. She bolted outside and came to an abrupt halt. Her eyes adjusted to the moonlit area. Three one-person tents lay in shambles. The contents of the backpacks were scattered on the ground. The body of one of the teens lay slumped over the log they'd used to sit on by the fire, while the other two lay sprawled on the ground. All moaning in pain.

A scream formed in her throat, but she stuffed it down. Forcing away the urge to run to them, she whipped around and rushed toward her tent to retrieve the Smith & Wesson from her pack. She had to help her boys, but not without a way to protect them.

Hands grabbed the back of her flannel shirt and flung her to the ground. She scrambled on all fours to escape and pushed to her sock feet.

A man spun her, wrapped his fingers around her throat and lifted her. In the dark, with the moonlight filtering through the trees and a ski mask covering his face, all she saw was the white of his eyes. "I'll be back for you after I take care of those boys. Don't go anywhere." Hot breath brushed her cheek. A second later, he tossed her against a tree.

Her shoulder collided with the rough exterior, and her head slammed into the trunk. She slid to the forest floor and toppled over. The veil of darkness hovered above. She fought against the abyss that threatened to take her under. Her eyes closed of their own accord. Feet shuffled and low voices poked at her half-conscious state, but she was unable to clear her muddled brain.

Blood dripped down the back of her neck. She blinked, but the haze refused to dissipate. She struggled with what to do. Her maternal instinct shouted at her to go to her boys, but in her condition, she'd never be able to protect them. She had to hide before the man returned so she could get help. If the man abducted her... No, she refused to let that happen. Joey and his friends needed her. They had to be okay. What would she do without Joey, her son in all the important ways? Her only connection left to Ryan.

A gunshot rang out in the night.

She jolted, sending bright white streaks flashing behind her eyelids. "Joey." She squinted, searching the campsite. The boys were nowhere in sight. Maybe more time had passed than she thought. They were there a minute ago. Weren't they? Had the masked man shot one of them? Her head pounded, reminding her of the man's threat to return for her.

Tori pushed to her feet. The trees spun around her. She shot out a hand to grab hold of anything to keep her upright but missed. She fell. Her hip took the brunt of her stumble. Blood whooshed in her ears. On her stomach, lying across the dirt and leaf-covered ground, she army crawled toward her tent. Pine needles stabbed her arms and legs, and small rocks dug into her knees and elbows. The pain—minor compared to the throbbing in her head. Nausea roiled in her belly. She swallowed back the bile threatening to come up. She had to hide before the man came back for her. She needed to get help for herself, along with Joey and the boys. Her phone—her only lifeline—she had to reach it and take it with her. She hoped it had a strong enough signal. It was iffy out in the woods, but what choice did she have?

The nylon material of the tent flap curled in her fingers, but the short distance had zapped her energy. She laid her head on her arm and took several deep breaths. Her eyelids lowered and she fought to keep them open. With a long exhale she shimmied her way into the opening and slipped her hand into her backpack. She retrieved her phone and stuffed it into her pocket, then clutched her weapon. If the man returned, she'd protect herself, but she hoped with everything in her she could escape and call for help. Reversing course, she dragged herself to the edge of the campsite. Once at the tree line, she hefted herself up against a trunk. On unsteady feet, she stumbled deeper into the forest.

Terrified the man who attacked her would find her, she burrowed deep under a thick brush. And if she hadn't given up on talking to God, she'd pray that the hole she'd crawled into wasn't the home of some critter who would want it back. Gun in her lap, she laid her head against a fallen log and closed her eyes. She'd make the call for help once her nausea subsided and she could raise her head without puking.

Clothes torn and nerves as tight as piano wires, every noise, every movement outside her hiding spot had her body tensing, making her head worse. As the minutes passed, fatigue set in. The exhaustion, along with the throbbing inside her skull, had her giving in to the darkness, letting it pull her into sweet oblivion.

The sun warmed her, chasing away the shivers that had racked her body during the night, but she fought against the morning light. She didn't want to move. She only wanted sleep. Allowing herself to drift, she jerked awake. The bright stream of light flashed in her eyes. She slammed them shut. The bass drum pounding against her skull intensified.

With a little more care, she pried her eyes open. Peeking through the slits she took inventory of her surroundings. The morning rays filtered through the branches. Flashes of the night's events came rushing back. But the biggest one stuck. The boys. She had to find her boys. Her breath caught in her throat. She needed help. Would 911 work out here?

Tears further blurred her vision. The desire to curl into a ball and sob overwhelmed her. Tired didn't begin to describe her state of mind. The past six years had taken its toll. *Ryan, why did you leave me? I'm tired of being strong. Joey is missing, and I don't know what to do.* Her deceased husband's words from a night years ago filled her mind. *If anything ever happens to me and you need help, call Michael Lane. He'll be there for you.* And Michael had. All the guys from Ryan's unit had come to lend a hand. At first, Ryan's traumatic brain injury changed his personality, then several months later a brain aneurysm took his life. Now, six years later, most of the men had drifted off into their own lives, only checking in occasionally—everyone except Michael.

Birds chirped from the colorful limbs above, pulling her further from her fuzzy state. Fingers to the back of her head, a sticky substance registered. A quick glance at the blood had her searching her memory for how she'd gotten the cut. The black hole in her mind gave way to no recollection other than hitting the back of her head on the tree and discovering the boys gone. Shaking off the confusion, she placed her gun on the ground beside her and dug into her pocket to retrieve her phone. She tugged a couple of times before she was able to retract the device. She wrapped her hand around her only way to contact the outside world.

Oh, please let there be service out here.

She tapped on speed dial number two and lifted it to her ear. The stuttered ringing almost made her cry with relief. "Come on, please connect."

"Hello."

"Michael." Her voice cracked.

"Tori, is—at—oo?" His broken words gave her hope.

"I need help. I'm hurt, and Joey's missing."

"Hurt? Where—you? Do—amb-ance? Did—911?"

"I'm somewhere off Broken Arrow Trail." Silence met her response. She'd pieced together his side of the conversation but had no idea if he understood what she'd said. "Hello? Michael?" The phone went dead. She placed a hand over her face. Why hadn't she tried 911 first? She punched in the numbers, but the phone didn't connect.

Her hand dropped to her side. The phone rested next to her leg. Had Michael gotten enough from the call to find her location? What if he hadn't?

A laugh bubbled out. Why would she expect life to be easy? It never had been. She'd lost her parents at an early age and lived with her grandparents, who loved her but didn't have the energy for a child. Then she'd married young and raised a toddler alone while her husband deployed. And, poof, what had seemed overnight, she was a widow with a teenager. She sighed. That's how her life rolled—one hardship after another.

Without the energy to move, she closed her eyes. Tears trailed down her cheeks at the unfairness of it all. Her only hope was that Michael found her before whoever destroyed the camp and threatened her returned.

"Tori? Tori!" Dead air met Michael Lane's ear. He sat on his couch and resisted the urge to chuck the phone against the living room wall. He'd failed Tori over the last year during his recovery from his near-death experience. The boat explosion during one of his DEA investigations had left him with PTSD and an inner ear problem that snuck up on him at the most inopportune times. Plus, the collection of wounds on his body had wreaked havoc with his physical abilities. The physical therapy he'd endured had been brutal.

Wrapped in his own pain from his injuries and the devastating loss of his career, he hadn't visited her at home much. Although, he'd taken her and Joey out to eat a couple of times, and they'd spent a Saturday supporting his buddy Roger Howe with a community day at the man's dog training center. The online local newspaper had written a great article about the search and rescue service Roger provided, along with multiple pictures of the event. He and Tori hadn't escaped the photographer that day. Their picture had ended up as part of the training center highlights in the write-up.

Ducky, his golden retriever air-scent dog with extra special talents, nosed his arm and whined. Michael ran his fingers through Ducky's fur and stared at the beige-colored walls. The dog had an uncanny sense of when Michael needed help. Whether to ground him in the moment or stabilize him when his inner ear went haywire. Ducky had been a blessing from the moment the pair met.

"Ducky, my man. Tori needs us."

The dog's head tilted, and his eyebrow equivalent arched.

"Come on. Let's pack and call Roger." Dialing his Army buddy's number, Michael strode to his closet. He collected his hiking gear and Ducky's supplies as the phone rang.

"Yo, Lane. What's up?" Roger's normal cheerful tone filled the line. His friend had found the love of his life during his Army days and now had the sweetest six-year-old little girl, Darby. Along with a thriving dog training center. In many ways, Michael envied the man, but after his *accident*, he didn't have much to offer a woman. Who would want a man with physical problems and no job, who had never been quite enough for those in his life?

"I'm heading out with Ducky."

A belly laugh filled Michael's ears. "I can't believe you let Darby name that dog."

A smile curved on Michael's lips. "As if I can say no to my honorary niece."

"True. She is special." Roger's voice turned serious. "I haven't received a search and rescue request from the county. What's going on?"

"Tori called. I didn't catch the full conversation. The call kept breaking up. But she's somewhere on Broken Arrow Trail and something's wrong."

"Do you need an extra team? Toby and I are available." Toby, Roger's German shepherd tracking dog, and Roger were one of the best teams around.

"Let me get a feel for the situation first. I don't want to embarrass her if it's a minor issue like a sprained ankle. You know how independent she is. She mentioned Joey, but I have no idea what she said. The connection was awful." Michael added protein bars and several just-add-water entrée packages to his bag, along with multiple water bottles.

"I'm surprised she got any service on that trail."

"You and me both, brother." He closed his backpack and

double-checked that his sleeping bag was secure. He brought it more for safety's sake then for sleeping under the stars.

"What are your plans as far as a scent for Ducky to follow? I suppose you could run by her house."

"I'd prefer not to take the extra time in case something is seriously wrong. I'm making an educated guess that she parked her car at the trailhead. I'll Slim Jim it and pray she left a sweatshirt or something in her vehicle. Otherwise, it'll be a lengthy search."

"Sounds like a plan. At least the weather isn't a concern. It's not supposed to get below freezing for several days. It won't be warm at night, but it won't kill either. Even so, I hope you find her fast. Keep me posted. You know the guys will drop everything to come help her. It's the least we can do." Roger's words struck him in the heart like a dagger.

Ryan's sacrifice had saved the unit. Most of the men had suffered minor injuries. All but Ryan. He'd paid dearly with a traumatic brain injury that had changed him and ultimately killed him. Tori deserved a medal for sticking by Ryan's side. His buddy's personality had changed, and he'd become more aggressive with certain triggers. Michael owed it to Ryan to watch over her. Besides, he'd promised his friend. Michael had dropped the proverbial ball after the explosion. That neglect ended now.

"Copy that." Michael adjusted Ducky's harness then added supplies to the saddlebags that he'd attach to the dog's vest when they arrived on scene. Once certain he had everything they'd need, he shoved the leash into one of the many pockets of his cargo pants. "Ducky and I are out of here. I'll call when I find her car."

"I'll be waiting. If you don't find what you need, let me know, and I'll run to her house." With that, Roger hung up.

"Come on, Ducky. Let's go find Tori."

The dog's tail wagged hard enough to knock himself off balance. Michael could've sworn the dog smiled.

He opened the back door. Ducky torpedoed outside, sniffed at the path to the truck and sat next to the driver's side door. The furball tilted his head as if to ask what was taking so long.

House locked and secure, Michael strode down the gravel path to the vehicle, stored his gear and boosted Ducky into the back seat. The dingbat dog would jump onto the bed but refused to get into the truck without help. The little diva. Michael shook his head at the ridiculousness of it all and slipped behind the wheel. He put the truck in reverse then turned and aimed the vehicle down the lane and out of his property.

He appreciated the open land around his home. It helped with his panic attacks when the memories hit hard. Many nights he sat out on his porch and looked at the stars. The view gave him a sense of peace when the events of the past got too hard.

Thirty minutes later, he pulled into the trailhead parking area. The lot sported only one vehicle—Tori's SUV. He peered out the front windshield. The leaves on the trees had turned colors. The gold, red and orange made the forest appear like it was on fire. A sight that never got old.

He glanced over his shoulder to the back seat. "Stay here, buddy. I'll be right back." Michael grabbed the Slim Jim tool off the passenger seat and slipped from the truck. He popped in his earbud and dialed Roger.

"You find it?"

"Hello to you too. And yes. It's where I guessed it would be." He slid the tool down the window inside the rubber seal and maneuvered it to pop the lock. "Success."

"Anything?"

"Hold on, would ya? I just got it unlocked. Give me a minute." Michael shook his head, but he understood Roger's urgency. He ducked into the back seat and scanned the interior. "Pay dirt. I found a sweater."

"Doesn't surprise me. That woman doesn't go anywhere without one."

"She says she gets cold inside stores and restaurants." He recalled several dinners with the guys where she'd donned a sweater after ordering her meal.

"Tiffany's the same way. Must be a girl thing." The softness that laced Roger's voice at the mention of his wife hadn't gone unnoticed.

What would it be like to have that kind of love? He shook off the thought. Been there, tried that and got his heart stomped on. He placed Tori's sweater in one of the bags he'd brought with him. "Time to go get her."

"You have your SAT phone, right?"

Michael rolled his eyes. "Yes, Dad. I have my satellite phone."

"Ha ha. Very funny. Call when you can. If I don't hear from you in the next twelve hours, I'm sending out a team."

"Got it."

"Be safe."

"Will do." Michael disconnected and stored his earbuds. He strode to his truck and opened the door. "It's time to go to work, Ducky."

The dog jumped from the vehicle, sat and gave a quick bark.

"Yeah, I know, you're ready." A smile tugged on Michael's lips.

Ducky's pink tongue dangled from the side of his mouth as he panted. In the nine months Michael had had the dog, he couldn't remember a time when the creature hadn't looked like he was smiling. Except for maybe when the dog tried to dupe him into a second dinner and Michael told him no. Every time Ducky gave him those sad eyes, he almost gave in.

He slid the backpack onto his back and clipped Ducky's saddlebags onto the dog's harness. "All right, Duck my man, time to find Tori."

The golden retriever sat, full attention on him.

Michael opened the bag and gave the dog the command to get the scent. "Check."

Ducky sniffed the contents of the bag. Michael pulled the sack away and closed it. After securing it in the largest pocket of his tactical pants, he sucked in a deep breath and looked into his dog's dark eyes. "Find."

Nose in the air and tail wagging, Ducky circled Tori's SUV then shot off toward the trail.

Michael jogged behind him, letting the dog do his thing. The area Tori had hiked concerned him. He knew from his days with the DEA that drug runners had a trail snaking through these woods. He might have to loop in his ex-DEA partner, Melissa Jones or MJ for short.

A mile later, Ducky exited the dirt path and circled back. Michael's inner ear chose that moment to go wonky. He stumbled. Ducky loped to his side and pressed against his leg, stabilizing him. "Thanks, boy." Michael placed his hand on the dog's head. He prayed the topsy-turvy motion stopped soon. He didn't have time to baby his inner ear.

Ever since Michael agreed to be part of Roger Howe's search and rescue program and accepted Ducky as his, the dog had assisted him with the residual effects from the explosion—vertigo due to his inner ear and PTSD—neither of which he cared to publicly admit continued to affect him. Except for the medical team that treated him and his ex-supervisor, no one knew the extent of his struggles. Roger and MJ had their suspicions but had yet to confront Michael.

"I think I'm good now." He patted Ducky's head.

The dog smiled up at him.

"You're pretty proud of yourself, aren't you." Ducky's tongue lolled to the side. Michael retrieved a water bottle from his pack, offered his dog some in a collapsible bowl then drank some of the water. Ducky hadn't mastered drinking from a squeeze bottle yet. A skill they still worked on. Certain that he'd taken care of Ducky's needs, he stowed the items. "Come on, you big nut, back to work."

Ducky plopped down on his rear, ready for the next command.

"Find."

The dog sniffed the air and hurried forward down the path.

Michael jogged after the golden with an extra dose of caution, not wanting to trigger his vertigo again.

Sweat poured between his shoulder blades into a stream down his back. The fall temperatures hadn't hit the sixties, but the excursion mixed with the humidity made for a toasty search. Michael swiped his forehead before the salty droplets managed to sting his eyes.

He checked his watch. Four hours had passed since he'd heard from Tori. And unless she had hiked deeper into the forest than he suspected, they should be coming upon the campsite soon. Especially with his dog taking a straight line to her scent.

Ducky lifted his nose higher in the air. The black tip of his snout twitched, and he took off running.

Please, let him have found Tori.

Picking up his pace, he rounded the curve and came to a halt. Where did that silly dog go? Ducky yipped. Michael turned to his right and stooped under a branch. The sight before him almost took him to his knees. Tucked inside a burrow, Ducky sat next to the hole and nudged Tori's hand with his nose. Head leaning against the tree, Tori remained motionless. Her phone rested on the ground next to her thigh, and her weapon lay in her lap. He peeled his gaze from her and took in the surroundings. Blood drops spotted the ground. Her blood. He examined her current state. Scratches littered her arms and legs that were exposed through tears in the fabric of her shirt and pants. But her face had him sucking in a harsh breath. Several scrapes and bruises dotted her cheeks and forehead. Her red hair hung limp and tangled at her neck.

"Tori." He strode to her hiding place. When she didn't respond, he cleared away a section of brush and crouched next to her. He jostled her arm. "Wake up, Tori."

Ducky whimpered his concern. The dog army crawled into the brush and nestled in beside her.

"I know, boy." Michael clasped her fingers and rubbed small circles on the back of her hand, careful not to irritate any wounds. "Tori. I need to see those blue eyes of yours."

Her eyelids fluttered.

"That's it." His pulse rate settled a bit.

Her eyes opened. It took her a few moments to focus. "Michael?"

"Yes, Red. I'm here." He took his first deep breath since he found her.

"Haven't called me that in a long time." Tori's breathy words worried him.

"I'll have to remedy that." He held the inside of her wrist and took her pulse.

She nodded and winced.

Between her speech and the response to moving her head, Michael's concern rose several notches. "I'm assuming you hit your head. I'm going to check it out. Is that okay with you?"

"You're loaning me your dog." Her hands moved in a steady rhythm over Ducky's fur.

He chuckled. "Yes, Red. Ducky is all yours for the moment."

"Thanks."

"Can you answer my question? I'd like to look at your injuries?"

"S—okay." She shivered under his touch.

He retrieved her sweater from his pocket and draped it over her. "All right, then, hold still." As gently as possible, he examined her arms and knees through her ripped shirt and jeans. He'd do a more thorough assessment later. "Lean forward a bit."

She complied and dipped her chin to her chest.

He ran a hand over the back of her head.

She hissed at his touch.

When he found a large goose egg along with a sticky mat of hair, he narrowed his gaze. The gash on her head that had bled and dried answered a few of his questions. But not the main one. How had she hit her head?

"Tori, what happened to you? And where is Joey?"

She licked her dried lips. "Something attacked me. J and boys...gone."

"Boys?"

"Joey and two friends."

Great. Three missing teens. Michael inhaled. No time to think about that now. Tori came first. She might have more information once she could think straight. And that right there, her foggy thoughts, worried him. The injuries to Tori didn't appear extreme. His experience told him that she had a concussion, but it shouldn't be severe. Michael smacked his palm to his forehead. He should hand over his first responder card.

"Hold on, Red." He dug through his backpack, found a fresh water bottle and mixed a packet of powder containing electrolytes into it. "Here. Drink this." Where had his brain gone? The woman had spent the night and all morning with a head injury, and if her dry lips were any indication, without food or water.

Bottle placed to her mouth, he tipped the container, allowing the cool liquid to quench her parched throat.

She pushed the water away. "Thank you."

After placing the container next to her leg, he pulled a protein bar from the front pocket of his pack. "Nibble on this, but go slow."

Without argument, she took a small bite and chewed. She fumbled with the water bottle and drank a little more.

He struggled not to help her. He'd always thought she was too independent for her own good, but he figured she'd ask for assistance if she required it.

Several minutes later, Michael assessed Tori's condition again. Her eyes seemed a bit brighter. It was amazing how quickly dehydration could set in, and how it affected people. "While we let the food and drink settle to give you energy, tell me what happened."

"We went camping." Her hand holding the remainder of her protein bar halted halfway to her mouth. She blinked. "Well, that's obvious. Sorry. I'm still on the slow loop."

"No worries, Red. Take your time."

She continued to stroke Ducky's head and back. That dog was a ball of comfort wrapped in silliness when off duty.

"I brought Joey and two friends camping. He's been a little down lately." She sighed. "Who am I kidding? A lot down. I thought coming out in nature might help." Her eyes drifted to the sky.

He placed a hand on her arm. The kid must have hit a low spot if Tori decided to go camping. The woman wasn't the outdoorsy type. "Did it help?"

She brought her focus back to him. "It seemed to. We started our camping trip a couple of days ago, and during that short time, I've seen the old Joey surface. Then last night a noise woke me. When I exited my tent, I found the site a mess and the boys laying hurt." She sucked in a breath.

"What happened next?"

"Someone or something grabbed me and tossed me against the tree." Her free hand smoothed over the goose egg on the back of her head then drifted to her throat. Red marks marred her fair skin. How had he missed that? "That's how I got the knot on my head. I knew I had to get help, but I don't remember anything else. I woke up tucked in the brush with the boys nowhere in sight. That's when I called you."

"Did you call 911?"

Her brow furrowed as she stared at Ducky. "No. I don't think I did."

"Why not call them first?"

Her eyes met his. "Because I knew you'd come to my rescue."

He jerked like someone slapped him. Coming from a woman who stood strong and refused to lean on anyone or ask for help, her statement filled a few cracks in his battered heart. "Thank you for trusting me."

"I hate bothering you, but I'm worried about Joey and his friends." She sat straighter. "We have to find them."

"We will. I promise." Michael patted her forearm. "How about we find your campsite and see if there are any signs of the boys." After she finished her snack and water, he collected the trash and stuffed it in his backpack.

She accepted his offered hand and stood. He maintained his grip while she gained her balance. "I'm good, thanks."

He studied her and then nodded. She tucked her cell phone in her pants pocket.

"Since you don't have a holster, I'll store your weapon in my pack." He took her silence as an agreement. Probably not the best idea to step on her independence, but he'd apologize later.

The creases in Tori's brow deepened. "I'm not sure how to get back."

"Don't worry. We'll find it." He motioned for her to follow and called Ducky. "Come."

Ducky trotted to his left side, but the little traitor stayed within inches of Tori's leg. Michael smiled. The dog knew who needed him the most right now.

Michael continued to pick his way through the thick foliage, shocked at the distance Tori had run in the dark last night. They'd hiked a good ten minutes already. How far had she gone? A few moments later, he ducked under a grouping of limbs. The trees opened to a small clearing. Camping equipment lay strung across the campsite. Blood drops dotted the ground. Not enough for concern, but the fact there was no sign of Joey or his friends bothered him.

Tori stepped to his side and sucked in an audible breath. "Michael?"

Without thinking, he wrapped an arm around her shoulders. "Ducky is great at his job. And Roger is a call away. He and Toby, his German shepherd, are the best tracking team around. We'll find them. I promise."

"But will they be alive?" Her question came out as a whisper.

"Tori, stop. You can't think that way."

She tensed. "Sorry. I'll do better."

He wanted to smack himself for making her hide her vulnerability. "That's not what I meant. All I'm saying is don't give up hope."

Arms hugging her middle, her eyes pleaded with him. "What do we do now?"

"We check in with MJ." His gaze traveled the exterior of the campsite. His past experiences told him to be wary.

"Your ex DEA partner, Melissa Jones? Why not just call 911?"

He debated whether to tell her the truth about Wildfire State Forest. But she deserved to know what they were up against. "Certain sections of this forest are known for drug runners. The DEA has had eyes and ears in these parts for quite a while. MJ would know where the traffickers are located or at least have an idea. I have no intention of putting other searchers in danger until I have more information." He punched in MJ's number. Even though he was no longer part of the team, he had remained good friends with MJ and her husband.

"Agent Jones."

"Hey, MJ, it's Michael."

"Michael, how are you? And why are you calling from an unknown number?"

"I'm good. And it's my SAT phone."

"Well, I'm guessing that means you're out in the wilderness."

"Wildfire State Forest. A friend of mine was attacked, and three teenage boys are missing."

"Oh, man. Where?"

"Off of Broken Arrow Trail."

MJ released a long hiss of breath. "Don't do a full search and rescue."

"I figured, but do you have new information?" He glanced at Tori, who stood watching him while he continued his conversation with MJ.

"You know I can't tell you that."

He clenched his jaw. He hated not being a part of the team any longer. "Humor me."

"Let's just say the boys and I are planning a fun trip out there to meet new friends."

He closed his eyes. A raid. "You've got to be kidding me."

"Nope."

Michael rubbed his forehead in a useless attempt to relieve his building tension headache. "When?"

"In a day or two. The wheels are in motion." The timing of her warning couldn't have been worse.

"As a professional courtesy to you and the guys, I'm letting you know that my friend Tori and I are taking a peek around for her son and his friends."

"Copy that. I hope you find them. But be careful. I wouldn't want the *wildlife* to take a chunk out of your hide."

"Noted. I'll call later."

"Do that. I'll let my buddies know what's going on. We might be able to help, but I can't guarantee it."

"I understand." He appreciated the thought and effort MJ would put into the assist.

"Good. Gotta go." MJ hung up.

"What did she say?" Tori ran a hand down Ducky's back.

"Not much," he mumbled.

"Michael. I know better. You look worried."

"I'm not lying. She was cryptic, but I got the gist of what she tried not to say."

"So?"

"We can't call in a search party. They're planning a raid

soon. If we make a lot of noise, the drug runners will move locations or attack anyone who threatens their business."

"Oh." Tori worried her bottom lip.

"However, I do need to update Roger."

Her shoulders sagged, and she nodded.

Michael examined the campsite while he called his friend. "Did you find her?"

Michael shook his head at Roger's abrupt answer. "I did. She's okay, but things aren't good. Joey's missing."

"Toby and I are on the way."

"No. Don't. Not yet."

Roger hesitated before he responded. "Something I should be aware of?"

"Let's just chalk it up to a work thing."

"Dude, you were DEA. I don't like the sounds of that."

He ran a hand over the back of his neck. "As you shouldn't."

"What's going on?" Roger asked.

Shoe prints covered the ground near the edge of the campsite to his right. He studied the evidence and visually followed the trail. From what he concluded, all three boys left the area on foot, telling him they'd all survived the initial attack. Beyond that was anyone's guess.

He returned his attention to Roger. "I can't tell you. You'll have to trust me on that. Tori and I will do this on our own for a bit and keep a low profile. I trust Ducky's ability. We'll find them." Ducky peered over at him when he heard his name, but the dog didn't leave Tori's side.

"I don't like it."

"Me either, but making a lot of noise will get people killed. I refuse to be the reason."

Roger sighed. "Copy that. I'm here if you need me."

"Thanks, man." Michael disconnected and focused on Tori.

Fatigue lined her features. He worried about her, but what concerned him the most was the cryptic message from MJ. His friend had left him bread crumbs to the fact that the State

Forest Drug Task Force had a mission in play. He prayed the raid would take down the head of the drug business in the area, but the timing was awful and made him wonder if there was somehow a connection to the boys.

"You really think we can find them?"

"I do. I'll find items that Ducky can work with." The internal tug-of-war of concern for Tori's concussion and the need to find the boys twisted his gut. Maybe he could drop her off at his friend Jackson's cabin, but it was about an hour away. Closer than her car. But either would take time they didn't have.

"I see that brain of yours churning."

"I'm worried about you. You're hurt."

"Finding Joey and his friends is the top priority."

Michael proceeded to scan the area for viable scent items. He collected a sweatshirt, a stocking hat and a T-shirt from the different areas of the campsite, confirmed with Tori he had an object from each boy, and placed them in individual bags for Ducky to use later. "Head injuries are nothing to mess around with. At least allow me to get you settled at a cabin not far from here—forty minutes, maybe. I'll drop you off and start searching."

"No. I feel better already. My head is down to a dull ache. And it'll take more than a day for my bruises and muscles to forgive me, but I can live with the discomfort if it means finding my son. Don't argue with me. I *will* be a part of the search."

A deep growl rumbled from his chest.

"And there's the bear you're famous for." She tried a smile but only had marginal success.

"Not funny, Red."

She shoved her fists onto her hips. "You can't deny it."

Unfortunately, he couldn't. The guys had nicknamed him Bear years ago. For whatever reason, any time he got frustrated he made a sound that resembled a growl. The guys howled with laughter the first time it happened. Soon after the nickname stuck.

"All right. You win. This time. But don't get used to it. If I think your injuries are getting worse, I reserve the right to march you straight to the cabin."

Tori folded her arms across her chest. "Fine."

He knew that stance. His statement was anything but fine. He strode to Tori's side and prayed the boys hadn't become prey to the drug runners. If so, the possibility of finding any of them alive was reduced to slim to none. He shifted to face her, "Ready to start—"

Tree bark exploded between them. Splinter needles stabbed his cheek. The report of a gun echoed through the forest.

"Run!" Michael pushed her into the trees. "With me!" He yelled the command to Ducky and sprinted after Tori, his dog hot on his heels.

Chapter Two

Tori's breaths came hard and fast as she sprinted through the trees. She dodged roots and fallen limbs, putting distance between herself and whoever had shot at her and Michael. Branches snagged her clothes and the ground threatened to trip her, but she refused to stop until Michael told her to. She had to survive. Joey and his friends were missing. They needed her now, more than ever.

Her head throbbed, and her body ached from the original attack. And her nerves sizzled from the close call with a bullet. Afraid to ask what more could happen, Tori clamped her mouth shut and focused on not spraining an ankle or breaking a leg.

Michael gripped her hand and tugged her off the narrow dirt path deeper into the woods. Limbs reached out like long fingernails and raked across her cheek.

Footfalls followed them. Another shot pierced the air.

She threw her arm over her head and whimpered but held tight to Michael's hand.

Ducky weaved in and out of the bushes, leading the way.

Tori hoped the dog knew where he was going. Ducky disappeared behind a thicket of trees.

"Come on," Michael whispered and yanked her behind him.

Her toe caught on a rock. She pitched forward. He spun and caught her in his arms.

He leaned close to her ear. "Follow me."

She crouched down, crawled into the tucked away space in the brush behind Michael and plopped down beside Ducky.

Finger to his lip, he pointed to the opening. She fought to slow her breathing.

The leaves crunched. Black boots appeared beyond the tangle of branches and brambles.

Michael tightened his arm around her, and she burrowed her face in his flannel jacket. What did this person want? She lived a simple life. Work, taking care of a teenager and making ends meet. Nothing special. Michael rubbed his hand up and down her back. She appreciated the comfort.

The person who'd shot at them—she assumed anyway—walked in a circle then stood mere feet from where Michael had tucked them away. A few moments later, the assailant moved out of sight.

They sat, unmoving, letting time pass until Michael finally released her. "Wait here. Don't make a sound. Ducky, stay." The dog lifted his head then huffed and laid back onto his paws. Michael scooted out from their hiding place. A couple minutes later he returned. "I think we're good." He held out his hand.

She accepted the gesture. "Are you sure?" Nothing about the situation felt safe. Straightening, she dropped her arms to her side.

"Pretty sure."

"Not what I wanted to hear." The man's comment had her clenching her fist.

He lifted his shoulder. "It's what I can give."

Honest, but annoying. But she'd prefer straightforward over sunshine and roses. "Fair enough." Breathing easy for the first time in well over thirty minutes, she sucked in precious air.

Ducky nudged her hand and whimpered. "I'm okay, boy." She brushed her fingers across his fur.

Michael's intensity belied his nonchalant words as he led her away from the brush and bramble that had saved them. She understood why he'd been so good at his job in the military. He maintained a focused awareness. Sometime later, he found a spot hidden out of sight and sat. He rummaged through his backpack, produced two more water bottles, along with a couple of protein bars, and patted the ground next to him. "Have a seat and refuel. You need the calories for our search. But go easy on the water. I brought enough when I thought I'd be hiking out of the woods. Not dodging bullets."

She had to admit her hands shook like leaves in a storm, but was the cause her blood sugar or fear? Either way, she needed the energy. Without further coaxing from Michael, she brushed leaves from a spot on the ground. Kind of stupid after sleeping in a hole last night, but the idea of sitting on creepy crawlies hit the top of her not-fun list. Convinced nothing would bite her, she lowered to the dirt and accepted his offer. "Thanks." She'd drink half and save the rest for another time.

"No problem." He placed his Glock next to his thigh before he took care of feeding Ducky and giving him water. Once the dog had his fill, Ducky moved to her side and Michael took care of himself.

She hadn't missed the way Michael scanned the trees while tending to his dog. Nor the way he kept his weapon close. She ran her hand down the golden retriever's back. The dog rolled over, silently requesting a tummy scratch. She nibbled on her bar and obliged the fur baby.

A few minutes later, she finished the snack and patted the dog's belly, making a sound like thumping a watermelon. She chuckled. It was hard to maintain stress around the loveable mutt. "Now what?"

Michael brushed his hands together, dusting off any crumbs. "We get Ducky on the case."

When the dog heard his name, he flipped over, lifted his head and panted. The same doggy smile she'd witnessed earlier greeted them.

The edge of her lip tugged upward. "He's a happy one."

"That he is. The world is his friend whether people want to be or not. He growls when he detects a threat, but I've only seen him lunge at someone once. The dude had moved toward Roger's daughter, Darby. Ducky didn't like it and made his opinion known. That's why I'm comfortable staying here for a moment. He'll warn us if he senses anyone nearby."

Her shoulders relaxed a bit at that news. "Smart dog."

"Very. But dumb as a stump too. The furball will look in the mirror and get spooked at his own reflection." Michael shook his head. "Sometimes I wonder about him."

Tori chuckled. "Give the boy a break. He's just a baby."

"A big baby. He thinks he's a lap dog." At Michael's claim, Ducky crawled onto her lap.

"Oof. Dude, you're a bit big for this." But she couldn't resist allowing him to stay and wrapped her arms around his neck. His comfort soothed her battered nerves.

A few moments later, Michael tucked his weapon into his holster, cleaned up their mess and stood. He wiped the dirt from his pants and extended his hand. "Ready?"

"More than." Sitting around, although necessary, had fed into her worry. Tori shoved Ducky from her lap and pushed to her feet. She groaned when her muscles decided to protest. "Sorry. I'm a little sorer than I thought."

"I have no doubt about that. You took a pretty good hit to your head. And those scrapes and bruises have to hurt."

She feathered her fingers over her cheek. The sting had lessened but hadn't disappeared. "They do, but I'll be okay."

"I know you want to keep going until we locate the boys, but please tell me if you need to stop. We'll head to the cabin. It'll be a hike. It's on the edge of the forest with other vacation homes in the vicinity but not too close."

She studied him a moment. Part of her knew he was right. If she ignored the aches and pains, especially if they got worse, she wouldn't be any good to Joey or his friends. She might be strong-willed, but she wasn't careless. "I will."

"Good. I'm glad." Trash and supplies taken care of, Michael removed a bag from his pack. He opened it. *"Check."*

Ducky sniffed the contents and sat.

Michael secured the scent object. His gaze met hers, and he arched a brow.

Yes, she was ready to find Joey. The sooner the better. However, with the man who'd chased them still on the loose, it scared the daylights out of her. She nodded.

"Find."

Nose in the air, the dog took off through the trees.

"Better not get too far behind. He gets a little put out when I'm too slow."

She chuckled. "Lead the way."

He took off in the direction that Ducky had gone.

Tori exhaled and followed. Running wasn't her thing, but to find Joey, she'd climb the highest mountain if she had to.

What seemed like hours later—but in truth only twenty minutes or so had passed—Michael held up a fisted hand. She recognized the hold your position motion left over from his Army days. She'd seen Ryan do it many times out of instinct.

Ducky sat and gave two quick barks at the brush to the left.

"What did he find?" she whispered.

"Not sure." Michael strode to Ducky and crouched. "Good boy." He scratched the dog's head. A few moments later, he returned to her side, holding a torn piece of navy blue cloth with dried blood. "Does this look familiar?"

Her heart pounded against her rib cage. "That's Andrew's. He was wearing a navy flannel shirt last night."

"We're on the right track then." Michael collected the piece of material and dropped it into a small plastic bag that he'd produced from the many pockets of his cargo pants.

"But where is he? And where's Joey?" She spun in a slow circle, scouring the forest for anything to lead her to her son.

The blood concerned Michael, but the evidence that Andrew had come this way relieved him. He prayed Ducky found the kid—soon. He tamped down the temptation to yank the satellite phone from his pocket and call MJ for details about the dangers she hadn't stated earlier. With three or four teams searching the area, they'd find the teens in no time—or maybe not. If the drug runners were involved... He shook his head. No. He refused to go there. But the thought lingered on the edge of his mind. Although, it was the answer that made the most sense.

Ducky sat and tilted his head as if to ask, *What are we waiting on?*

The man with the gun continued to concern him. Shooting at them *was* something a drug trafficker would do.

After an inspection of their surroundings, he gave Ducky a scratch under his chin. "Let's keep moving."

"I'm right behind you." Tori threw her shoulders back. A movement he knew all too well. The determined set of her jaw spoke volumes. The woman was unstoppable when she put her mind to something.

"All right, Ducky, it's back to work."

The dog's pink tongue dangled from his open mouth.

Michael retrieved the bag and held it out. "Check."

Ducky's nose sniffed then went in the air.

He tucked away the bag and lifted his hand palm up. "Find."

The dog circled to where the scrap of material had caught on the branch. He sniffed again and took off through the brush.

Tori's eyebrow lifted. "Guess he found the scent."

"That he did." Michael adjusted his backpack, preparing to jog through the woods. He tapped the holster on his hip, confirming his Glock was ready and available. "Let's go, before he gets irritated."

She followed him through the trees, keeping her eyes out for a threat. "He can't be that bad."

"Oh, he is. He's a diva." Michael smiled. "But I wouldn't change a thing. He's my buddy."

Tori kept pace with him. "I can tell. He seems protective of you."

"That's one way to put it." Ducky helped him in ways people didn't understand. Michael spotted the dog up ahead, sitting on his haunches inside a section of brush. "Hold up."

Tori stopped beside him. "What is it?"

His finger to his lips, he slid his gun from the holster and whispered, "Ducky's ignoring us."

"I take it that's not normal."

"Not at all." He motioned for Tori to follow him behind a tree. "Stay quiet until he moves." Michael had no idea what caused Ducky's behavior, but he refused to disregard it. The dog had instincts that continued to shock him at times.

Tori clutched his arm. Her hand trembled. He knew her well enough not to call attention to it. Michael turned his head and listened for what had caused Ducky's reaction. The longer they sat, the more concerned he got for them and his furry friend.

"Do you think the attacker found us?" Tori's breath brushed against his ear.

He shrugged. "Maybe. But it could be a wild animal." He prayed the drug traffickers hadn't homed in on them.

Branches rustled beyond his dog's hiding spot. He and Tori waited in silence for several more minutes.

Finally, Ducky glanced in their direction and panted. Whatever the dog had sensed was gone. Ducky trotted toward them.

"Seems he deems it safe to proceed." Michael held his Glock close to his leg, prepared for unwanted company. The way Ducky hid and sat motionless was a new one for Michael. He filed it away for future reference. He eased from behind the tree trunk and strode in Ducky's direction. Tori followed, staying on his six.

Once he reached the golden, Michael squinted at the area that had held his dog's attention. Nothing stood out as odd. Why would someone watch them, and not take a shot at them? Assuming the noise had been a person. An animal made more sense. He patted the furball's head. "Ready to work?"

Ducky turned in a circle with excitement.

"Find," Michael commanded.

Once again, they trailed behind the dog as he searched for who Michael now knew was Andrew. He prayed they'd find the teen alive and well. But he wasn't holding his breath on the well part. At this point, he'd be happy with alive.

They ducked under tree limbs and dodged bushes. His dog had stayed inside the thick of trees and avoided the open spaces. Michael wouldn't complain. It kept them unexposed. The dense brush poked and scratched their skin, but they had avoided more severe damage.

The temperatures were cool and the humidity livable, but the excursion of tracking behind Ducky made for a warm day. Sweat dripped down Michael's temple, and he swiped it away. He slowed and pulled even with Tori. "Doing okay?"

Her ragged breaths gave him his answer, but he let her respond. "I'm good."

"That's why you're panting worse than Ducky?"

She playfully smacked his arm. "Stop that."

"I'll call Ducky, and we can take a break."

She shook her head and stumbled, righting herself before she face-planted on the forest floor. "No, I want to keep going. That man out there is hunting us. What if he's hurting the boys?"

He clutched her bicep and halted their progress. "Tori, we'll be vigilant, and I have no idea where Joey and his friends are and what is happening to them. But you can't power through. You'll end up dropping where you stand and will be of no help to the boys."

Tori placed her hands on her lower back and sucked in air. "Fine. You win."

"I'm not trying to make you mad. I'm only trying to get you to see reason behind stopping for a moment." He released his hold on her arm.

"I know." Her tone sounded as though the fact frustrated her.

Ducky barked twice.

Michael jerked his head toward where his dog signaled. "I think he's found something." He prayed it was one of the boys and not another piece of clothing.

She exhaled. "Then let's find out."

They jogged through the trees and exited into a small clearing. The space—a great place for an ambush—sent Michael on high alert. He held his arm out, stopping Tori from continuing.

"What is it?"

Michael scanned the area but found nothing amiss. "We're getting closer to the known drug trail. I'm not taking any chances, that's all." Satisfied nothing or no one lingered on the fringes, he motioned for her to follow.

Ducky sat at the edge of a small cliff, alerting him to something below.

"What do you think he's doing?" she asked as she strode to join the golden retriever.

"My guess is there's something or someone down below. I don't want you to get too close, okay?"

Tori stared at the dog. "You think it's Andrew?"

"Could be. But I'm not going to assume. I want proof."

The two of them moved closer.

"Michael, what's that?"

"Stay here." He examined the thin wire that lay loose along the ground. "It's a trip wire. And someone tripped it." He stood and scanned the surroundings again.

"Red, call Ducky and make him stay with you."

"What's wrong?" He hadn't missed the quiver in her voice.

"Looks like someone is setting illegal traps. I don't want him caught in one."

"Someone?"

"Possibly the drug runners. At least that's my guess. If anyone gets too close to their business, the traps deter them. Or hurt them. Take your pick."

"Ducky, come here, boy." She patted her thighs. "Come on."

The dog looked at him for approval. "Go on."

Ducky loped to Tori, who praised him and rewarded him with lots of pets.

Michael moved with caution to the edge of the overhang and looked down. A teenage boy lay motionless on a rock ledge about eight feet below. Blood caked his head. Thankfully, he hadn't rolled off the landing and fallen the twenty feet farther down. But the head injury worried him.

"Anything?"

"Yes. I'm guessing it's Andrew. He's unconscious and has a head wound."

"Can you get to him?" She took a step.

He held up his hand. "Don't come any closer." He pulled Ducky's leash from his pocket and tossed it to her. "Clip that on him. He should listen to you, but I'm not taking any chances."

She did as he instructed. Her eyes met his. "Michael?" The worry in her tone raked across his heart.

"I think I can get down there, but I'd prefer to wait for backup. He's close to the edge of a ledge, but unless he moves, he isn't in danger of falling off." Michael shucked off his backpack and placed his weapon on top of it. He moved closer to the drop-off and peered down then extracted the SAT phone from his pocket. "I'm going to place a call for help."

"What about what Melissa said?"

"We don't have a choice. Andrew needs medical attention. I'll call MJ and have her arrange for assistance so she can monitor how it's done, but Andrew can't wait." Michael took a step closer and leaned forward to get a better read of the situation. The earth gave way.

His hands flew in the air, and his back hit the ground. He tumbled down the slope. The phone fell from his grip, flew over the cliff and out of sight. His shoulder smashed into the ledge, threatening to pitch him in the direction of his phone.

Chapter Three

"Michael!" Tori's heart stopped when Michael disappeared over the edge of the cliff. She sprinted toward the drop-off and skidded to a stop a few feet from the chunk of ground that had given away. He had to be okay. If not, she had no idea what she'd do. How would she get help? Her cell phone, for all intents and purposes, was a brick out here. She was alone in the forest with no clue of her location. Running for help wasn't an option. And what about the drug traffickers that Michael had mentioned? Her pulse pounded against her skin.

She grabbed the dog's leash before he decided to bolt to his owner. "Ducky, stay."

The dog whined but obeyed.

She strained to see below, but from where she stood, she couldn't see anything. "Michael?"

"Don't get too close."

She closed her eyes in relief and gripped Ducky's leash tighter. "We're several feet from where it gave way."

"Good. Be careful, the ground could be unsteady on either side of that section as well. I don't want you to fall." A groan met her ears.

"Are you hurt?" She fisted her fingers in Ducky's fur.

"I've been better." From what she could tell from the scraping and brushing sounds, he was moving around.

She shifted forward but halted. She wouldn't put herself in danger. Michael needed her. Although, she had no idea how she'd help him. "Can you call someone?"

"No can do. The SAT phone is gone."

Tori fought the desire to sit and bawl like a baby. The situation with Michael and the boys required her to stay strong like she had her entire life. Falling apart wasn't an option. "What can I do?"

"Give me a minute."

The silence—only broken by the shuffle across the dirt.

She hated not knowing what was happening. "Michael?"

"Yeah?"

"Can you please talk me through what's going on? I can't see much from where I'm standing." She hated to admit it, but his voice calmed her. The exposure from the open area behind her and being alone had her peering over her shoulder, searching for her attacker.

"I will, just stay back." He grunted. "I crawled to Andrew, and I'm taking his pulse."

"How is he?"

"Pulse is steady. He's got a gash on his head. And his skin is cool to the touch."

She scraped her teeth across her bottom lip. She hated head wounds. "Has he moved?"

"Not since I joined him." Michael chuffed. "Not exactly how I wanted to rescue him."

"Speaking of, how are we getting the two of you off that ledge?" She ran her hand over Ducky's fur to settle her nerves.

"That's a great question."

She leaned a little farther and spotted Michael's leg. The fall had torn his pants and blood seeped into the material. "You didn't tell me you were injured."

He moved to her line of sight and peered up at her. His face was smudged with dirt. "I thought I told you to stay back."

"I am. There's space between me and the slope. When you're farther out, I can see you without risking the fall."

"Okay, but don't move any closer to the edge."

"Stop complaining and enlighten me on how we are going to get the two of you up here." Tori hoped he had a plan. Ducky was great company, but she wanted Michael by her side. The realization hit her smack in the chest. Throughout most of her life, she hadn't leaned on anyone. Even with Ryan, she'd stood tall and handled everything on her own. She'd had to with him deployed most of their marriage. Tori returned her attention to Michael and the situation at hand.

His gaze swept the area then back to her. "There's a rope in my pack. Get it out."

"On it." Tori hurried to where he'd left the backpack. Digging through the contents, she found what she was looking for then eased to the drop-off and held up the rope. "Now what?"

"Loop it around the tree and toss both ends to me." He pointed to her left.

Her gaze followed his finger. A tree grew at an angle toward the small cliff. She made her way to the trunk and pushed on it out of curiosity. It appeared sturdy, so she looped the rope around the base and tossed both ends to Michael.

"Got it. Is it secure?"

"I circled the bottom of the tree. There's a big branch about two feet above the rope. It shouldn't move up or down too much."

"Good."

She scooted closer and peered down at him. Michael fashioned something that looked like a lasso. "What are you doing?"

"I'm going to put this—" he held up the rope "—around Andrew and hoist him to you."

The man had to be kidding. She glanced at the tree and then

at the drop-off. How on earth would she get a teenage boy bigger than her over the edge? "Are you sure it's going to work?"

"Not really, but what choice do we have?"

He had a point. They had to try. "What do you need me to do?"

"Keep an eye on the rope and tree. If it snags or starts to fray, let me know. Once I get Andrew to the surface, pull him away from the edge."

Michael made it sound simple, but she knew better. "Okay." She turned to check on Ducky. The dog stayed dutifully in his spot. "Ducky, your owner has a lot of faith that I can move a sixteen-year-old boy." Ducky tilted his head and his ears perked up. "But I'm not so sure."

"What did you say, Red?" Michael called from below.

"Nothing." Tori refused to admit she had confided in his dog. She jutted her chin and peered down. "Tell me when you're ready."

Michael groaned as he moved Andrew into position. He sat and caught his breath from the exertion. His actions showed signs that he had injuries from the fall—more than just the one she'd seen on his leg. She knew the man. He'd never admit such a thing when Andrew needed his help. The guy was as selfless as they came.

"How's Ducky? Is he calm or pacing?"

She glanced at the dog. "He looks like he's smiling."

"That's good. If he gets agitated, you take him and my weapon, and hide."

Yeah, that helped her nerves. Not. "Got it." She bit back her concern and waited, refusing to hurry him along.

"Time to get Andrew out of here." Michael stood and began hoisting the unconscious teen. He grunted with each pull.

The boy's head and shoulders came into view, but she couldn't go to him yet or she'd tumble down the slope like Michael had. "A little farther." A few more feet gave her the room she required. "Hold the rope still."

"Hurry."

She scooped her arms under Andrew's and braced her feet. "Okay, keep going."

The rope continued to move, giving her the assistance she needed to drag the teen onto solid ground. She backpedaled, straining with each step. "Stop."

"Is he safe?"

"Yes." She loosened the rope a bit from where it had tightened around Andrew's chest. The boy probably had rope burns from the rescue, but she'd take that over him dying on that ledge. "What next?"

"Take the loop off him and pull the rope up."

"What about you?" Even though she had no idea what Michael had planned, she did as he asked.

"I'm coming. Don't worry."

Don't worry? Her life had been a lesson in worry. But she had experience hiding it from her family and friends. She had to tap into those skills. Allowing herself to fall apart wouldn't do either one of them any good. After she finished removing the rope, she looked down at Michael and held up the braided cord. "Done."

"Tie a loop around the tree and slip the other end through it. Tug on it to make sure it's tight, then toss it to me."

With a quick look at Ducky to make sure he hadn't moved and his demeanor hadn't changed, she strode to the tree. She hugged the trunk to reach around it, then grabbed the end of the rope and fastened it. Loose end in hand, Tori eased to the edge and tossed it over to Michael. "It's on."

He yanked on the line and nodded. "Feels secure. Coming up."

Unable to help herself, she lay on her stomach and peered over the edge. Eyes glued to her friend, she chewed on the inside of her lower lip. He pressed his feet against the rock wall and walked up it while pulling with his arms. His grunts mixed with moans made her stomach twist in knots. His foot slipped,

and she gasped. He caught himself and continued the trek up
the rock wall. Refusing to watch any longer, she scrambled
to her feet and paced a ten-foot path near Ducky. Some friend
she was. What if he fell?

She glanced at Andrew, who still hadn't moved. Michael
had risked his life to help the kid. And what had she done?
Left him alone to make the climb without her support. She
pushed aside her concerns and laid back down to continue her
vigilant watch over him. "You're almost there."

Once at the top, he pulled hand over hand until he lay flat
on the ground and rolled to his back.

Tori crawled next to him and brushed sweaty hair from his
forehead. "You did it."

"Yeah, give me a minute." His chest heaved. "I'll go ahead
and admit it now. I'm out of shape."

She knew better. He'd put on muscle since his injuries from
the boat explosion. Roger had told her that Michael had taken
his physical therapy to a new level. "I doubt that. But we can
argue the point later."

He nodded. After a few moments, he sat up and scooted to
Andrew. "He still hasn't moved?"

"No. And that doesn't give me warm fuzzies about his condition."

Michael glanced over at his dog. "Ducky, come." Seventy
pounds of golden retriever sat in his lap with his fantail on
high. Michael ran his hand over Ducky's head and down his
back in a steady rhythm. "Could you please grab my pack? I
don't know about you, but I need a drink."

"I didn't exert myself like you did, but I could use some
water." She rummaged through the bag, retrieved the two already opened bottles, and handed one to Michael, along with
Ducky's collapsible bowl. In the short time she'd watched the
pair, she knew Michael would take care of his partner first.

"Thanks." He poured water into the dog's bowl and guzzled the remainder of the bottle while Ducky drank his share.

"I hated moving Andrew like that, but his head injury and our location, along with the lower temperatures, dictated that I do so."

"He's alive. That's the most important thing." She exhaled. "I wish we could call for help."

Michael's shoulders sagged. "I'm sorry."

She jerked her gaze to him. "For what?"

"For dropping the phone. It's my fault we're stuck here alone."

She placed her hand on his arm. "Michael. I didn't mean it like that. You had no way of knowing the ground would give way."

"Still." He shrugged. "What about your cell?"

She dug it out of her pocket and checked the bars. "No service."

"I figured. I'm not sure how you got through to me the first time." Michael's gaze traveled along the tree line. "We're closer to the drug runners' trail than I like. Since they've carved a trafficking path out here, it makes the most sense that these guys are the ones who attacked you and took the boys. So, I'm assuming it's one of the enforcers that's hunting you down. We have to stay out of his crosshairs. Time to move. We've been here too long."

"How? Andrew can't walk." Tori took a deep breath. "Hand me my weapon. I'll stay with Andrew while you go for help." She hated the thought. In fact, it terrified her. But what choice did they have?

"No way. I'm not leaving you for some maniac to pick off. We're getting out of here together."

"Do you really think it's the drug traffickers who are responsible for the attack?"

He nodded. "I do. It's what makes the most sense."

Her gaze shifted to the tree line. The gravity of the situation ramped up a notch. "What do you need me to do to help us get out of here?"

"You'll have to schlep my pack, and I'll fireman carry Andrew." Michael stood and brushed off the seat of his pants. His movements—slower than normal.

"I can do that." She screwed the cap on the bottle. "What do you think happened to Joey and Kurt?"

His expression hardened. "I'm choosing to believe they escaped like Andrew did."

"What if we're too late?" Tori was torn. Andrew required medical attention, but her son was out there—somewhere—lost, hurt or dead. She whimpered.

"Red, please don't. If we could continue the search I would."

"I know." And she did. But it didn't make it easier to walk away.

"Let's get moving. The faster we take care of Andrew, the faster we can search for the other two boys."

It was then that Tori noticed him favoring his right arm. The man had rips in his jeans and in his shirt sleeves. Blood and dirt caked the rims of the torn holes. She fought against the instinct to examine his wounds from the fall. Instead, she hefted the backpack over her shoulders, bouncing to adjust the way it lay on her back, and tightened the straps. The movement sent a zing from her previous injuries through her bruised body. The extra motion made her stumble backward. She caught her balance, hooked her thumbs under the straps and shook off the lingering effects of her attack. The pack weighed more than she anticipated, but since Michael planned to carry Andrew, she wouldn't complain about the extra load or her boo-boos. She'd take a deep breath and become what everyone expected. Strong and determined. Oh, to let go and show her true feelings for once. But she didn't have that luxury—never had.

Michael bent and as carefully as possible hefted Andrew over his shoulder. He straightened and groaned.

"Are you sure about this? If not, the offer still stands to hide us and go for help." She hated the idea of being alone with her assailant on the loose, but she'd do it out of necessity if she had to.

"Not with the gunman still out there. We'll go to the cabin together, get Andrew medical help and make a plan to search for Joey and Kurt." He adjusted his grip on the teen's leg. "No way am I leaving you out here without protection and sunset coming in a few hours. I've got this. I'm not completely useless. Ducky, come." The dog trotted to his side, and Michael jerked his chin, indicating the direction to go. He staggered the first couple of steps. Ducky pushed into his leg, and after a moment, the pair strode forward together.

What had she said to provoke that comment? Michael was one of the most capable men she knew. She shook off the confusion and hurried to catch up with the duo. "How far is the cabin?"

"I've spent a lot of time in this forest, so I have a general idea of where we are. I'd say it's about an hour away, give or take, but it will depend on if we run into trouble."

"What a pleasant thought." Tori gazed at Andrew's limp body. Her thoughts swirled with *what ifs*. What if she'd stayed and fought for her boys? What if she hadn't insisted on taking Joey camping? What if she'd asked for help from Ryan's unit? What if she still had God to turn to? The last thought stole her breath. Why did life have to be so hard?

No! Stop with the pity party.

She had to stay strong and focus on the here and now. The outcome of Joey and the others depended on her. Her gaze explored the dense trees along the narrow dirt trail Michael forged ahead of her.

Who wanted to hurt her? And the better question—why?

Chapter Four

The path opened enough for Tori to walk next to Michael. Ducky plodded between them, tongue hanging to the side. Her hand smoothed over the dog's fur, warming her fingers. The action grounded her and settled her spiraling thoughts. Michael had found Andrew, but Joey and Kurt were still missing. The small amount of food she'd consumed threatened to come up. Her son. Where was he? Tears pushed behind her eyes, causing her head to pulse from her earlier injuries. The cuts and scrapes on her arms and legs throbbed, but the aches didn't compare to the pain in her heart.

She hated asking for fear of Michael's answer, but she had to know. "Do you think Joey and Kurt are still alive?" Her voice cracked on the words.

Michael slowed. "I honestly don't know. But since the person or persons didn't kill them outright and leave their bodies, I'd say it's a good possibility. We need to focus on that."

She sucked in an audible breath and jerked her gaze to him.

He cringed. "Sorry. I didn't mean to sound so cold."

"No. That's okay. Thank you for not mincing words." She appreciated him not treating her like a delicate flower. Her entire life she'd confronted troubles head-on. Oh, how she'd love to curl up in a ball and cry—and had on a few occasions in private—but she'd refused to do that in front of Michael. He and everyone else in her life expected her to be rock-solid in the face of challenges, so that's what he'd get.

He adjusted his grip on Andrew's legs and gave her a sad smile. "Nevertheless, I'm sorry."

She waved him off. If he kept apologizing and looking at her like that, she'd lose it. "Let's keep moving. I want to get Andrew to the cabin and get him medical attention, then find the rest of my boys."

"Do they spend a lot of time with you?" Tension oozed off Michael, and the crease between his eyes deepened as he continually assessed their surroundings.

"Joey, Kurt and Andrew are inseparable. They hang out together all the time." A smile tugged at the corner of her mouth but didn't fully form. All the terrible possibilities swirled in her mind. Even fond memories couldn't shove aside her maternal worry. "I love having them around. Sure, I'm still Mom, but they treat me like... Well, like I matter to them, and they seem to enjoy me being with them." Her footsteps faltered. She knew what Michael was doing. Keeping her focused and not stewing about her troubles. She appreciated it, but her thoughts were never far from her boys.

"When Ryan told all of us in his unit how you two got married and immediately took custody of Joey, we thought he was nuts. Eighteen, newlyweds and raising a two-year-old. Not to mention his deployments." Michael shook his head. "But you two seemed to make it work."

She shrugged. What choice did she have? She'd loved Ryan, and that's what life required of her. "I look back, and I won't lie, it was a lot. But we refused to let Joey go into foster care if we could help it. I love that boy like my own. He's my son in every way."

"You're amazing, Red." His soft, sincere voice warmed her heart.

"I'm not. But thank you." When was the last time she felt cherished? Ryan had loved her. She had no doubt about that. But they were young, and perspectives changed over time.

Ducky planted himself in the middle of the path and bared his teeth. A deep low growl rumbled from him.

Michael maneuvered into the bushes, lowered Andrew to the ground and retrieved his weapon. "What is it, boy?"

The dog shot off toward a thick of trees.

"Don't move. Stay hidden." Michael took several steps in the direction where Ducky had disappeared from sight.

Tori's thoughts went on a rampage through her head. Michael was convinced her tormentor had to do with the drug dealers using the forest. What had she and the boys done to garner their attention? Or did her circumstances possibly have nothing to do with those lowlifes who preyed on others?

Trees rustled around her. She grabbed Andrew's hand. "It's okay. Michael will be back soon." She hoped. What would she do if he didn't return?

Michael stepped into view, his dog trotting next to him. The furball sat, and he patted Ducky's head. "It's clear. Come on out."

She wiggled from her spot and stood. "What was it?"

"I'm not sure. He doesn't normally do that. Except with leaves and butterflies, he's pretty chill. I wonder what set him off."

"I hope whatever it was had four legs and not two," Tori muttered. The idea of the man who'd hurt her and taken her boys finding them terrified her.

"It was time to give Andrew a break from hanging upside down. It's not good for his head. But I don't want to stay here long. We should keep moving. Ducky's actions concern me." Michael dug his fist into his lower back and arched. A series of pops accompanied the stretch.

"You should feel better after that."

His quiet laugh—a wonderful sound. "Must say, it eased the

ache. Time to go." He pulled Andrew's limp body to a seated position and lifted him over his shoulder. His hand shot out and pressed against a tree. Ducky rushed to his side. A few moments later he stood straight. "Come on. But stay quiet. I didn't find anything or anyone, but I don't trust that whatever bothered Ducky is gone."

She nodded. She had no intention of putting a target on them.

The two walked in silence with the dog by their side for several more minutes.

Branches rustled ahead, and footfalls filled the quiet.

Michael halted his progress and held up a fist.

Tori stopped and listened for anything significant. A noise she didn't recognize came from her left. A chill slithered up her spine. Her heart pounded. Had the person after her found them?

"Follow me," Michael whispered. His stride quickened. Twenty feet later, he ducked into a hole within a rock formation.

She joined him and blinked, allowing her eyes to adjust to the dimness, and took in her surroundings. A cave. And not a tiny one either. She squinted. It appeared to have a couple of offshoots from what she could make out. "What if whoever is out there follows us in here?" She kept her question low and soft.

Michael placed his finger to his lips and motioned for her to come with him.

A little deeper into the cave, he turned left and tucked into a corner. He lowered Andrew to a prone position and massaged his shoulder. The poor guy had to be miserable, especially after the fall. Ducky lay beside the teen as if to say, *I dare you to hurt him.* "If we stay out of sight, I don't think he'll find us."

"You saw him?"

A small sliver of light from the opening allowed her to see

Michael shrug. "More of an impression." The words—so quiet she had to lean in to hear.

She removed the pack but maintained her grip on the straps in case they had to flee.

Leaves crunched near the entrance of the cave.

Tori froze and stared at Michael. His hand flew to his weapon.

A thunk and hiss jerked her attention in the direction of the opening.

Michael rushed to the edge of their hiding spot and peeked around the corner. His gasp sent her heart racing. He launched himself at her and threw her to the ground, covering her and Andrew with his body seconds before the world exploded.

Dirt particles threatened to cut off Michael's airway. He coughed and coughed again. He tucked his face closer to the ground, searching for a small pocket of semi-clean air. The bubble he found was a blessing. He took a sip of oxygen and another. His thoughts spun, along with his head. The explosion had triggered his vertigo and his PTSD. Panic clawed its way up his throat, stealing more of the air. The horrors of the boat explosion swirled in his mind like a vortex. He inhaled and counted to ten. When that didn't work, he did it again, and again until his heart rate moved away from stroke level.

His mind caught up with what happened, and he jolted. "Tori?" Had he even said her name out loud?

"Here." He felt her move, pushing on his chest, more than heard her muffled answer.

He lifted from his protective position and rolled off her. A groan fell from his lips. The dust had settled, allowing him to breathe easier, but the light had disappeared. Nausea chose that moment to churn in his belly. A wet nose nudged his arm, followed by a swipe of a tongue. "Ducky." His dog laid his snout on his shoulder. The hot breath against his neck was a familiar, comforting sensation.

A hand patted his arm and moved to his face. Tori cupped his cheek. "Michael, I can't see anything. So, you have to tell me. Are you okay?"

"I will be." He hoped.

"Not helpful. Talk to me."

He swallowed hard. "The blast triggered my messed up inner ear." And brought back all kinds of terrible memories, but no need to tell her that.

Her thumb caressed his cheek. "What caused the explosion?"

He'd lean into her touch if he wouldn't puke in the process. "A pipe bomb."

"Excuse me?" Her voice shot up an octave.

Ouch! The increased volume and pitch of her words shot a dagger through his temple, sending his head on another roller coaster ride. He inhaled through his nose, tamping down the reaction. "Whoever we heard took advantage of us ducking into this cave. I saw a pipe bomb at the entrance. It must have collapsed the opening. Ergo no light and lots of dust." He sucked in air and blew out between pursed lips. "We have to check on Andrew. There's a flashlight in my pack. Can you get it while I figure out how to sit up without barfing?"

Tori's humorless chuckle came from his right. "Please don't, or it'll be two of us losing our lunch."

"How did you raise a toddler if vomit makes you sick?" Yeah, so what if he'd chosen to ask the question to delay moving. He'd take the extra time.

"You do what you have to do as a parent whether you like it or not." Her hand left his face, and the warmth next to him fell away, replaced by the damp cool air of the cave. He heard a scrape against the dirt floor, and then the metal slide of the zipper.

Michael patted Ducky's head and gave the dog a gentle push. "Scoot over, boy."

The furball huffed his irritation but moved off Michael's shoulder.

Michael placed his hands beside his hips and gritted his teeth, preparing for the onslaught of dizziness. He pushed to a seated position and scooted to place his back on the rock wall. Okay, not too bad. Maybe his head wouldn't sideline him. And the nausea *had* lessened a bit.

"Got it."

The flashlight clicked on. The bright beam sent streaks of white lightning across his vision. He winced and slammed his eyes closed.

The shaft of light moved from his face. "Sorry. I didn't mean to hurt your head."

He waved off her concern. "I don't have a concussion. It was only the intense light right in my eyes."

"Again. Sorry about that."

He eased his lids open and scanned the interior of the cave illuminated by the flashlight. He moved with caution to Andrew's motionless form and placed two fingers against the teen's neck. His shoulders sagged with relief. He thanked God he'd covered the boy with his body before the bomb went off. "He has a pulse and seems to be breathing fine."

"Good." Tori sniffed. Was the woman crying? "But how are we getting out of here and getting him the medical attention he needs? Plus, we have to find Joey and Kurt. I'm really worried about them."

Yeah, me too, honey. Me too. "Hand me the flashlight, and I'll go assess the damages." Assuming he could stand.

"Are you sure about that? I mean, you said your inner ear is wonky."

"Red, I'm fine. The effects of the blast are fading." And they were, but the anticipation of reliving the Tilt-A-Whirl in his head made him cringe.

She held out the light. "Please, be careful."

"It'll only take a couple of minutes. Don't wander off." He used the rock interior to steady his movements and stood. The world hadn't spun, so he'd count that as a win.

Ducky rose and leaned against him. The dog had been more than a search and rescue dog, so much more. He'd saved Michael's sanity after his *accident*. The one where someone tried to blow him up. "Okay, Ducky, my man. Let's go check out the damages." His dog tilted his head and looked at him, then tilted the other way and looked at Tori as if trying to decide who to stay with. Michael chuckled. "Come on, boy. I might need your help." He hated taking Ducky away from Tori, but if his vertigo returned, his dog was his lifeline.

Flashlight sweeping a path, he and Ducky made their way toward the entrance. He swung the light top to bottom of the pile of rocks and whistled between his teeth. They were not getting out that way. The pipe bomb had collapsed the rock opening. Small boulders filled the exit.

Michael swooped the beam deeper into the cave. His fingers ran through Ducky's fur as he studied the dark tunnel ahead. A way out? Maybe. He'd investigate before he dragged Andrew and Tori deeper into the unknown. *Please, God, let there be another exit.* "Let's go break the news to Tori, boy."

The pair strode to the alcove that saved their lives.

Tori sat holding the teen's hand. She glanced up at Michael. "Are we stuck?"

"The entrance is blocked. But there might be another way out."

"How?"

He jerked his thumb over his shoulder in the direction deeper into the darkness. "Some of these caves have two or three outlets."

"Then let's go."

"Hold on. I don't want to move Andrew until I'm sure." He crouched beside her and bit back a groan. "I'll go investigate. But that means you'll be here alone. I don't want to leave you." Yeah, he knew he sounded stupid. Stay and not get out and possibly let their attacker find them in the cave. Or go and find another possible exit. No brainer, but apparently his brain had malfunctioned.

She lifted her chin. Determination shimmered in her eyes. "We'll be fine."

"I'll have to take the flashlight."

"I figured that one out already. What choice do we have?" She shrugged.

"True." He gathered his pack and pulled out a water bottle and protein bars. "Let's refuel, and then I'll head out. Sorry, but we'll have to share the water. I'm running out. I hadn't planned for us to be on the run."

She waved a hand. "I don't care about sharing. I'm just grateful you have any left. I could use a drink. Especially after all that dust."

Michael dropped his chin to his chest. Why hadn't he thought about that earlier? Once again, he hadn't been enough—done enough—for another person he cared about. "Sorry."

The crease in her forehead deepened. "For what?"

"Oh, I don't know. For not taking care of you." He rolled his eyes at his stupidity and carelessness.

"I'm a big girl, Michael. I knew where the water was. I could have gotten it myself if I'd really needed it."

"I suppose. But I should have taken care of you." He'd promised Ryan, and lately, he'd failed to do a good job. "Here." He handed her the drink, letting her take what she needed, then poured Ducky some into his water dish and guzzled the rest. "I'll be back as soon as I can. Pray I find a secondary exit."

Tori snorted.

"What?"

"Nothing."

He narrowed his gaze at her. What was that all about? He

shook his head and promised himself he'd question her later. Hand braced on the wall, he rose and brushed his hands together, clearing the dirt from his palms. "Hang tight." He retrieved the flashlight from where he left it on the ground and set off to find a way out. "Ducky, come."

The dog huffed then took his time getting to his feet. Ducky ambled to his side.

"So, you're coming with me?"

The dog stared at him with those sad eyes that melted his heart. But Michael had learned to stay strong against Ducky's persuasive powers.

"Let's go, Mr. Dramatic."

Ducky stayed next to him as they made their way through the tunnel.

"Duck, I'm worried about Andrew. And we have to find the other boys. And did you see the cuts and bruises on Tori? Not good, my man." Great, he was having a full-on conversation with his dog. Maybe he'd hit his head harder than he thought. Nah, who was he kidding? He'd talked to his dog like a human from the second he brought the mutt home.

Michael swept the beam along the ground and up the sides of the cave. Nothing but rock, dirt, bugs and spiders. Ick. He had an aversion to the eight-legged critters. But nothing compared to his buddy Doug Olsen and snakes. He chuckled. Man, his friend hated those things.

A glow up ahead quickened his steps. When he found the source, he came to a halt. Branches and dirt filled a hole to the outside.

"What do you think, Ducky?"

The dog's snout lifted. "Whoo, whoo, whoo, whoo."

"Sometimes I think you're part husky with the way you talk." He smiled and patted Ducky's head. Michael moved closer to assess the exit.

Fresh air mixed with the aroma of loam filtered through

the hole. Michael tugged on a limb. The branch broke free and rocks and dirt tumbled in.

He jumped out of the way. The sediment settled, and he stepped back to the opening. "We have a way out, Duck."

His dog slanted his head one way and then the other.

"What, you don't trust me?" Michael exhaled. There he went again, talking to the dog like the furball would answer him.

After removing enough debris to crawl out, he pointed to a spot inside the cave. "Sit. Stay."

Ducky ambled to the location he'd indicated, sat and huffed.

Michael wiggled through the hole and got to work clearing an opening that would accommodate him and Andrew. Sweaty and dirty, he reentered the cave. Ducky remained where he'd commanded, but the dog must have gotten bored because now he was lying down with his snout on his paws.

"Time to get Tori and get out of here." He patted his thigh twice. "Come." Ducky stood, stretched in a downward position and fell into step beside him.

On their way to get Tori and Andrew, Michael made a plan in his head. He'd get them to the cabin and call for help. Then he'd double his efforts to find Joey and Kurt.

"Michael?" Tori's soft question echoed off the walls.

"We're back," he called out. Being in a complete blackout and not knowing what was happening had to terrify her.

"Good." A small quiver in her voice made him pause.

"Is everything okay?" He swept the light around the cave.

"It's fine. I'm just not a fan of dark caves." She lifted her palms and shrugged. "What can I say?"

He chuckled. "Why don't we get you out of here, then? Ducky and I found another exit. It took longer than I expected since I had to move some branches to expand the size of our way out."

Tori stood, brushed off her pants and hiked the backpack onto her shoulders. "I'm ready whenever you are."

He glanced at the teen. "Has Andrew roused at all?"

"Not a peep. I'm worried about him and the other boys."

"Can't say I'm not, but we'll be at the cabin soon. We'll get Andrew the help he needs then continue to search for Joey and Kurt." Assuming they avoided their attacker. He gave her the flashlight and hefted Andrew over his shoulder. "Keep the light ahead of us, and follow me."

She pointed the beam of light several feet in front of him. "Lead on."

Ducky stuck to his leg as they meandered their way through the cave to the secondary exit. Michael had to dip down to carry Andrew through the opening. He stumbled a bit but kept upright. Once outside, he straightened and readjusted his cargo.

Tori exited and sighed. "Hello, fresh air."

"I'll admit, I wasn't fond of that cave." He gave her an exaggerated shudder.

She chuckled, but it was forced. "Where are we?"

"I'm not exactly sure, but the lake's right over there." He pointed about fifty yards away to the body of water that made his skin crawl. "We'll hike along the tree line. It should drop us off at the cabin. It's on the outskirts of the state forest. We should be far enough away from the drug runners not to bring attention to ourselves. There are other cabins scattered nearby in the area." The trees would keep them tucked away and not out in the open as they hiked. Plus, the larger the distance between him and his personal nightmare of the lake, the better.

"I'll be glad when we get there and call an ambulance for Andrew."

Michael jerked his head toward the body of water, motioning her in the direction to head. "Come on. The sun is setting. I'd like to avoid traipsing through the dark as much as possible."

They moved together along the tree line, hidden from sight but still following the shore. The tactic made sense. But the water made him itchy from the inside out.

A storm cloud of exhaustion hovered over Michael from the weight of Andrew on his shoulders and the aches from the fall. He closed his eyes for a moment and sighed at the sight of the cabin in the distance. Dark had settled in, but at least they were close.

"Almost there," he whispered.

Tori had remained quiet on the hike, and he appreciated it. The last thing he wanted was to bring attention to their location in case the person after them had discovered they'd escaped the cave.

The trees angled closer to the beach. The sound of small waves lapping along the shore increased, sending a wave of panic through him. His heart rate spiked, and he fought to keep his respirations normal. His knees buckled. He struggled to maintain his balance. Ducky pressed against him. The dog's action stabilized his steps.

"Michael, are you all right?" Tori clutched his arm. "We can stop for a minute if Andrew's getting too heavy."

Nice of her to think his misstep was because of Andrew. "The cabin's up ahead. I'll be fine." He heard her frustrated sigh and glanced at her. His heart twisted at the disappointed expression that flittered across her face. Add another mark to his "how many times can I let someone down" record.

The flash of a shadow disappeared behind a thick of trees ahead and to his left.

Michael held up his fist, signaling Tori to stop. Ducky lowered his head. A deep growl rumbled from him. "Leave it," Michael whispered. Ducky stopped with the noise, but his stance didn't relax, confirming what Michael had caught a glimpse of—someone sneaking around in the woods.

"Is it safe to continue to the cabin?" Tori whispered.

Was it? The figure hadn't come from the vacation home. It had appeared and disappeared in the trees. Not the area directly around the property. "I'd rather be there than out here in the open. But be alert." The situation had him running scenarios in his mind. If the shooter had found them, why not finish them off? Why sneak back into the woods?

The remaining distance had him hypervigilant. Between the lake sounds and the shadowy figure, Michael's nerves hummed. He skirted around to the back door. "Lift that bear statue. The key is in a case under the base."

Tori followed his directions and presented him with the key.

"Go ahead and unlock the door. We'll keep the key with us until we leave."

Without a word, she opened the door, and they stepped inside. The dark interior put him on edge. His law enforcement background had his skin crawling to clear every room of the house, but first, he had to find a place to lay Andrew down.

"Do you think it's safe to turn on the lights?"

He thought for a moment. "My friend Jackson uses this cabin frequently, so it being occupied isn't out of the ordinary. Plus, there are other cabins nearby. But let's be careful and not light it up like a Christmas tree. A lamp or two should be okay." The cabin had no direct ties to either Tori or him. And the connection to Jackson wasn't direct. Jackson's uncle had given him the cabin, but the title was under a trust. The shadow a little while ago was an anomaly. Michael never got a good look, so it could have been an animal, for that matter. But with everything going on, he'd continue his vigilance. "There should be a switch on the other side of that wall in the living room. Use that one."

The small glow from the moon through the windows allowed Tori to find the switch. He laid Andrew on the couch and rolled his shoulders. He winced. The fall had banged up his arm pretty good. But nothing too serious.

Tori's eyebrow arched.

Okay, so yeah, his body had reminded him in a loud way of the discomfort. Not much he could do other than admit it. "Just a few bruises and sore muscles. Nothing to worry about."

She rolled her eyes but kept her opinion to herself.

"I'm going to clear the house. Stay with Andrew. Don't leave this room." He removed the Glock from his holster.

"You think someone's here?"

"Not really, but I'm not taking any chances with your safety."

She nodded.

He searched each room and came up empty. *Thank You, God, for her compliance. I don't have the energy for a confrontation.* Finger on the edge of the curtain in one of the bedrooms, he pulled it back an inch and peered out into the darkness. He stood motionless, his gaze roaming the edge of the property, searching for movement.

Confident they were alone, inside and out, he returned to the living room. "Everything is good to go. Time to find the phone and call for help."

"Would you please get a washcloth so I can clean Andrew up?" She brushed the teen's hair from his forehead with a practiced mother's touch.

"Sure." Michael headed to the kitchen. He picked up the receiver on the landline and called 911. Once he confirmed the dispatcher had the ambulance on the way and requested no lights and sirens out of an abundance of caution, he placed a call to MJ.

"Agent Jones."

"MJ, it's Michael."

"Michael. Where are you? I called the SAT phone several times, but you didn't answer. And whose number is this?"

"Slow your roll." He'd forgotten how MJ could spin up when she hit the worry zone.

"Answer my questions."

"Yes, ma'am. I lost my phone when I fell off a small cliff."

"You did what?" Her pitch hit an octave an opera singer would be proud of.

"Let me finish."

"Fine."

"We found one of the boys…" Michael explained what happened but left out a few details.

"An interesting hike back. I hear a bigger story behind that."

"There is, but it'll wait until later." He rubbed his temple. Once MJ got her teeth into him, he'd spill the events without holding back. Tenacious. Too gentle of a word for her.

"Agent Smith and I are on the way to the area. I have information for you but discussing it over an unsecured line isn't a good idea. We'll use the cabin as a command center. Two birds one stone. And all that."

"Copy that. We'll be waiting." The line went dead. Michael glanced at the receiver and shook his head. That woman was a top-notch agent but could be as annoying as a circus of fleas on a dog.

He placed the handset back onto the cradle, gathered supplies for Tori and joined her in the living room.

"How's he doing?" He handed her the bowl of water and washcloth.

"He came to for a second and muttered something about the shooting and Joey then passed out again. I'm worried." She gently wiped the dirt from the teen's cuts.

Since anything he said would be hopes and wishes, he remained silent and found the thermostat and turned up the heat to eliminate the chill in the cabin.

A while later, the hum of an engine and the crunch of tires on the gravel road grabbed his attention.

"Finally. I'll go let the paramedics in." Michael strode to the door. After checking to be sure it was safe, he stepped outside. The cooling temps hit him, and he stuffed his hands in his pockets. His gaze traveled to the trees.

Red and blue light bounced across the property. He closed his eyes. At least they'd got the message about no siren. The cabin was far enough away from the drug runners' area that he shouldn't worry. But he couldn't help but wonder if the commotion would bring the attacker to their location. And if it did, could they survive long enough to find the other boys before it was too late?

Chapter Five

Tori wrapped her arms around her waist, keeping herself from shattering into a million little shards as the paramedics loaded Andrew into the ambulance. Her gaze tracked the truck as it pulled away from the cabin and disappeared around a corner, leaving her alone with Michael and her thoughts.

She had no idea what to do with the bottled panic that threatened to explode like a shaken two liter bottle of cola. The paramedics had treated her and Michael and gave her a word of warning about her mild concussion. She'd thanked them and turned the focus onto Andrew. They assured her they'd take good care of the teen, but her mom instincts wanted to be by his side. Yet if she went, where would that leave Joey and Kurt?

After Michael had finished his phone calls, she'd called Kurt's mom, letting the woman know about her missing son and that law enforcement were doing everything possible at the moment. Tori refrained from adding that it was the DEA that wasn't allowing a full search. Then she called Andrew's parents about his condition. She had to pull herself together not only for the boys, but for the other hurting parents. Weakness—not an acceptable trait. Especially now. Responsibility and strength were her gig. And she did it well, even if she hated it.

"Andrew will be okay." Michael placed his hand on her shoulder and squeezed.

"He's a tough kid." She lifted her chin, refusing to let the tears win.

"What did his mom and dad say?"

The conversation had been tough. His parents had held it together, but she could tell they'd fall apart as soon as they hung up. She would have. "Said they'd meet him at the hospital and thanked us for rescuing him."

He nodded, but remained quiet. Finally, he sighed. "It's late. Why don't you go shower and change clothes while I wait for MJ?"

Tori pulled the hem of her shirt straight out. "And change into what? It's not like I have a suitcase or even my backpack."

"There are extra sweats and T-shirts in one of the dressers. Jackson won't mind. Besides, I have a feeling MJ will come prepared with something that will fit you. Or at least fit better than what's in those drawers."

"A hot shower sounds wonderful. I'll take you up on that." She had to retreat before he witnessed her falling apart. Her son was still out there in the cold. Hurt? Scared? Either option had her heart pounding, but the idea of both made her dizzy. "I'll be back as soon as possible so you can clean up while I stand watch."

Michael opened his mouth as if to object, but simply nodded. "Take the forest room."

"The what?"

"Each room is decorated in a theme or a unique color. If I remember correctly, the room is dark green and tan with pictures and accessories of forest critters. It's rather calming, at least to me."

"I can see where it would be—if you like nature." She did but from a comfy chair on a deck.

"I take it you don't."

"That's not it. I've just never had the time to learn how to navigate the world of camping and hiking. I'm not exactly comfortable out in the middle of the woods."

"Then why did you bring the boys?"

"Because that's what Joey needed." She'd stuffed her concerns of the unknown aside in hopes that her son found his way out of the depression that had recently consumed him.

"You're a great mom."

She shrugged, not so sure Michael was right. She tried, but doing everything alone was exhausting, and she knew she messed up on a lot of things.

He dipped his chin and peered into her eyes. "You *are* a great mom. Never question that. Now go. Clean up. Be careful of your bandages. We'll redress any of the cuts and scrapes if they come off once you're done."

Tired of fighting the tears she refused to let him witness, she nodded. "Which one is it?"

"The room's this way." He motioned for her to follow.

She trailed behind him and entered the door he indicated.

"I'll be in the living room if you need me."

"Thanks." She closed the door and collapsed against it. Tears fell like a waterfall down her cheeks. Why did life have to be so hard? If she lost Joey, she had no clue how she'd survive. Ryan's loss had almost gutted her, but she'd stood strong and given the world the impression everything was all right. To the people around her, she appeared to have a backbone of steel and could handle anything that came her way.

The truth? She hadn't been okay since her parents died all those years ago and she'd moved in with her aging grandparents.

"Get it together. You don't have time to fall apart. Joey and Kurt are counting on you." Great. Now she was talking to herself.

Mustering all the energy she had, she pushed to her feet and dug through the dresser. She collected a long-sleeved T-shirt and sweatpants, not caring if they matched as long as they were warm. Clothes in hand, she moved into the en suite bathroom and flipped on the light.

The mirror mocked her. A woman with dirt, cuts and bruises on her face, along with hair that would make Medusa proud, stared back at her. Red puffy eyes and dried tears completed the vision.

Wow. Hot mess didn't come close. She wondered what Michael thought of her now. Thankfully he hadn't witnessed her breakdown. She fought against the temptation to cover the mirror with a towel and turned on the shower. Time to get her act together and clean up.

Twenty minutes later, dressed in fresh clothes and her wet hair hanging limp on her shoulders, she opened the bathroom door. Steam rolled from the room. The hot water had restored her energy, at least a bit until the fog on the mirror vanished and her reflection greeted her again. Red marks marred her face, and the gash sliced across her forehead, skin glued together compliments of the paramedics. The bruises on her cheek and along her neck—a stark contrast against her fair complexion. She studied the person in the mirror. It was almost as if another woman stared back at her.

She exhaled. Time to put on her mask of invincibility and face Michael. She stepped into the hall and froze. The angle into the other room gave her a line of sight but kept her hidden from view.

A woman she assumed was MJ stood in the living room, leaning against the far wall with her arms crossed facing Michael. "Is she okay?"

Tori felt like a stalker but couldn't move. They were talking about her, and she had to know what Michael would say.

He ran his hand through his hair. "Honestly, I don't know. She's the strongest woman I've ever met."

MJ raised a brow.

"Present company excluded."

"That's what I thought." The woman grinned.

He shrugged. "She seems quieter than normal. I'm worried, and I'm never worried about her. She always lands on her feet and is ready to fight. But this…" He swiped a hand across the back of his neck. "This bothers me."

The banter between them and Michael's concerns twisted her stomach in knots. Why did she care the two had an easygoing relationship? It wasn't like she and Michael were more than friends. And when had she given him reason to think she wasn't okay? The man had enough struggles in life without her adding to the mix.

She sneaked back into the bedroom and closed the door with a soft snick. Placing her back against it, she slid to the floor and covered her face with her hands. Her she was again, battling to not lose her hard-fought control. The day had taken its toll. Joey and Kurt were still missing, and Andrew was at the hospital. To make matters worse, she had to protect Michael from her fears and despair.

Ryan had told her about Michael's ex-girlfriend dumping him and how the man had internalized it as a failure. Once the dust had settled from the breakup, Michael had responded by becoming a player. Too many women, too little time, and all that ridiculousness.

During their time in the forest, the strong urge to run into his arms and let him share her pain of losing Joey had shocked her. But she had no intention of adding to his emotional misery with her reaction or her baggage. So, here she sat on the carpet alone, like always, holding back the gut-wrenching wails that threatened to let loose.

What was taking Tori so long? Michael glanced down the hallway, debating whether or not to check on her. He'd sensed a shift in her during their hike to the cabin. Almost as if a shield had lowered and vulnerability had taken over.

"You owe us details." MJ pushed off the wall and headed to the main part of the cabin.

Michael stood for a moment and contemplated MJ's question. Was Tori okay? Honestly, he had no idea. Which made him mentally run through every conversation they'd had together.

Continuing to spin the thought around in his mind, he joined the small contingent of task force members in the kitchen. He recognized DEA agent Earl Harper, and of course, he'd seen Agent John Smith outside checking the perimeter, but he hadn't met Indiana conservation officer Wesley Reynolds until tonight.

"Hey, man, how's it going?" Earl greeted him with a bro hug that consisted of a couple of big slaps on the back.

Michael rolled his shoulder, shaking off the discomfort of Earl's greeting. "I'm doing okay."

"Yeah, yeah, can we stop with all the touchy-feely stuff and get down to the nitty-gritty?" MJ flopped onto a chair.

He and Earl laughed. If he hadn't witnessed the way MJ interacted with her husband while she and Michael worked together, he'd say she had no emotions in her body.

She pinned him with a glare. "Spill it. What happened out there?"

Michael sat at the other end of the table. He'd taken a shower in one of the other bedrooms once the team had arrived. The hot water loosened his stiff muscles, but now he felt every ache and pain from his and Tori's adventure. He glanced around the table. All eyes focused on him. He took a moment to collect his thoughts.

"Ducky and I were hanging out at home." He started with the glitchy phone call and how he found Tori hiding in the brush. Then he filled them in about where he discovered Andrew, his own fall, and how they got the teen off the ledge. The part about the cave and the explosion raised a few eyebrows. He finished off the statement with how they ended up at the cabin and called the ambulance for Andrew. "I'm worried that the boys are either involved with the drug runners, or they stumbled upon something they shouldn't have."

John had joined them during his rundown of the events. The man leaned against the counter near the sink and scratched his jaw. "It's possible, I suppose. If that's the case, why not just kill the kids and Tori?"

Michael cringed.

"Sorry."

"No. You're right. I've thought the same thing." And he had. But hearing it out loud made the severity of the question a little more brutal. He, of all people, knew just how ruthless drug traffickers could be. He had the scars—inside and out—to prove it.

"You do know we still can't call in a full search party for them, right?" MJ laid it out in no uncertain terms.

"I know. I've explained the basics to Tori. She doesn't like it, but she understands that we'd put the boys at greater risk if the drug runners have anything to do with their disappearance." He rubbed at the ache in his chest. He loved Joey like family, but more importantly, he was letting Ryan down by not protecting his buddy's wife and son. Disappointing everyone—again.

"Could it have something to do with the missing hikers?" John asked.

"What missing hikers?" Michael's gaze zeroed in on the man.

"A couple of people have gone missing and never been found. I doubt that has anything to do with this, but I'll fill you in later just in case."

Michael trusted MJ so he'd wait on that information. "How soon until you raid the drug camp?"

"Another day. Maybe two. We're waiting on word from our undercover agent. As soon as that happens, we're going in." Earl approached with two mugs of coffee.

"Then I'll pray the agent calls sooner versus later. Thanks."

Michael accepted the cup from Earl. Warmth infused his skin. He closed his eyes and inhaled. The bold aroma cleared the cobwebs from his tired brain. His gaze connected with each officer in the room. "I grabbed a few items from the camp and plan to take Ducky out in the morning to see if he can find Joey and Kurt. Think you can get someone to process the campsite and the cave without tipping off the players of the raid?"

"I'll handle that. Once I make a call, I'll grab a map. You can point out where you think the site and cave are, along with the ledge. That tripwire makes me edgy. It screams of the drug trade." Michael's new acquaintance, Officer Wesley Reynolds, pulled out his cell phone. "It won't be as thorough as I'd like since the officers will have to collect evidence while playing the role of hikers, but we'll get it done."

Michael took a sip of the warm brew. "I appreciate whatever you can do."

The man lifted a hand and nodded before he walked outside with his phone to his ear. Earl and John dispersed from the cabin, checking the perimeter while Reynolds made the call, leaving him alone with MJ. He and his ex-partner moved to the living room.

Michael lowered himself onto the recliner. His bruises ached from sitting on the hard wooden kitchen chair. He glanced over his shoulder, wondering why Tori hadn't reappeared.

"Give her a minute to regroup." MJ snuggled into the cushion of the couch. "So, what's the story between you two?"

He turned his focus to MJ. "Not much to tell. I served with her husband. He asked me to watch out for her if something happened to him." He lifted his hands, palms up. "He died six years ago. She called. So, here I am."

"Uh-huh, right." MJ rolled her eyes.

"Seriously. We are friends at best." Sure, he found her attractive. And she had a servant's heart. All he had to do was remember how she'd put her entire self into caring for Ryan and Joey. The woman was selfless and independent.

"That's too bad."

His brow scrunched. "What does that mean?"

"Because, dummy, you're a great guy."

He shook his head. "Nah, I'd just mess up a relationship." He had no doubt about that. His past was littered with mistakes where he just hadn't measured up to expectations. "Besides, she doesn't need anyone. I've never met a more driven woman than Tori."

MJ grunted.

"Again, what does that mean?" The woman was starting to irritate him.

She grabbed a pillow and hugged it to her chest. He studied his friend for a moment. She had a contented glow about her, and that made him happy. "It means that everyone needs someone to lean on from time to time."

"Do you?" He'd seen her before she married Steve and now after. He thought he knew the answer to his question.

"Hello? Have we met?" She rolled her eyes again. It seemed to be her favorite response to him. "Being a woman in a male-dominated career is hard. Even if your team respects you, there are always those that wait for you to mess up. You worry that the facade of strength you present will fail. When I met Steve, he chipped away at my outer shell. He gave me a safe place to let my guard down and be me."

"I'm glad you found Steve. But that's not Tori." He leaned forward and rested his elbows on his knees. "She's a take-charge and do-it-yourself type of person. The guys and I have offered more times than I can count, but she never calls us."

"Michael. I'm sure she's a highly capable woman. But have you ever considered that she gets tired of doing it all by herself? Maybe she'd like help but is afraid to ask for it for some reason?"

He straightened. "Why on earth would she be afraid? MJ, that doesn't even make sense."

"Sure, it does. From what you said, she's had to be strong, and that's what everyone expects of her."

"But we've told her we'd help." He realized his voice sounded like a petulant child, but, at the moment, he couldn't care less.

MJ pinned him with a glare. "And I told you to call if you needed anything after your injury. Have you called me?"

He slouched back into the recliner. No, he hadn't called his partner or his team. He hadn't wanted to look weak. Not wanting to face the reality of what MJ had forced upon him, he stood. "I'm going to go check on her."

"Just think about what I said."

He strode down the hall to Tori's room. Hand lifted to knock, he froze. He leaned his ear next to the door.

Sniffs came from inside.

The sound shocked him. Tori never cried. Well, except for Ryan's death. He and his brothers in arms had all shed tears that day.

Could MJ be on to something about Tori needing support?

He rested his forehead on the barrier between him and the woman he was coming to care about and closed his eyes. *I'm so sorry, Ryan. I messed up. I promise to do better with Tori. And I'm going to find your son.*

Seemed that Michael never quite met expectations—was never enough for his friends and family. He sucked in his self-doubt and knocked. "Tori? Is everything okay in there?"

"Um. Sure. Give me a second." The door opened a couple of minutes later. Her eyes were red and slightly puffy, but the injuries on her face and neck stole his breath.

He decided against commenting on her tear-streaked cheeks and focused on her cuts and bruises. "Part of the task force team is here, waiting to talk to you about what happened."

Her shoulders sagged. "Then lead the way."

The fatigue in her expression bothered him. Maybe MJ was

right. He tucked away the concern to examine later. "Come on. Let me introduce you to everyone."

They strode down the hall into the living room. Earl and Wesley had returned from outside, but John had yet to come in. He and Tori sat on the couch, and he took care of the introductions.

"Nice to meet all of you." Tori's soft voice surprised him.

He jerked his gaze to hers. He'd never experienced the timid young woman in front of him. Maybe MJ's theory had merit. "MJ brought you clothes for tomorrow."

"I appreciate that. I don't think I can search for the boys in this." She swept a hand from her shoulders to her feet. The sleeves had been rolled several times to shorten the length, and he'd guess she'd done the same with the waistband of the sweatpants since they weren't falling off her.

He wanted to tell her to stay at the cabin and he'd search for the boys. But Tori would never agree to that. "On that note, let's get started."

MJ took the lead. "Michael explained what happened. The rest of us have discussed different possibilities as to why. But we'd like to ask you a few questions."

At that moment, John Smith came in from outside and hung up his jacket. "After thinking about it, I say Michael made someone mad. I mean seriously, who could be angry with her?" John pointed to Tori then turned to Michael. "Who was it, dude?"

"No one." Okay, that was a lie. He'd made a lot of people angry over the years. "This has nothing to do with me. I wasn't even there." But John had brought up a possibility he hadn't considered.

"If you two are finished—" MJ's brow arched "—I'd like to get some answers."

John waved at her like swatting a fly. "Go ahead, Ms. Bossy Pants."

MJ stuck her tongue out at John.

Man, he missed the comradery of working with these people.

"As I was about to ask, Tori, can you think of any reason someone would want to hurt you or the boys?" MJ focused on Tori.

She swung her head side to side. "No. I work as a receptionist all day, and I take care of Joey the rest of the time. You know, homework, food, chauffeuring him around. Well, until now. He just got his license, so I guess I won't be doing that anymore." The dejected way she dropped her chin to her chest had Michael's heart splitting into two pieces.

"Was he or the other boys into drugs?" Earl asked.

Tori's head jerked up. Her eyes widened. "You think that's what happened?"

"Not necessarily, but it's worth considering." Michael appreciated Earl's almost apologetic tone.

She sighed. "Not that I know of. And I'm pretty tuned in to that sort of thing because of Ryan and Joey's mother."

John lifted a hand and patted the air. "Wait. I'm confused. I thought *you* were Joey's mother."

"Yes and no." She bit her lip and shifted her gaze to Michael.

He took over the explanation. "Ryan and Joey were brothers with a slew of years between them. Their drug-addict mom lost custody of Joey when he was two years old and Ryan was eighteen. Ryan and Tori married young and filed for custody of Joey. He's lived with them ever since. So, in essence, Tori is the only mother Joey's ever known." He laid his hand palm up, hoping she'd accept his comfort.

Earl's wide eyes would have been comical if the topic wasn't so serious. "Whoa. That had to be rough. Eighteen, married and an instant mother."

Tori laced her fingers with his and squeezed. "It wasn't easy, but we didn't have any other options."

"Add to that Ryan joined the Army and deployed soon after." Michael glanced at her. "She's one strong lady."

The men all nodded in agreement, but he hadn't missed MJ studying Tori's reaction.

Tori shrugged but maintained her connection with him. "Thanks, but not really. You do what you have to do."

MJ leaned forward and rested her forearms on her thighs. "You're positive the kids aren't involved in drugs."

The creases in Tori's forehead deepened. "I don't think so, but anything is possible, I guess. I mean, I do work full days, so maybe I missed something."

"We'll keep the possibility open but move on. Did you run into anyone else while hiking and camping?" MJ continued.

"No. I don't recall seeing or hearing anyone."

"Okay, MJ, spill. What do you have on the missing hikers?" Michael asked. When MJ had mentioned the disappearances earlier while in the kitchen, it had set a fire of concern deep in his belly.

Wesley Reynolds raised a finger. "I'll take that one." He grabbed a computer tablet beside him. "There were two in the last six or seven months." He tapped the screen. "A fifteen-year-old boy, Kevin Hartmann. He was camping with his father and a friend not far from Tori's campsite. According to the father, the kid went into the woods to explore and never returned."

"Did you expect foul play or an accident?" Michael asked.

"We haven't ruled out either. We searched for a week and found no trace of the kid. The investigation is still ongoing, but has slowed." Wesley returned his attention to the tablet. "The other was Barrett Gardner, a forty-one-year-old male last seen entering the state forest six months ago at the same trailhead you mentioned where Tori entered. No one realized he went missing until he didn't show up for work on the following Monday. His ex-wife described him as an avid hunter. The thing is, she'd moved out a year before due to erratic behavior."

"Did she elaborate?" MJ asked.

"Said he had a traumatic brain injury due to a car accident. It changed him. She feared for the safety of their teen-age son after Barrett lost his temper and shoved her into the wall, giving her a mild concussion. She said it was an accident but refused to put her son at risk." Wesley glanced up. "Could Barrett be going after teenage boys?"

Tori clasped her hands in her lap. "TBIs don't make people evil. They make them confused and change them in ways we can't understand. My guess is that he had no idea how to deal with his frustration and acted out without thought of the consequences. I doubt he wanted to hurt her."

Wesley opened his mouth, but Michael shook his head, warning the man to stop.

"I still say we keep Barrett on the list." Earl held up his hand. "The teens might have said or done something that made him lash out."

Michael couldn't disagree with that. "We also have the drug runners. Is it possible that one or more of the boys saw something they shouldn't have?"

"Anything is possible. But when? I was with them the whole time," Tori said.

"True." Michael scratched his jaw. "I'm just spitballing here."

MJ stood and paced. "Since we're on the topic of the drug trade, what about your last drug bust, Michael? I know Wade and his second-in-command are dead, but what about another one of his minions trying to get revenge on you?"

"Then why attack the boys and Tori? I wasn't with them." MJ's idea had merit, but he had no idea how it connected to Tori.

"And if we're talking revenge, my question from earlier stands. Who have you made mad?" John, who'd been silent to this point, piped in.

"Too many to count. When drugs are involved, people do stupid things. I've arrested men and had their wives and girl-friends promise to kill me. People have been killed during raids, and the families threaten retribution. It's the life of a DEA agent. You know that."

"Some are sad." MJ's gaze connected with his. "Like Robert, the innocent man who stepped in front of his drug dealing cousin to save his life only to lose his own. His wife was devastated, and his son, Devin, took it hard too, but never seemed to blame law enforcement. And don't forget that father—what was his name? The one who blamed everyone for his son's death even though *he* put his own child in danger."

"Jeffrey." Michael would never forget those cases that MJ mentioned.

"That right." She shook her head. "Sometimes I hate our job."

The room grew quiet. The heater hissed in the background, and the tick of the clock over the fireplace grated on Michael's nerves. He'd done the job to serve and protect. But the horrible consequences of people's actions had become the main characters in his nightmares. He remembered each and every one of those cases—in detail. The ones with young children and teens gnawed at his heart the most. Maybe being unable to return to his chosen career wasn't an all-bad thing.

"What we have is a lot of possibilities that we can't rule out, and nothing solid." Michael hated stating the obvious, but they were no closer to figuring out what happened to the teens than they were when Tori and he entered the cabin.

Tori pushed from her seat, limped to the window and laid her forehead against the glass. "I understand we need to consider the who and why, but I don't care about all that. I just want my son and his friend back."

The pure and utter pain radiating off her ripped the air from his lungs. Without further thought, he went to her and rested his hand on her shoulder. "First thing in the morning we start searching again. If it's the last thing I ever do, I'll find them. I promise you that." Maybe he shouldn't commit to things he had no control over, but what else could he do? Tori had to get her son back.

Michael peered into the night, hoping he hadn't made a huge mistake. *God, please don't let me fail her.*

Chapter Six

The dirt trail in front of Tori rated a four out of ten on her personal difficulty scale. But the scrapes on her knees stung at a seven beneath the fleece-lined leggings that Melissa had brought for her last night. Each step stretched the raw skin, causing it to burn. Good thing Michael had insisted on covering the road rash with bandages or the discomfort would be worse. However, neither the scrapes nor the goose egg and gash on her head that throbbed in time with her heart hurt like the sandpaper grit of her eyes or the ache in her heart.

Last night, she'd hidden in her room and cried from physical exhaustion, her injuries, the missing boys, but most of all, she was tired of being alone and doing everything by herself. Michael had stepped in without question and put his own safety at risk for her. His actions chipped away at her independence. Would it be so bad to rely on someone else? Someone like Michael? She'd always liked him as a friend, but truly trust him to be there for her? Maybe.

She shook off the direction her mind had taken and focused on putting one foot in front of the other as she followed Ducky down the dirt path. Even though her body ached from head to toe, she refused to allow her stiffness to stop them from finding Joey. He took priority over her discomfort. She ducked under a limb, narrowly avoiding another scratch on her face. *Gah! Get your head in the game, girl.*

"Ducky, come." Michael called the dog to his side. "You look ready for a break, Red."

"I'll admit it. I am. But I don't want to slow him down."

"None of us can go nonstop. Including Ducky." The dog trotted over and pushed into Michael, demanding pets.

Glad for the suggestion to rest, she sagged in relief. "Then find us a place to sit for a minute."

Michael's gaze scanned the area. "There. That looks like a good place to stay out of sight." He pointed to a large downed limb tucked within the trees.

She took a step and stumbled. Ducky rushed over and leaned into her leg. The pressure helped steady her. The dog really did have amazing instincts.

Michael gripped her elbow on the opposite side of Ducky. "Are you okay?"

She peered up at him. Why hadn't she noticed his deep chocolate eyes before? A girl could get lost in those things. Whoa. Her exhaustion must be worse than she thought. This was her husband's best friend. Her friend. Nothing more. It never could be. He played the field, or at least had, and she kept the world closed off. "Um...yeah... I'm good now. Thanks."

"If you're sure." He didn't look convinced.

She straightened her spine and hoped her body didn't prove her to be a liar. "Positive."

He released her arm and held out his hand, pointing her in the direction of the log.

Too tired to care if bugs or spiders had made a home on the large piece of wood, she lowered her aching body. "You think we'll find them before our attacker finds us again?"

"I don't plan to let that man get his hands on you. We will find the boys." Michael hadn't hesitated. "I haven't let my guard down, and Duck's on to something, but he hasn't quite been able to catch the full scent. For lack of a better explanation, time has passed so he's hunting it, not following it. If that makes any sense."

"Kind of. But it doesn't matter to me how, as long as we find Joey and Kurt." Birds chirped overhead, and leaves rustled around her. Every little noise twisted her nerves to the breaking point. Here she sat, in the middle of the forest searching for Joey and hiding from a killer. She fought the desire to scream. "I just want my boys home and no one trying to hurt us."

"Ah, Red, I know you do. I'm sorry I'm not able to find the boys faster." Sympathy oozed through his words.

She glanced at him. The dejected expression lasted a fleeting second, but she'd seen it. "Michael, I have every faith that you'll keep me safe. And I know you'll find Joey and Kurt. But I'm not disillusioned that when we do, everything will be roses and butterflies. They might be hurt, or worse." She couldn't bring herself to say the *D* word.

"I'll do my best to bring them home." He stood, slung the backpack on. "We've stayed here too long. I want to get moving. I don't want to make you an easy target."

"What a pleasant thought." She pushed to her feet and groaned. All the aches in her body chose that moment to remind her they existed.

Hand hovering on his Glock, Michael scanned their surroundings then patted Ducky's head. "Ready, boy?" The dog peered up at him with the ever-present doggy smile. He opened one of the large pockets of his tactical pants and retrieved the T-shirt he'd used earlier when they'd started the search. "Check."

Ducky sniffed the item and sat. His tail fanning the dirt, he was excited to work, or so she assumed.

Hand out, palm up, Michael gave the command. "Find."

Ducky's nose went in the air, and he took off.

When she lost sight of the dog, she shifted to face Michael.

"Shouldn't we run after him or something? Aren't you afraid he'll get lost?"

"Nah. He'll keep us within hearing distance. But I'd prefer to keep at a quick clip. I don't want to slow him down."

"Then let's get going." Glad she didn't have to run, Tori strode alongside Michael at a fast pace. The trees reached out and snagged her clothes like fingers determined to grab her. Her heart rate ramped up the farther into the woods they went. Sure, the exercise had increased her pulse, but the forest seemed to press in on her, stealing her breath. She expected a shot to ring out or the person who tried to kill them to jump from the foliage and end her life. Add to that, her heightened concern for Joey and Kurt.

Ducky shot through the trees. They picked up the pace.

"Ducky's a great dog." She sucked in air and tried to hide the fact the exertion had winded her.

"One of the best." So unfair. The man's breathing seemed normal. Compared to hers.

"He's a happy boy." As if Ducky heard her talking about him, he came trotting back to check on them.

Michael stumbled and Ducky bolted to his side and plastered himself to Michael's leg. He gave the dog a couple pats on the head. Soon Ducky moved away and took off again.

"He seems to know when someone needs help."

"What do you mean?" Michael's shoulders tensed.

"The way he leaned into me back there." She jerked a thumb over her shoulder. "And just now with you."

"He..." Michael blew out a breath. "He senses when people are about to lose their balance and places his body in the right position to give support."

Interesting. She'd heard of service dogs that did that, but not a search and rescue dog. However, she had limited knowledge about that too. "Did you teach him that?"

"I guess he's just a natural." The man stiffened. "Come on, let's keep moving."

Tori peeked over at Michael. The man's demeanor had shifted. He was hiding something. Was it about the boys? Or had he sensed something or someone? Her gaze drifted to the dense foliage. Where was the man who tried to shoot her?

Michael trod behind his dog. Tori had come too close to knowing the truth. His inner ear had almost given him away. Thanks to Ducky he hadn't face-planted, but his stumble raised questions. Not about him—yet—but Tori was like a puppy with a chew toy. Tenacious beyond words. He hated what the explosion had done to him, both physically and emotionally. His career had disintegrated before his eyes. And his mind played games with him on a good day. Water and abrupt loud noises triggered his post-traumatic stress, and the PTSD triggered anxiety attacks. He huffed out a breath. No job. A medical condition that came and went as it pleased. And he avoided large bodies of water like a coward. He was a mess.

The woman's strength continued to amaze him. Ryan had been a blessed man to have her by his side. Someday, maybe God would provide him with a woman like Tori. The only difference... Yes, he wanted an independent woman, but his heart also desired someone who needed him. Then again, he hadn't been enough for his ex-girlfriend and others in his life. He always fell short of people's expectations.

"Michael?"

"Yes."

"I just now realized you're using Joey's T-shirt."

He nodded, unsure what she was getting at.

"Ducky has his scent, doesn't he?"

"Seems to." Michael had never developed the ability to read women. One would think being around Tori he'd at least have figured out the basics of his friend. But no. He placed his finger under her chin and lifted. "What are you getting at?"

"You mean we might actually find him?"

He ran his hands up and down her arms. "I told you we would. Have a little faith."

She snorted.

Ouch. He knew he'd failed a lot of people over the years, but to hear her doubt him... That hurt. "What? You don't believe me?"

"No, I believe *you*. I'm not so into the faith part."

Now that surprised him. "I thought you and Ryan held the same belief in God."

"We did—once. Then life happened." She shrugged like it was no big deal.

He remembered a similar reaction earlier. How had he missed so many things in her life? *You never should have promised to look out for her. You've only messed it up, like always. And this. It's huge.* Well, that had to change. He couldn't let her down anymore. First, he'd work on finding Joey, and while they searched, he'd tackle her dwindling faith issue. He'd find a way of digging without putting her on the defensive. He hoped.

A discussion he planned to have, but he'd hold off a bit longer. "Let's catch up with the furball."

He jogged behind his dog, careful of each step so as to not twist an ankle. Ducky veered to the right. Michael dipped under limbs, following his dog deeper into the trees. He glanced over his shoulder, checking Tori's location and condition. She stayed focused and never complained. Not even with her worry for Joey. Ducky froze ten feet ahead of him. The dog's head jolted up, and his ears rotated forward.

Michael's hand went to his weapon on instinct. He held a finger to his lips.

Tori's eyes widened.

He eased forward. He placed his hand on Ducky's head and whispered, "Leave it." He turned to Tori and motioned for her to follow. "Tuck inside those bushes and stay out of sight. I'll leave Ducky with you. Don't come out unless you know it's me."

Worry lined her features, but Tori nodded and wiggled into the brush.

"Duck, stay with Tori."

The dog gave him the side-eye then crawled onto Tori's lap. Michael lifted a few branches over their hiding spot. Once satisfied, he slid his Glock from the holster and slipped into the trees away from his dog's focus. If their attacker had found them, he wanted the element of surprise, coming in from the opposite direction.

In stealth mode, he picked his way through the brambles and stepped with a light foot on the dried leaves that created the forest floor. His eyes were in constant motion. There. In the distance. A figure outlined by the sunlight dipped under low hanging branches, moving in a pattern that suggested he was hunting. Michael skirted around the area, aiming toward Tori. He had to get her out of here.

Michael eased the limbs from the spot where he'd left Tori and Ducky. He kept his voice low as to not attract attention. "Time to go."

Tori jolted and stifled a scream. "Scare me to death, why don't you. What did Ducky hear?" she whispered.

"A person."

She scrambled to her feet. "The guy after me?"

"Uncertain. But if I had to guess, I'd say that would be an affirmative. It's time to move on. I want to put some distance between him and us." He waved her to follow and took off in the opposite direction, away from Joey's scent and from where he'd seen the stranger. Once sure they'd avoided the person in the woods, he'd circle back. Glock in hand, he stayed on alert and prayed the man he'd seen didn't find them.

Ten sweaty minutes later, Michael halted near a copse of trees. "I think maybe—"

A twig snapped in the distance. He spun and leaned to the

side to search for where the noise had originated. A whoosh and thunk met his ears. He whipped his head around. The tip of an arrow had embedded itself into a tree trunk, and the shaft wavered from the abrupt hit.

He grabbed Tori's hand and jerked her farther into the woods. "Keep your head down."

Another arrow whizzed by.

Michael drew his weapon and held it to his leg. He and Tori ducked under branches and dodged downed logs. Ducky came flying in from the left and joined them.

The crunch of leaves under his boots echoed in the trees. Stealth wasn't in his vocabulary, escaping was. He'd worry about the ramifications later once they put distance between them and the shooter.

Another arrow whoosh passed his head. He ducked out of instinct, but if the killer had aimed better, he'd be dead.

Tori whimpered. Her hand tightened. "How many arrows are in his quiver?"

"My guess? Six. That's a standard quiver size. But I could be wrong. Keep running." If Michael had accurately guessed, the shooter still had three remaining.

Hand clasped with Tori's, Michael weaved his way through the forest. Never going in a straight line. Tori's breathing came in short pants. He had to stop soon for her to catch her breath, but not yet.

Several minutes later, he slowed and pulled Tori into the crevasse of a huge boulder. Glock leveled at the opening, he wrapped an arm around her waist. Ducky circled his legs and stuck close.

Tori collapsed into him. "Is he gone?" Her quiet words came between sucks of air.

"I'm not sure," he whispered back. He strained to listen for evidence that the man had found them. The latest attempt on her life concerned him. His protective streak caused an internal debate that warred in Michael's brain. Take her back to the cabin and hide her away from danger? Or continue the search with her by his side? He knew what she'd say, but his fear of letting her down had his heart racing. Too many times in the past he'd made wrong decisions. Or so his ex-girlfriend and family had told him, along with others. Nothing but a disappointment. He refused to add Tori's opinion of him to that column of his life. His heartbeat galloped in his chest, pounding on his breastbone.

Ducky whined at his side. The furball sensed an anxiety attack sneaking up on him.

He took a few deep breaths, settling his pulse into a normal rhythm, and patted the dog's head. "It's okay, boy. I'm good." He'd agreed to train with a search and rescue dog last year and gained the equivalent of a service dog in the process. He thanked God every day that Roger had partnered him with Ducky. The dog had saved him both emotionally and physically more times than he could count.

"Do you think it was the same guy from the cave? I mean, one was an explosive, and this was a compound bow. Or at least I'm assuming that based on the velocity of the arrow."

He raised a brow at her observation and knowledge. The woman continued to surprise him.

"What? Ryan liked to hunt. He'd talk about it before and after each time he went out."

"That's true. I just didn't expect you to listen to the details." Michael scanned the woods. He'd allowed himself to become lax. Not anymore. Tori's life was too important to him. "Different methods could mean different attackers. However, it could also speak to someone who has hunting experience, along with knowledge of explosives. Ex-military. A demolitions expert who hunts on the side. Or even our drug runners might have familiarity with both. It's hard to tell."

"Great," she huffed. Her eyes narrowed. "Come to think about it, that arrow missed you by an inch or two. It hit several feet from me. Does that mean our assailant is after you now?"

She had a point. Why the switch in targets? Not that Michael minded. He'd rather have the sights set on him than her. "That brings up interesting possibilities. For now, let's stay alert and continue our search." And he would be hyperaware of their surroundings like he should have been all along. He'd made a commitment to his best friend a long time ago to watch out for Tori, and right now, he had to step up his efforts to keep that promise.

The lack of movement during their quiet conversation gave him hope they'd lost the attacker. "I haven't heard the guy in a while. Let's get back to our search, but let me take a look first."

She gazed up at him. "Be careful."

"Always. Ducky, stay." He slipped past her and eased from the gap in the rock. Handgun at the ready, he transitioned to stealth mode and examined the surrounding area. Nothing appeared disturbed nor did he see footprints. Confident, at least as much as possible, they'd eluded the person chasing them, Michael returned to the place he'd hidden Tori.

"Red?" He peeked into the crack. "I think he's gone—for now."

She released an audible breath and joined him. Ducky followed and sat by his feet.

"Do you think we really lost him?" Her eyes scanned the trees.

"For the moment. But don't let your guard down."

"Believe me, I won't."

"Then let's get Ducky back to work." The dog's fantail swished on the ground, scattering pine needles, leaves and dirt. He gave the furball the scent again. "Ducky, find." The dog trotted off. Nose in the air, Ducky zigzagged through the woods. Michael squeezed Tori's hand for encouragement. "Come on. Let's see what he finds."

Ducky quickened his pace.

Michael increased his speed. Unwilling to be unprepared, especially after narrowly escaping the arrows shot from a compound bow, he gripped his Glock. His gaze drifted from his left to his right and back, no longer concerned about the uneven ground. He refused to drop his vigilance with the attacker nearby. Been there, done that, about got a one-way ticket to eternity for it.

"Doing okay?" he threw over his shoulder.

"Fine. Keep going." Her audible heavy breathing told him a different story. "Don't worry about me."

Yeah, like that would happen. He glanced back at her, debating if he should stop. He hated to since Ducky had caught the scent.

He hit something hard, and his foot slipped. A snap of metal met his ears, followed by a shooting pain slicing up his lower leg. He pitched forward and landed on the ground hard. His Glock dropped from his hand.

Streaks of white lightning flashed behind his eyes. Nausea churned in his belly. He swallowed the bile pooling in his throat.

"Michael!" Tori dropped to her knees next to him. Her hand warmed his shoulder, grounding him from the pain. "Can you move?"

Could he? He honestly had no idea. After sipping in oxygen to get a handle on the intense burn in his leg, he took a deep breath. "What happened?" He shucked out of his pack and rolled onto his back. Slivers of blue sky peeked through the canopy of the trees.

"You hit the edge of an animal trap." She moved to examine his wound. "By the looks of your pant leg, the teeth scraped grooves into your skin, but thankfully it didn't clamp onto your ankle."

"Feels like a thousand bee stings." He pushed up with his arms behind him and leaned on his hands. Spotting his Glock, he slid it close to his side.

"I can imagine. It got you good." She rummaged through the backpack and extracted the first aid kit and a water bottle.

"Hold still and I'll get you cleaned up." Tori hiked up his pant leg, exposing the cuts. "Yikes. The teeth on that trap carved deep gouges in your ankle."

He had no desire to look at the mangled skin. "Do I need stitches?"

"I'll have to clean it first before I can make that determination." She handed him a prescription dose of ibuprofen and arranged the supplies while he swallowed the tablets. "Ready?"

Not really. He'd prefer to let the medicine kick in first. But they couldn't wait that long. "Sure." He gritted his teeth when the cloth raked across the gashes. The water Tori poured over the injury soothed the throbbing for a moment. She patted the area dry with gauze, applied ointment and wrapped the lacerations.

"I placed several sterile pads under the gauze roll. I'm hoping the bleeding will stop soon. It's not bad, but..." She shrugged.

"It'll help clean it out." He flexed his ankle and winced. If he'd stepped straight on the metal trap, he'd have a bigger problem than slices in his skin. "Guess I'll have to make sure my tetanus shot is up to date." And maybe a regimen of antibiotics. The thought of the rusty metal piercing his flesh sent a shiver down his spine. He'd spent enough days in the hospital after the explosion. He had no desire to step foot in one for a long time to come.

Ducky had returned and sat beside him, tongue dangling from his mouth. His buddy's actions relieved one stress. He needn't worry about the person shooting at them for the time being. As long as Ducky stayed relaxed, they should be good to go.

His thought returned to his injury. The idea of standing made him cringe, but the longer they waited, the harder it would be to find the teens.

"Okay, boy. Help me up." Ducky stood and braced himself. Michael placed one hand on the ground and one on Ducky. He pushed off the forest floor and used his dog for stabilization. Once upright, he tested his leg. A zing of lightning zipped from his foot to his hip, but the pain was bearable.

Tori stuffed the kit into the pack and slipped it onto her back. "Are you able to walk?"

"Yeah." He wasn't excited about it, but he'd endure. They had a job to do. Joey and Kurt took precedence over his boo-boo. "Hand me the pack, and we'll continue searching."

"I've got it." She glared at him, daring him to argue the point.

"All right, Ducky, back to work." He held his arm out, palm up. "Find."

The dog darted through the trees.

"Let's go." Michael clenched his jaw and half jogged, half limped after Ducky. Of all the stupid things, stepping on a trap topped the list. And he was paying for his inattention. But who had placed a trap in the thick of the trees? He knew people hunted illegally, and he'd heard rumors that drug runners used them to keep unwanted animals and humans away similar to the use of the trip wires.

Or—he hated that his mind went in that direction—someone had placed traps specifically to capture other humans. Too many possibilities to know for sure. And he hated the inability to put the pieces together.

A single bark broke through the trees, interrupting his internal lecture and thoughts.

Michael's heart kicked up a notch at Ducky's signal. "He's found something."

"Do you think it's Joey?"

"I don't want to get your hopes up."

"They already are."

He had no explanation for Ducky's response other than he'd found her son, unless Kurt had borrowed Joey's shirt and his scent was what Ducky had followed. But there was no way to know until he laid eyes on his dog's find.

God, for Tori's sake, please let it be Joey.

The pair hurried to a small clearing. Michael's heart threatened to stop beating. He grabbed Tori's arm, halting her from moving closer.

Ducky sat next to a pile of leaves and whined. Not a typical response when he found a victim alive. Add to that, Joey was nowhere in sight.

His stomach dropped. There was only one reason his dog would react that way. *God, please let Joey be alive under all that.* He clutched her shoulders and turned her to face him. "Stay right here."

"You think he's under there, don't you?" Tears pooled on her lashes.

"I'm not going to speculate until I take a look." At least not out loud. He dipped his head and peered into her blue eyes. "Promise me you won't go any closer."

She glanced to where Ducky sat then to him. "I promise."

Michael inhaled, held it, and released a long slow breath. Time to discover who or what lay hidden beneath the pile of leaves and twigs. He limped over and knelt next to Ducky. "What do you think, boy?" *Please, don't let it be Joey under this mess.*

He brushed the leaves away and uncovered a baseball cap. The dark blue hat sported the Brentwood High School mascot. He pivoted and held it up.

"That's Joey's." Tori hugged her waist. The agony that laced her features would have taken him to his knees if he hadn't already been there.

"Give me a minute." His heartbeat drummed under his breastbone.

Several swipes later, the face of a young man stared at the sky with lifeless eyes.

Tori's worst nightmare had come to life. She stood frozen in place where Michael had left her. First Joey's cap, now part of an exposed body. Hair the same brown as Joey's. Her son was gone. She had nothing left in life. Her husband had died six years ago and now Joey. Tears burned her eyes and emotion clogged her throat. A sob escaped, then another. Her knees buckled.

Arms surrounded her and kept her from falling. Michael's breath warmed her ear. "It's not him."

She struggled against his hold. She wanted to run to her son and beg him to wake up. But deep down she knew that would never happen again.

Michael cupped her cheeks. "Did you hear me, Red? It's not Joey."

She flipped her gaze to him. Had she heard him correctly? "It's not?"

"No, honey. It *is* a young man, probably in his early twenties, but it's not your son. And even though I don't know Kurt, this guy's too old."

"You're sure?"

He nodded. "The guy looks nothing like Joey."

Her body sagged against him, soaking in his strength. Having someone to support her was new. She had done it all on her own for so long. She pushed back. "I want to see him with my own eyes." Hand up, she stopped him from protesting. "I trust you, but I need to prove it to myself."

For a moment, she thought he'd argue the point, then he nodded. "Watch where you step. Ducky and I have already compromised the scene when we uncovered the body, but I'd like to leave it as intact as possible."

The pile of red, yellow and orange leaves tormented her. Knowing what Michael said and confirming it were two different things. "I'll be careful." Her gaze shot to the exposed body. God wouldn't be so cruel, would He? Yeah, she didn't have a lot of faith in that question. Her life had proven that.

"Are you ready?"

She resisted the urge to say no. It was time to face reality the way she always had. Head on. Tori threw her shoulders back. "I'm good." The leaves crunched beneath her boots. The walk felt like the length of a marathon. She peered down.

Unseeing eyes stared into oblivion. Her hand flew to her heart. The young man had no resemblance to her son or Kurt. She took her first deep breath since Ducky had alerted on the body. "It's not Joey."

Michael snaked his arm around her and tugged her close.

Tori turned her face into his shoulder, and for the second time, she accepted the comfort he offered. She dug deep to find the strength not to cry. Did it make her a bad person for being glad the guy in the leaves wasn't her son or his friend? Maybe. But she couldn't deny her relief.

She inhaled and stepped from the solace of Michael's arms. "Now what?"

He steered her away from the dead body. "I call it in and have Officer Reynolds take care of the scene and let him know about the crossbow incident." Michael retrieved his new SAT phone that MJ had given him. "Stay close and stay alert. I have no idea if your attacker did this or someone else." He waited for her to agree then turned his attention to his call.

Her gaze traveled to the young man who'd lost his life, and she ignored the conversation going on next to her. How had she found herself in this dilemma? What had she done to become the target of a madman?

Chapter Seven

The longer Michael stayed with the body, waiting to turn over the scene to the conservation officers once they arrived, the quieter Tori became. Not to mention, the itchier he got about being exposed to her attacker. He hated that she'd witnessed death in such a fashion, but was also relieved the person buried under those leaves wasn't Joey or his friend Kurt.

"Once the officers get here, we'll head to the cabin and take a break for the night since we'll run out of light if we keep going. Until then, I'm going to grab reference photos of the scene." He pointed to a nearby log. "Go on and have a seat while we wait."

Without a single word, Tori complied. Her gaze, the classic thousand-mile stare. She'd shut down a few minutes ago. Michael hadn't seen her like this before. She'd always presented herself as unflappable.

He'd give her a little time to come to grips with what she'd seen and experienced. He held the phone MJ had given him as a backup and limped to the body. Fire shot up his leg. He grimaced from the pressure on his wound with each step. A second round of ibuprofen sounded amazing right now, but that would have to wait for another few hours. The prescription dosage he'd taken had barely put a dent in the pain.

As to not disturb the scene any more than he already had, he stood several feet away and snapped pictures from different angles. Finished, he turned and surveyed the area. His eyes roamed the trees and brush, searching for danger. Either from the man who'd attacked them on multiple occasions, or whoever had killed the young man. Assuming it wasn't the same person. With drug traffickers, you never knew. The entire situation had him on edge. His SAT phone buzzed. He read the text.

Wesley: ETA four minutes on my guys.

Michael: Scene secure. Theirs when they arrive.

Wesley: Copy that.

Michael eased next to her. "Red?"

Her gaze drifted to him, and she blinked.

"Officer Reynolds texted. The officers are a few minutes away. We'll leave as soon as we each give them a quick statement."

"Good. You need to get back to the cabin so you can clean that wound and bandage it properly. And maybe some ice for the swelling and more ibuprofen for the pain." Tori's normal all-business side had returned, along with color in her cheeks.

A hot shower and pain meds sounded fantastic, but he pushed the thoughts from his mind. He couldn't ignore the continued threat. He had to keep his wits about him until he reached the cabin and had backup.

Two men pushed through the brush forty-some feet ahead.

Michael drew his weapon. He refused to assume they were the good guys until proven otherwise.

"Lane?" the one on the right said as they approached.

He nodded. "Credentials."

The two extracted their wallets and produced identification.

Michael holstered his Glock and shook the men's hands. "Thanks for coming."

"Not a problem. I'm Officer Gregor, and this is my partner, Officer Newman."

"Michael Lane, and this is Tori Campbell."

"Good to meet you both, but I'm sure you'd like to get out of here." Gregor pointed to Michael's ankle.

He glanced at his blood-soaked ripped pants. "You could say that."

"Then let's get down to business. Where's the body?"

"Over here." He motioned for them to follow. "My search and rescue dog alerted on that pile of leaves."

"SAR? Not HRD?" Officer Newman crouched by the lifeless young man.

"He's an air-scent dog not a human remains detection dog. He hit on a baseball cap owned by the teen we are searching for, not the body." Ducky stuck close, and Michael patted his head. The poor thing had worked hard today. He deserved a special treat. One he'd get once they returned to the cabin.

"Got it." Officer Gregor pulled out a phone. "Why don't you give me a rundown on what happened while Newman talks to your girl, and we'll take it from there."

His girl? Tori wasn't his. But he had to admit, he liked the sound of it. "Take it easy on her. She's been through a lot. And I'm not just referring to today."

Newman nodded. "Will do."

Michael faced Gregor. "Ready?"

"Whenever you are." The officer hit record.

Michael proceeded to give him a timeline of everything that occurred up to and including the discovery of the body while the officer documented his words.

Gregor slid the phone into his pocket when Michael ended his statement. "Once we finish, we'll send the report to Officer Reynolds. I'm sure he'll share our findings with you."

"I appreciate it." Michael said his goodbyes and joined Tori. "Doing okay?"

Her eyes remained glued to the young man's body. She shrugged. "What choice do I have?" she muttered.

Uncertain if the words were meant for him or not—and

he'd guess not—he ignored her comment. He held out a hand, and she placed hers in his. She pushed to her feet and swayed. Ducky rushed to her side. "Take a second. You've had a long day."

"So have you." She ran her fingers through the dog's fur. Her countenance shifted, and she straightened. "I'm not a weak little girl."

"I'm not saying you are. In fact, quite the opposite." MJ's words rattled around in his brain about how staying strong was exhausting. He'd taken notice of Tori's reactions since his and MJ's conversation. His ex-partner was on to something, but how did he navigate those waters without making things worse? "It's okay to lean on someone from time to time. You don't have to shoulder everything on your own."

Tori's eyebrow arched. "Really? And how often have you asked for help?" She waved her hand like swatting a fly. "Forget I said anything. Let's get out of here."

Her words had hit their mark. He did tend to be a lone wolf, so to speak. Not that he didn't like people—quite the contrary. Before life had put him through the grinder, his friends had tagged him as a social butterfly. He'd loved large groups of people. But he'd let too many people down not meeting expectations. Never enough for his ex-girlfriend no matter what he did. Not to mention his parents. Disappointed with his choices—it didn't matter that he'd followed his heart—they'd disowned him. That had been a hard reality to swallow. How could someone do that to their own child? Add to that, his inability to keep his friends safe. The incident with his Army unit, more specifically Ryan, had gutted him. And now Tori. He'd failed to see her struggles, which had ultimately led her to the situation at hand.

Frustration coursed through him. Why hadn't she turned to him or one of the guys? Any one of them would have come running to her aide. If only she'd confided in him. He would have dropped everything to help. Right. As if he'd disclosed his problems to his buddies or her. Maybe it was time to open that box and let out his anxieties.

He mulled over telling her about his struggles. But if he expected anything from her, he had to rip the proverbial bandage off his insecurities. With the officers not far away, he felt a measure of safety to stay and have the conversation. Even then, he examined his surroundings. There had been no sign of the attacker, but the man did seem to appear out of nowhere. He shook off the fearful thought. If he planned to tell Tori about his medical issues and concerns, he'd better get on it. Now was the time to confess his shortcomings before they headed to the cabin.

Keeping his voice low, so as not to be heard by the men working with the body, he released a long breath. "Tori."

Startled, she stumbled. He grabbed her arm to keep her upright, and Ducky scurried to assist.

"Sorry about that. I guess I'm a bit more tired than I thought." Pink crept into her cheeks.

"Do you need to sit back down?" His leg screamed at him, but he ignored it and focused on Tori.

"No. I'm fine." She waved him off. "What were you about to say?"

Michael ran a hand over the back of his neck. "Before we get to the cabin, there's something you need to know."

She tilted her head. "What's that?"

"I feel guilty that I haven't been around much since my accident." If you could call someone trying to blow him up an accident. He mentally rolled his eyes.

"Don't worry about it. Joey and I are—were—doing fine."

"It doesn't excuse my lack of contact." Michael shifted his stance, his leg aching almost as much as his heart. He'd pushed too many people away over the last year. This was it. The truth had to come out if he expected her to trust him with all things. "I kind of went into a hole and never came out. I haven't been honest with the guys or you about why I walked away from my career with the DEA."

Tori's attention jerked to him. "What do you mean?"

His boss and his doctor knew, but he hadn't told the whole truth to anyone else. He shifted to face her. "I have an inner ear problem. Vertigo strikes whenever it decides to. I can't predict it. Ducky's been a godsend." The dog's ears perked up. Michael scratched the furball's head. "Yes, I'm talking about you, boy."

"The way he leans in to help you maintain your balance?"

"Exactly. And then some." Might as well put it all out there. If he expected her to let him into her world, he had to be willing to share. "I'm guessing you noticed my discomfort when we walked near the lake."

Her gaze locked with his. The intensity was almost too much to handle. "Yes. But I didn't want to pry."

"Ever since the explosion and subsequent injuries, I have post-traumatic stress."

"The *incident* during deployment changed all of you. I saw it seep into your everyday lives. But I take it this is different."

He nodded.

"PTSD is nothing to be ashamed of." Her hand cupped his cheek. "You know that, right?"

He fought the yearning to lean into her touch. "Yes, but for me, it's more than that. Between the inner ear issues and the flashbacks, along with intense panic, my life has changed drastically. I no longer have a job and have no idea what I'm going to do. I can support myself due to my military benefits and my disability retirement from the DEA, but I don't have anything to offer to a committed relationship. That's why I—"

Her eyes grew wide, and she dropped her hand like his skin had burned her. "Oh, my, you have a girlfriend on the side, don't you."

"What?" He scrambled to make sense of her statement. Then it hit him. His playboy past rolled at him like a runaway truck. She still thought he had a string of women in the wings. "No. I don't do that anymore. Haven't in a long time. Not since an Army chaplain sat me down and challenged me. I didn't like the version of me he presented."

"But Ryan said..." She scraped her teeth along her bottom lip and looked away.

"Red, please." He placed his finger under her chin and lifted. "I'm not that man. I don't even date anymore."

Her blue eyes studied him. "Well, that's good. Not the dating part, but the one-night stands."

When had he given her the impression that he still lived that way? That chaplain had saved Michael from self-destruction after the incident while on deployment. Not long after, God had become his center, thanks to Ryan. The man had a TBI, but throughout all the changes in his thought process and personality, his friend's faith had never wavered. Michael rested a hand on her shoulder. "I hate that you have that opinion of me."

Her hand once again caressed his cheek. "I'm sorry I never asked."

"You shouldn't have had to. It should have been evident." He leaned closer. He'd never noticed the gray flecks that enhanced her blue irises. He'd admired her tenacity for years, but over the past couple of days, he'd seen her in a whole new light. One that intrigued him.

Her thumb caressed his cheekbone. "You've checked in on me frequently, but we've never really shared beyond a basic friendship."

Guilt filled him. He'd promised Ryan he wouldn't look at Tori as anything other than a friend. And he was failing in a spectacular fashion. He stepped back, breaking the moment. He refused to betray his friend by going against his wishes.

Disappointment flashed across her features. Had she wanted him to kiss her? No. He was kidding himself. What would she want with a man who no longer had a career?

"I will remedy the lack of help for you and your son later.

For now, I intend to find Joey and the other teen. But we'll have to wait until morning before we continue."

She drew back her shoulders and set her jaw.

Oh, he'd made her mad with his switch from soft to operator mode. Of that, he had no doubt. She hadn't deserved his hot and cold attitude. But he was struggling to make the right choices this time around in life. Disappointing others came at too big of a price.

"Come on. Let's get back to the cabin."

"Lead the way." She motioned for him to go first.

He waved at the men working and limped from the crime scene. As they trekked through the forest, he split his attention between Tori and the threat against her. How did he keep her safe? Tucking her away while he searched was the best answer, but she'd never go for it. But hiking through the woods with a target on her back wasn't a great option either.

The silence that lingered between them set his nerves on edge. However, it allowed him to focus on the sights and sounds of nature, confirming no one followed them.

"Do you think he's still out there?" Her words were barely loud enough for him to hear.

"Yeah, I do. I'm praying we don't attract his attention."

"Is that why you're moving randomly through the woods?"

He glanced at her and raised an eyebrow.

"What? I may not know where we are or how to get to the cabin, but I'm not clueless either."

Tori had nailed it. He'd zigzagged them through the trees, not sticking to any one direction. "I don't want to make it easy on the person after you to lie in wait along the trail."

"Makes sense."

A rustle to his left stopped him. He grabbed Tori's arm with one hand and his Glock with the other. He tugged her behind him and searched for the origin of the sound. Seconds ticked by. Nothing happened, and no one appeared. Now he was being just plain paranoid. But the oddity stuck with him.

His gut said the noise wasn't an animal, but why hadn't the person attacked?

"Come on. Let's get to the cabin." He released Tori but refused to holster his weapon. The whole situation had his mind spiraling with the *what ifs*.

They hiked in silence for another twenty to twenty-five minutes when he veered toward the path to their destination. The trail opened farther.

Unlike last night in the dark, their destination came into full view. The ranch-style log cabin sat in the clearing. Five steps led from the ground to the front door. A large wrap-around porch with rocking chairs invited visitors to come and relax. But it was the lake and dock behind the house that gave Michael pause. His nightmare, come to life. How would he navigate his biggest PTSD trigger? Sure, he'd hiked along the shoreline, but it had been in the dark. Hearing the waves lapping the shore had been bad enough. Now he had a full view of his nemesis.

Bushes rattled next to them, and a person stepped out with a gun drawn. "Freeze!"

He leveled his gun at the person. Ducky growled beside him, and Tori's hands flew into the air. It took a moment longer than normal, but his brain engaged. He lowered his Glock and patted the dog's head. "Leave it. Yo, MJ. Put the weapon away."

"Well, if it isn't Agent Lane, the prodigal son." MJ smiled and holstered her weapon.

"Not an agent anymore, and you know that." Yeah, he hadn't been an agent since the explosion, and it killed him to admit it. But MJ continued to call him that.

"Pfft. I've told you before, that's a technicality."

A rather large one, but he appreciated MJ's acceptance.

MJ eyed him from head to toe. "Looks like you ran into a bit of trouble since we saw you last night."

"That's an understatement. I'll give you the full rundown

once we get inside, but the bottom line is trouble found us, and I discovered a trap the hard way."

"Wesley told us about the body." MJ's eyes narrowed at his blood-soaked pant leg. "I want to hear the unabridged story, so let's get moving."

Their small group strode to the cabin.

"What are you still doing here?" For the first time since that morning, Michael relaxed—at least a bit.

"After meeting you here yesterday, we decided to use this place as a command center until we get word from our inside source."

"Any news on that front?"

MJ's head swung side to side. "Nothing. I'm hoping we hear soon."

Michael held on to the rail and limped up the stairs to the cabin.

Once inside, MJ pointed him toward the couch. Without arguing, he hobbled over and sank into the soft cushions, hoping his leg would function when he got up again. He patted the spot next to him, and Tori dropped into it. Her entire body sagged with what he could only guess was a relief to be off her feet.

MJ sat on the edge of the chair diagonal from him. "So, what happened out there?"

He launched into the details of their experience. When he got to the part about finding the young man's body, he noticed Tori's jaw twitch. He looked a bit closer. Her eyes glistened with tears. The story no doubt had brought back the memories of assuming the person who had died was Joey.

"Now you're caught up." Michael laid his head back. "It's been a long day."

MJ stood and pointed toward the bedrooms with en suites. "Why don't you two grab hot showers while I collect the first aid kit. Same rooms as last time."

He had no intention of putting up a fuss. His body ached, but more importantly, he had to clean the gashes on his leg before the dirt caused an infection. Tori had done her best, but with limited supplies, she couldn't do what a full wash with running hot water could. "Sounds like a plan."

Tori nodded. "Excuse me." She hurried from the room.

MJ watched her leave and flipped her gaze to him. "That woman is holding it together by the thinnest of threads."

"Do you blame her?" Of course Tori was on edge.

"No. But she needs someone to lean on, or she'll break." MJ glared at him, challenging him to disagree.

For the first time, Michael saw Tori for the hurting woman underneath the titanium wall she'd built around herself.

"I hear you. And I'll do what I can." Michael pushed to his feet and groaned.

MJ stood. "You good?"

"Just stiff. Take care of Ducky for me?"

She nodded. "I know where his food is. I'll get him fed and give him water."

"Thanks." He patted his dog on the head. "Stay with MJ."

Ducky's eyes shifted from him to his ex-partner from where he'd taken up residence by Michael's feet.

"Yes, you need to stay with MJ. I'll be back in a few." After a quick wave at MJ, he hobbled down the hall. He paused at Tori's door and lifted his hand to knock. Sobs came from the other side of the barrier. He dropped his hand and rested his forehead against the wood. MJ was right. *God, how do I get her to open up before she falls to pieces?*

The gut-wrenching sobs tore him to shreds. He cared for Tori more than any friend he had, even his ex-girlfriend.

He straightened at the realization that his heart had gotten involved. Something he'd vowed to never let happen again. And the fact had scared him more than he cared to admit.

Tori hugged her knees and let the tears flow. Exhausted from the hiking, the fact her son and his friend were missing and being strong her whole life. She wanted someone to share the burdens with. Ryan, the only person she'd ever entrusted with her deepest emotions, was gone. Had been for a long time. Even before he died, they'd lived in separate worlds. Him on deployment the majority of the time, and her raising his baby brother along with keeping the home front running. Being a military spouse wasn't easy, but when you're eighteen...that made everything even harder.

After her meltdown, she'd dragged herself to the shower and cleaned up. Working the brush through her hair, she stared at the woman in the mirror. When had life become a series of devastating events? Since forever. But to be honest, part of that was her fault. She'd built impenetrable walls after the first couple of years with her grandparents. Nana and Pops loved her, and she adored them, but the couple had struggled to raise a young girl. Terrified they'd give up and place her in foster care, Tori decided then and there to never put pressure on them for fear of losing the only family she had left in the world. The strain that was put on her as a teen had formed her independent, private mentality. A lifestyle she continued to cling to.

One last swipe of the brush, and she eyed her reflection. She'd hidden from reality long enough. After placing the brush on the counter, she made her way to the living room and spotted MJ in the kitchen.

"Feel better?" MJ stood at the counter pouring hot water into a mug.

"Much." Tori scanned the rooms. "Where's Michael?"

MJ jutted her chin to the back door. "Out on the porch."

"Did he take care of his leg?" She'd intended to help him, but her pity party had lasted longer than she planned.

"After he cleaned it in the shower, I put antibiotic ointment on the cuts and replaced the bandages for him. The gouges are ugly, but not serious. As long as it doesn't get infected, he'll be okay." The agent dunked her tea bag in the cup.

Tori deflated with relief. "Good. I was worried about him."

"As you should be." MJ's tone held a bite to it.

"Excuse me?" What had she done to deserve the woman's annoyance?

"Look. I'm sorry. I don't really know you, but I understand you. Holding the world at arm's length. Doing it all on your own. That was me until I met my husband. Not leaning on your own strength and letting someone help is freeing."

"I don't..." Don't what? Understand? She knew exactly what MJ was talking about. She'd relied on herself for so long, that she'd lost the ability to be anything but superficial to her friends. She'd kept her hurts, fears and dreams bottled up, never sharing with anyone. "It's not that easy."

"Sure it is." MJ rested her hip against the counter and sipped her tea. "You simply decide to open the door and let that man in." She tipped her chin toward the back deck.

She shook her head. "He doesn't need my pain. He has enough of his own."

The cup halted halfway to MJ's lips. "Michael talked to you?"

"Yes." She had no idea how much she should share without his permission.

"Huh. Then he trusts you. He allowed you to see his vulnerability. That's not easy for him. Don't you think he deserves the same from you?"

Ouch. This agent didn't pull any punches. "I'm not sure I know how."

MJ shrugged. "I can't tell you what to do. That's something you have to choose. But I'll tell you this. That man is as kind and sweet as they come. He's sacrificed a lot to help others but doesn't feel worthy of praise. And with the person after you, and Joey and Kurt still missing, it's most likely making matters worse." The agent strode over and patted Tori on the shoulder. "Just think about it. I'll be in the study working if you need me."

Tori watched MJ saunter off and replayed the conversation

in her mind. Michael had trusted her with his secrets that he'd kept from the guys in his unit. She knew firsthand how tight those men were. If he found it within himself to be vulnerable with her, then maybe she could let him in.

Not giving herself time to think, she eased onto the back porch. Her eyes raked over her surroundings. With the lake in front of her and the woods to the right, her steps faltered. Being out in the open plucked at every one of her nerves. The person who'd targeted her was still at large, and Joey and Kurt remained missing. Even with her mind spiraling out of control on her situations, she owed the man who'd saved her life, so she wrangled her panic into submission.

Michael stood there, white-knuckled grip on the railing, staring at the water.

"Hey, how's the ankle?"

He shifted to face her. Tension lined his features. His jaw clenched to the point she worried he'd break a tooth.

She hurried to his side. "Michael, what's wrong?"

He jerked his head toward the lake.

Oh. She closed her eyes. How had she missed it? His PTSD with the water nearby. "From what you shared, I know the lake isn't comfortable for you. Why are you out here?"

"Trying to tell myself that I can be near water and not panic."

She ran a hand down his arm. "And how's that working out for you?"

He chuckled, but there was no humor to it. "It's not." He stiffened. His eyes narrowed as he studied the woods. Lacing his fingers with hers, he tugged on her hand. "I don't trust your attacker. Let's move out of sight from prying eyes."

Without hesitation, Tori followed him to the covered portion of the porch and eased onto the love seat. "If you're not dealing with it well, then why are you out here?"

"I have to do this." He returned his attention to the water lapping along the shore.

A soothing sound to her under normal circumstances, but for someone who'd endured the injuries and pain he had… "You know, a wise man once told me, you don't have to be strong all the time."

"I'm thinking he's not trustworthy when it comes to advice like that. He always falls short of what people need. Why would you listen to him?"

Tori grabbed his bicep and jerked him to face her. Michael had been nothing but supportive. He'd risked his life to save her and Andrew. He planned to continue the search for Joey and Kurt even though he'd hurt his shoulder and cut up his leg. "Why would you say that?"

He shrugged off her grip and stared at the ground. "I've never been enough. I blew it with my ex-girlfriend, and she ran off and married my best friend. Well, my ex-best friend now. You lost your husband because I didn't keep Ryan safe. I should have noticed the warnings but didn't. Then I went off the deep end and took home every girl I could find while on deployment. And Remember Doug Olsen? His wife, Tabitha—who wasn't his wife at the time—about lost her life when I missed the danger signs and got caught in the boat explosion. I messed up, and she had no one to turn to. I'm just happy it worked out, and Doug came to her rescue. And let's not forget how I disappointed my parents by not following their plan for my life. They disowned me when I joined the Army to get away from the pressure, and then when I didn't re-up, I went into law enforcement. Another thing they wouldn't have approved of. But by then it didn't matter. I'd already lost them."

Running out of steam in his rant, he ran a hand along the back of his neck. "I just couldn't stand the thought of a business degree and taking over my dad's accounting firm. I would have died inside sitting at a desk all day. But look what all that got me."

"Michael, you didn't cause Ryan to die. And you can't anticipate everything like the explosion. Sure, dating all those women wasn't the best choice, but from what you've told me, you owned it and moved on. You're not that man anymore." She rested her hand on his shoulder. "As for your parents, no one should be told what to do with their life. That was your decision, not theirs. They should never have put that pressure on you. And they are the ones who threw away the opportunity to know their honorable and selfless son. That's not on you."

He sat in silence for several minutes. His eyes darted back and forth at a spot in the distance as if searching for an answer. "Maybe. It doesn't excuse that I haven't kept you safe or found Joey yet."

"You and Ducky are here trying to rescue my son. It's not your fault he's missing." Her heart hurt for her son, and her fear they wouldn't find him alive consumed her thoughts, but this man hadn't let her down. He had to know that. "No, we haven't found Joey and Kurt, but I'm alive because of you. You're an amazing man. Why can't you see that?" She'd shake sense into the man if she thought it would work.

His gaze met hers. "Is that your honest opinion or are you saying what you think I need to hear?"

The words slapped her across the face. "Why would you say that?"

He exhaled. "You tend to show people what you want them to see, not necessarily what is true."

Okay, so that hurt. But he wasn't wrong. Tori had a decision to make. Tear down her self-constructed walls or stick with the status quo. Michael had confided in her about his fears and self-doubt. He deserved to see the real her. But the idea scared her to death. She hadn't been the authentic Tori since her youth. Except with Ryan. Even then, she'd held back so he could do his job in the Army without worrying about her or Joey.

"I'm telling the truth. You *are* an incredible man. I'm sorry

you feel like you have to question me. I want to change that."
She pushed the love seat glider into motion. Tucked away next
to the house gave her a modicum sense of security, but being
outside sent shivers racing up her spine. She wanted to continue the discussion, so she stuffed down her concerns. Michael wouldn't put her in danger.

His gaze scanned the area. He must have felt the exposure
too. "I didn't mean to put you on the spot."

She shook her head and gripped the cushion on either side
of her legs. "You didn't. Of all people, you deserve honesty."

He stayed quiet, for which she was grateful. The silence allowed her a moment to gather her thoughts.

"Before my parents died in a car crash, according to my
mother, I was a motormouth. She'd laugh at my nonstop talking, but she never made me feel bad. She listened for as long
as I had something to say." A smile tugged on Tori's lips. The
memories warmed her insides. Oh, how she missed her mom
and dad. Years had passed, but she hadn't forgotten the love
they shared as a family. "I had dreams. Big dreams. I wanted
to become an actress. Dad signed me up for acting and dance
lessons. He made sure I had everything I needed to succeed.
Then the car accident happened that took both of them from
me. I went to live with my grandparents. They're wonderful
people, but older than the average grandparents for someone
my age. They weren't prepared for a sulky preteen. I was too
much for them to handle at their age."

Michael placed his hand on hers. "I'd say they did a pretty
good job raising you."

"They did." She stared at his hand. The touch sent warmth
flooding through her chest. The simple act of support brought
tears to her eyes. "At that point, I realized I had to make life
easier for Nana and Pops. I stopped my race car of a mouth
and never complained. I was too worried they'd either send
me away, or I'd cause them to leave me like Mom and Dad

had. So, I took the burden off them. I kept everything inside and never, not once, gave them any reason for concern. From that day on, I refused to ask for help."

"That had to be tough on a young girl."

"Especially one who loved to think out loud. But I did what I had to do and became independent and private."

He smoothed his thumb over the back of her hand. "What about your dreams?" His attention split between her and their surroundings. He hadn't stopped his visual perimeter check since she'd joined him on the porch.

Her stomach flip-flopped at the reason for his alertness. Joey had rarely left the forefront of her mind. She chuffed. "Yeah, those days are gone."

"Why?" He shifted on the seat to face her.

"I have a son and bills to pay. Plus, dreams change with age and experiences." Her pulse increased. Would she have a son to worry about once this—whatever this was—was over? She forced down her wayward thoughts. "I'm not that same girl anymore."

"What's your new dream?" He flipped their hands and laced their fingers together.

Tori couldn't deny how wonderful the connection felt. She considered his question for a moment, not wanting to brush off the answer. "I guess I'd like to find someone to share life with. I've been on my own for so long. Sure Ryan and I had a few years, but we were rarely on the same continent."

"I can understand that. Deployment is tough for those overseas. But it's hard on those at home too." Michael continued to rub his thumb in circles on the back of her hand. "Take that wish a little farther. If you can find that special person, would you want more kids?"

Tears sprang to her eyes. When she was a teen, she hadn't questioned whether or not she'd have children. She'd wanted a houseful. Being an only child had sparked that desire. But her only son was missing, and she wanted him back with a desperation she couldn't put into words. Thinking about a life without him tore her to pieces. "I just want Joey back."

"I know, Red. And I want him back in your arms too. But when he comes home. What about then?"

Would she ever wrap her arms around her son again? She sighed and focused on Michael's question. "Probably not as many as I originally wanted, but yes. I'd love to have a few more kids." The older she got she knew that might not happen.

"What else do you want in life?"

Even with her life out of control, the comfort of Michael's touch made her believe in things she thought she'd never have. Like total honesty with someone. "I confess. I'm tired of being and doing what everyone expects of me. I want to be able to be myself."

"I'd like it if you'd let me see the real you."

Tori swallowed the emotion that had built up. She might want that, but she wasn't quite ready to agree to show her true self. Time to place the focus on anywhere but her. "Enough about me. What about you?"

He jolted. "What about me?"

"What do you want to do with your life now that you are no longer with the DEA?"

His thumb stopped moving, and he straightened in his seat. "My job is over not by choice but by necessity. I don't have a backup plan. And at the moment, it's hard to look beyond my physical and psychological limitations."

"Don't be so hard on yourself. It seems as though you've focused so much on what you can't do that you haven't considered what you *can* do." Why couldn't this man see what she and everyone else could?

"Maybe. I just feel worthless. Especially now with Joey and Kurt still out there."

Just like that her own pain fell away and her heart shattered for him. "Oh, Michael. Don't attach your worth to your job.

You'll find another career that you love. I know you will." She placed her hand on his arm. "You'll figure it out. And I know you'll find Joey and Kurt." She believed it. She had to. Anything else would rip both of them to shreds.

"Maybe we can help each other figure out life once we find the boys."

"I'd like that." The idea of sharing her struggles with someone soothed something deep inside her.

Michael's muscles tightened under her fingers.

"What's wrong?" She studied his face. Something had brought forth the intensity of the agent and military man he'd once been.

His gaze scanned the tree line. He stood. "We've stayed outside too long."

She spun toward the area beyond the cabin. "What did you see?"

"Nothing." His eyes narrowed at a spot in the distance. "But I've got a hinky feeling, and it's not going away. I want you inside."

"Then let's go." She followed him through the back door.

He flipped the dead bolt and turned out the lights as he moved to the living room.

MJ stepped from the office with John beside her. She halted when she came face-to-face with Michael. "What?"

"We're exposed."

"Got it." MJ grabbed John's arm and pulled him toward the front door. Tori had no idea what secret language the two had used. "You play invisible, and we'll play the happy couple." The two agents disappeared outside.

"Care to explain?" Tori waved a hand toward the door.

"If anyone's watching, they'll see MJ and John. A couple enjoying a vacation. Hopefully, that will hide our presence here."

"Makes sense." Assuming the attacker hadn't followed them to the cabin. Tori exhaled. The past couple of days had been too much for her sanity. She sat on the couch in the dim light while the agents did their thing and wondered how a simple camping trip had turned into a nightmare.

Chapter Eight

After securing the Velcro straps on Ducky's vest, Michael stepped from the cabin into the crisp morning air and let the dog explore. He blinked the lingering haze from his vision. Sleep had eluded him last night. His ankle had ached no matter what position he tried to lay, and his mind reeled from his run-away mouth. A mental and physical combination that wasn't conducive to rest. He'd shared more with Tori than he'd ever done with anyone since the horrible day his parents told him not to return home—ever.

He'd shocked himself when he opened up to Tori about his medical issues and his PTSD. He'd broken the promise he'd made to himself that he wouldn't release that information to anyone. Then this situation with Tori came along to bring them closer, and apparently, he couldn't stop talking. But he had to admit, a weight had lifted yesterday when Tori had defended him.

He took a deep breath, allowing the cool fall air to clear the remaining cobwebs from his brain that the two cups of coffee had missed. The sensation of someone watching had disappeared at some point during the night, but he refused to dismiss the possibility. He scanned the edge of the property, searching for a clue as to what might have caused the internal warning.

"Hey, everything okay?" Tori joined him on the front porch. She zipped the winter jacket MJ had brought her then shoved her hands into the pockets and bounced on her toes. "It's getting downright chilly out here."

"I checked the weather this morning. Daytime temps are dropping, but it won't hit freezing for a couple more days. Nights are cold, but not deadly—yet." He prayed they found Joey and Kurt before the cold front that promised snow hit. Otherwise, his assurance that he'd locate the teens might turn a rescue into a recovery.

Tori scraped her teeth along her bottom lip. A gesture he'd come to recognize as a sign of *I'm worried, but will never say it out loud.* "If we don't find the boys soon, they won't be alive, will they?"

How did a person answer that question when a mother asked? He sighed. "Since we've opened the door to honesty between us, I'm not going to sugarcoat it. We have to find them soon, or it'll be a recovery if they're out in the elements when the storm hits."

Tori gasped.

Maybe he misjudged the situation and shouldn't have been so blunt. "I'm sorry. But I didn't figure you'd want it painted in bright colors and lies." His dog returned to his side and sat next to him like a sentry. He ran his fingers through Ducky's fur. Michael hadn't pushed to start their search due to the low-lying fog that had rolled in during the early morning hours. But now that it had begun to burn off, it was time to move.

She stared at the woods that created the boundary to the property. "As hard as it is to hear, I'd rather know the truth."

He nodded. "I figured that."

Her shoulders sagged and she shifted to face him. "When are we leaving?"

"Five minutes?" He had to grab the pack he'd placed by the rocking chair to his right, but other than that, he was ready for the search. He hadn't wanted to waste time once the fog lifted.

"That works for me. I'll go finish getting ready." Tori entered the cabin, leaving him alone on the porch.

"Duck, my man. I hope you're ready to work. We're running out of time."

The dog looked at him, panting with his normal doggy smile.

"You are the happiest guy I've ever known." Michael scratched him under the chin. "God blessed me the day he put you in my life." He knew of people with PTSD who had service dogs but hadn't considered his mental state severe enough. Boy had he been wrong. Ducky had changed his quality of life.

The cabin door squeaked open, and Tori rejoined him. "I'm good to go when you are."

"Then let's get to it." He slid his backpack on and pointed to the tree line. "I want to take a look over there before we start our search."

"You think someone watched us from there last night." Tori hadn't asked but stated what he feared.

"Yes. But that poses a lot of questions. Why hover and not attack? It seems out of character for the person determined to hurt you." Michael clomped down the steps and headed toward his target.

Tori strode next to him. "I hadn't thought of that."

Too many things weren't adding up. They approached the trees, and his ingrained instincts kicked in.

He held out his arm, stopping Tori. "Red, hang back and let me examine the area first. Ducky, stay." Michael commanded the dog and moved toward the trees. At the edge of the foliage, he knelt and stared at a spot on the ground.

"What did you find?"

"A boot print." He air-traced the imprint with his finger but didn't touch the evidence. He stood and pivoted until he positioned himself in the line of sight. Same as the person who'd left the print. Michael scanned the cabin and the surrounding property. Someone with a large shoe size had stood here facing the cabin with a full view of the back deck, including the tucked away corner where they'd sat. A shiver zipped down his spine. He and Tori had spent a lot of time out there. The person could have easily taken a shot, either with a gun or a crossbow, and hit their target without an issue. Why hadn't they?

Michael joined Tori and Ducky. "I'm not sure what to make of it, but there is no doubt that someone watched us last night."

Tori rubbed her arms. "To what end?" He hated the distress in her tone. The woman had enough to worry about without adding a stalker to the mix.

"I have no clue. The whole thing doesn't make sense." A killer and a stalker? He shook his head. No, that didn't compute.

She bumped her shoulder to his. "I'm glad I'm not the only one confused."

He had to smile. He liked seeing this side of her. The one that said what she thought instead of measuring every word or action. "We should get Ducky to work, then we can brainstorm." Among other conversations. Her lack of faith bothered him, and he planned to uncover why she'd turned away from her beliefs.

"Then let's do it."

Michael removed the bag with a stocking cap inside. "We ran with the T-shirt yesterday. I'm afraid he'll take us back to the same spot so I'm giving him a new scent. Let's hope the two boys are together."

Her shoulders drooped. "I know I shouldn't put priority of Joey over Kurt, but it's hard not to."

Hand on her arm, he squeezed. "Don't do that. It's not that you don't care about Kurt. Your mother's heart is aching for Joey, and that's okay. I have every intention of locating both of them."

"Thank you. I guess I'm losing faith that we'll find them."

Tucking that choice of words away, he opened the bag and

held it out to Ducky. "Check." The dog got a good whiff. Michael turned to Tori. "Ready?"

She nodded.

"Find."

Ducky's nose went in the air, and he took off through the woods.

"Come on." He gestured for her to join him and followed his dog. Branches reached out like fingers to grab them and tangled roots threatened to trip them as they hurried to keep up with his dog. Sweat trickled down his temples, even with the temperatures hovering in the low forties.

Twenty minutes had passed and Ducky stayed on the scent. Tori had paced alongside him or directly behind him, pending the width of the trail. Her heavy breathing concerned Michael, but they didn't have the luxury of stopping often. Which was a bummer since his ankle throbbed in time with his heartbeat. But he shoved the discomfort aside. His number one goal—to find Joey and Kurt, no matter how much pain he was in.

He turned his focus to Tori and the discussion he was determined to have. "Since we have a moment, I have a question for you."

Her boots crunched beside him. "What do you want to ask me? You know all my secrets now."

Not all of them. "I know you and Ryan shared a belief in God. He talked about it a lot. At the time, I didn't understand, but now I do. What happened to your faith?"

Tori stumbled.

Michael grabbed her elbow before she fell. "Red?"

The lingering silence killed him. He wanted more than anything for her to open up. But he knew how to be patient and give her time—he didn't like it, but that's what she needed. So, he waited.

Ducky zigzagged his way deeper into the trees then back

to the narrow dirt path—over and over. A strange behavior, but the dog appeared to be on the trail.

Tori released a heavy sigh. "It's not that I don't believe anymore."

"Then what is it?" He slowed his pace. Ducky wouldn't get too far ahead. Of that he was sure. The dog hated for Michael to be out of sight for long.

"I suppose the best way to explain it is that my trust in God evaporated. Life got hard when I lost Ryan. And with everything that had happened with my parents and grandparents, I didn't believe He cared anymore."

Michael tugged her to a stop. "So, you literally did everything on your own? No help from anyone with your day-to-day living, plus you muscled through the hurt without turning to God?"

She lowered her gaze to the ground. "That about sums it up."

He placed his finger under her chin and lifted. "Red, He hasn't turned His back on you. You can trust Him to ease the pain."

"Then why has everything in my life been so hard?" Her voice rose with each word.

Michael rubbed his hand up and down her arm. "I can't answer that. But I do know that God has big shoulders. Be honest with Him. Tell Him you're angry, and let Him comfort you."

Tori closed her eyes and shook her head. "It's not that easy."

"But it is." He slid his hand into hers and laced their fingers together. "Let me ask you this. If you got mad at me, would you walk away or would you tell me about it?" He knew exactly what she'd do. He'd lived it several times since they'd met years ago.

"Oh, I'd tell you about it, all right." The corner of her mouth tipped upward.

"I have no doubt about that. I've heard you lay into Ryan, and I have my own battle scars from your ire." He chuckled at the glare he received. "Face it, you're the stereotypical red-head. That gorgeous red hair is a warning."

She playfully backhanded him in the stomach.

"Oof. Thanks a lot." He rubbed the spot where her light tap had struck.

"You deserved it."

He smiled, happy to see her out of her funk, even if it was temporary. "I admit it. I did."

The crease in her forehead deepened. "I'm not that bad, am I?"

"No, Red, you're not." He cupped her cheek and stared into her blue eyes, mesmerized by the intensity he found there.

"Why do you call me that?"

"Red?"

"Yes. Ryan never did, so it's not like you picked it up from him."

The nickname was for him and him alone. He recognized the truth now. How did he explain that no matter what he'd promised his friend, he'd teetered on the edge of feelings for Tori for the last couple of years?

"It's not very original, but that name for you is mine." He lifted a strand of her hair that had escaped her cap and held it between his fingers. "Your hair—it's beautiful just like you." Staring at her mouth, he wondered what kissing this woman would be like. He leaned closer. The snap of twigs broke the moment. He stepped back and glanced over his shoulder.

Ducky ran full speed toward them, a snarl on his lips.

Michael reached for his Glock and tucked Tori behind him, searching for what had triggered his dog.

One minute Tori had peeled away another layer of herself to Michael about her lack of trust in God. The next she'd melted into a puddle at his touch. No one had touched her like that for years. He'd cut through the walls she'd constructed since her youth and had shown her she wasn't alone. And she thought for a second that Michael had planned to kiss her. Then Ducky came out of nowhere breaking the connection, sending fear racing through her veins.

The dog grabbed Michael's shirt in his teeth and yanked him toward the dense foliage. Her fingers twisted into the fabric of the back of his shirt, terrified to let go. She'd temporarily forgotten about her troubles. A nice reprieve, but reality had returned front and center.

"What's wrong with Ducky?"

"I have no idea, but I'm not ignoring his warning. Stay quiet." Michael placed a hand on the dog's head. "I'm coming, boy."

Ducky let go but nudged his leg as if to say, *Hurry up.*

Tori followed Michael into the trees, never releasing her grip.

"Get down out of sight," he whispered.

She lowered to her knees on the cold ground. The chill seeped through her fleece-lined leggings. A shiver slithered from her legs to the top of her head. A reminder that a cold front was heading their way.

Once she had moved out of sight from the trail and ducked behind a large pile of brush, Michael crouched beside her. She didn't miss the grimace. The pull on his ankle had to be killing him. She tapped him on the shoulder. When he turned his head to face her, she mouthed, "Are you okay?"

He leaned into her ear. "I'll be fine."

The warmth of his breath rushed across her cheek. Her heart rate increased. The man turned her inside out. Not because of his handsome good looks, although, that didn't hurt. Seriously, who wouldn't be attracted to the six-foot, brown-haired, brown-eyed, swoon-worthy man? But that wasn't what had her giving up her solitary mindset. It was Michael's protective side. His heart—the size of Alaska. The man cared for people, and she'd trust him any day of the week. He was that solid. Now, if only he'd realize it.

A low rumble came from Ducky, who lay next to Michael. "Shh, boy." Michael laid his hand on the dog's back.

Voices filtered through the trees and along the path.

Tori peeked through the branches, careful not to expose herself. Two men with guns roamed the trail. One was taller than Michael, the other a bit shorter. Both scanned their surroundings as they walked.

"We need to finish our perimeter check and get back. Boss has plans for us."

"Did he say what?"

The tall guy shook his head. "No. I think he has plans for us to *clean up* his dirty work, if you catch my drift."

"I hate doing that. Let me run the drugs all day long. Anything but *that*."

"He learned the business from Tommy Wade. What do you expect?"

"Fine. I don't like it, but I'm not going to be next on his list."

The tall guy slapped the shorter one on the back. "Then let's get this over with."

The two disappeared around a curve in the path.

A little while later, Michael checked his watch. She peered at his wrist. Twenty minutes had passed since the two men had moved out of sight.

"Do you think it's safe?"

Michael glanced down at Ducky, who lay happily panting by his side. "Seems to be if Duck's mood is any indication."

"Speaking of, do you think he reacted that way because of those men?" Her legs had cramped. The need to move overwhelmed her. But she refused to be the weak link and get them killed. Michael had to be in worse shape than her.

He nodded. "That's my guess. And from the sounds of it, we're close to the drug traffickers' location."

That concept made her queasy. "Since Ducky searched in that direction, do you think he hit on one of the boys?"

Michael pursed his lips and exhaled. "I do, but those men

concern me. We're too close to the drug trail to continue without backup."

"So, what are we going to do?"

"I think we should lay low until the drug bust."

"Do we know when the raid is planned?"

"Last I heard, it was tonight. I'll give MJ a quick call to confirm."

A couple minutes later, Michael pocketed his SAT phone. "Tonight is a go."

"Until then?"

"I hate to say it, but we backtrack a bit and find a secluded place to wait."

"You know best." Her stomach dropped at the thought of waiting any longer to find her son and Kurt. However, Michael's experience trumped hers.

He grunted.

She cocked a brow, challenging him to argue with her. Because this was a fight she'd win. She was done allowing him to degrade himself.

Arms crossed over his chest, Michael met her gaze. "Fine. I'd like to set up far enough to stay out of the way, but not so far we can't jump in as soon as the task force clears the area."

"Like I said, you know what's best. I'll follow your lead." She motioned for him to go ahead.

Ducky stuck close to Michael's leg as he limped in the direction from where they'd come.

What was that old saying? Two steps forward, one step back. Tori glanced over her shoulder toward where Ducky had alerted. The urge to scream and ignore better judgment to find her boys hung heavy over her.

Stuffing the impulse away, Tori trudged after Michael. Desperation had set in, but common sense stood strong. She wouldn't do anything to get the boys killed.

As they walked the narrow dirt path, ducking branches and dodging fallen trees, the conversation about God rolled in her mind. For the first time in years, Tori considered praying. Her boy was out there with an attacker on the loose, and at the moment, she was helpless to do anything about it.

Chapter Nine

"Police."
"Police."
"Put down your weapons."
"Freeze."

A cacophony of commands penetrated the air not far from where Michael had tucked Tori out of sight. The pair had sat along with Ducky for several hours waiting for this moment. When MJ had confirmed the time of the raid, he and Tori moved closer. He had no intention of delaying the search longer than he had to. He'd maintained a safe distance, but the noises seemed to bounce around the dense forest.

Gunshots rang out, accompanied by more shouting.

Michael jerked with each crack of gunfire. His heart rate increased and sweat beaded on his upper lip. His body anticipated an explosion. He closed his eyes and took three deep breaths to stave off a panic attack.

A weight pressed against his chest, and fur tickled his face. Ducky lay on him with his snout resting in the crook of Michael's neck. Deep pressure therapy. Another untrained task Ducky performed. God had known what Michael needed. He couldn't be more grateful for this dog. The heaviness of

Ducky's body, similar to a weighted blanket, kept Michael grounded in reality away from the horrors of his past.

"Michael?" Tori's voice pulled him out of his drifting.

He blinked, bringing his surroundings into focus. The concern in the depths of her blue eyes twisted his heart. "I'm okay, Red. I promise."

She scraped her bottom lip with her teeth. "If you're sure."

"I am." Or he would be once his anxiety faded. He tilted his ear in the direction of the raid. Things had quieted down, but loud voices remained a staple at the scene. His phone vibrated in his pocket. He dug it out and held it up to Tori. "It's MJ. Hold on." He tapped the accept button and put the phone to his ear. "MJ?"

"We have everyone that we've found in custody. But Joey and Kurt aren't among them. Normally, I wouldn't let a civilian come close, and I'm referring to Tori, not you. But with that storm coming in, those boys have to be found soon. Get Ducky over here."

"We're on it. I don't have anything denoting search and rescue, so tell your team not to get trigger-happy."

"As if. We're better than that, and you know it. But I'll pass the word." The line went dead.

Michael shook his head at her ridiculousness. Oh, how he missed working with that woman. "MJ cleared us to go in. Stick by my side. They're still working. We don't want to get in the way."

"I'll agree to almost anything if it means finding Joey and Kurt." She scrambled to her feet and extended her hand.

He stared at her small fingers. The anticipation of agony thrumming through his leg had him holding back. But he had a job to do, and he refused to let Tori down—again. He accepted her offer and grasped her hand. Hauling himself to his feet was an experience in pain. He'd sat too long. His ankle had stiffened and the cuts pulled. A long stream of air blew through his pursed lips, settling the intensity.

Tori gripped his hand tighter but said nothing.

Once the initial zing of pain dimmed, he took a deep breath. "Ducky."

The dog pushed on his leg.

"Ready to work, boy?"

Ducky's tail whacked against the log Michael and Tori had used as a backrest.

Michael removed the stocking hat that led them here from his pocket. He had switched up the scent items since Ducky had found the body with the T-shirt. "Check."

His dog sniffed and stuck his nose in the air. The furry antennas otherwise known as ears twitched.

With the hat tucked away, Michael held out his arm, palm up. "Find."

Ducky took off like a shot.

He turned to Tori. "Remember, stay close." After she nodded, he hurried after Ducky, trusting her to keep her word and not stray from his side.

The moon glowed in the night sky, giving the scene an eerie vibe. Law enforcement officers swarmed the area. On a mission, Ducky appeared oblivious to the chaos and wove around agents and handcuffed drug runners sitting on the ground. Michael hobbled as fast as possible with Tori next to him. The questioning looks would have been comical if the situation was different. Ducky zoomed into the woods and out of sight. A moment later, a single bark filled the night air.

"Is that his signal that he found someone?"

"Yes. And unlike last time, there's no whining." During one other search and rescue he and Ducky had performed, besides the guy they found in the pile of leaves, the person hadn't survived the initial fall. Ducky had the same reaction. He barked and then whined. Almost as if the dog mourned the death.

"Meaning?"

"The person is alive."

Tori stumbled, caught herself, and continued to jog along-side him. He hadn't missed the quick intake of air.

They rounded the curve where Ducky had disappeared mo-ments ago and found him sitting in front of a section of brush. Michael slowed and moved next to his dog, patting him on the head. "Good boy."

The dog laid down and did his doggy army crawl thing to-ward the brush.

Tori flanked Michael's other side. "What's he doing?"

"Hang right here. Don't come closer until I know what's going on." Michael drew his Glock and held it at his side. No need to startle anyone by aiming at the targeted area, but he wanted to be prepared for anything. He moved closer and crouched beside Ducky's head. Using his phone flashlight, he swept the tangle of branches.

Wide eyes stared at him. The young man pushed backward in a poor attempt to increase the distance between them. The guy reminded him of a trapped animal.

He crouched on the balls of his feet but positioned his in-jured leg out a bit to ease the ache. He kept his tone soft and smiled. "You must be Kurt."

If possible, the kid's eyes got bigger.

"I'm Michael, and this furball—" he brushed his hand down Ducky's head and neck "—is Ducky. We're search and rescue."

"You're Agent Lane, aren't you?" The kid's teeth chattered.

He wanted to get the teen out and warmed up, but he wouldn't rush it. "Just Michael Lane. I'm no longer with the DEA."

"Joey talks about you and how you've hung out with him after his papa Ryan died."

"He's a good kid. Speaking of, do you know where he is?"

"You mean, you haven't found him?"

Michael shook his head. "We need your help. Andrew fell and hit his head. He's alive and at the hospital. He woke up for a moment but wasn't able to give us any information. Do you have any idea where Joey is?"

"No. When the man took him, we got separated."

There was more to that statement, but for now, his priority was Kurt. "I'd like to hear more about what happened, but I have someone with me who's anxious to see you."

"Who is it?"

"Tori Campbell. We've been trying to find you since you disappeared from the campsite."

"Mrs. C?" There was a noticeable wobble in the teen's voice.

Michael smiled. "She's right behind me, waiting for us. Rather anxiously I might add. What do you say we get you out of the brush so she can see for herself that you're okay?"

The teen cradled his left arm against his middle and scooted on his rear toward Michael.

"What happened to your shoulder?" He shined the flashlight at the discoloration on the teen's shirt.

Kurt wiggled from his hiding spot, and Michael helped him to stand.

The kid wobbled.

He put his arm around the boy's waist. Only then did he realize the severity of the shivers racking Kurt's body. Whether from the temperatures or shock, warming the teen up shot toward the top of the to-do list.

"Thanks." Kurt leaned into Michael for support. "The guy who took Joey shot at me and hit me in the shoulder."

"Once Mrs. C hugs you and sees for herself that you're alive and, all things considered, well, we'll get you a blanket and have the paramedics take a look at that wound."

"Something to drink and eat would be appreciated too."

Michael chuckled. "I think that could be arranged." The duo took two steps toward Tori.

Her hands flew to her mouth and a small squeak emerged. She hurried to Kurt and threw her arms around him.

The kid grunted at the impact then tucked his face in the

crook of her neck and sobbed. The outward emotions of the teenage boy gutted Michael.

"You're okay. I've got you." Tori rubbed her hand up and down the kid's back. "We'll get you to the hospital and call your parents. Everything's okay now." Tears streamed down her cheeks. Her pleading eyes met Michael's.

He nodded. "Red's right. You'll be home soon."

Kurt lifted his head from Tori's shoulder and sniffed several times. "You call her Red?"

"Out of everything going on, that's what you latch on to?" Michael gaped at the kid.

The teen shrugged then grimaced.

"Well, you have seen the color of her hair, right?"

"Oh, yeah, and the temper that comes with it." Kurt cringed. "Sorry, Mrs. C."

For the first time since the search and rescue ordeal started, Tori laughed. A full-on belly laugh. She flanked his other side. "You're not wrong. Come on. Let's get you checked out." She tipped her chin to see over Kurt's head. "There's an ambulance or something here, right?"

"Or something. Paramedics should be on-site, but they use a different mode of transportation out here. A medic unit wouldn't make it through the woods, even with the path cut by the drug runners." Michael moved the three of them plus Ducky in the direction of where he expected the medical help to have set up.

"Whatever is available to help Kurt is fine. I want him taken care of." The mama bear inside Tori had begun to peek its head out.

"I won't lie, Mrs. C. My shoulder hurts, and I'm cold and hungry. But I'm okay."

"And you'll stay that way." Tori's statement held a "don't argue with me" tone.

When they approached the hubbub of activity, MJ strolled over along with John Smith. "Ducky was right again."

"That he was. MJ, John, this is Kurt. Kurt, I'd like you to meet Agent Melissa Jones aka MJ, and her partner, Agent John Smith."

"I can't tell you how awesome it is to meet you." Michael felt the tension release in Kurt's body.

MJ chuckled. "I'm sure it is."

"Medics are this way." John waved at them to follow. "Later on, we'll need a statement from you, Kurt, but at the moment, we're focused on the drug traffickers."

Kurt looked to Michael for approval.

He nodded. "After the paramedics assess his injuries, I have my own questions. How about you guys wait until he's at the hospital for your statement?"

"That works for me. There's no rush since we got this mess to clear out." MJ slapped Michael on the back. "You'll let us know if the information he has is something we should be aware of?"

"Of course." Michael knew the importance of collecting evidence and witness statements. He'd lived that life for years. He'd help MJ and John in any way he could.

"Then we'll leave you to it and get on with arresting these slimeballs." MJ patted Michael on the back again, then she and John strolled away.

Kurt watched the duo leave and turned to face Michael. "She's scary."

Michael chuckled. "Can be. But she's one of the best at what she does." He pointed to the all-terrain vehicle not far away where the medics stood. "Over there." A few moments later, he helped Kurt to sit on the ATV bed.

The paramedics slung a wool blanket over Kurt's shoulders, set up an IV and got busy treating him. A through and through bullet hole to the teen's shoulder. Michael prayed the damage was minimal. "Ready to tell us what happened?"

Kurt's Adam's apple bobbed. "Mrs. C had gone to bed and the three of us stayed up talking. We had just put out the fire when a man came out of nowhere swinging a log at us. I don't remember much until he took us by gunpoint into the woods. Joey elbowed the guy in the face and yelled at us to run. Andrew and I took off. I looked back and saw him clock Joey over the head with the butt of the gun. Then he aimed it at us and fired. He hit me in the shoulder. Andrew came back to help, but I told him to hide and go for help as soon as he could and that I'd do the same. So, we split up. I had no idea what happened to Joey or Andrew after that. I just tried to survive until help arrived. Then I ran into the drug runners' territory and couldn't escape without being seen."

The kid had endured incredible pain but had kept his wits about him. Michael hated to push, but the more he knew the better. They still had to find Joey. And based on Kurt's recollection, Tori's son was in trouble.

Tori's eyes filled with tears at Kurt's account of the attack at the campsite. Her Joey hadn't escaped the madman's clutches. And the worst part, no one had a clue where the assailant had taken her son. Why didn't she stay and fight? She mentally chided herself. Because if she had, they'd probably all be dead. Her gaze drifted to the night sky. Trees rose up around her and the moon shone bright, illuminating the area where the task force took custody of the drug runners. The stars dotted the black background, pulling her attention from the conversation. Her mind wandered to her once strong faith in God. When had she turned her back on Him?

It had started when Ryan returned home injured with the TBI that had changed him. She'd maintained her relationship with God, but as time passed, she focused on doing everything herself. The day-to-day communication had slowly disappeared until it was nonexistent. Could she trust God again and regain a relationship with Him?

"I want to transport him as soon as possible. That gunshot

wound requires more than what I'm trained for." The para-medic's words refocused Tori on Kurt.

"I understand. But I'd like to go through his story one more time before you leave." Michael folded his arms across his chest. "Do we have time for that?"

The second medic nodded as he adjusted Kurt's IV. "Make it quick."

"What else do you need to know?" Kurt adjusted the sling supporting his arm with the gunshot wound.

"I'm clear on the events at the campsite and immediately after. But where it gets thin is between you running from the attacker and how you ended up hiding in those bushes over there." Michael jerked his head in the direction they'd come from.

Kurt sighed. The poor kid sounded like he had the weight of the world pushing down on him. She tamped down the urge to wrap him in a hug but clasped his hand and held tight instead.

"At first, I tucked in between a couple of boulders and prayed the man who took Joey wouldn't find me. I put pres-sure on my shoulder to stop the bleeding but ended up passing out. When I woke in the morning, cold and in pain, I knew I had to get help. Not only for Joey and Andrew, but myself too." Kurt stopped his rundown of the events. His eyes glazed over as if stuck in the past.

"You're doing good. Keep going so Michael has all the in-formation." She gave his fingers a gentle squeeze.

The teen's gaze shifted to her, and he nodded. "I tried to move as quietly as possible, but honestly, I doubt I succeeded. I was surprised the bleeding had stopped, but once I started moving again, it trickled down my arm. I got turned around in the woods. I thought I was heading toward the car, but instead, I ended up running into the drug traffickers' path. That's when I heard two guys arguing about drugs. I peeked out. One of them was wearing Joey's baseball cap. The hat he had on when the man took him." Kurt's forehead scrunched.

"Then one dude shot the other and buried him under leaves."
Kurt's eyes widened, and he turned to Tori. "Mrs. C. you have
to find that guy. You can't leave him out there. I should have
done something, but I didn't know what to do." The desperation in his tone tore her heart to shreds.

"Kurt, honey, you did the right thing by staying out of sight.
You couldn't have saved him. You would have only gotten
yourself killed." Her chest tightened, squeezing the air from
her lungs. She easily could have lost Kurt if he'd acted.

"Maybe."

"I'm right, and you know it." She brushed a strand of hair
off his forehead. "Officers recovered his body. You don't have
to worry about him any longer."

The kid's shoulders drooped. "I'm glad he's not laying out
there alone anymore."

Oh, the heart of this kid.

Michael cleared his throat. "Don't worry, the officers took
good care of him." He waited a moment to allow Kurt to regain his composure then continued. "Can you tell me what
happened next?"

Kurt winced when the paramedic cleaned around the wound
on his back. "I hid in the bushes until the guy with the gun
left."

"Was it the same man who took Joey?"

"No. Different guy. But he talked about his boss wanting
the man dead. Could the *boss* be the person who took Joey?"
Kurt's words slurred. The pain medication they'd put in his
IV started to take effect.

"It's possible. If you saw him again, could you identify
him?" Michael asked.

"I'll never forget his face or what he did." A lone tear trickled down the teen's cheek.

"Later, once you're on the mend, we'll work on a compos-
ite sketch."

Kurt closed his eyes and opened them. "I want to help, but I'm tired. Are we almost done?"

Tori raised a brow.

Michael nodded. "Just one last thing. How did you get to that hiding spot where Ducky found you?"

"As soon as the guy left, I ran. Again, the wrong way and ended up here. I crawled into the space and prayed for help."

"Sounds like someone listened to you." Michael patted the kid's knee and smiled.

The corner of Kurt's mouth tipped upward. "Happy for that."

"I'm sure you are." Michael looked at her. "Anything you want to ask or say?"

Tori struggled to find her voice. Hearing Kurt's fear had gutted her. "Go ahead and rest. I'll be by to see you once we find Joey."

The young man gripped her hand with more strength than she thought possible. "Please, find my friend."

She leaned in and kissed the teen's cheek. "We will." Tori nodded to the paramedics. "Get him to the hospital, and please, let him call his parents on the way."

"We'll take good care of him." They loaded him in the back of the ATV bed, and a few minutes later they headed down the carved-out dirt path.

An arm wrapped around her shoulders. "He'll be fine."

"I know. But it's hard to see him in pain." And she wasn't just talking about physical. "Now what?"

"From what Kurt said about the argument and the boss, I'd say everything revolves around these drug runners. But until we get eyes on Joey and confirm the identity of the person who took him, I can't say with confidence."

"How do you think that man who died ended up with Joey's cap?" Several scenarios came to mind, and none of them were pleasant.

"I have no idea. But if I were to guess, I'd say either Joey lost it and that guy found it, or the man took it from Joey, meaning they were together at one point."

"I prefer the answer that he escaped and lost it when he ran away. But that's wishful thinking on my part." But grasping on to that theory gave her hope.

"I'd love to tell you he's hiding out there waiting for us to find him, but I'm not going to pretend he's not in danger." Michael cupped her cheek, and she leaned into his touch.

His caress was a little too comforting for her sanity. She stepped back, putting a bit of distance between them so she could think, and spun in a slow circle, watching the activity of the task force. "Do you think Joey's here—somewhere?"

"It makes the most sense." Michael guided her to a place to sit. "Let MJ and the others do their jobs, and pray they find Joey safely tucked away in one of the drug runners' caves."

Tori pulled her jacket tighter around her and stared off into space. Pray. Could she? And she didn't mean the *thanks, God*, or *please, help me*. But a true conversation, laying her heart out to Him and trusting Him to have her back. Trusting His plan to be what is best. Maybe a simple prayer would help her get started again.

God, Joey needs you. Please be with him and show us where to find him.

There. She'd done it. Took her first step back toward God, whom she once talked to every day like a best friend.

MJ strode toward them, her head down and her hands stuffed into her pockets.

Tori nudged Michael. "That doesn't look good."

He straightened. Tori noticed the grimace as he eased to a stand. "What's the verdict?"

"We're continuing to search, but overall, I'm confident that we've swept up all those involved. Everyone's in custody. I'm sorry, but there's no sign of Joey. John and Earl are interrogating the players now about Joey, but so far, no one is acknowledging him. They're the best in the business. If anyone can get answers, it's those two."

Tears burned behind Tori's eyes. She'd counted on finding her son here. Now they had nothing to go on.

"Thanks, MJ. Let me know if that changes." Disappointment filled Michael's voice.

"You know I will."

"Since I'm no longer legal to be a part of this and refuse to give these drug runners a loophole to get out of the charges, I'm trusting you to get answers. I'll take Tori to the cabin. And now that the raid is over, I'll call Roger and set up a full search for first light." He glanced at the dark sky. "The weather will become a challenge if we don't move soon."

"You won't have pushback from us. In fact, I know a few on the task force that'll want to come help once we get this mess cleared up. I'll have Wesley notify his department about Joey. Come morning, when it's safe for all involved, you'll have all the help you'll need."

Michael held out his hand, and MJ grasped it. "Thanks. I'll send you the details as soon as I have them."

MJ nodded and moved to Tori. "I really hope you find Joey tomorrow."

"Thank you." What more could Tori say? MJ had helped when and where she could while waiting on the raid. And Tori appreciated it. "We'll leave you to your job and get out of your way."

"See you later." MJ strode away, whistling to get another officer's attention, and met the guy halfway.

"Ready to get some rest before we hit it hard tomorrow?" Michael asked, not taking his eyes off the remaining activity from the drug trafficking raid.

"If it helps me find Joey, then I'll do whatever it takes."

"Then let's get going." Michael removed his flashlight from his pack and called Ducky over from where the dog had plopped down to rest. The golden fell into step next to him.

Tori joined the pair. The hike through the forest in the dark set her nerves on edge, even with the flashlight sweeping across their path, illuminating the way. But more than anything else, she wondered if she'd ever see her son again.

Chapter Ten

The dim light in the cabin gave the interior an eerie glow. The silence between them on the hike back bothered Michael. He understood Tori's disappointment in not finding Joey but had no clue how to comfort her. After hanging their coats near the front door, he'd fed Ducky and let him out to do his business. With the dog now lying on the floor, snoring, Michael collapsed on the couch and pushed farther into the cushions. Using the coffee table as a footrest, he propped his throbbing leg onto the flat surface. The pillow under his foot cradled his ankle and gave him a small amount of relief.

Michael placed a call to Roger.

"Howe."

"Hey, Roger, it's Michael."

"Where have you been? MJ gave me a few updates, but are you okay?"

"Yeah, Tori and I are fine." He glanced at his torn-up ankle. "Maybe a little battered and bruised, but nothing time won't fix."

"I'm glad to hear that. I was starting to worry."

Michael sighed. "We found Joey's friends, Andrew and Kurt, but there's no sign of Joey yet."

"Say the word and Toby and I are in on the search."

"I'm calling in the favor. We need help."

"No favor. That's what we do. Especially for friends."

"Thanks, man." Michael felt a little lighter now that he knew Roger would join them tomorrow. "First thing in the morning we're heading out."

"Where do you want us to meet you?"

"Remember Jackson's cabin?"

"Sure do. We'll be there at oh five thirty."

He glanced at his watch. Five thirty in the morning would come awfully fast. "We'll be waiting." Michael ended the call.

Head tipped back on the sofa, he stared at the ceiling. He'd thought for sure they'd find Joey tonight. Oh, he was glad they'd located Kurt, but his heart ached along with Tori's that they hadn't discovered Joey's whereabouts. With Roger and Toby's help, the probabilities rose. And knowing Roger, he'd pull in a few other teams as well.

Tori returned from the bathroom, settled next to him and laced her fingers with his. "Have you heard anything about how Kurt and Andrew are doing?"

"Nothing recent. At the last report, Andrew was awake and talking. As for Kurt, he'll recover. I wish he hadn't had to wait so long for medical attention. Infection is a real possibility. He'll probably be on some serious antibiotics for a while. He was smart to hide. It could have been so much worse."

A hum of agreement came from Tori. She matched his position and exhaled.

The heater droned in the background, filling the silence. A quiet that left him alone with his thoughts. Michael had no words. So far, he'd failed Tori and Joey. Then again, he and Ducky had located two of the three boys. Just not the one that would heal Tori's heart. It wasn't enough. He was letting his buddy Ryan down. Michael had promised to take care of the man's family, and he'd missed major warning signs for both Joey and Tori. Add to that, Michael had come to care for her more than he should. But he reminded himself that Ryan had based his demands on the playboy Michael used to be. Not on the man he had become.

"Where is Joey?" Tori's voice caught.

He draped his arm around her shoulders and tugged her close. "I don't know, honey. I wish I did. But I can promise you Ducky and I won't stop looking until we find him. And Roger and Toby are joining the search tomorrow."

At the mention of his name, his dog lifted his head. When Michael didn't respond, Ducky huffed and rested his snout on his paws. His golden-reddish tail swished, fanning across the floor.

Tori sighed. "I miss my son."

He kissed the top of her head. "I know you do." His insides warmed at her confession and acceptance of his touch. Maybe they could have something more when this nightmare ended.

The SAT phone rang, and he answered it. "Lane."

"Hey, Michael, it's MJ."

"Hold on. I'm putting you on speaker." He tapped the button. "Go ahead."

"We're still processing the scene, but I can say for certain that these guys didn't take Joey."

Tori sat up. "How do you know that?"

"We've done initial interviews with the lackeys. They're all sharing enough information to take down the big boys in this operation. None of them have any knowledge about a hostage. However, a couple guys overheard orders to kill the guy you found buried in the leaves."

"So, he was part of the drug trafficking?"

"Yes. According to most of the worker bees, he went missing. So far, only the two knew about the directive to kill the kid."

Tori jerked her gaze to him. "So, whoever Kurt saw shoot the man isn't the person who kidnapped Joey?"

"That's my take on it," MJ said.

"I've been out of the game too long. I would have tagged someone you've arrested for all the trouble."

"There is one detail that we should keep in mind."

"What's that?"

"We know for a fact that Lance Kingman, one of Tommy Wade's low-ranking boys, is trying to step in and take over Wade's failed drug business. He's not one of the main dealers, but according to those we've questioned, he's attempting to claw his way to the top of the food chain. Unsuccessfully, I might add." A rustling sound came from MJ's end. "Hold on a minute."

Tori slumped in her seat. "Who's Tommy Wade?"

"Wade was a major drug dealer that I worked hard to take down a year ago. The explosion happened right around the time I had proof of his murderous ways."

Tori nodded. "Your Army buddy Doug and his new wife, Tabitha, were involved, right?"

"Yes."

"So now that Tommy's gone, this Lance guy is stepping in?"

"Sounds like he's trying." Michael shrugged. When he walked away from his career, not by choice but by demand, he hadn't stayed current with the DEA cases.

The crease between Tori's eyes deepened. "Does he have a vendetta against you?"

"He might. I took down his boss, but never had any face-to-face contact with him."

"Okay, I'm back." MJ stopped their conversation. "I really don't think the attacks on you had anything to do with the drug operations here. Granted, Lance is in the wind, so I wouldn't rule him out."

"If not them, then who?" Tori asked.

"Could the whole thing be random?" Michael didn't think so, but he had to consider all options.

Tori twisted to face him. "What do you mean?"

"Let's consider Barrett, the man with the TBI. What if you triggered him by hiking and camping in his safe zone?"

"It's possible, I guess. But why would he continue to come after me?"

MJ jumped in. "I'm just throwing it out there, but maybe you remind him of his wife. I've seen a picture of her. She has red hair like you. With his brain injury, he could be having difficulty separating you from her."

Tori's brow furrowed. "I suppose, but I feel like that's a reach."

"MJ, does Barrett have any experience with explosives?" They had considered him due to his disappearance and medical condition but hadn't focused on his skillsets.

"Good call. The man who trapped you in the cave had to have some knowledge. Although, you can look up stuff like that online now. Hold on." A few moments later, MJ cleared her throat. "Barrett worked construction. Demolition is one of his specialties."

"Don't mark him off the list." Michael struggled with the randomness, but he also couldn't ignore it.

"I don't like him for it, but maybe I'm biased." Tori toyed with the hem of her shirt. "Who else could it be?"

"Other than a long list of angry family members of those I've put behind bars?" Michael sighed. The suspects were endless.

"You've got a point. But narrow it down. Are there any that stick out as more than the standard 'you ruined my loved one's life'?"

Yeah, well, that list was long too. Michael considered the options. "Holder's wife threatened to kill me."

Tori's eyes widened. "What did you do?"

"I arrested her husband on drug charges. Nothing out of the ordinary, but she flipped out. Blamed me for her husband's poor choices."

"Well, that's just dumb," Tori chuffed.

He shrugged. She spoke the truth, but it didn't change the fact that he'd taken the blame for many men and women who he'd arrested over the years.

"What about Pratt?" MJ threw in.

"Yeah, Jeffrey Pratt was beyond angry." Michael rubbed his thumb back and forth on Tori's hand. "In a way, I don't blame him."

Tori's eyebrow arched.

"During the drug raid, I shot and killed his son. It didn't matter to Pratt that he was the one who put his son in danger by bringing him into the drug business, or that his son fired on me first. The man lost it. He threatened revenge."

"Do you know where he is now?" Tori asked.

Michael shook his head. "No. Most criminals are just blathering when they say things like that. No need to take it to heart." If he did, he'd never step foot outside again. "Does Pratt have knowledge of explosives and hunting?" Michael no longer had access to the DEA records. He had to rely on his old partner.

"Hang on. I'm checking." A few moments later MJ came back onto the call. "Yes, to both. He was in the Army for a short stint and played with stuff that went boom, and he's also an avid hunter."

"He's a definite maybe." Michael chuckled at Tori's "you've got to be kidding me" look. "What?"

She smiled and rolled her eyes. "Anyone else?"

The group continued to run down possible suspects. Which included Tommy Wade's attorney and her father. The father had promised retribution after his daughter was convicted of attempting to kill Tabitha, his friend Doug's wife. And the man had experience with all weapons, including explosives.

"Keep the attorney's father on the list." Michael rubbed his forehead. "See? Too many to count."

"Those are the main ones I can think of. I'll keep noodling on it though. You two play it safe tomorrow when you start searching in the morning. Don't let your guard down. Not until we find Joey. I have a hinky feeling about this," MJ said.

"Me too. Let us know if you find out more information."

"Will do. Talk to you soon."

Michael disconnected the call. He agreed with MJ. "My gut says something's off with this whole situation. I can't put my finger on it. Since MJ and the guys aren't here, I'd prefer if you slept on the couch tonight, and I'll take the recliner. I don't want you out of my sight."

"Whatever you think is best. I'm not going to argue. I trust you."

Earlier, he'd begged for her to believe in him, but now he doubted the wisdom in that. He didn't deserve her trust. Not when he'd come up short finding the most precious person in her life.

"Stay here while I check all the locks." He stood and walked away.

He hadn't done enough for her or Joey, and it grated on him. Maybe once the entire fiasco was over, he'd revisit his feelings for her, but for now, he had to keep his distance. Keep his focus. If either died under his protection, he had no idea how he'd cope.

Doors and windows locked, Michael ambled to the living room and sat on the recliner. He'd taken extra time in hopes Tori fell asleep before he returned. And she had. Elbows on his knees, he covered his face with his hands. A washed-up DEA agent with emotional and physical limitations. Plus, a track record of letting people down. Why on earth would Tori ever be interested in him? He closed his eyes. His problems didn't matter right now, and he was selfish for even going there. His complete concentration should be on Tori and Joey's lives.

God, how do I protect Tori when I have no idea who's behind the attacks? And please, keep Joey safe wherever he is. You've given me a strong sense of intuition. Right now, I have a bad feeling about how this will end. I need Your help, more than ever.

He dug into his pocket and set the SAT phone on the end table to keep it from digging into his thigh while he rested, then settled into the chair with his Glock in his lap. He stared at the shadows that dotted the walls and ran through all the suspects again.

Who would come after him, and if they did, why target Tori and Joey? He drifted off, the tangled conundrum swirling in his mind.

Eyes closed, Tori listened to Michael's soft snores. She'd lain there pretending to be asleep when he returned from securing the cabin. His change in demeanor had struck hard. One minute he'd comforted her and the next, he pulled away. It was slight, but she'd noticed. Regrets about opening up to him and becoming vulnerable for the first time in her life came crashing down. Had she made a mistake?

Tears pooled on her lashes. If he'd changed his mind about a relationship beyond a friendship, then she'd honor that. She'd stuff her feelings down deep like she always had and become the person he and everyone else expected. After all the practice she'd had in her life, it wouldn't be difficult. But having the hope of a partner in life who really knew her ripped away shredded her insides. Why had she ever thought that she'd finally be able to be herself?

With a quiet sigh of resignation, she relaxed and allowed sleep to pull her under.

Something wet tickled Tori's hand. She brushed it off and shifted into a new position to go back to sleep. The wet hit her hand again, accompanied by a soft whine. Ducky. She rolled over and brushed her fingers across his back. "What is it, boy?"

Smoke hit her lungs, and she coughed. What in the world?

She pushed to a seated position and winced at the stiffness from her injuries.

A haze filled the cabin. Ducky barked.

"What's wrong with Ducky?" Michael's voice had a deep gravelly tone from his sleepy state.

She coughed. "I'm not sure. But it's smoky in here." Did the damper on the fireplace snap closed? She didn't remember lighting a fire when they arrived.

The alarm of the smoke detector pierced the air.

The recliner footrest popped down, and Michael coughed. "Tori, get out of here! The cabin's on fire!"

The dark cloud in the room grew heavier. Flames crept along the wall from the direction of the bedrooms. A fire had taken hold on the other side of the house and moved so quickly they hadn't had much warning. No wonder they hadn't noticed until the air was thick with smoke. She bolted from the couch and jammed her feet into her hiking boots she'd left beside the coffee table, not taking the time to tie them. Thankful she hadn't loosened them more than necessary when they made it to the cabin.

Michael grabbed her hand and yanked her toward the back door. "Ducky, come!"

For the first time in a long time an urge to pray formed on her lips. Not that "I'm going to try" prayer from earlier, but a full-on desire to talk to God.

She stumbled outside behind Michael. Her feet hit the deck, and she flew down the five steps. Once on the ground, Michael let go, and they sprinted away from the cabin with Ducky loping in front, leading the way.

At a safe distance from the fire, Tori faced the vacation home and placed her hands on her knees. She inhaled and exhaled, regulating her pulse. "He found us."

"We don't know that. It could have been an accident."

No way. Her gut said the attacker had targeted them. If Michael hadn't insisted that she sleep on the couch instead

of the bedrooms where she was sure the fire had started…
She couldn't go there and keep her sanity. "Do you really believe that?"

He stayed quiet a moment then shook his head. "No. Which
worries me about being out in the open." His gaze roamed
the tree line. Ducky leaned against his leg. "It's okay, boy."
He turned to her. "I'll call 911 and report the fire. After that,
we find a place to wait out of sight." He slid his hand into his
pocket. "You've got to be kidding me."

"What's wrong?"

"I took out the SAT phone and laid it on the end table by
the chair because it was poking me in the leg. When we ran
out, I forgot I'd done that."

"So, we're on our own?" The hope inside her deflated.

"It appears that way. Unless I can get a signal on my regular cell phone." He pulled out the smaller device and held it
up. "Nope. Nothing."

She shivered, realizing they didn't have their coats. The
long-sleeved shirt and sweatshirt helped, but the night temperature seeped in.

Orange and red flames shot from the roof of the cabin.
Tori stared, mesmerized by the destruction. From what little
she understood about fires, she knew the entire building had
gone up fast. Windows shattered, followed by an earth-shak-
ing explosion.

The blast knocked her to the ground. She struggled to her
feet, seeking out Ducky and Michael. The dog paced a five-
foot section of the yard a short distance away. Michael pushed
to his hands and knees not far from her. The moonlight along
with the blazing cabin brightened the night sky, enough for
her to witness the panic in his gaze. The explosion. Of course.
A trigger for his PTSD.

A figure rushed out of the woods close to the lake and
swung a bat-like object at him.

"Michael!" Tori had missed the guy's initial approach since she was concentrating on Michael's reaction.

He turned in time to avoid a strike to the head, but the assailant connected with his back and shoulder. Michael hit the ground with a thud.

She scrambled backward, but before she could take her first step, an arm wrapped her waist and dragged her into the woods.

"Michael!" She flailed in the guy's grip, kicking, twisting, screaming, but his hold was too tight.

"Stop fighting. You will not win." The man clamped a hand over her mouth and shoved a gun to her temple.

Her breath came in pants behind his huge hand.

A deep growl echoed through the night. Ducky stood several feet away, teeth bared. He stalked forward, ready to attack.

"Tell the dog to back off, or I'll shoot him." The man moved his weapon from her and aimed it at Ducky.

Tori's heart shattered. That dog meant everything to Michael. She couldn't—wouldn't—let him get hurt. "Ducky, stay."

The growls continued, but the dog stopped moving.

"That's a good girl." Her attacker returned the barrel of the gun to her head and entered the woods near the lake.

The guy's patronizing words raised her fury. She'd find an opening and then make her abductor pay for his actions. She hoped.

Branches crunched beneath her attacker. Her legs dangled to his side. He held her at an awkward angle, but she knew she wouldn't be able to get enough power behind her kicks to inflict damage. But she had to make a move if she wanted to survive.

Tree limbs scraped across her cheeks as they plunged deeper into the forest. She rested, gathering her strength, giving the illusion that she'd conceded, but she refused to give up without a fight.

Timing her efforts with the man's relaxing state, Tori reached up and raked her fingernails across his face. The man howled. He dropped her to the forest floor. She crawled on all fours then pushed to her feet and ran. Branches slapped her face and twisted roots tripped her, but she stayed upright. A scream built in her throat, but before she released it her body slammed to the ground.

Her attacker flipped her over, wrapped his hands around her throat and squeezed. Twigs jammed into her scalp. She opened her mouth, but nothing came out.

"Feisty one, aren't you." Blood dribbled down his uncovered face. She stared into his anger-filled eyes. "You shouldn't have done that." The pressure on her neck increased and closed off her airway.

She clawed at his hands without success.

Tears sprang into her eyes. This was how she was going to die. The clothes she'd worn were now in ashes at whatever was left of the cabin. Michael had no scent for Ducky to follow. No way of finding her. An idea popped into her head. She had to hurry before she lost consciousness. Her energy seeping away, she yanked the band from her hair and let it fall from her fingers.

God, please help me. Let Michael find the hair tie so Ducky can track me. I trust You.

Her first heartfelt prayer in years. She hoped God listened and didn't turn His back on her because of her foolishness when her world fell apart.

Darkness tugged at the edge of her vision, and her muscles went limp.

Chapter Eleven

As if the explosion that knocked him flat hadn't turned his world upside down enough, triggering the start of a panic attack, someone had beaned him. The tree limb—it could have been a baseball bat for all that mattered—had missed a full blow on the intended target, his head, and hit his shoulder. A bruise had already begun to form. Thankfully the attacker had only grazed the back of his head, but, man, it hurt like crazy and made his world fuzzy. Michael fought through the fog that had collapsed over him and struggled to make his arms and legs cooperate. He had to get to Tori. She'd yelled his name. Or so he thought. Between the knock to his skull and the roar of the blazing cabin, he wasn't 100 percent sure what he'd heard.

Ducky's deep rumble urged Michael from his dazed state. His dog had a protective streak, and he only growled when he sensed danger. Whatever agitated the furball couldn't be good. Michael pushed to all fours and staggered to his feet. His gaze landed on the cabin.

Fire consumed the structure at a rapid rate. A sinking sensation hit his stomach. The attacker had expected them to be asleep in the bedrooms, not in the living room. The guy had choreographed the blaze so they'd die in their beds with no way out. He'd done something right by having Tori spend the night on the couch. If he hadn't listened to his gut, they'd all be dead. Michael prayed someone around the lake saw the flames and called for help.

He blinked away the muddled mess in his brain and scanned the area for Tori. Nothing. She'd vanished into the night. Ducky stood facing the tree line adjacent the water, a snarl on his lips. Whoever had hit him over the head must have taken Tori.

Once again, Michael had failed. His abilities were not enough to keep her out of the hands of a madman. He had been right there and still hadn't protected her.

He stumbled toward the lake. His heart rate skyrocketed. Flashes of the boat exploding danced in his mind. Heat singed the hair on his arms. His body was thrown against the dock and then deep into the water. The struggle to escape. Fear of drowning. The horrors while in so much pain he wanted to die. He struggled to shake off the flashback.

Of all his failures, his inability to protect Tori and find Joey struck hard. Right now, Tori's life was on the line, and he refused to let her down. He didn't have the privilege of allowing his fears to take over his abilities. Tori needed him to dig deep and find the courage to face his inadequacies. Ducky pressed against him. His hand dropped to the dog's head, almost as if a magnet drew it there. The warm fur grounded him. He closed his eyes, inhaled and counted to ten. If he focused on finding evidence of where Tori had gone and not on his surroundings, he could do this.

The moonlight reflected off the water, giving him the light he needed to do a brief examination of the shoreline. No obvious shoe prints. He stepped closer to the water. His legs shook at the memories. The nightmare wavering just beyond reach.

Ducky hadn't left his side, doing the job no one had trained him to do. The dog's instincts and actions were the only reason Michael wasn't in a full-on panic.

Several more deep breaths slowed his pulse. *Focus on the*

here and now. Michael concentrated on what the situation demanded, refusing to let the effects of the events drag him under. He moved along the shoreline and examined the ground for clues indicating which direction to search. No footprints marred the sandy dirt. She hadn't come that way. He straightened and stared at the tree line. His best guess from the lack of evidence where he stood and his dog's previous intense stare into the trees—the guy had taken Tori into the woods.

"Duck, I wish I had a scent for you to follow." He glanced at the blazing cabin. All their clothes and possessions were now up in flames. How in the world would he and Ducky track her?

The dog whined.

"I know, buddy. I'm worried too." He patted Ducky's head. "I guess we're doing this the old-fashioned way. Come on." He led the dog to the edge of the trees that surrounded the once tranquil, beautiful cabin. His tracking skills were rusty at best, but he trusted that God would give him the wisdom to get through this mess.

He retrieved his personal cell phone from his pocket. Even though it had no service bars and since the Wi-Fi was toast by this point due to the fire, he had no ability to contact the outside world. However, the flashlight on the device came in handy. Oh, how he wished he'd grabbed the SAT phone when they'd escaped the inferno. But it was probably a mangled, smoldering hunk of plastic by now as well. MJ attempting to call and not receiving an answer was the only hope for immediate assistance.

God, please let her curiosity that she's known for kick in. I could really use some help about now.

With the light pointed at the ground, Michael traipsed deeper into the woods with Ducky at his side. A snapped branch here, and a footprint there, guided him along the same path the kidnapper took. At least he hoped that was the trail he was following. He came across a section of disturbed leaves and twigs accompanied by several drops of blood. Almost as if someone lay hurt on the ground. His mind ran through different scenarios. Maybe, just maybe. The possibility—a reach, but what choice did he have?

Michael tapped the largest part of the depression, hoping for the best and that Ducky could get a scent from where the person had lain. Ready to give the command for his dog to sniff, his gaze drifted to the left of the spot. He squinted and shone the light in that direction. Under a scattering of leaves lay the cream-colored hair band Tori had worn earlier.

She'd left him a way to find her. He could kiss the woman. The thought stopped him short. Who was he kidding, he'd wanted to kiss her for some time now, but Ryan's foxhole words had pushed away the longing. He'd refused to let his friend down. But that was before he'd met God and had a chaplain make him take a long hard look at how he was destroying his life with his revolving door of women. Now that he'd acknowledged his destructive path, he respected the women in his life and tried his best to protect them.

Pushing the memories aside to analyze later, he lifted the hair tie with a stick and held it out for Ducky to get a whiff. "Check."

The dog's nose twitched, and then he lifted his head and wagged his tail with enough enthusiasm the action almost knocked him over.

He patted Ducky's head. "Find." The dog sniffed the air and took off through the woods.

Every ache and pain in Michael's body dimmed as he concentrated on the search for Tori. He held the phone steady, allowing the flashlight app to light the way. He jogged behind Ducky, trying his best to keep up. He dodged branches that reminded him of fingers reaching out to grab him. Leaped over tangled roots, until his ankle gave out and he came close to falling on his face. But determination fueled him on, so he kept going despite the increasing stab of pain.

The phone vibrated in his hand.

Michael jolted to a stop. "Ducky, come." His dog returned to his side. Michael glanced down at the screen. One bar. Eyes to the treetops, his gaze drifted to the sky. How in the world had he received a text from MJ out here? Whatever the reason, he thanked God for the cell service, no matter how small. He opened the message.

Cabin reported on fire. You okay?

We escaped. Tori abducted.

Heading to cabin now.

Ducky is searching. Any news on remaining drug runners? He'd love to know what he was up against once he found Tori.

All drug runners accounted for.

His fingers flew over the keys. Even Lance Kingman?

Yes. Found him two counties over. Arrested three days ago.

Not Tori's attacker.

Doesn't appear that way.

Michael sighed. One more suspect taken off the list. He shifted to relieve the pressure on his leg. The gashes throbbed if he stood in one place too long. The bar on his cell disappeared. No. No. No. He had to get more information from MJ. He moved back, praying he hadn't lost the connection to his ex-partner for good.

The bar reappeared. His shoulders sagged in relief. Have you heard about anyone else on our list?

Holder's wife is clear. She's in the hospital with pneumonia.

He hated to hear of the woman's ailment, but it helped them narrow down the possibilities. Although, she could have hired someone, so he refused to eliminate her completely. What's the news on Barrett?

Nothing.

And Pratt?

Again, nothing.

So those two remained as suspects. His phone vibrated again while he pondered the information.

And Tori's clear. No hidden enemies.

He hated digging into Tori's life like that, but they had to know. His fingers froze on the keys. Wow, the guy must have hit him harder than Michael thought. How could he have missed the obvious?

Not trying to kill Tori this time. Kidnapped her.

That changes everything.

Yes, it does. The idea of someone targeting him didn't seem as farfetched now. But why take Joey and Tori?

How did he put you two together?

His mind scrambled to make sense of everything.

Online article and picture.

He remembered the photo of her kissing his cheek. An innocent gesture, but the guy could have taken it as a relationship. They'd had to do damage control around town when the rumors hit. That had to be the connection. Hurting those who were close to you—a common danger when dealing with vengeful criminals.

Must have been some picture.

Not funny.

Sorry.

He wouldn't hold it against MJ. Most—probably all—law enforcement officers had inappropriate humor at times. It kept them sane when things around them turned ugly.

Keep digging. Service sketchy but I'll try to text. And pray that the messages would go through. Continuing the search. Later.

Stay safe.

"Okay, my man, let's save Tori and figure out who wants revenge on me." The thought left him cold. He'd failed another person he cared about because of something he'd done. Then again, he'd only done his job. He hadn't made a mistake. It was high time for him to quit beating himself up over every little thing. Determined to change his way of thinking, he inhaled and slowly let the air out of his lungs. Palm out flat in the direction Ducky had originally gone, Michael gave the dog the command to continue. "Find."

The dog lifted his head and scurried through branches and bushes. Michael followed, the phone the only thing lighting the path. With the lack of broken limbs and the undisturbed forest ground, he knew the abductor hadn't brought Tori this way, but Ducky didn't track on the ground, he trailed through the air, following the scent. How many times had the dog taken him through thick brush on a search? Too many to count, and he had the scars to prove it. But his dog had always found the victim they searched for.

Ducky came to a clearing just inside the edge of the woods and sat.

Michael spun in a slow circle, shining his phone flashlight. What had the dog alerted on? He narrowed his gaze, hoping to find the source of Ducky's warning. There, in the brambles, a piece of material. He moved closer, aiming the light at the object. A sliver of Tori's shirt.

He ran a hand down Ducky's back. "Good boy." Michael reached into his cargo pants pocket and extracted a dog biscuit from the handful he'd resupplied earlier. "That deserves a treat."

The dog took the offered food and gulped it down.

"Dude, ever hear of chewing first?" Typical Ducky, a canine vacuum. Michael held his hand out in a stop gesture. "Stay." If the bad guy came through here, he must be close. The lake sat on the other side of the trees. He could hear the waves lapping along the shoreline. Michael crouched and ducked through the branches. There. Just beyond the expanse of sandy dirt. He squinted to make out as many details as possible. The moonlight trailed through the dark sky, revealing a boat with... one...two people aboard. The one who moved from the boat onto the dock was no doubt the person who abducted Tori.

The other person had red hair. Even in the dim light, he could see the color. Tori. Her head drooped and bobbed with the movement of the vessel. Was she alive? And if so, for how much longer?

A rocking motion stirred Tori to consciousness. The term awake was subjective. Her mind wandered, trying to make sense of what happened. Flames. Michael falling to the ground. Ducky growling. Panic clawed at her throat, and tears pricked behind her eyes, but she shoved the response away. She refused to dwell on the things she couldn't change. She had to focus on the here and now. Just like she had her entire life.

She fought the fog inhabiting her brain and listened for a clue as to where her abductor had brought her. Waves slapped against a firm barrier. Each time, her body swayed. Near the lake, or on it. She wasn't sure. And the concept of opening her eyes had bad idea written all over it. Her throat hurt where the man had strangled her, along with every other injury she'd endured over the last few days. The sinking temperatures sent shivers racing through her. The storm coming on the horizon must have moved faster than anticipated.

The thought of moving made her stomach twist, but she had to find a way out of her current situation. Joey counted on her staying strong. She blinked away the haze only to find the dark of night. The soft glow of the moon helped orient her. The outline of the shore in front of her and the lake at her back. She sat on the deck of a medium-sized boat. Not a small fishing boat, but not a cabin boat either. Some kind of deck boat was her guess. Back against a hard object, she let her gaze roam the area.

"Momma T?"

Tori jerked her head to her left. The sweetest and most terrifying sight came into focus. "Joey?" Tears pooled on her lashes and a couple sneaked down her cheeks. "Are you all right?" She lifted her hand to cup his face, but her motion stopped before she reached her goal. She yanked, but her arm didn't budge. A quick glance down explained why. A rope she hadn't noticed until now wrapped her arms close to her body. The entire contraption was attached to a metal bar that ran the length of the transom.

"I'm so cold. The guy who grabbed me tied me up and left me here. And my wrist hurts. I think I sprained it when I tried to fight him off." The teen's teeth chattered.

"Oh, Joey, I know you did everything you could." Her heart broke for her son. She'd worried about the temperatures while he was missing and hoped that he'd had protection from the weather. Apparently not.

"I'm not gonna lie. I'm scared." Tears streaked down his face. "I know I should be stronger, but I'm not."

What had she done to her poor son? Her *I can do it all and nothing affects me* attitude had bled off onto the person she'd vowed to protect and love since she and Ryan took custody of him at two years old. "Joey, it's okay to admit you're afraid."

"You don't." He sniffed and wiped the tears with his shoulder. Their abductor had tied them in a similar fashion. Neither could move far.

Michael's words about her independence slapped her across the face. "I made a mistake. I've tried to show everyone I could do it all myself. To be what others expected. I was wrong. Michael's shown me that."

Joey jolted. He raked his gaze across the shoreline. "Uncle Michael's here?"

"Somewhere out there." She jutted her chin toward the trees. "He and Ducky won't stop until they find us." A prayer lingered on the edge of her thoughts. Should she? Why not continue what she'd started. She'd vowed to herself not long ago to grab ahold of the faith she'd once allowed to dwindle into nothing. *I'm sorry for letting our relationship fade. I need You now more than ever. Please let Michael find us. If not for me, for Joey.*

"I hope so. If anyone can find us, it's Uncle Michael." Joey shook from the cold.

She forced a smile but worried about his body temperature. "He is pretty amazing." If only he'd see the same thing about himself.

"Ah, I see you're awake. Good." The man who'd taken her stepped onto the boat, making it rock.

The rolling motion did nothing to help her already queasy stomach. "Why are you doing this?" Sure, curiosity had made her ask, but if she kept the guy talking it would give Michael more time to find her.

He crouched beside her. His features were barely visible in the dim light. The man leaned in. "Ask Agent Lane." She flinched away from his hot breath. He ran his knuckles down her cheek. "So pretty."

She jerked her head away. His touch made her want to puke. "Always so feisty."

She dug deep to find the unflappable woman inside. With more attitude than she felt, she sneered at him. "You've said that before."

"Because it's true." He shrugged. "And I kind of like it. It'll be more fun to watch you squirm when the time comes."

"What are you planning to do?"

"Ah, now, come on, darlin'. Where's the fun in telling?" The man tipped his head back and laughed. "But I'll give you a hint. You won't feel a thing." He glanced over his shoulder.

Tori's gaze followed his. She sucked in a breath.

"What is it?" Joey strained to see around the man who held them captive.

She swallowed hard. Her son wasn't in a position to see the explosive device. Did she tell him and add to his stress or keep it to herself? The mama bear inside her screamed to protect him. But he deserved the truth. She jutted her chin at the madman in front of them. "He's rigged the boat to explode."

"As in blow up?" Joey's voice rose an octave.

"Yes, dear boy, when your mama's boyfriend shows up. He'll get a front-row seat." The man had moved to the device and fiddled with the wires.

Joey swung his gaze to her and whispered, "Boyfriend?"

She shrugged. "Michael?" Tori whispered back. How had their attacker made that connection? They'd never dated. Sure, he'd taken her and Joey out to eat a few times a month. But it was nothing beyond a friendship. Although, now that she looked back, she and Michael had played around the edges of a relationship without realizing it.

The knowledge Michael and Ducky were searching for them, or at least she assumed so, slowed her racing pulse. "If we're going to die, don't we deserve to know the truth of why you are doing this?"

The man whipped around. "You *are* a lively one."

Joey snorted. "That red hair isn't for show. I should know."

One part of her wanted to laugh, and the other part wanted to hug her son for staying strong. "Yeah, you should." She returned her attention to the man who planned to blow them up. "What's wrong with me wanting to know who's going to kill me and why?"

The guy studied them for a minute then placed his fists on his hips. "Fine. It's not like it makes a difference to me."

From what she concluded from his words, he planned for Michael to watch them die. So, until he arrived, they'd stay alive. She mustered all the courage she had. Determination— natural to her as breathing. But since she and Michael had shared their insecurities, her veneer had chipped. She inhaled and found that rock-solid woman beneath the surface. "Then let's start with your name. Or do you prefer Coward?" She raised a brow, taunting him.

"Why you..." He marched over and raised his arm.

Before his action registered, the back of his hand connected with her cheekbone. Her head whipped to the side. White lights streaked across her vision. Her jumbled brain tried to make sense of what just happened.

"Don't touch my mom!" Joey's voice penetrated her muddled thoughts.

She hadn't counted on that reaction. Her intention was only to make him angry enough that he'd spill more details than he planned.

Her face hot and already swelling from the abuse, she blinked away the tears. "I'm okay, Joey." Well, she'd started the harassment, might as well finish it. At this point, she had nothing to lose. "See? A coward. Hitting a defenseless woman."

The man who'd repeatedly threatened her crouched in front of her. "I can see why Michael likes you. What man doesn't love a challenge? But I'll warn you now, you'll regret crossing me."

Okay, so maybe poking this particular bear wasn't a great thing to do. She softened her tone. "What's your name?"

He pinched her chin hard enough to leave bruises, stared into her eyes and then shoved her away. "Name's Jeffrey Pratt."

Her stomach clenched. Michael had shot the man's son, if she remembered correctly. The man appeared to be out for revenge. "How did you find out about Michael and me?"

Joey jerked his head in her direction, and his eyes widened. With an almost imperceptible shake of her head, she stemmed the question from her son. When Jeffery made another scan of the area, she mouthed, *Play along.*

"I've searched for him for the past year. Then I heard about his *accident* and saw the online article. Poor DEA agent, he can't ruin people's lives anymore. Oh, wait, ex-DEA agent." The maniacal laugh that emerged from Jeffrey sent shivers up her spine. "The picture of you kissing him at the open house for that dog training center set the plan into motion."

Kissing him? She closed her eyes and exhaled, remembering that moment. He'd apologized for his lack of presence in her life and promised to make a point to come around more often to hang out with Joey. She'd kissed his cheek as a thank-you. A reporter chose that moment to snap a photo. A few from the community had questioned her and Michael's relationship, but she'd set them straight and ceased the rumors. Apparently, Jeffrey hadn't gotten the memo.

"So, this is all about revenge?"

"No. This is about justice. He took something precious of mine. I'm taking two important people from him and making him watch."

The explosion at the cave, the arrows and the cabin fire confused her. "If you wanted to kidnap me, why try to kill me?"

An inhuman growl burst from Pratt. "When you proved to be harder to get my hands on than anticipated, I'd given up on my original plan. Killing you and Michael had been enough. Then you escaped the cabin fire, and I had the opportunity to follow through and make Michael suffer. I decided to take it as a sign."

Well, that explained why his methods had flip-flopped more than a fish on the riverbank.

Pratt sneered. "So here we are. Now, enough chitchat. I've got things to do." He chucked her chin with his knuckles. "Don't go anywhere." His laughter filled the night air as he stepped off the boat into the darkness.

Tori aimed her gaze at the explosives. The blocks of what she assumed were C4 stared back at her. How would they escape? Did Michael have experience with explosives? Tori rolled through her memories of Ryan's unit and each man's expertise. But she came up blank.

God, please don't let Michael get hurt. Help him find us so he can save Joey.

She'd love to live. To admit her feelings to Michael and show him what a wonderful man he was. But if that couldn't happen, she'd settle for Joey being able to grow up and have a future.

Chapter Twelve

The ingrained ability to move without a sound through enemy territory came in handy. Michael crouched at the edge of the tree line. Ducky sat motionless next to him. A small swish of the dog's tail—the only unnatural forest noise. Michael's heart thumped beneath his breastbone, threatening to break free as he watched the boat holding the woman he'd come to care deeply for. *Right.* Who was he kidding? The woman he loved. Truth be told, the woman he'd secretly loved for a long time. Along with her son, whom he adored.

He glanced at Ducky. The dog sensed his tension but obeyed every command. Ducky's antenna ears perked forward.

Michael jerked his gaze back to the boat. The man who'd boarded not long ago stepped onto the dock and disappeared into the night. He had a decision to make. Go and rescue Tori or circle around and try to find the maniac who had abducted her? Each choice carried a danger.

Mind made up, he whispered next to Ducky's ear. "Stay."

The dog shifted his gaze to him, then back to the boat as if to say, *You can't be serious.*

He cupped his hand under the dog's snout and stared into his black eyes. "I mean it, Ducky. Stay."

The dog huffed and plopped down.

Dramatic much? Michael rolled his eyes but praised the furball. "Good boy." He stood and wove his way to the dock, taking cover behind trees and bushes along the way. His boots hit the sandy dirt. Packed enough his foot didn't sink, but loose to the point he'd leave prints. Not ideal, but he planned to get in and out with Tori and worry about the bad guy later.

After a quick examination of his surroundings, he stepped onto the boat and stopped in his tracks. "Joey," he whispered.

"Uncle Michael. Help. Some guy named Jeffrey hurt Momma T." The stress in the teen's tone worried him.

"Jeffrey?"

"Jeffrey Pratt," a soft, feminine voice slurred.

Michael spun toward Tori. Something was wrong. He turned on his cell phone light and lifted it to her face, careful not to shine it in her eyes. The red swollen mark on her cheek stole his breath. "He did that to you?"

She shrugged. "He didn't like being called a coward."

Michael closed his eyes. Of course, she'd spouted off. "Oh, Red. That mouth of yours."

"What can I say? I bring out the best in people." The corner of her mouth lifted, and she grimaced.

He cupped her cheek, and she leaned into his touch. "I think we need to work on your idea of best."

"Maybe."

Joey grunted. "Jeffrey was right. You two *are* into each other."

"Yes," he and Tori said in unison.

He whipped his gaze to her. Had she really agreed? "We'll discuss this later. For now, we have to get you guys out of here." Michael retrieved a knife from his cargo pants and cut the rope, releasing it from the metal bar. He moved to untangle the cord from Tori.

"I've got it. Help Joey and get him out of here. Don't worry about me."

Yeah, like that would happen. He made quick work of the restraint and assisted Joey to his feet. The teen tottered. Plus, Michael hadn't missed the shiver that had consumed the boy's body. The temperatures continued to drop, and Joey wasn't dressed for the colder weather. "Get your balance, and tell me what's wrong."

The teen grabbed hold of Michael's arm and steadied himself. "I hurt my ankle. I think it's only a sprain, but I can't walk on it."

"Take him. Go!" Tori whisper-shouted. The rope remained around her torso, but she'd made good progress freeing herself.

He focused on Joey. The quicker he got the teen to safety, the faster he could return to help Tori. He lifted the boy's arm around his shoulder. "Lean on me, and let's get you out of here."

Joey complied but threw a glance over his shoulder. "What about Momma T?"

"Don't worry. As soon as I get you to safety, I'll come back and help her. And knowing her, she'll be right behind us." Michael hated leaving her, but arguing with her was a lost cause. He assisted Joey onto the dock and hobbled him up the shore, aiming for where he'd left Ducky. Once he deposited the teen with his dog for protection, he would hustle back to get Tori away from the boat in case Pratt returned.

Ducky shot to his feet. Head down, a growl built in his throat.

"It's okay, boy. It's only Joey."

The golden was a protective thing, which Michael appreciated. Once the dog recognized Joey, his head lifted, and his tongue dangled from his mouth while his tail acted like a fan on high.

Michael lowered Joey to the ground and took extra time he didn't have to prep a hiding spot. He knew Tori's main concern had been for Joey, and he wouldn't let her down.

The teen patted Ducky's head. "Hey, big guy. Did you miss me?"

The furball answered with a lick across Joey's face. The kid chuckled at the greeting.

With a burrow carved out inside the brush, he signaled Ducky to sit. "Crawl in. I want you out of sight. And whatever you do, don't come out until I say so. I'm leaving Ducky with you. He'll keep you safe."

"Just help Momma T." The teen scooted his way into the opening and tapped the ground beside him. "Come here, Ducky."

The dog's black eyes peered up at Michael, asking for permission. "Go on." Ducky edged in and laid his head on Joey's lap. "Stay with Joey." He added a pile of twigs and branches to cover the entrance of the hole he'd created then rushed back to the dock.

He stopped dead in his tracks. Michael drew his Glock and pointed it at the drug dealer he'd once put behind bars. The same man who blamed him for his son's death.

Pratt's arm snaked around Tori's neck, and he held a gun to her temple. "Hello, Agent Lane."

"Let her go, Jeffrey." His training kicked in. He kept his arm steady and stowed his emotions—or at least tried.

The man jabbed the barrel deeper into her skin. Tori whimpered and tried to pull away from the offending metal, but Jeffrey held her too tight.

The vulnerable cry that filled the night air twisted his stomach. The thought of losing her terrified him. He'd pushed her away before the fire. His own fear that he wasn't enough as a man—scratch that, as a person—had dictated his response. They both had claimed feelings for each other moments ago on the boat. Something that had healed a piece of him. Time to let go of his insecurities and trust God. Why had it taken so long? Who knew?

"You've already messed things up by taking the boy. So, I

guess watching her die will have to be enough." Pratt backed toward the dock, half dragging Tori with him.

She struggled to keep her feet under her as she clawed at his arm around her neck. "Bomb. Leave. Take care of Joey." Tori squeaked the warning.

Had he heard her correctly? A bomb? But where? It was then that he noticed a black box in Jeffrey's hand next to her throat. The boat. And Jeffrey was getting closer and closer to the threat. He had to take the man out, but how? He couldn't take a shot. The light of the moon allowed him to see general shapes and movement, but not details. If his aim was off by an inch, he'd kill Tori.

God, I could use Your help here.

A gunshot rang out, and Pratt dropped to the ground, clutching his shoulder. The black box had flown from his hand.

Michael swung his Glock in the direction of the discharged weapon. A tall bulk of a man marched from the tree line. Gun aimed at Pratt.

"Stop right there!" Michael held his gun on the man. He had no idea what had happened except that Tori was free from her captor. She stumbled across the uneven ground. He held out his arm.

She collapsed into him. "We have to get out of here. The boat is rigged with explosives."

The guy who'd saved Tori's life ignored Michael's weapon and hurried to Pratt. The man lifted Jeffrey to his feet. "He hit the switch. The detonator is live. I've got him. Take your lady and go."

It was then that Michael noticed the flashing red light glowing on the ground. He wouldn't argue. He had no clue how long of a delay Jeffrey had programmed the device for. "Come on, Red."

They hurried to the woods into safety behind the trees. The large man and his cargo were not far behind.

Just as they reached the tree line, the boat exploded, knocking the group to the ground from the concussive force. Michael lifted his head and shook off the wave of dizziness from the explosion. His gaze focused on what used to be the dock. Debris rained down and pounded the area outside the trees.

Ducky barked twice, but he maintained his position hidden from sight.

"Where's Joey?" Tori's muffled voice barely penetrated his hearing.

Michael clutched her shoulder and dipped his chin, ignoring the ringing in his ears. He peered into her blue eyes. "With Ducky. He's safe." Man, he felt like he was yelling. And maybe he was.

She nodded her understanding. "I want to see him."

"And you will. But not yet." He helped her to stand and pivoted to face the man who'd come to their rescue. "Who are you?"

The guy pushed to his feet and faced him. "Name's not important. That guy—" he pointed to Pratt, who lie unconscious on the ground "—has hounded you for the last couple of days."

Michael narrowed his gaze. He wished he had more light than the moon provided so he could see the man better. Maybe identify him. "How do you know that?"

The guy shrugged. "The woods are my home."

Tori sucked in an audible breath and straightened next to him. "Wait. You're Barrett."

Barrett? The man with the TBI who went missing over six months ago?

The guy jerked his head to Tori. "Yes, ma'am." Michael didn't miss the hesitation.

Tori stepped toward Barrett. "You're hiding out in the woods because you're afraid."

Barrett took a step back as if she'd slapped him and raised his weapon. "How did you know that?"

Michael drew his Glock. He shouldn't have trusted the man even if the guy had saved Tori's life.

* * *

Tori recognized the panic in Barrett's actions. Oh, how she wished she could see his facial expressions. He reminded her of Ryan after his traumatic brain injury. The uncertainty. The fear. The inability to regulate his emotions. Deep down, she knew that Barrett didn't mean any harm. His brain had reacted. She wanted to go to Joey and prove to herself that he was okay, but she had practice—a lot of it—from dealing with Ryan.

"Barrett." She kept her tone soft. "It's okay. You can relax. We aren't going to hurt you."

"Answer my question." His arm stayed rock steady. The gun never wavered.

Michael's arm wrapped around her waist and pulled her closer to him. "We researched different angles as to who might have been after Tori. Your name came up."

"Why? How did you find out about me?" Barrett's confusion ramped up.

She maintained her even tone. "You are a missing person lost in the woods."

Barrett's voice caught. "Someone is looking for me?"

Tori nodded. "Your wife and son filled out the paperwork when you didn't return from your camping trip. But I'm guessing you left with the intent of not going back."

Barrett checked on Pratt, who hadn't moved since the explosion, then shifted his focus to her. "How do you know these things?"

"My husband, before he died, suffered a TBI. It changed him." Boy, was that an understatement. He'd come back unable to control his emotions and angry at the situation as a whole. It took them weeks to figure out their new normal. And even then, things changed on the daily for them.

Barrett touched the back of his head like the injury still existed.

"The thing is, I loved him even when we had to figure out a new way of life."

Barrett's arm lowered. "But I hurt her. I couldn't stay. I couldn't take the chance I'd injure the people I love."

"Barrett, listen to the lady." Michael squeezed her side. "She knows what she's talking about. Ryan was my friend. I had no idea how to reach him when he got agitated. But Tori did. She fought to figure it out. Through her love and patience, Ryan found a way to be happy."

Michael had shocked her with his words. He'd noticed and never said anything. "Once Ryan and I both accepted his difference in thought process, we had a good life for as long as it lasted."

Barrett's shoulders slumped. "What happened to him?"

"A brain aneurysm." Tori remembered that moment like it had just happened. "I went to work one day. When I got home, he was gone." She inhaled and took several seconds to get her emotions under control. "The doctors said it wasn't instantaneous. My guess is that he didn't heed the warning signs, thinking the TBI caused the excruciating headache."

"Yeah, I can understand that."

"Barrett, you're not alone. You have a wife and kid. Don't throw that away." Michael practically begged the man.

Barrett lowered his weapon. "I guess I should quit hiding from reality."

Tori took a long breath. She felt Michael's muscles relax.

"Can you keep an eye on Pratt there?" Michael gestured to the man who'd targeted her. "Tori wants to see her son."

"I've got him covered. Go find your boy."

"Thanks, Barrett." Now that the danger had receded, she felt the urge to grab Joey and hold on tight. "Michael? Where is he?"

"Come with me." He led her to a pile of brush and branches. One by one, he tossed them to the side. A furry head poked out. "Good boy, Ducky." Michael ruffled the fur on the dog's head, flopping his ears back and forth.

"Momma T?" Joey's voice had never sounded so good.

"I'm here." A cold breeze kicked up, sending a shiver snaking up her spine. She hugged her waist. The cold bit into her clothes. Unprepared to run from the cabin, she'd only had time to shove her feet into her boots. Her coat, hat and gloves were now destroyed by the flames.

"Are you okay?" Joey asked. He remained hidden within the brush.

Michael continued to move the barrier between them as they talked.

"I'm good. We're safe now."

"But I heard the explosion." Joey's voice quivered.

She wanted to wrap him in her arms and never let go. "No one was hurt. Well, except for Jeffrey."

Ducky shot out from the hole and pressed against Michael's leg.

"Michael, are you okay?" She'd seen the dog respond to his stability issues before.

He laughed and stroked the dog's fur. "I'm fine. It's Ducky who's a little needy."

Joey crawled out and fell into her embrace. "I'm so sorry." He trembled in her arms.

She rubbed her hand up and down Joey's back, both comforting and warming the teen. "For what? You had no control over what that man did." She glared in the direction of the unconscious man who'd threatened her son's life.

"No, but I should have been stronger. I should have helped you."

And there it was again. She'd modeled the wrong behavior. She pulled away and cupped his cheeks. "Being strong is okay, but you also have to know when to trust others and ask for help."

The teen stared at her. "Who are you, and what have you done with my mom?"

She threw her head back and laughed. A full-on belly laugh

that hadn't happened in years. In fact, she couldn't remember the last time.

Joey turned to Michael, concern written all over his face. "See what I mean? Something's wrong."

"I think for the first time in a long time, something's right." Michael joined them and wrapped them both in his arms. "And I plan to see that it stays that way."

"If you're sure," Joey mumbled, cocooned within her and Michael's embrace.

She couldn't help the tears streaming down her cheeks. Her son was safe. She and Michael had a lot to talk about, but she knew he cared about her as more than a friend. And for the first time since that scared little girl moved in with her grandparents and had to become the glue that held the trio together, a weight had lifted. She gazed into the night sky. *Thank You.*

A few moments later, Michael released them. "I need to get back to Barrett and see if I can get a message through to MJ. Pratt's shoulder and head require medical attention, and I, for one, want to go home and get a nice hot shower."

Tori smiled hard enough to make her cheeks hurt. Of course, that wasn't difficult with her swollen face. "Come on, guys, let's take care of business and go home."

"And there she is. Ms. Bossy," Joey teased.

It might take time to work through the events of the past few days, but she planned to do it with both Michael and Joey by her side.

Chapter Thirteen

Red and blue lights bounced off the trees lining the dirt road. Michael took a deep breath, locking down the panic rising in his throat. Going near the boat at the dock spun up his anxiety. Flashbacks had reared their ugly selves, but he'd managed to free Tori and Joey. After getting Joey to safety and discovering Tori with a gun to her head, he'd almost lost his ability to function. He had God to thank for getting him through the living nightmare. And now that they had arrived where the cabin had once stood, he could finally breathe.

His buddy Roger Howe, who he'd called earlier in the night about helping with the search for Joey, rushed toward him. MJ must have contacted Roger about the close call for him to come in the middle of the night. "Is everyone okay?"

Michael sunk his fingers into Ducky's fur. The dog hadn't left his side since he had released him from guarding Joey. Ducky's instincts were right on. Michael required the tether to the present. If allowed, his mind would tumble into the past. "It was an adventure."

Roger snorted. "In Michael speak that means you had several close calls."

He shrugged. Pretty much. "I don't want to let Ducky go."

Perspiration popped on his upper lip despite the dropping temperature. The idea of his furry friend not being by his side threatened to throw him into a tailspin. "But could you take him? The hospital won't be too happy with his presence." The thought of dealing with the events of the past couple of days without his canine best friend jabbed at his heart. He blinked back tears. He was man enough to admit that his emotions were all over the place and Ducky grounded him. But he had to be realistic about the situation. Plus, Tori and Joey needed him.

"No problem. I'll take him home, clean him up and make him a nice warm bed by the fireplace." Roger studied Michael a moment. "As soon as you're free and home or somewhere you can have Ducky, I'll bring him to you." His friend clasped his shoulder. "Any time of day or night. I know he's more than a SAR dog to you."

Michael shouldn't be surprised at Roger's deduction. His friend's ability to read people was off the charts. "Thanks, man."

"You'd do the same for me." Roger snapped his fingers. "Let's go, Duck. I have a five-year-old who will be thrilled to see you."

Michael gave Ducky one last head rub and lifted his palm up, fingers pointed at Roger. "Go."

Ducky tilted his head as if to ask if he was okay. The amount of communication that dog could do with a simple look amazed him.

"I'm fine. Go on."

The dog trotted to Roger's side and accepted pets from the man. Like all goldens seemed to think, everyone was a friend. And Ducky was no different. The boy was as gentle as they came. But if he perceived a threat—watch out. He had a vicious bark, and when he bared his teeth the dog looked downright mean.

Michael stuffed his hands in his pockets. "I'll call."

"We'll be waiting." Roger strode to his truck with Ducky by his side.

He sucked in a deep breath and returned to the cars where he'd left Tori and Joey with MJ. The crisp night air stung his lungs. He itched to leave the forest. A place that had once been a refuge for him. In the past, on days that his PTSD had hit hard, he'd go hiking in the woods to clear his head. Always with Ducky by his side. He already missed the mutt.

Joey and Tori stood with wool blankets wrapped around them, leaning against MJ's vehicle. Tori huddled in on herself with her arms crossed, waiting in the cold for him to return. The sight almost took him to his knees. No woman had ever cared enough to sacrifice for him. If he and Tori dated, she'd give him 100 percent of her attention. He'd seen it with Ryan. And he intended to give her the same. Assuming she didn't change her mind once she had time to think. He prayed she didn't.

He swallowed past the lump in his throat. Tonight could have turned out much worse. "Hi."

She tilted her head. "Hi to you too. Everything good?"

"Yes." His hands shook as he opened the back passenger door for Tori. He already missed his dog's comforting presence. But he'd deal. He had to for her and Joey's sake. "Time to get you and Joey checked out at the hospital."

"I hope you're on that list as well." She cocked an eyebrow, challenging him to disagree.

If his body didn't ache with a vengeance, he'd brush off her concern. But as it stood, he'd welcome the medical attention. "Me too."

"Good. And thank you for rescuing Joey." Tori slipped onto the seat and swung her legs inside.

"Of course." Michael's throat clogged with emotion. He closed the door before he collapsed into a pile of goo from the weight of the situation. He could have lost Tori and Joey today. And that didn't sit well with him. He cleared his throat.

"Joey, take the back seat next to Momma T. She'll need you close, even though she probably won't admit it. So deal with it."

The teen chuckled. "I have no problem with that." He leaned in and whispered, "Don't tell her, but I kind of need the same thing."

Michael smiled, happy to hear the young man's admission. Now he understood why the teen hadn't waited inside the car. He helped the boy around to the other side. Joey's limp was more pronounced since he'd walked on it to the clearing. "Let's get you both to the hospital and checked out."

"That goes for you too, Mr. Your leg has gashes in it. And let's not forget the tumble you took down the cliff." MJ glared at him.

Joey whipped his head up. "What?"

"A long story." He opened the door. "I'll fill you in later."

"I'm holding you to that." Joey ducked into the car and slid next to Tori.

Michael secured the door, turned to face MJ and folded his arms across his chest. He plastered a scowl on his face.

"Oh, lose the attitude, grumpy pants." She motioned for him to get in the car. "You aren't invincible."

"I've already promised Tori I'd see the doc."

"Glad to hear it. If you'd have disagreed, you would have had a fight on your hands. I saw how Ducky supported you."

Yeah, his dog had assisted him and held him together on the walk here. He'd have to navigate the world without him for a few hours.

Might as well admit it. MJ wasn't stupid. "He seems to know when I'm struggling."

"He's good for you." MJ jerked her thumb over her shoulder at the car. "And so are they."

"I read you loud and clear."

MJ speared him with a look. "And?"

"And, that conversation has to happen between Tori and

me first." He refused to mess things up before they started by making assumptions.

"Copy that. Hospital time." MJ jiggled her keys.

He sighed and got into the vehicle. Seat belt on, he rested his head on the headrest.

"Do you think I'll be able to see Andrew and Kurt?" Joey asked from the back seat.

MJ adjusted the heater and put the car into gear. "From what I've heard, they are both doing well. I see no reason you can't visit them."

"Good. I'm worried about them."

Michael shifted so he could see into the back seat. "I'm not going to gloss over things. Andrew has a head injury, but according to what MJ has told me, he's awake, and the doctors agree that he'll recover. As for Kurt, he has a gunshot wound to the shoulder. Again, he's expected to recover with minimal side effects."

Joey let out a long sigh. "I just feel so bad."

"Why? There's nothing you could have done to prevent what Pratt did."

"I guess." The teen turned his attention out the side window.

Michael recognized the guilt. He'd lived with it for a long time. When Joey said nothing else, Michael gave Tori a sad smile and faced forward. Later, he'd have a discussion with the teen and help him navigate those feelings.

The dirt road turned into a paved county highway, and the trees that lined the path thinned.

The quiet drive gave Michael too much time to think. How could hours feel like days? His mind ran in circles, replaying everything that happened since the fire at the cabin. He'd almost lost the woman he loved. Yes, he admitted it. No, he refused to hide the fact any longer.

God, please let her look past my failings and be willing to give me a shot at a meaningful relationship.

When they had a moment alone, he'd confess his feelings to her and let her decide what the future held.

After the hospital visit, which included confirming Andrew and Kurt would recover from their injuries and an examination by the emergency department doctor, Tori sank onto her couch and hugged her throw pillow. She'd never understood the phrase "home sweet home" until now. She pitied anyone who told her to move. Head back and eyes closed, she thanked God for protecting everyone she cared about. She released a long breath. It was nice to have open communication with Him again.

"Doing okay?"

She lifted an eyelid. Michael stood with one hand on the back of the sofa. A soft smile on his lips. "I've been better, but it could have been a whole lot worse if not for you."

"I'm just glad you and Joey are home."

"Me too." Tori patted the seat next to her. "Have you heard from MJ?"

He eased onto the couch, tossed the extra pillow onto the coffee table and propped his injured ankle on it. "A few minutes ago. John Smith questioned Pratt. It's just like he said. He was out for revenge on me and saw our picture. He assumed you were my girlfriend and planned to use that to his advantage. He admitted when he couldn't get to you, he changed tactics and tried to kill us. But when the fire he set failed, he took advantage of the situation and continued with his original plan."

"That's what he told me on the boat." She let the truth of how close she'd come to dying set in. "It's amazing what one photo can do. That image not only started a rumor around town but sent a killer after Joey and me."

Michael grunted. "It makes me furious he targeted you."

She reached for his hand. "Michael, it's okay. We're all alive. It wasn't your fault. Please let it go."

"I suppose." He linked their fingers together. "What did I do to deserve you?"

"You can't be serious."

"I am."

"You are the most selfless man I know. You are there for every one of your friends and anyone who needs help."

"That's just being a kind human being."

"Not everybody thinks that. Don't you see? That's what makes you special."

"Maybe." He sat in silence. His gazed locked on the wall.

She joined him, staring at nothing. "I'm worried about Barrett. He saved my life. I hate a life in the forest for him. Is there a way to help reunite him and his family?"

"Already in motion, Red. MJ and I are on it. Barrett will receive the medical attention he needs, and we've contacted his wife and son. It's the absolute least I can do after he watched out for us in the woods. His family's on board with our plans and promised to be by his side."

"Good. That's good." Relief flooded her system. She hadn't realized how tense she'd become over Barrett's situation. "I don't think people understand how hard it is on someone who knows they aren't the same but can't do anything about it."

"From the way it sounded, his family promised to be there for him every step of the way. They have a long road ahead, and the wife is still worried about her and her son's safety, but she still loves Barrett and wants to see him get the help he needs."

Tears pooled on her lashes. "He broke my heart when I found out he'd hidden in the woods to keep his wife and son safe. I pictured Ryan out there alone."

"Oh, honey, you were the rock that my friend needed after the incident overseas. And Barrett will be taken care of. You can relax, everyone is safe now, and Pratt is behind bars." Michael brushed his thumb along the back of her hand.

She inhaled and released it slowly. Life had spun out of control, but with Michael by her side, she felt grounded.

"Are you really okay, Red?"

"Now that we're home, and you're here with me." Head resting on the back of the couch, she rolled to look at him. "What about you? I know your leg still hurts, but how are *you* doing?"

"To be honest, it's like I can breathe again now that you and Joey are out of danger."

The admission had her sitting up and staring at him. "That had to hurt."

He chuckled. "Hey, I'm a work in progress when it comes to revealing my feelings."

"Right there with ya, my friend." She grinned.

Michael's smile faded. "Is that all we are, Red? Friends?"

How did she answer that without tripping into her insecurities? Fear of rejection was alive and well. "Where's Joey?"

"Are you avoiding the conversation?" Michael's shoulders drooped, and he jutted his chin toward the hallway. "He's asleep in his bed. Between the aches and pains, dealing with the cold and using the crutches for his sprained ankle, he's wiped."

"Thank you for getting him settled. I'm glad he's able to sleep. He went through a lot. He needs the rest." She stared into Michael's brown eyes. Eyes that held caution.

His gaze didn't waver. Knowing him, he'd wait her out, and her energy was nonexistent. Might as well lay it all out there. Sidestepping his question wouldn't be possible. "Ryan and I were so young when we got married. Then having parenthood thrust upon us, we barely had time to grow up ourselves. He understood my past. At least what I allowed him to see. But granting someone access to my deepest darkest secrets and dreams hadn't happened—ever. You're the first I've allowed to break through that barrier."

He linked their hands and squeezed. The silent encouragement was more necessary than he could possibly understand.

"To answer your question, I'd really like to be more than friends. But I'm scared to dream."

"Believe me, I understand that sentiment." He shifted to face her and tucked a wayward strand of hair behind her ear. "I'll be the first to admit that I'm a mess. I have no job. PTSD that I fight every day. And an inner ear issue that frequently impairs my physical abilities. I don't have much to offer you. If I'm honest, I'm not enough for any woman."

"Michael. You're more than all that. You've stayed by my side since Ryan's injury and death. Never once complaining about stepping in and helping Joey." She cupped his cheek. "You risked your life for me. And above everything else, you've let me in. What more could I want?"

"Are you kidding? Pratt had you in his crosshairs because of my past. If I wasn't around, you'd never have been in danger."

"Oh, Michael. You carry too much on your shoulders." This was it. The defining moment. "You're everything I want—everything I need. Why can't you see that?"

"You're more than I ever could have dreamed." His brown eyes held hope and a bit of fear. "Are you sure?"

"I'm positive. For the first time in my life, I feel like I can let go and be me." She smiled. "Assuming you're ready for that."

His hand covered hers. "I think I can handle anything you throw at me, Red." He closed the distance and brushed his lips against hers. A light, soft graze. Almost like dipping a toe in the water before diving in.

Her belly fluttered at the warmth of his touch. She hadn't been kissed in years and had forgotten how much she craved the closeness. Hand to his chest, she leaned in.

Responding to her gesture, Michael deepened the kiss and ran his fingers through her hair. He pulled back and rested his forehead against hers. "That was worth the wait."

Tori couldn't help but smile as she caught her breath from the mind-altering kiss. "I completely agree."

"I've spent my whole life trying to be enough so those closest to me will love me."

"Michael, you're the man I need. The man that I love."

"I am? You do?"

The shocked look in his eyes made Tori chuckle. "Michael, you're everything I want. I love you."

He tilted his head and snuck another quick kiss. "And I love you, Red." He ran his knuckle down her cheek. "Tori Campbell, would you go on a date with me and give this thing between us a try?"

Tori closed her eyes and soaked in the love and acceptance of the man next to her. Never had she thought her dreams might come true. But Michael had opened that door and held out his hand to help her step through. Whatever the future held, she thanked God for the man beside her. "I'd be honored."

Epilogue

Six months later

Tori collapsed onto the soft leather couch, leaned her head back and closed her eyes, reveling in the moment of quiet. The guys from Michael's unit, along with MJ and her husband, Steve, had descended on her home first thing this morning, buckets, toolboxes and ladders in tow. So much for a peaceful sunny April Saturday. And since she'd decided not to hide her true self anymore, she'd said as much. Until they explained they'd come to help with repairs around her house and property. Including tuning up her car and replacing the tires—at no cost to her.

Beyond grateful for their thoughtfulness, she'd retracted her grumbling and moved aside and let the hordes in. She'd pitched in where they'd allowed, and now, seven hours later, her muscles resembled jelly.

Joey's laughter filtered in through the window she'd opened to vent the odor from the freshly painted hall bathroom. The change in her son since the guys committed to stopping by more often after the nightmare camping trip in the fall had been drastic. His playful happy attitude had returned. Of course, some of that had to do with Michael. His constant presence hadn't gone unnoticed, especially by her.

"What's that smile for?" Michael leaned over the couch and captured her lips.

When they broke the kiss, she patted his cheek. "Just thinking about you."

"I like that." He waggled his eyebrows.

"Oh, for the love of everything, would you two stop." MJ sauntered into the living room.

"As if you and Steve are any better," Michael challenged the woman.

Tori loved the banter between the ex-law enforcement partners. She'd gotten to know Melissa better over the last few months. The woman had become a friend—a true friend. Not the superficial kind she'd once had. She was getting better at letting people see the real her.

"Whatever." MJ dropped onto the recliner, her legs hanging over the armrest. "But you're not wrong." She threw her head back and laughed.

The boisterous woman had shocked Tori at first. She'd witnessed Melissa in work mode, but spending time with her and her husband had been enlightening.

"Not wrong about what?" Doug Olsen strolled in with his arm around his wife, Tabitha.

"MJ and Steve's public displays of affection." Michael rested his hands on Tori's shoulders. He knew her well. She craved the connection. If he was close, he held her hand or caressed her arms. He made contact in some way, giving her what she needed to feel cherished.

She blinked back tears. Her life had changed, and she loved the direction it was heading.

"Whose PDA are we talking about?" Roger and his wife, Tiffany, joined the group, along with Frank, Justin and Landon from the Army unit. Joey must have stayed outside with Ducky.

"MJ and Steve," the others said in unison.

"Hey, like any of you have room to talk," MJ protested.

When Steve leaned down and kissed Melissa, the room erupted in laughter.

Once they quieted, Tori cleared her throat. All eyes shifted to her. "I can't thank you enough for coming today. You all are too generous with your time and purchases." The tires they'd bought for her car had surprised her, but the lumber to fix her fence and the shingles they'd replaced on the roof... Just wow.

"You're important to us. And that's what friends do. They take care of each other," Landon said.

She didn't miss the look between Landon and Justin. What was that all about?

"Come on guys, let's get things cleaned up while Michael starts the grill. I don't know about y'all, but I'm starved." Frank patted his belly.

"You're always hungry." Justin laughed.

"True." Frank shrugged and headed toward the door.

The group cleared the room, except for Melissa, who lounged in the recliner.

Michael sat next to Tori on the couch. "Are you doing okay? They can be a lot."

"That they can. But they're a great group of friends." She patted his hand. "I'm good."

"I better go start the grill before the vultures swoop in." Michael gave her a quick kiss and headed to the back deck.

"You two seem happy." Melissa grinned like a fool.

"We are." Tori propped her feet on the coffee table. "Can I be honest with you?"

MJ's eyebrow raised. "Isn't that what we do?"

"True. I'm still getting used to the openness in friendships." She had to admit, she loved not hiding behind a false front. "I never thought I'd have my dream. True friendships and a relationship with Michael."

"Have you two talked about the future?"

She shrugged. "In general terms. I think he's hesitant since he doesn't have a job."

"That man needs to get over himself," Melissa grumbled.

"I agree. But I'm not going to rush him. He's still processing the changes life has thrown at him."

"You're good for him. And as someone who cares deeply for that man—I put my life in his hands more times than I can count—I appreciate you looking out for him. I only want the best for both of you."

"Thanks. Someday maybe he'll realize I don't care about the fluff. Just him. Until then, I'm good with where we are." But, oh, how she wanted more with the man who had stolen her heart.

Burgers sizzled on the grill, and Ducky played fetch with Michael's buddies in the backyard. Life couldn't get much better than this. He held the spatula in his left hand and slid his right into his pocket. His fingers touched the one carat emerald-cut diamond solitaire he'd purchased weeks ago. The timing had to be right. Or so he'd thought. Right now, he didn't care anymore. He'd settle for a moment alone to pop the question.

A bang jerked his attention to his left.

Justin had dropped a five-gallon bucket on the sidewalk. "Sorry."

Michael had confided in his friends about his PTSD. They'd all taken it in stride and helped him whenever it hit hard. He waved off his friend. His pulse rate had spiked. Not at the loud noise, but at whether or not Tori would say yes to his proposal.

He lifted his face to the sky. The sun warmed his cheeks while the slight breeze whispered through the trees, keeping the temperatures perfect for a cookout.

"Hey, dude." Landon moved beside him and slapped him on the back. "Given my offer any thought?"

"Yeah, you could say that." He shook his head. "I can't stop thinking about it."

"Then why don't you take me up on it?"

Landon and Justin owned a security business, and Frank was one of their employees. They contracted jobs from the installation of home security systems to private investigations and everything in the middle. Landon had offered him a job as a PI with their company two weeks ago. Stunned didn't begin to describe his response. "I can't keep from wondering if your offer is out of pity."

His friend's eyes widened. "Are you kidding me? You are the last person who needs pity. The offer is legit. With your experience, you'd be an asset to our company."

Okay, so he still had a few self-esteem issues, but he was working on those with Tori's help. Michael flipped the burgers. "I've looked into the PI license. It shouldn't take me long to jump through the hoops."

"Then you'll take the job?" The hopefulness in Landon's voice made Michael smile.

Why prolong the answer? He'd decided about two minutes after Landon had asked, but his insecurities had held him back. Not anymore. Time to live life again. "Yes."

Landon grabbed him in a big bear hug and pounded his back with friendly slaps. "You won't regret it."

He laughed. "I think I already do." Smoke floated from the grill, reminding him not to burn the burgers or Frank would disown him.

"Is dinner about ready? I'm dying over here." Speaking of the bottomless pit, Frank joined them.

"All done." Michael plated the meat. "Here, take that to the table."

Frank accepted the tray, and he and Landon sauntered off.

Tori wrapped her arm around his waist. "What was that all about? Did Landon rearrange your spine?"

Michael couldn't quit grinning. He was at peace with his new job. "Almost. The man doesn't know his own strength."

"So?"

He scanned the yard. "Come with me." He laced their fingers together and tugged her around the corner of the house.

"Where are we going?"

"Somewhere private."

She laughed. "Around those guys? Impossible."

"Don't I know it?" Once alone, he placed a chaste kiss on her lips. "I love you. You know that, right?"

"And I love you too."

He smoothed the crease between her eyes. "Landon and Justin offered me a job as a PI with their company."

Excitement danced in Tori's blue eyes. "And?"

"I took it. You're looking at a private investigator. Or at least once I obtain my license."

"That's amazing. I'm so proud of you for taking that step."

"You know what? Me too. But I couldn't have done it without your support over the past six months. You've made me feel whole again." This was it. He took a deep breath and lowered to one knee.

"Michael?"

"I thought my life was over after the explosion, and I'd grow old alone." He swallowed past the lump in his throat. "Then you showed me that I could still have everything I've ever wanted. A woman who loves me and a family."

Her eyes widened.

"You are everything I've always wanted and needed. I've talked with Joey, and he's okay with this." Here we go. Why was he so nervous? He lifted the engagement ring. "Red, will you fulfill my dreams and marry me?"

Tears rolled down her cheeks. She nodded. "Yes."

Michael slid the emerald-cut solitaire onto her finger. He stood and gathered her in his arms.

Whoops and whistles erupted.

Michael held Tori close and turned.

His buddies—their friends—cheered from the corner of the house. Even Ducky, who stood beside a grinning Joey, barked in excitement.

"I think they approve." Michael chuckled.

Tori shifted in his hold. Her blue eyes sparkled with tears. "I know I do."

The chaos in the background faded. Michael dipped his head and touched his lips to hers in a kiss that spoke of love and a future neither dreamed they'd ever have.

* * * * *